New York Times and *U*

Caridad Piñeiro is a Jers

and is the author of nearly fifty novels and novellas. She loves romance novels, superheroes, TV and cooking. For more information on Caridad and her dark, sexy romantic suspense and paranormal romances, please visit caridad.com

The Texas-based author of more than thirty novels and novellas, **Colleen Thompson** is a former teacher with a passion for reading, hiking, kayaking and the last-chance rescue dogs she and her husband have welcomed into their home. With a National Readers' Choice Award and multiple nominations for the *RITA®* Award, she has also appeared on the Amazon, BookScan and Barnes & Noble bestseller lists. Visit her online at colleen-thompson.com

Discover more at millsandboon.co.uk

DANGER IN DADE

CARIDAD PIÑEIRO

COLTON'S K-9 RESCUE

COLLEEN THOMPSON

MILLS & BOON

First Published in Great Britain 2024
by Mills & Boon, an imprint of HarperCollins*Publishers* Ltd
1 London Bridge Street, London, SE1 9GF

www.harpercollins.co.uk

HarperCollins*Publishers*
Macken House, 39/40 Mayor Street Upper,
Dublin 1, D01 C9W8, Ireland

Danger in Dade © 2024 Caridad Piñeiro Scordato
Colton's K-9 Rescue © 2024 by Harlequin Enterprises ULC

Special thanks and acknowledgment are given to Colleen Thompson
for her contribution to *The Coltons of Owl Creek* series.

ISBN: 978-0-263-32258-3

1224

DANGER IN DADE

CARIDAD PIÑEIRO

To my amazing daughter and son-in-law, Sam and Dan.
Wishing you all the best on the addition of Axel Scott!
May he bring you immense joy!

Chapter One

The pit bull nearly yanked Brett Madison's arm out of its socket as the dog jerked its head back and forth, thrashing forcefully, the pressure on his forearm punishing.

"*Pust,* Mango. *Pust,*" Sara Hernandez commanded, and the dog instantly released his arm and sat, staring at him as if ready to attack again.

Sara strolled over and bent to rub Mango's head affectionately, ruffling her short, glossy white-and-tan fur. "Good girl, Mango. Good girl," she said and fed Mango a treat as Brett slipped off his baseball cap and wiped sweat from his forehead. Despite the mid-December weather that had brought a cooling breeze through the doors of the training ring building, the dog bite suit was hot thanks to its weight and padding.

"Do you think she's ready?" he asked Sara, the K-9 trainer who South Beach Security had hired nearly seven months earlier to run their new K-9 training center just outside Miami.

Sara smiled and chuckled. "Mango's ready. What about you?" she asked and shot him a look from the corner of her eye.

Brett dragged a hand through the short, damp strands

of his high-and-tight cut and shook his head. "Possibly. It's only been three weeks that we've been working together."

"A solid three weeks and you've had a K-9 partner before," Sara said and skimmed a hand down his arm to reassure him.

"I worked with a K-9 during my time in the Marines, but it's been a while," he said and rubbed Mango's head as well to reward the dog for her good behavior. It was while working as a military policeman that he'd met SBS acting chief Trey Gonzalez and then served with him during a second tour in Iraq. A tour that they'd both survived, although the scars remained.

"I think you and Mango will be happy together," Sara said and slipped the muscular dog another treat.

Brett unzipped the suit and slipped out of it. The cooler air bathed his sweat-drenched clothes, rousing goose bumps on his overheated skin. He rubbed his arms to wipe them away and then accepted Mango's leash as Sara handed it to him.

"You're ready," Sara said, reassuring him yet again.

"I am," he said and glanced down at Mango, who cocked her head to the side and peered at him with joyful cinnamon-brown eyes and a friendly grin, her tongue lolling out of her mouth.

"You are, too, Mango," he said, almost as if to convince himself. It had only been three weeks since Sara had paired him up with the pit bull and while the dog had performed amazingly well during their training, it would take more work and time together for him to feel as if he and Mango would be up for anything Trey Gonzalez might assign.

His friend Trey had reached out to him months earlier while he'd been working as a police officer in a sleepy North Carolina town. He'd liked the quiet at first after the trauma from his tour of duty but had been feeling lost and dissatisfied after several years.

When Trey had called with the opportunity to join him in

Miami, he'd jumped on it. The fact that Trey now trusted him with one of the coveted positions in their new K-9 training program spoke to the fact that Trey was pleased with what Brett had done so far with South Beach Security.

As Sara and he walked away from the training ring, he noticed Trey's cousin and Sara's new fiancé, Jose Gonzalez, leaning against the doorframe of the building, a broad smile erupting on his face as it settled on Sara.

She hurried to Jose's side and kissed him as he wrapped an arm around her waist.

When Brett approached, he held his hand out and said, "Congratulations on the engagement, Pepe."

"*Gracias.* Congrats to you as well on the promotion to the K-9 division," Jose said as he shook Brett's hand.

"Thanks. I hope I don't disappoint. I know Trey is keen on the K-9s taking off for the agency," Brett said. He owed Trey for believing in him after what had happened in Iraq.

"It was a rocky start what with the serial killer here at the kennels, but I'm sure you and the other agents Sara trains will be up to the challenge," Jose said and playfully squeezed Sara closer.

"I know Brett and Mango will be up for anything," Sara said, no indecision in her voice.

Brett smiled and dipped his head in appreciation for her trust in him and his new K-9 partner's capabilities, which were a testament to her training skills.

As they walked toward the former kennel owner's home where Sara was living with Jose, Brett bid them goodbye and peeled off to head to his car, Mango loping at his side. He buckled the pittie into the front seat and rubbed her head affectionately. The dog responded with a happy lick of his face and a doggy grin.

He was grateful for the dog's love since he knew the pit bull's powerful jaws and muscular body could inflict quite a lot of punishment if necessary. His forearm still ached from the earlier bite, and he was sure he'd have a bruise by the next day even with the padding in the suit. In a real-world situation, extensive thrashing combined with the bite could cause considerable damage.

"You're my girl, Mango," he said and massaged her head and shoulders again to reinforce the relationship with his partner so that when the time came on assignment, he could trust her to do as commanded.

He just hoped he would have a little more opportunity to train with Mango before that time came. More than anyone, he understood the dangers of not being prepared and what the cost would be, he thought as he rubbed a spot by his collarbone. Beneath his fingers, the ridges of scars were a painful reminder of the price of failure.

But not now. He would be ready when the time came.

THE NIGHT HAD been a killer.

Two of her line chefs had called in sick and a delivery of her porterhouse steaks had gone missing, prompting a last-minute menu change.

Her sous-chef, Melinda, pressed a glass of wine into her hand. "Here, Chef. You need it."

Anita Reyes accepted the glass and peered around her restaurant's kitchen.

All the dinner tickets had been cleared off the rail, and despite being down the two chefs, the others had still been able to clean as they cooked, leaving the kitchen relatively in order.

"Things look pretty good, Chef," she said.

Melinda nodded and gestured toward the back door. "They do, and the butcher promised to get us those porterhouse steaks for tomorrow. Why don't you get some air and enjoy that wine while we finish up."

Anita had been running around all night filling in for the missing line chefs while still doing her own job of making sure that the orders were perfect and ready to go out to diners. Her feet and back ached and sweat dripped down between her shoulder blades from the heat in the kitchen.

A breath of fresh air and sip of a fine wine sounded like heaven.

She pushed through the back door and onto the small landing in the narrow alley between her restaurant and the hotel behind her.

The late-fall night wrapped her in nippy air, making her shiver as it chased away the warmth of the kitchen. The street noises from busy Ocean Drive and Collins Avenue were almost nonexistent in the alley thanks to the buildings sheltering it on either side.

She sat on the stoop, leaned against the brick of the building and sipped the wine, a tasty cabernet franc they'd been lucky to find at a local distributor. The floral vintage pleasantly slipped down her throat, and she breathed a sigh of relief that her killer night was almost over.

Long minutes passed as she relaxed but soon responsibility called her to return to her kitchen and make sure everything was in order so they could start all over again for tomorrow's lunch and dinner crowds. As tired as she was, she reminded herself how lucky she was to have attained her dream of owning her own restaurant, and a successful one at that.

Varadero, her Cubano-Latino fusion restaurant, rarely had an empty seat and dinner reservations were fully booked for the rest of December and into the new year, pulling a smile from her.

But that meant lots of arduous work, and as she slowly rose to return to the kitchen, the door of the hotel across the way burst open as a man flew out and tumbled onto the rough ground in the alley. The man scrambled to his feet, as if ready to run, but a second later a masked man rushed through the door, grabbed him and wrapped an arm around the man's neck.

She recognized the unmasked man as one of the hotel's owners, Manny Ramirez.

Anita froze in place, shocked by the scene playing out before her as the two men grappled in the darkness of the alley. She had no doubt it was a fight to the death as light suddenly gleamed on a knife blade in the masked man's hand.

He punched the knife into Manny's side and, in a growly voice, said, "You know what we want."

Manny grunted and abruptly bent over from the pain of the knifing. That seemed to break his attacker's hold for a hot second.

A mistake, since Manny was able to take a swipe at his attacker's head. His hand connected and ripped off the mask. Exposed and clearly annoyed, the man tossed Manny away, pulled a gun from beneath his black denim jacket and fired.

A perfect circle marked Manny's forehead as he stood there for a shaky second, surprised by death before he collapsed.

Shock stole Anita's breath, and the sharp sound drew the killer's attention.

He whipped around to stare straight at her, as shocked as she was.

A heartbeat later, he pointed the gun and fired.

She ducked as the bullet whizzed by her head and bit into the brick. A chip flew off and grazed her cheek, propelling her to flee as the warmth of blood trickled down her face.

The man aimed at her again and she tossed her glass of wine at his head.

A perfect strike.

It stunned him long enough for her to dash into her kitchen. Locking the door behind her, she screamed, "Call 911!"

Chapter Two

The police detective standing across from her seemed better suited for a modeling gig than a cop's life.

Detective Williams was over six feet tall with a lean, muscular physique, ice-blue eyes, boyish dimples and chestnut-colored hair with thick, rumpled waves that fell onto his forehead.

"Do you think you could identify the man who shot at you?" Williams asked, pen poised over a small notepad.

In her mind's eye, the scene she had witnessed barely an hour earlier replayed itself like a movie, pausing at the spot where the mask had come off and then again when the killer had turned his attention to her. She rewound and replayed that section and nodded.

"I'm sure I can."

"Are you sure? I mean, you only saw him for what, a few seconds?" Williams pressed, his gaze narrowed as he scrutinized her.

Her answer was immediate. "Without a doubt. I'll never forget what I just saw."

With a nod, Williams looked toward the two police officers who had been the first ones on the scene in response to her 911 call. He waved a hand in their direction, and when they approached, he said, "Detective Gonzalez has arranged for a sketch artist to work with Ms. Reyes. Please take her to headquarters while I coordinate with the CSI team."

"Yes, sir," said Officer March, a petite young Latina, before turning to her. "If you wouldn't mind following us to our cruiser?"

"Of course," she said, even though the thought of leaving the safe space of her restaurant had her gut clenching with fear.

"I'll lead the way," said Officer Garrett, a strapping Anglo six-footer with shoulders as wide as the doorway and gingery blond hair.

Anita stood and followed the policeman outside, where several other officers kept back a crowd of bystanders who packed the sidewalk and spilled onto the street. It created a traffic backlog of the cars that normally cruised up and down Ocean Drive, wanting to be seen as well as to see what was happening along the popular strip.

There were just so many people, she thought, searching the crowd for the face she had seen in the alley. She had watched one too many crime dramas and knew the suspect often hung back to watch what the police were doing at the crime scene.

For a second, she thought she saw him, and stopped short, heart pounding so hard it felt like it was climbing up her throat.

Officer March immediately came to her side, partially shielding Anita's body with hers. "Do you see something?" she asked.

Peering around again quickly, Anita shook her head. "No, I guess not," she said and continued to the cruiser, where Officer Garrett had opened the door.

She slipped into the back seat, expelling a relieved breath, comforted by the protection of the police cruiser.

But as the car pulled away from the curb, she kept a sharp

eye on the crowd, feeling the continued presence of the killer chasing her until they were blocks away and almost at Miami Beach police headquarters on Washington Avenue.

Breathing easier, she settled back into the seat and closed her eyes, but as soon as she did, that night's images flashed through her brain again. The fight. The knife. The perfect little circle in Manny's forehead before he became a lifeless heap on the ground.

She shuddered, wrapped her arms around herself and rocked back and forth, shocked yet again that she'd watched a man die that night.

That she'd almost died.

The cruiser came to a stop in front of the police station, and a second later Officer March slipped from the car to open her door. But as the young Latina stepped onto the sidewalk, a sedan screeched to a halt beside them and the windows on the cruiser's driver side exploded, sending glass flying everywhere.

Officer March hauled Anita down behind the protective barrier of the police cruiser.

"Shots fired. We need backup," she shouted into her radio and returned fire on their attacker.

The sharp retort of the gun had Anita covering her ears and hunkering against the vehicle body for protection.

Officer March cursed beneath her breath. "Officer down. Officer down," she screamed into the radio as, with another angry squeal of tires, their assailant's vehicle peeled away.

Anita shot to her feet in time to watch the late-model Mercedes fishtailing as it sped off.

Officer March raced around to the driver's side of the vehicle, and Anita followed, helping the young officer move her wounded partner to the ground.

"I'm okay," he said with a grimace even though he clearly

wasn't. Blood leaked from his shoulder and the many cuts and scratches on his face.

Officer March bent to apply pressure to the wound, but a mob of other officers and EMTs rushed in to take over. "We've got this," an EMT said as he went to work on Officer Garrett.

"Let's get you inside," Officer March said, and a phalanx of officers surrounded her as they rushed across the plaza in front of the station and into the modern-looking building.

When they burst into the lobby and the officers spread out to take defensive positions at the door, a very pregnant woman walked up to her.

"Ms. Reyes, I'm Detective Gonzalez. Please follow me," she said, but as Anita took a step, her knees suddenly buckled, too weak to support her.

Detective Gonzalez and Officer March were immediately at her side, slipping their arms through hers to offer stability.

"I'm sorry. I feel so stupid," she said.

But Detective Gonzalez reassured her. "It's okay. *You're* okay. We've got you now. It's not every day someone tries to kill you."

No, it wasn't every day someone tried to kill you. Twice. But she wasn't ready to die.

She drew on every ounce of courage she possessed, straightened her spine and walked with the officers to an interview room.

MIDNIGHT PHONE CALLS were generally not good.

Tonight's call had been no different, Brett thought as Trey and he pulled up in front of the Miami Beach police station.

Crime scene tape surrounded a police cruiser with bullet holes in the doors and shot-out windows. Glass littered the street along with gun shell casings that a CSI team had marked for collection.

A small splotch of blood also stained the pavement and Brett hoped the size of it said the officer had survived the shooting.

Inside the station, they quickly cleared security and went to meet Trey's wife, Detective Roni Gonzalez. Because of her pregnancy and a bout of bed rest a month earlier, Roni was on desk duty but still working cases.

Roni was waiting for them by her office door along with a cover-model-handsome thirty-something man Brett assumed was her partner.

"Good to see you again, Trey," the man said and shook his boss's hand before turning to him and saying, "Detective Heath Williams."

Brett shook his hand. "SBS K-9 Agent Brett Madison. This is Mango," he said and gestured to the pit bull sitting obediently at his feet.

"Nice to meet you," Williams said as Roni waved them into her office.

"What's up? You need our help?" Trey said and stood by the side of Roni's desk as she sat and rubbed a hand across her baby belly.

"There was a murder tonight in South Beach. We have a witness who the killer tried to take out right in front of the station," Roni said and handed Trey a piece of paper.

"This is the guy?" his boss said, and when Roni nodded, he handed Brett a police sketch of their suspect. A thirty-something man, either Caucasian or Latino, with a strong jaw, sharp, thin nose and small scar beneath one eye. Short-cropped dark hair in a precise fade made Brett think ex-military.

"Pretty bold to try to take someone out right in front of the station," Brett said and handed the sketch back to Roni.

"We feel the same way. That's why we're working on finding the right safe house for our witness, because we think this guy won't stop until she's dead," Williams said and leaned his hands on the top rung of a chair in front of Roni's desk.

"I guess you want to use the penthouse," Trey said, referring to the space that Brett had heard was reserved for the Gonzalez family when they worked late nights or clients who were either visiting or needed extra security.

Roni nodded. "Just for tonight. If this guy knows I'm on the case and knows the Gonzalez family—"

"Hard not to know them in Miami," Williams said with a shrug of wide shoulders and a touch of facetiousness.

Roni ignored her partner and continued. "He'll probably assume that's what we'll do and might try to go there. We're worried he'll do that while civilians may be present. That's why we're working on finding another safe house. But we can't get that done for another few hours."

"Say no more. Since I figured this was very urgent, Brett and Mango are also here to help protect your witness," Trey said and gestured in their direction.

Mango's ears perked up at the mention of her name and Brett reached down to rub her head. "Mango and I are ready," he said and hoped it didn't sound like he was also trying to convince himself.

"Great. We have an initial witness statement and the sketch. By early morning, we'll be able to move the witness to a safe house. With your help, if that's okay?" Roni said.

Trey nodded. "Whatever you need, SBS is here for you and Miami Beach PD."

"It's appreciated, Trey. This is going to be a high-profile case. Reporters are already leading with this on the local news because the victim is well-known and we had a very public shoot-out in front of the station," Williams said.

Roni lumbered to her feet, her pregnancy belly making her slightly unbalanced, which made Trey slip an arm around her waist.

"You feeling okay?" he asked, clearly still in protective mode considering Roni's issues a month earlier.

"Feeling like a beached whale," she said with a carefree laugh and swept her hand across the large mound of her belly.

With his concerns relieved, Trey motioned for them to head out the door. Once Roni and he were in the lead, Williams, Mango and Brett followed them to an interview room at the far end of the hall.

Roni knocked to announce herself and at the "Come in," they entered.

A shocked gasp filled the air as he stepped inside.

"Brett?" the woman said and as he met her gaze, her surprise transferred to him.

"Anita?" he said and muttered a curse.

Chapter Three

"You two know each other?" Roni asked, her narrowed gaze skipping from Anita to Brett and back to Anita.

Intimately, Anita thought, and heat rose to her face, but her embarrassment was quickly replaced by anger at seeing the man who had ghosted her so many years earlier. A man she'd loved with all her heart.

Body tight with tension, she gestured to Brett and, in what she hoped was a neutral voice, said, "I was a cook at a place not far from where Brett was stationed in North Carolina."

"Anita made the best chicken and rice I've ever tasted," Brett said with a forced smile that was bright against his dark, well-trimmed beard but didn't quite reach up into his chocolate-colored eyes.

"It's on the menu at my restaurant," she said, trying to keep the conversation sounding friendly, although with a quick look at Roni, she thought the other woman had caught on that things were anything but friendly between her and Brett.

"Maybe when this is all over, I can get a plate of it," Brett said, sounding chill as well.

"I'd like that," escaped her before she could bite it back. The last thing she wanted was to spend any more time than was necessary with the marine who had broken her heart.

"Hopefully this will be over quickly," Trey said and clapped Brett on the back.

"I'd like that also," she said, wishing for the same thing.

"We're arranging for a safe house, but in the meantime South Beach Security will help in safeguarding you tonight," Roni explained.

"We're taking you to our offices on Brickell Avenue. We have a secure penthouse there. Brett and his K-9 partner, Mango, will stay with you until you move into the police safe house," Trey said.

Brett and her alone together tonight. Luckily not much was left of the night, since Brett and she had never been able to keep their hands off each other. But she'd learned the painful lesson that passion alone wasn't enough to keep a relationship going.

Hopefully the dog, a thick-bodied, medium-sized tan-and-white pit bull, would play chaperone and provide a buffer to keep them from making a mistake they would regret in the morning.

"If you're ready, Trey and Brett will run you over to the SBS offices," Roni said and gestured to the door.

"Ready as I'll ever be, but before I go, I wanted to know how Officer Garrett is doing," she said, mindful of the officer who had been injured earlier.

Roni smiled in appreciation of her concern. "He'll be fine. Bullet went through his shoulder without doing much damage."

"Good to hear. Please thank him for me."

"I will," Roni said and motioned for her to follow the two men and the dog out of the room. They made their way through the labyrinthian halls of the police station to a more secure back exit to the building.

A big, black unmarked SUV sat at the curb, ready to transport her to SBS's secure space.

She prayed Brett and his boss could keep her safe so she could get back to the restaurant that was her life. She'd toiled and worked too hard to let what had happened tonight keep her from her dream.

Brett helped her into the back seat and then harnessed Mango into the seat next to her, issuing the dog a command. The pittie instantly obeyed and sat, obviously well trained and obedient.

They pulled away from the station and were quickly traveling down Washington toward the causeway that would take them up and over Biscayne Bay to Downtown Miami where SBS apparently had their offices. As they drove, she kept a keen eye on the vehicles in and around them, but so did Trey and Brett.

It was clear both were on the lookout, their gazes constantly darting around to take in everything going on as they pulled onto Brickell Avenue. She caught a glimpse of a plant-filled courtyard decorated with Christmas lights and a nativity scene in anticipation of the upcoming holiday. The courtyard was in front of a large glass-and-stone structure, and they drove into an underground lot for the office building.

After parking, Trey and Brett hesitated, making her wonder until Brett said, "We need to make sure we weren't followed."

Long minutes passed until the two men were seemingly satisfied that it was safe to exit the vehicle.

"Wait for us," Brett said, not that she planned on going anywhere without them.

He and Trey immediately charged into action, exiting the vehicle and removing Mango from the dog's seat. Trey checked the area to make sure it was secure before Brett swung around to her side and opened the door.

He stood by her car door, hand close to the holstered gun

at his belt while the other held Mango's leash as the pittie stood tucked tight to Brett's leg, as ready for action as her partner.

She stepped from the car and was straightaway sandwiched between Trey and Brett, who provided protection until they slipped inside the building's stairwell and hurried up the staircase to the lobby. Brett opened the door and delayed for a moment, making sure the area was clear before they hurried across the lobby and to the security area.

Trey paused to say something to the two guards there, and they did a quick look in her direction and nodded.

As they walked to the elevator bank, she heard the click and static of radios as one of the guards relayed instructions to other security people in the building.

Inside the elevator, Trey used a badge to grant access to the penthouse floor, reached into his guayabera shirt pocket and handed Brett a badge. "This will clear you to enter."

"Thanks," Brett said and slipped the badge into his shirt pocket.

In what seemed like only seconds, they soared to the penthouse, which Anita guessed was about twenty stories up from the vista visible outside the windows that made up two of the walls of the immense open space. The downtown buildings jutting up into the night sky seemed harsh against the delicate palm tree fronds dancing on a night breeze and the shifting, crystalline waters of Biscayne Bay. Bright moonlight kissed the bay, making the water glitter like diamonds in the dark. Here and there, Christmas lights were visible inside offices in the buildings and on the buildings themselves. A few of the offices even boasted Christmas trees with gifts beneath. Maybe Secret Santas like they did in her restaurant, she thought.

Inside the penthouse, elegant modern furniture somehow created a comfortable atmosphere, making her almost feel at home, especially as she took in the high-end kitchen at one side of the large area. It had everything a chef would need to make a gourmet meal, not that she would be staying there long enough to cook.

Trey gestured toward the kitchen area and said, "The fridge is fully stocked in case you're hungry. I imagine you didn't have time to eat tonight. There are clean clothes in the second bedroom if you want to shower and change into something more comfortable and get some rest."

"I'd like that," she said and offered him a weak smile in thanks.

Trey nodded and clapped Brett on the back. "I'll let you get to work. The guards are on alert down below and as soon as Roni has the address for the safe house, we'll move Anita there."

"Mango and I will make sure she's safe," Brett said and shot a quick look in Anita's direction.

She had wrapped her arms around herself tightly, and even though it had been way too many years since he'd last seen her, he had no doubt she was barely holding it together. Her face was pale, the lines as tight as her body, which vibrated from the tension.

He didn't blame her. Most people rarely witnessed a murder and were almost killed themselves, especially twice in one night.

Reaching out, he trailed his fingers down her upper arm and said, "Why don't you take a hot shower. It'll help you relax."

She opened her eyes wide and shook her head. "I'm not sure how I'll ever relax."

He understood. He'd felt the same way after his first battle as a soldier. He'd never killed a man, much less almost been killed. It was something that you never forgot. That settled in your soul, staying with you no matter how hard you tried to shake it loose.

As her gaze connected with his, she seemed to also understand and took a step closer, as if seeking solace, but then abruptly jumped away.

He got it. Being close would bring back too many memories. Remind him of how her body fit naturally to his, like they were two pieces of a puzzle meant to be together. It would feel like a homecoming, but that was the last thing she probably wanted after the way things had ended between them.

Instead, he said, "It's going to be all right. The police and SBS will keep you safe until we catch this guy."

She bit her lower lip, nodded and flipped her hand in the direction of the far side of the room. "Trey mentioned a second bedroom. Is it that way?"

He shrugged. "I've never been up here, but I'm guessing that's the way," he said and followed her to the far side of the space where three doors were visible. When they reached the second door, he stepped ahead to check the area, not wanting to take any chances, although he trusted that the building had been well secured even in advance of their arrival.

Sure enough, they had nothing to fear, and with that he left Anita to shower and returned to the large open space, Mango tucked against his leg.

He unleashed the pittie, rubbed her head and rewarded her with a treat for her good behavior. Searching through the kitchen cabinets, he located a bowl, filled it with water and set it out. Mango eagerly lapped up a drink.

Since he could also use a pick-me-up, he made a pot of coffee, and thinking that a full belly might help Anita relax, he gathered what he needed from the fridge for a Western omelet and started cooking.

He had just finished flipping the omelet when Anita

strolled out in University of Miami sweats that were way too big for her. She'd had to roll up both the sleeves and legs of the sweats. The loose folds of the fabric hid the curves he knew were beneath the fleece, and that was a good thing. He'd loved to explore those curves way too much when they'd been together.

Her hair was damp, making it the color of rich cocoa. The darkness of her hair made her amazing green eyes pop against creamy skin. An angry two-inch-long scrape on one cheek marred her otherwise flawless face.

He was about to skim a finger across that wound, but pulled back, certain that was too intimate a touch. Much like this moment was becoming a painful reminder of other mornings spent with her when they'd been a couple.

To break that too-personal feeling, he busied himself with getting plates and cutlery as she sat at the kitchen island.

"THAT SMELLS GREAT," Anita said, watching Brett putter around the kitchen and return with place settings he set on the counter.

He went back to the stove, grabbed the frying pan and came over to scoop out pieces of the omelet onto the plates. After he did that, he said, "Coffee?"

She shook her head. "I don't think I could sleep if I had coffee," she said and then added with a harsh laugh, "Although I don't even know how I can think about sleep with someone trying to kill me."

He laid a hand on hers and squeezed in reassurance. "We'll keep you safe."

She acknowledged his statement with a quick dip of her head, unable to muster the optimism he possessed. But the aromas from the omelet, sweet pepper and onion mingling with the creamy eggs made her stomach grumble with hunger.

"It looks and smells great. You always made a good omelet," she said and immediately wished she could take the words back because they reminded her of what they had once been to each other.

"Thanks. I had a good teacher," he said, and his words elicited the happy but unwanted memory of her showing him how to flip the eggs restaurant-style. There had been lots of runny eggs on the stove and floor, but also a lot of laughter and love.

When he had gone, she had missed that laughter almost more than the sex, although the sex had been...

Fighting that recollection because it created an ache deep inside her, she asked, "How did you end up in Miami?"

He shrugged those wide, almost impossibly broad and muscular shoulders. "I wasn't up for another tour and got a job at a local police force. I was working there when Trey reached out to me about joining SBS."

Motion from the corner of her eye caught her attention. The pit bull moved away from a water bowl and settled herself close to Brett's feet with what sounded like a happy sigh. "And ended up with a K-9 partner."

Brett smiled, bent and rubbed the dog's head and shoulders, which prompted Mango to roll over and present her belly to him, tongue flopping out of her mouth. Her tail wagged enthusiastically, smacking loudly against the wood floor. He rubbed her belly, laughing at the dog's antics.

"Mango's a good dog. Smart. We've only been paired for about three weeks, but she'd been well trained before that," he said with a final rub and returned to finish the last of his omelet.

She dug into the food as well since the fuller her belly got, the drowsier she was getting despite her earlier comments about sleep eluding her.

Brett, apparently picking up on how she was battling to keep her eyes open, said, "Go get some rest. I'll clean up."

In the old days, they'd had a rule that whoever didn't cook had to clean, but those were the old days and now they were in new and uncharted waters. Still, there was comfort in remembering those old patterns even if they were breaking them and even though she didn't want a repeat of those yesterdays.

"Thanks for cleaning and thank you for the omelet. It hit the spot," she said, rose and was about to head to the bedroom when Brett's cell phone rang.

He answered, listening intently. Nodding, he said, "Got it. I'll bring her down."

Swiping to end the call, he said, "The safe house is ready faster than expected. We're good to go if you are."

"I'm good to go," she said although she wasn't sure she was. Despite how things had ended between them years earlier, there was a sense of security and comfort with him there. Going to the safe house felt like taking a step off a cliff. But if that was what she needed to do to have this whole ugly episode finished so she could get on with her life, she was ready to do it.

But was she ready to deal with Brett's sudden return to her life?

Chapter Four

Brett leashed Mango and led the way from the penthouse to where Trey waited for them in the lobby.

"Miami Beach PD has chosen a safe house in Aventura. Small condo in a complex on Marcos Drive," Trey said and handed Brett a printout with the details of the location.

Brett flipped through the pages, wincing at the photo of the ground-level windows, making it easy for anyone to take a shot into the condo. "Doesn't seem all that secure, and I thought they were worried about civilians?" he said and handed the papers back to Trey.

"Killer doesn't know where we're headed and apparently this was the best choice available on short notice. Aventura police are already guarding the location."

With a reluctant nod and quick glance back at Anita, he said, "I'll feel better once we check it out."

"Agreed. Let's get going," Trey said and pushed off to lead them across the lobby and to the parking garage. At the entrance to the stairs, he paused to make sure the area was safe and did the same once they entered the garage.

The men became human shields to protect Anita, surrounding her until they had her out of harm's way in the SUV with Mango sitting beside her.

Trey was at the wheel, alert for any movement out of the

ordinary as they pulled onto Brickell Avenue. He turned in the direction of I-95 for the short fifteen-minute-or-so trip to North Miami Beach and the condo in Aventura. In no time they were moving along the expressway. Traffic was light in the very early morning hours, and like Trey, Brett kept an eye out for a possible attack, but all was calm.

As they exited for North Miami Beach and the hospital, a car quickly raced up behind them on a side street.

"Watch your six," Brett warned Trey, who nodded and confirmed, "Roger that."

Trey pulled to the right and slowed, cautious until the car whipped around them and sped off.

"Just someone in a rush," Brett said and relaxed a little as Trey made the last few turns and finally pulled up in front of the complex for the safe house.

It was a nice-looking building with condos that boasted good-sized patios. Unlucky owners faced the parking lot, but those on the opposite side of the building had gorgeous views of the condo's pool and the waters of Maule Lake, Eastern Shores to the left, Greynolds Park to the right and, in the far distance, Oleta River State Park.

It was those views that worried him since they'd be hard to protect against anyone with a rifle who wanted to shoot into the safe house, although he had noticed heavy metal hurricane shutters in one of the photos Trey had given him earlier.

As they neared the entrance to the building, he noticed the Aventura police car parked in front, but instinct had him reaching out to grasp Trey's arm and say, "Let's wait for them to approach."

Trey nodded and slowly inched up behind the police car but with enough space to maneuver around it in the event of an emergency. *Never let yourself get boxed in*, he remembered from his time in the military.

No activity from the cruiser greeted them when Trey

stopped the car, making Brett's gut tighten with worry. Turning slightly in the seat, he said, "Keep your head down, Anita."

She slinked down in the back seat and Brett said, "I'll go check with them."

He hopped out of the car and walked the few feet to the police car. The window didn't open as he approached, heightening his fear that something was horribly wrong.

He was a foot from the driver's door when he realized both officers were slumped over, clearly injured. Possibly dead.

Backpedaling, he had barely reached the SBS SUV when a shot rang out and pinged loudly against the hood of the vehicle. Exposed, he crouched down, raced to his door and hopped back in as another bullet tore into a wooden column by the front entrance of the condo building.

Trey whipped away from the parking lot and raced back onto the street to escape the shooter, who managed another shot against a side window and then the rear window, but luckily the SUV's bulletproof glass held.

Speed-dialing Roni, Trey said, "We were attacked at the safe house. Two officers are down. Send the EMTs."

Roni muttered a curse. "Sending help immediately. Williams will head there to see what he can find out. Where are you taking Anita?"

Brett jumped in with, "We could go back to the penthouse, but it would expose too many civilians to whoever is desperate enough to do something like this."

"Agreed. I'm taking her to one of our safe houses, only… How did he know where the safe house was?" Trey pressed.

A troubled silence followed until Roni said, "We'll see who had access to that info here and in Aventura."

"*Gracias.* I'll see you later," Trey said and ended the call.

Brett was worried about how the leak had happened, but before he could say anything, Anita spoke up.

"Do you really think someone at the police station leaked the location?"

Trey shrugged as he quickly backtracked to I-95. Once he was on the highway, he said, "This shooter—or whoever hired them if it's not the guy you saw—may have the connections to get that info."

"Where are we going?" Brett asked, concerned that whoever it was might also be able to find the location of this new safe house.

"We have a place in Homestead, not far from the air force base. We'll keep Anita there until we figure out what's going on," Trey said and pushed the vehicle's speed on the highway while also staying vigilant to see if anyone was following them.

Brett did the same, watching for anyone or anything that seemed suspicious. Thinking that whoever had shot at them had done it from a distance and probably would not have had time to get into a car to chase them.

But he didn't like such uncertainty because the two officers had been shot at close range, which meant someone else might have been nearby as well.

"I think there are two shooters. One who attacked the officers and another one who shot at us."

Trey dipped his head from side to side as he considered Brett's question. "I agree. It would explain the injured officers and how someone was also taking potshots at us from a distance."

"Great. Two people trying to kill me," Anita said from the back seat, and Mango must have sensed her distress since the dog did a little whine and laid a paw on Anita's thigh.

"Thank you, Mango," Anita said with the barest hint of a smile.

"Whatever is happening, we will protect you," Trey said and shot a quick look at Brett, who reluctantly nodded.

While he'd signed up to work on any assignment South Beach Security would give him, he'd never expected that it would involve Anita. They had a history, and that history might make things difficult. It could even open a world of hurt if old emotions rekindled between them.

But he bit his tongue, thinking about what would be necessary to safeguard the house until they could figure out who was after Anita and end the threat.

The drive to the SBS safe house in Homestead was nearly an hour, which gave him way too much time to think about the danger Anita was in and how he and Mango were going to protect her, especially if there were two people working together now.

Those thoughts were still whirling through his head as Trey pulled off the highway and navigated the streets leading to a smallish one-story, coral-colored cinder block home. It was a street with well-kept homes, many of which boasted Christmas lights and decorations for the upcoming holiday. The safe house did as well, making it look just like any other home in the neighborhood.

Once Trey had slipped into the driveway and parked, his boss took a moment to peer all around before he said, "I'll open up and make sure it's clear."

"Mango and I will hang back until you give us the go-ahead," Brett said and went into action, opening the back door and freeing Mango so she could hop onto the concrete pad of the driveway.

Trying to act naturally, he walked Mango along the edge of the drive, letting her relieve herself while he waited for Trey to return. All the time he was on high alert, vigilant for anything that seemed out of the ordinary.

When Trey hurried out a few minutes later, he came to Brett's side and handed him the keys to the house.

"Everything is good inside. You're going to need some

groceries and other supplies. While you get Anita settled, I'm going to make a quick run to the store. They'll be open at seven," Trey said and gestured toward the car, where Anita patiently waited.

"Do you think my guarding her is a good idea?" Brett asked in low tones so only Trey could hear, still worried about the complications of spending time with Anita.

"I understand your concerns, but you obviously know her better than anyone else and that's a good thing. It can't be easy for her and if I'm not reading the signals wrong, you care for her," Trey said, clearly determined that Brett stay on this assignment.

"And that's the issue. Emotion clouds your judgment. We both know where that could lead," Brett replied, worried that feelings could get in the way of his decision-making as they had once with disastrous results.

"I know you still blame yourself, but it wasn't your fault, Brett," Trey said and laid a hand on Brett's shoulder, offering reassurance.

"It was my fault. I dropped my guard—"

"Like any of us would in that situation. I trust your judgment," Trey said and peered back toward Anita. "I think she trusts you, too," he quickly added.

Brett tracked his gaze to where Anita sat, staring out the window at the two of them. "I'm not sure that's true, not that it matters."

"It does matter, but I need to get you those supplies," Trey said and jangled the car keys in his face to signal it was time to get going.

With a reluctant nod, Brett clicked his tongue to command Mango, who had been patiently sitting at his feet, to walk with him to the car. After a quick glance around, satisfied everything was still safe, he helped Anita from the SUV.

"Thanks. It was getting a little warm in there," she said as he led her into the home, locking the door behind them.

Once inside, she stood in the living room and did a quick twirl to peer around the space. "This is home for now?"

"For now. Trey went to get some supplies, but hopefully you'll be able to go home soon," Brett said, understanding her concerns.

"I hope so. I can't be away from the restaurant for that long. I need to call my sous-chef and explain. Give her instructions on what to do. I also need to call my parents so they won't worry," Anita said and pulled her phone from her pocket, but Brett quickly laid a hand on hers to stop her.

"I'm pretty sure the police asked you to shut it off and not use it," Brett said.

Anita nodded. "They did, but I really need to let my people know what's happening."

Brett stroked his hand across hers to calm her, but she jerked her hand away, clearly uncomfortable with his touch. "Wait until Trey comes back. He may have a burner phone you can use. We don't want someone tracking your phone to this location."

ANITA NODDED, understanding the why of it even as she started to pace worriedly across the length of the living room.

Her sous-chef could handle things for a day or two, maybe more, if the two line chefs showed up for work. But if not, they'd have to make arrangements for temps and she'd have to change the daily menus. Order supplies.

Brett's hand at the small of her back stopped the whirlwind of worries that had been circling around her brain.

She faced him, shaking her head in apology. "I'm sorry. I have a lot on my mind."

He offered her a sympathetic smile and said, "I could

smell the wood burning from way over there. I understand, but it'll be okay."

"The restaurant is my life, Brett. I've worked so hard and now…" Emotion tightened her throat hard, making it almost impossible to breathe, much less talk.

"It'll be okay," he repeated and went to stroke a hand down her arm but then yanked it back, clearly remembering how she had shunned his touch earlier.

A bump by her leg had her looking down to where Mango was rubbing her head against Anita's calf, also trying to comfort her.

Their care lightened the weight of worry in her soul. Wiping away tears, she smiled feebly and, in a choked voice, said, "It's going to be just fine."

"It is. How about we get the lay of the land and see the rest of the house?"

She nodded and together they did a slow stroll around the one-story building to learn the layout, locating the primary bedroom with its private bathroom. Two other bedrooms shared a Jack and Jill bathroom. A nice-sized eat-in kitchen was right off the living room in the open-concept space. Glass sliding doors by the kitchen table opened onto a patio and nicely landscaped backyard. A white vinyl fence secured the yard and they stepped out into the early-morning light to scope out the backyard.

In all the rooms and the yard, Brett took his time to let Mango nose around, and at Anita's questioning look, he said, "I want her to be familiar with the scents here."

Although he didn't say it, she got it. *In case someone came here who didn't belong.*

They had just returned to the living room when Mango's head shot up and the dog hurried toward the front door and stood there, vigilant. A low, vibrating growl erupted from her at the sound of a car pulling up.

Brett walked to the window closest to the door and drew aside the curtain to reveal the SBS SUV sitting in the driveway. The driver's door opened, and the rear hatch lifted. Trey went to the back and then walked to the front door, carting several large bags.

Brett commanded Mango to heel and opened the door for Trey, who jerked his head in the direction of the car and said, "There are a few more bags in the back."

Brett and Mango flew into action, heading outside to bring in the rest of the purchases as Trey took his haul into the kitchen.

As Trey unpacked, Anita helped him stow the food in the cabinets and fridge, her mind already racing with what she could cook with the various ingredients. Cooking might help keep her from worrying about all that was happening.

"I see Roni has trained you well," she teased since he'd managed to buy a perfect assortment of fresh foods and staples to complement the pantry items she found as she stored things away.

"Very chauvinist of you. I'm actually the cook in the family," Trey teased back with a boyish grin on his handsome face.

"Then Roni is a lucky woman," Anita said.

Trey smiled and quickly added, "The stuff in the cabinets is fresh. We change it out regularly since we never know when we'll need to use this safe house."

A couple of minutes later, Brett and Mango returned with the rest of the supplies. She laughed as she realized Mango was carrying a bag in her powerful jaws.

"She wanted to help," Brett said with a chuckle and toss of his broad shoulders.

As Brett unpacked, she realized those bags held food for Mango as well as toiletries and clothing.

"I thought you might want to change and guessed at the sizes," Trey said as Brett held up T-shirts and jeans.

"Thank you, but I'm hoping I'll be home and in my own clothes soon," she said. That only earned worried looks on both men's faces.

"I hope so, too," Brett said as he opened the refrigerator to stow the milk and cream Trey had purchased. Of course, just the fact that Trey had laid in enough food for a week warned her that going home soon would be unlikely, which reminded her that she had to call her sous-chef and make arrangements for her restaurant and staff and call her parents to tell them she was okay.

"Brett said you might have a phone I could use to call my people and my parents and let them know what's happening," she said.

"I do. I'll get it for you," he said and left her and Brett alone in the kitchen to finish unpacking.

As they put away the last of the groceries, Brett said, "You'll be back at work before you know it. Don't worry."

She gritted her teeth and nodded. What was the sense of arguing when she knew it wouldn't change a thing about her current situation.

Trey returned to the kitchen and handed her a cheap-looking cell phone. "You can use this."

Taking the phone from him, she hurried from the room to have some privacy for the call.

Chapter Five

Brett watched Anita go, understanding her worries about her business, but he had his own concerns, namely keeping her alive.

"I get the feeling you think this might take some time," Brett said.

Trey nodded and leaned close. "Roni called. No leads on this guy. They're running his police sketch against all the databases, but so far nothing. I have Sophie, Robbie and John Wilson working on it as well."

Trey's tech guru cousins worked miracles for SBS and Wilson, Trey's new brother-in-law, had a supercomputer and programs that had helped the police and SBS on various occasions. If they couldn't make something happen quickly, he didn't know who could.

"That's great. What can I do to help?" he asked.

With a shrug, Trey replied, "Besides keeping Anita safe? Once I leave here, I'm going to find out why someone would want Ramirez dead. You're welcome to help me with that."

"If there's a computer here—"

"There's a laptop on the desk in the second bedroom. You can access our network with your own credentials. If you find anything—"

"I'll keep you posted," Brett said just as Anita returned to the kitchen.

"What do we do now?" she asked.

"Brett and I, as well as the rest of the SBS team, are working on identifying the suspect you saw. For now, just get some rest and stay alert," Trey said and hastily added, "I should go back to the office to oversee things."

"I'm not sure I could sleep, but I'll try," she said.

"Take the first bedroom with the bathroom. I need to use the computer in the second room," Brett said with a flip of his hand in the direction of the far side of the house.

Anita nodded, snatched up the clothing that Trey had bought and hurried from the room again. At the sound of the bedroom door closing, Brett said, "She's barely holding it together."

Trey nodded. "Understandable, but luckily she has you. You know her and what she'll need to face this."

Face this? Brett thought. Even he felt the weight of the uncertainty, but he would help her in any way he could.

"I'll take care of her."

Trey nodded and bro-hugged him. "As soon as we have anything, you'll be the first to know."

Brett dipped his head in acknowledgment and said, "I'll start searching for any dirt on Manny Ramirez."

With that, he walked Trey to the front door. Once his friend had left, Brett locked the door and returned to the kitchen to feed Mango before he started researching the hotel owner.

The pit bull greedily gobbled down the kibble, making Brett laugh.

He bent and rubbed the dog's sides after she finished and teased, "How you don't choke is beyond me."

The dog answered him with an almost knowing grin and a kibble-scented lick of his face.

"Let's get to work," he said and issued a hand command for the dog to follow him to the second bedroom, where, as promised, a laptop sat on a small desk.

He tried to make himself comfortable on the wooden chair, but his holster kept on banging on the furniture's side, forcing him to remove it and place it on the desktop. Powering up the laptop, he started with simple searches on the internet to get a sense of who Manny Ramirez had been.

Luckily, a local magazine had done a piece on Ramirez as part of a Latino Heritage Month celebration. The article was a glowing tribute to how Ramirez had escaped Cuba as a young boy during the Mariel boatlift in 1980 and earned scholarships to a local university known for its hospitality management program. After graduating with honors, Ramirez had launched his career by laboring in low-level positions until he'd worked his way up to management roles in a variety of boutique hotels. He'd used those as a launching pad for jobs with a large luxury chain until somehow finally purchasing a run-down South Beach hotel with a business partner. Together, the men had turned the location around and made it one of the most well-known properties in the area.

It seemed like a success story on its face, but something niggled Brett's consciousness. Mainly, how the two men had managed to find the money to buy the building, which even in its shabby state had to have been worth a great deal of money.

Searching the web, he found a website that listed similar properties for sale and whistled as he discovered a hotel in the area that was on the market for well over twenty million dollars. A lot of money for two men who hadn't owned any property before that.

Unless, of course, they had partners who had bankrolled

the purchase, he thought, mulling over that possibility and who might be involved.

That had him returning to his research until Mango raised her head from where she had been sitting at his feet.

"What is it, Mango?" he asked, then rose and grabbed his holster, slipping it back on his belt.

Mango immediately raced toward the door of the primary bedroom, where she pawed at the bottom of the door, clearly sensing that something was wrong.

Hand on his gun, Brett listened at the door. A strangled cry rent the air, worrying him. He knocked on the door. "Everything okay in there?"

ANITA WIPED AWAY the last tears of the crying jag she'd allowed herself. Straightening from the bedspread, she hurried to the door, all the while hoping Brett wouldn't take note of the tears.

He hated tears. Hated to see women cry. He'd let that slip once when they'd been lying together after making love. Not long before he was supposed to ship out to Iraq, which had been the reason for her tears that night.

Sucking in a deep breath, she forced a smile and opened the door.

Brett's gaze swept over her features, apparently seeing too much since he reached out and drew her into his arms, offering solace.

She didn't fight him this time since the warmth and feel of his body supplied a sense of security and homecoming she'd been lacking for way too long.

The long hours at the restaurant had left her little room for a personal life, and the few times she'd tried, the relationships just hadn't felt right.

Right, like what she was feeling at that moment, held in his powerful arms. No matter how it had ended between them, Brett had always been the one man who had made her feel like she'd found home.

"I'm okay," she finally mumbled into his broad chest when prompted by Mango butting her head against her leg.

She absentmindedly reached down to pet the pit bull, but then yanked her hand back, remembering that Mango was a service animal.

"I know I'm not supposed to treat her like a pet, only she's just so friendly," she said.

Brett inched away slightly and peered down at Mango. "She isn't a pet, but she's taken a liking to you, and she is here to protect you. Right, girl?" he said and bent to affectionately rub the dog's ears.

What looked like a grin spread across Mango's mouth and she bumped her head against Brett's leg, as if confirming what he'd said.

"She's really special," Anita said, tempted again to pet the animal, and at Brett's nod, she did, earning a doggy kiss on her hand.

"She is. Like I told you, I haven't had her long, but she's smart and fearless. When I took her through the obstacle course, she didn't hesitate to do things like the tunnel, which freaks out a lot of dogs."

"I'm glad to hear you're happy with her," she said, especially since she supposed Brett and Mango intended to work together for several years.

"I am," he said and wavered, focusing on her face intently. "Are you sure you're okay?"

Her smile came freely this time and she nodded. "I am. What were you doing?"

"Research into Manny Ramirez to figure out why someone would want to take him out," he said and rose to his six-feet-plus height, reminding her once again of his physical power and presence.

Why someone would want to kill Manny had been on her brain for hours. With a shrug, she said, "He seemed like a nice guy. He was very welcoming and helpful when I first opened the restaurant."

"What about his partner?" Brett asked.

Anita gestured toward the kitchen. "Why don't I make us some tea while we discuss him."

She always found tea calming, unlike coffee, which made her hyper.

Brett nodded and flipped his hand in the direction of the second bedroom. "Let me grab my laptop in case we want to look up something."

"Great," she said and hurried to the kitchen, where she located a kettle and a tea box filled with an assortment of brews.

She filled the kettle and set it on the heat, pulled mugs from the cabinets and laid them out on the table.

When her stomach did a little growl, she remembered that Trey had bought cookies, possibly because he knew his friend Brett had a wicked sweet tooth. Going to another cabinet, she found the package and placed several cookies on a plate she set in the center of the round table in the eat-in section of the kitchen.

The house was actually a great starter home with a kitchen that had her itching to cook. Then again, most kitchens had her itching to cook, and since it seemed they'd be there at least for the night, she intended to make dinner later.

Brett entered the room, placed his laptop on the kitchen table and flipped the lid open on the tea box. "Earl Grey for you, right?"

She nodded and smiled, comforted that he had remembered her favorite. In turn, she pulled out two black tea bags and handed them to him. "I know you think tea is dirty brown water—"

"And I like it as dark as I can get it," he said, then accepted the tea bags and placed them in the mug.

"I could make you coffee if you'd like," she said, but he waved her off.

"Dirty brown water is fine. I know tea calms you," he said with a chuckle.

She sat next to him to wait for the kettle to whistle and said, "You were investigating Ramirez?"

He nodded, swung the laptop around and powered it up again. "I am. We're trying to figure out why someone would want him dead. Did you know him at all?"

Anita tried to recall what she remembered about the man. "He and his partner bought the hotel about six months before I signed the lease for the restaurant. I understand most people in the area were happy about it because it would mean more tourists and possibly more business."

Brett nodded and asked, "Do you know how he got the money to buy it?"

Anita delayed, feeling awful about speaking ill of a dead man. But then again, wouldn't it be worse to let his death go unavenged? With a shrug and bobble of her head, she said, "Rumors said it was more than just Ramirez and his partner in the business."

"Meaning?" Brett asked as he typed something into the laptop, possibly his password.

"I heard from another hotel owner that there was dirty money behind the purchase."

Brett digested what she'd said. "Could be just bad blood because that owner was afraid of losing business to a new place."

She nodded. "Could be, but I heard it from more than one person who didn't have an ax to grind."

"And where there's smoke, there's fire," Brett said and typed something else into the computer.

"What are you doing?" she asked, leaning over to read what was popping up on the screen.

"Checking the property records to see if any mortgages are listed. If they are, that might dispel any rumors about the dirty money," he said and turned the laptop slightly so she could see the results more clearly.

"There's a mortgage listed. They got a loan from a bank," she said, but shook her head. "What about all the renovations? That loan barely covered the cost of the hotel."

"Are you sure?"

With a certain bop of her head, she said, "I remember the listing price because I saw it when I was searching for a restaurant space I could lease. Unless they got a huge deal, that mortgage was only for part of the purchase and none of the renovations."

"That confirms some of the info I found before. I'll send this to Roni and Trey and see what they can do with it," he said and tapped away on the computer to email his colleagues.

The whistle of the teakettle made her pop up, grab a pot holder and shut off the stove. She picked up the kettle and poured the hot water into the mugs with their tea bags.

While Brett wrote his email, she grabbed some cream and sweeteners for herself, since he took his dirty brown water as black as he could, and prepped her tea.

"What else do you know about Ramirez and his partner? Anyone they work with?" Brett asked.

Cradling the mug in her hands, Anita found the warmth was comforting, as was the citrusy fragrance of the bergamot. She dipped her head from side to side as she considered everything she'd heard about the hotel or the two men who owned it. There had been the rumors about the purchase, of course, but not much else, except…

"I think Ramirez liked to bet on the horses and sports games."

Chapter Six

"Gambling? Did he do a lot of it?" Brett asked, imagining the kind of trouble Ramirez could have gotten into if his luck hadn't been good.

She nodded. "He invited me to go with him to some big racing event. At Waterside Park, I think. He said he had friends with connections and a VIP suite."

Brett hopped online and went to the website for the racetrack. A number of events were listed, and he read them off to her. "International Derby. Hibiscus Invitational Meet. Paloma Challenge—"

She jabbed her index finger in his direction to stop him. "That's the one. The Paloma Challenge. It's some fancy racing, music and food event. Ramirez even hinted that if I went, he would make the connections for me to be one of the featured chefs for next year."

"Makes me wonder how much one of those VIP suites might cost," he said and whistled after a quick search on the internet revealed the price. "Luxury suites can run over fifty thousand plus catering and liquor."

"Ouch. His connections obviously had big bucks."

"Possibly dirty big bucks, you said, right? I'll send that info, too, and see if they can get the names of who rented those VIP suites," Brett said and drafted another email to Roni and Trey so they could do additional research.

He got an email back almost instantly.

Video meeting tonight. Twenty hundred.

Confirming he'd be available, he let Anita know about the meeting.

"I hope they've made some progress," she said, shoulders drooping.

"I know you're worried about the restaurant, but we need to keep you safe," he said and stroked a hand across her shoulders, offering comfort.

Her lips thinned into a tight slash, and she nodded. "I know. I'm just not used to being away and cooped up like this."

He remembered how she had been quite active, often jogging or hiking when she wasn't working at the restaurant where he had first met her.

Deciding that he'd already made some headway in their investigations and that he had to keep Anita sane for the moment, he jerked a thumb toward the rear of the house. "Mango could use some exercise. A walk isn't a good idea, but there is that backyard out there. We could let her have some fun."

Anita peered at the pit bull, who gazed up at her adoringly. "I'd like that."

He shut down the laptop, rose and grabbed some treats from a bag that Trey had bought.

"*Kemne*, Mango," he said and reinforced the command with a hand signal, moving his palm toward himself.

Mango immediately hopped to her feet and followed the two of them out the sliding glass doors to the small square of fenced-in yard behind the home. There were well-tended flowers planted around the edges, adding bright spots of color against the white vinyl fence and emerald of the tropical plants in the beds. By the back door was a mesh bag with an assortment of sports balls, and Brett took out a tennis ball.

He tossed it toward the back of the yard and before he could even utter the command, Mango was chasing after the ball and returning to drop it at his feet. "Good girl," he said and rubbed the dog's ears.

He offered the ball to Anita, who tossed it and laughed as Mango shot off to retrieve the object and eagerly bring it back to her. She bent to rub Mango's head and chuckled as the dog hopped up to lick her face.

"*Lehni*, Mango. *Lehni*," he said and pointed to the ground to reinforce his down command.

Mango swiftly obeyed, but Brett could swear the dog seemed unhappy that he'd instructed her away from Anita. To reward her for obeying, he fed her a treat and rubbed her head. "Good girl. I know you love Anita, but you have to listen to me."

Grabbing the ball, he tossed it again and they continued playing the game with him and Anita alternating the throws. It seemed to do Anita well to escape her thoughts about what was happening. Her face lost some of its paleness and a healthy pink glow spread across her cheeks. Her smile was bright and reached up into her green eyes, making them sparkle like a finely cut emerald.

She could distract him from what he had to do, and more than once he had to force himself to keep his mind on the area around them, vigilant for any signs of danger. Luckily the hour passed pleasantly with them playing with Mango and him reinforcing some of the commands they'd been working on together at the new SBS K-9 training facilities.

More importantly, the hour passed without a threat, and he hoped that would continue.

"We should probably head back in," he said, keen eyes

surveying the area around the backyard to make sure everything was secure.

At the door to the kitchen, he held out his arm to block Anita's entry, and at her questioning gaze, he said, "Just want to make sure it's safe."

Especially after what had happened just hours earlier at their supposedly secure safe house.

He opened the door and, with a hand command, confirmed the "go check" instruction with "*Revir*, Mango. *Revir*."

Mango raced into the house. The patter of her nails on the floor sounded loudly as she did a loop around the primary areas of the home. Quiet told him she had hit the bedrooms, which were carpeted, before the sound of her approaching again on the hard wooden floors indicated that it was safe inside.

The pit bull sat just inside the door, head tilted slightly as if to say, "Why aren't you coming in?"

"Good girl, Mango." He rubbed the dog's head and fed her a treat as Anita and he entered the house.

"I didn't realize you could train a dog to search a home like that," Anita said while walking toward the fridge.

"It takes some training, but it's useful. Psychiatric service dogs are trained to do that so they can reassure patients who are fearful of people being in their space," he said and leaned on the counter beside her as she started taking things out of the fridge.

At his questioning glance, she said, "I figured I'd start prepping some things for dinner. Cooking relaxes me."

He nodded and flipped a hand in the direction of the computer. "I'll get to work while you cook." He wanted to say that it would relax him to know they were making some progress on the case, but he bit it back, knowing it would kill the happy mood she was in.

With that in mind, he sat at the kitchen table, opened his laptop and logged in to the SBS network to continue his research.

THERE WAS SOMETHING calming about the way the knife cut through the carrots. The sharpness of the blade easily broke the flesh, creating nice sticks she chopped into smaller pieces for the stew she'd decided to make. Stew was comfort food and boy did she need comfort, although having Brett nearby, as complicated as that was, helped, as did Mango's presence.

She'd heard stories about the kind of damage that pit bulls could do. Luckily Mango seemed to like her, she thought with a quick look at the dog, who had settled herself at Brett's feet as he worked.

Armed with that sense of safety, Anita tossed the carrots into the pot, where she already had onions, celery and beef cooking in the fat from the bacon she had rendered to start the meal. Bacon always added welcome smokiness and salt.

She stirred the mixture, careful to cook it slowly, building a nice caramelization of the beef and vegetables in the pot. The brown bits would add a ton of flavor to the sauce for the stew.

When she was satisfied the mixture was ready, she deglazed the pot with some red wine, also courtesy of Trey's shopping. Roni was a lucky woman if Trey was this conscientious at home.

Scraping the bottom and sides of the pan, she got all the brown bits off, added stock and then her grandmother's mix of spices for her *carne con papas* stew. Oregano, pepper and bay leaves would add more flavor to the sauce. She'd add the potatoes later.

"Smells great," Brett said from beside her, startling her

and making her jump. She had been so focused she hadn't heard him approach.

"Just me," he said, then laid a hand on her shoulder and gently squeezed to calm her.

Heart pounding, she splayed her hand over her chest and said, "A little jumpy."

"Understandable," he said, so close, the warmth of his breath spilled across her forehead. The smell of him, so familiar, both restored calm and unsettled her.

It was difficult to have him so close. The hard feel of his arm next to hers. And his hand, so strong and possibly deadly, yet incredibly gentle as well.

It roused memories of the way it had once been between them, and as she looked up and met his gaze, it was clear he was thinking much the same thing.

She gestured with an index finger, pointing between the two of them. "This doesn't make any sense considering how things ended."

His lips tightened into a line as sharp as her knife. "I never meant for it to end that way."

She raised an eyebrow in both question and challenge. "With you ghosting me?"

Looking away, he abruptly shook his head and released a long, rough exhale peppered with an awkward rush of words. "I didn't mean to, only…the deployment wasn't going well and…you had mentioned a new job in another town. I didn't want to do anything that might hold you back."

It took a long moment for her to take in all that he'd said, but then she blurted out, "I'm sorry the deployment didn't go well for you but maybe talking to someone about it might have helped."

And she'd taken the new job mainly to get away from Brett and any memories of him.

BRETT WASN'T SURE that anything at that time could have helped him deal with what he'd experienced on the battle-field and the lingering effects of it.

"Maybe. It's not the kind of thing you share, especially with…civilians," he reluctantly admitted and quickly tacked on, "I wanted to look for you when I got back, but I couldn't. I wasn't the same man and wouldn't have been good for you. But I'm sorry I hurt you. I never meant to do that."

"And here we are now. What do they say? Fate works in mysterious ways?" she said with a shrug, then turned her attention back to dinner and covered the pot to let the stew simmer.

"It does, only…this isn't quite how I pictured a reunion and…"

His long hesitation had her glancing back up at him. "We can't trust anything we're feeling?"

He nodded. "You can say that. We've got a past and now this unpredictable present."

"But definitely not a future?" she pressed, narrowing her gaze to try to read what he was thinking.

The last thing Brett wanted to do was to hurt her, but de-veloping feelings for her again could make him hesitate when he had to act or take unacceptable risks. That had cost him once dearly. It was the reason he wasn't the same happy-go-lucky guy she'd once loved. For those reasons, he gave a final squeeze to her shoulder and whispered, "I'm not sure this is the best time to think about a reunion."

The muscles in her jaw clenched and her lips flattened into a slash of displeasure. Her eyes, those gorgeous emer-ald-colored eyes, lost any luster and grew cold and distant.

"You're right. It isn't," she said and pointed toward the kitchen table, where his laptop and papers sat, waiting for him.

"I'm going to get back to work." He didn't wait for her

reply before returning to the table and settling in to do more research on Manny Ramirez, his partner and any of the people he associated with at the races or his hotel.

In more than one photo he noticed the same few faces. He saved those photos to a file on his laptop and made a list of their names.

One name popped out at him: Anthony Delgado.

Brett hadn't been directly involved with the SBS case involving a possible serial killer at the location of the new SBS K-9 training center. He'd been working on another assignment, but he'd heard Delgado's name mentioned in connection with the kennel investigation.

He had no doubt Trey would immediately zero in on that name as well since it was way too much coincidence that a real estate developer with shady connections would also be tied to Ramirez.

Occam's razor. The simplest explanation is often the most likely answer.

Except that seemed a little too simple and obvious and stupid.

Why would Delgado do something to draw attention to himself?

Setting aside Delgado, Matt researched the other names on the list. Many of them were connected to horse racing and another name caught his attention: Tony Hollywood.

The mobster's name had been tossed around during another investigation a few months ago involving sabotage at a local racehorse stable.

SBS K-9 Agent Matt Perez was now engaged to the owner of the stable. He made a note in the file to have someone at SBS chat with Matt and his fiancée, Teresa Rodriguez, about the names on his list.

As he worked, the sound of Anita toiling in the kitchen and the smell of dinner accompanied him, creating a very homey and comforting environment. For a moment he could almost forget that they were dealing with a life-and-death situation…until he reminded himself that it was Anita's life at stake.

Anita, who I still care about more than I should.

He glanced in her direction. She was busy stirring something on the stove, slight frown lines across her forehead as she focused.

She had slipped into the cotton shorts and T-shirt that Trey had bought for her. They were slightly large but did nothing to hide her generous Cuban curves. Curves he was well familiar with and created an unwanted reaction that had him shifting uncomfortably in the chair.

He muttered a curse beneath his breath, but it had apparently been loud enough to draw her attention.

She stopped stirring and glanced in his direction. "Did you find something interesting?"

Chapter Seven

Yes, you.

He bit it back and instead said, "I'm wondering what you're so busy stirring."

The barest hint of a smile slipped across her face. "I remembered you liked cheesy polenta and thought that might be fun with the stew instead of rice."

"Totally fun," he said while reminding himself that nothing about what was happening was fun. But faking it made it easier to deal, especially for Anita.

Because of that, he shot to his feet and said, "I'll set the table so we can eat before the meeting."

THE MEETING.

Anita had gotten so involved with prepping dinner that she'd almost forgotten about the meeting. And about Brett. *Almost* being the operative word.

It was impossible to forget that the man she'd loved with all her heart was now just feet away. When he'd stopped writing or video calling her so many years earlier, she'd feared that he'd been killed, but after asking around, she'd learned that he was alive and well. Physically well anyway.

She'd gotten the sense from his earlier awkward response that the aftereffects of his deployment still possibly lingered.

She told herself not to care. Not to wonder how he liked being in Miami and working with his old friend Trey Gonzalez.

She forced herself to do what she did best, ladling spoonfuls of the polenta into large bowls and topping it with the beef stew, hoping it would soothe their nerves. To finish the dish, she sprinkled fragrant chopped parsley for a bit of freshness and frizzled onions she'd fried for texture.

She picked up the bowls and took them over to the table. After, she returned to the kitchen, grabbed the bottle of wine she had opened to cook and went to pour some for Brett.

He waved her away and said, "No, thanks. I need to stay clear."

She did a small pour for herself, more to savor it with the meal she'd prepared than to calm herself. She didn't think there was much that would help ease both her fear and the conflicting emotions about Brett.

Returning the wine bottle to the kitchen counter, she poured water for Brett and brought it to the table, where he was waiting for her to eat.

"Go ahead, please. Don't let it get cold," she said as she sat, but he held off until she was in her chair to fork up some of the polenta and stew.

As soon as it was in his mouth, he hummed in appreciation and said, "This is delicious. Thank you."

"You're welcome. I figured we needed some comfort food with all that's happening."

Brett nodded and forked up another big helping that he ate before he said, "I'm sorry this is happening, but we'll get you home as soon as we can."

"That would be great. I worry about being away from the restaurant," she confessed.

He hesitated for a second, ate another healthy portion and then said, "You always wanted your own place. When did you open it?"

"About three years ago. I started with a food truck and that did well. At one of the food and wine festivals in South Beach I made some connections that landed me on a few television cooking competitions. I was lucky enough to win," she said, then picked up her glass and took a sip of the wine.

"It wasn't just luck. You worked hard and you're a great chef," he said and fixed his gaze on her, as if he wanted her to see the sincerity in his words.

She smiled, appreciating his support. "Thank you. The competitions let me build a nest egg to open the restaurant, and once I did I got some nice reviews and more television appearances. It was demanding but worth it."

"Wow, I'm with a celebrity chef," he said, a note of playful awe in his voice.

Laughing and shaking her head, she said, "Not much of a celebrity but it is fun to be on television."

DEFINITELY MORE FUN than the way she might be plastered all over television now because of the murder, he thought, but didn't say, wanting to keep the discussion upbeat and casual. She'd had enough of death and destruction for the moment and would have more of it once they had their meeting later.

"I've never been on television. What's it like?" he asked and ate as she described the chaotic atmosphere of the televised cooking competitions, the pressure to win as well as the hectic moments as they filmed the segments.

He finished his bowl well before she did, rose and got himself another helping because the food was too delicious not to have seconds. But seeing she still had way too much on her plate because she'd been telling him about her television appearances, he said, "I'm sorry. I didn't mean to keep you from eating."

"It's not that. I'm a mindful eater. I guess it's a downside of being a chef. I'm always analyzing everything I eat. The mouth feel. If it's lush. The textures and taste," she said and finally scooped up a larger forkful.

He got it. He was always on the lookout for things that were out of place or could be dangerous to whomever he was protecting, he thought but didn't say.

Keep it casual, he reminded himself.

"You always could pick out all kinds of different flavors and textures when we went out for dinner," he said and winced, hoping his words wouldn't rouse unhappy memories.

A wistful smile drifted across her face. "We used to have fun..." she began, then shook her head and quickly switched gears. "How did you end up in Miami?"

With a shrug, he said, "It's a long story."

She wiggled her fingers in front of her in a come-and-share way. "I think we have all night at least."

He laughed harshly since he couldn't disagree with that. "I met Trey when we were Stateside, and I was working as an MP. When I deployed, I ended up working alongside him during our tour."

"You were both in Iraq at the same time?" Anita asked to confirm and resumed eating.

Brett nodded. "We were. It was hot, dusty and dangerous but we survived. When we came back, Trey headed home to Miami, and I stayed near the base. Found a job as a K-9 officer with a small local police force and did college part-time until I got my degree."

"I guess you didn't like being a cop?" she said, picking up his vibes.

With a dip of his head, he said, "It's much harder now, but I loved the job. Loved helping people. I just missed being near a big city. Small-town life wasn't for me."

"Why not go back to your family on Long Island?" she asked as she finally finished her bowl of polenta and stew.

He shrugged and said, "I was thinking about doing that

when Trey reached out to me. He'd taken over the reins at SBS and was starting a new division. He remembered my work with the K-9s and wondered if I would be interested in working with him."

"And the rest is history," she said with a laugh and shake of her head.

"The rest is history," he repeated and chuckled.

"And here we are," she said and held her hands palms up, as if to say, "What now?"

He wished he knew what would come next for them, but for now his sole focus had to be on keeping Anita safe. He couldn't allow any distractions that would keep him from that, including Anita.

"I'll help you clean up so I can get ready for the meeting," he said and jumped up.

"You mean so *we* can get ready for the meeting. I don't plan on just waiting around while someone tries to kill me."

She also stood, picked up their bowls and took them to the kitchen sink.

Admiring her determination, he said, "*We* will get ready."

He joined her at the sink and together they rinsed and loaded the dishes into the dishwasher, the actions a familiar pattern since they had done it so many times when they had been dating. As it always had, it calmed and brought a sense of peace he'd often lacked while serving in the Marines.

It was with that peace that they sat together at the table for the video meeting with his colleagues at SBS.

When the image snapped to life on his laptop screen, he transferred it to a nearby television, so they'd have a larger image. Trey, Mia, Roni, Robbie and Sophie sat at the conference room table in the SBS offices.

"Good evening," Trey said, beginning the meeting.

"Is it a good evening?" Brett said, hoping his boss and friend might have good news.

The grim look on Trey's face immediately provided the answer. "Unfortunately, we're not any closer to finding out how the safe house was compromised. Because of that, we're going to be keeping Anita at our location for the time being."

Brett nodded. "Understood."

"Good," Trey said and pushed on with the meeting. "We looked at the info you sent over. We uncovered much of the same information. Delgado came to our attention during the kennel investigations."

Brett knew there was possibly more and said, "What about Hollywood?"

Trey nodded. "When we helped Teresa Rodriguez with the attacks at her stable, we also learned about Tony Hollywood. He's a mobster the FBI believes is involved in some illegal activities at the racetrack. I put my money—no pun intended—on Hollywood having a connection to this murder given Ramirez's possible gambling."

"I think we should focus on Hollywood," Brett said and everyone at the SBS table nodded in agreement.

"Good. Because of that, we've reached out to the FBI agents who were investigating Hollywood to see if they can add anything to the mix," Trey said.

"We also have John running Hollywood through his program to see if it confirms our suspicions," Mia said, referring to her newlywed husband and the software he had created that could predict the possibilities of almost anything.

At Anita's questioning look, Brett leaned close and whispered, "I'll explain later."

With a quick bob of her head, the meeting continued with Roni joining in. "The FBI believes Hollywood runs some kind of gambling ring. Fixing races, loan-sharking, illegal betting. It's possible Ramirez was involved or owed Hollywood money and our suspect was sent to clean things up."

"I'm sorry to say this, Roni, but it seems possible that if

a police officer owed someone money, they could be pressured to supply information to Hollywood or his associates. Like the safe house location," Brett said.

Roni's face hardened and she frowned at his suggestion, but with the slightest nod, she reluctantly said, "It's possible. My partner, Detective Williams, is investigating that angle."

"Thank you, Detective. I know that can't be easy," Anita said, clearly reading the other woman's upset.

"It isn't, but we'll check every possible angle to make sure you're safe, Anita. Believe that," Roni said, then winced and rubbed a hand across her baby belly. "Sorry, the baby kicked. Sometimes I wonder if she wants to come out early and in time for Christmas," she said with a laugh.

Christmas, Brett thought. It was barely three weeks away, but the holiday was the last thing on his mind.

"Hopefully we'll all be home for Christmas," Anita said and shot Brett an encouraging glance.

"Hopefully," he echoed and wondered if he might somehow be spending Christmas with her as he often had in the past. He'd even taken her home to Long Island one Christmas, making his family wonder if she was "the one."

And she had been until everything that had happened in Iraq, he thought, and shook those thoughts from his head to focus on the meeting.

"In the meantime, Robbie and I are searching various sources for more information on Hollywood and his associates. We're also using facial recognition software to see if we get any hits against the artist's sketch of our suspect," Sophie said.

Robbie seconded that with, "We'll find something. I'm sure of it."

Brett didn't doubt that. Trey's tech guru cousins and fellow SBS agents were NSA-level smart. Together with Mia's tech genius husband, he was sure they'd find out more before the FBI or police would. They were just that good.

"I don't doubt it. I'll keep working at my end as well," he said, hoping he could also help to bring this investigation to a quick close.

Once that happened...

He didn't want to think about what that would mean for him and Anita now that they'd been thrown together again.

"Great," Trey said and clapped his hands as if to signal that they were done. His next words confirmed it. "Let's all get to work on these various leads, but also get some rest. We need to be sharp if we're going to break this case and get Anita home safe and sound for the holidays."

After everyone echoed his sentiments, Trey ended the video call, leaving Brett and Anita at the table, peering at each other.

"Are you okay with all that?" he asked, wondering what she might be thinking about their actions and how they impacted her life.

ANITA SUPPOSED SHE'D have to be okay with all that they were doing to keep her safe.

"What choice do I have? You said you'd explain about Mia's husband," she said, puzzlement on her face as she recalled Mia's mention of him during the meeting.

Brett nodded. "She married John Wilson, the tech billionaire, a couple of months ago."

"And he has some kind of magic program?" she asked, still confused by the connection to the well-known and eccentric billionaire.

"You could call it that. His program sucks in data from all over and analyzes it to predict the actions that might occur, the likelihood that suspects are involved in a crime. Even victims before they become victims. All kinds of things like that," Brett explained.

It seemed a little woo-woo to her, and while she wasn't a Luddite, she preferred things she could touch and feel, which was likely why she was a chef. She loved the hands-on aspect of cooking. It grounded her.

"It sounds almost sci-fi to me, but if it works..."

"It works. I've seen it in action, but it's still hard to believe although AI can do a lot of amazing—"

"And scary things," Anita jumped in. She'd seen deep fakes and other worrisome AI-generated elements.

Brett nodded. "Definitely scary so it's good Wilson is on our side. He lets SBS use his supercomputers for a lot of our work and that gives us a huge advantage over the authorities."

"I'm glad also. I'd love for this nightmare to be over quickly," she said and gestured toward the bedrooms. "I'm going to watch some television in my room. I don't want to bother you when you work."

"You can watch out here. When I'm concentrating, nothing bothers me," he said and jerked his head in the direction of the large TV mounted on the wall and the very comfy-looking couch with its soft, deep cushions.

She tracked his gaze to the couch and large TV. "Thanks, I will."

It wasn't because of Brett that she'd stay there, she told herself. No, it wasn't, she argued internally but at the same time she couldn't deny that having him nearby brought a maelstrom of emotions. Peace, comfort and that something else she didn't want to acknowledge yet. She was still working through the hurt caused by his ghosting her and reminding herself that she had her own life now. One she'd fought hard to achieve, and which didn't have time for any kind of relationship. Especially one as complicated as it would be with Brett.

Even with all those misgivings, she snuggled into the welcoming couch cushions and flipped on the television, surfing through the channels until she found one of those treacly sweet movies that drew her into the forgetfulness of happily-ever-afters. This one was about two chefs, their nieces and an unexpected cooking competition.

Perfect, she thought as she gave herself over to the entertainment and grew drowsy.

As her eyes drifted closed, the actors on the screen melded into her and Brett, bringing visions of a happy, carefree life. But as she closed her eyes, a sudden abrupt movement roused her.

Chapter Eight

Brett had been deep into the info on the screen when Mango's head shot up.

The pit bull stood and stared toward the sliding doors that led into the backyard and growled.

A shadow shifted across the darkness.

Brett shot to his feet as one of the glass doors shattered, sending shards flying into the room.

"Get down, Anita," he shouted and whipped out his gun, but before he could shoot, Mango launched herself at the intruder and clamped down on the man's arm.

He dropped his gun and it clattered onto the floor.

Brett issued the attack command to reaffirm Mango's actions. "*Útok*, Mango. *Útok*."

The man was screaming and beating on Mango's head with his free hand.

Brett took a step in the intruder's direction but suddenly a second man burst through the broken door, forcing him to confront the new attacker.

"Hold or I'll shoot," he said, pointing his weapon at the man, who didn't seem to care, maybe because he was wearing armor on his upper body.

Brett didn't have that advantage and raced behind the

kitchen island for protection, drawing him away from Anita as she huddled behind the couch.

Bullets slammed into the wood and quartz of the island, sending bits and chips of wood and countertop flying.

At a pause in the shooting, Brett surged to his feet and returned fire, striking the man mid-chest.

The man grunted from the force of the blow, stunned for a heartbeat, while a few feet away, his partner was still battling Mango, evening the odds.

The armored attacker fired once more, driving Brett to duck beneath the kitchen island again, but he couldn't stay there, leaving Anita unprotected.

He jumped up and fired at the second intruder's exposed legs.

One of the bullets struck home.

The intruder muttered a curse in Spanish and grabbed at the wound.

In the distance, sirens rent the night air, growing louder as they sped closer.

"Vamanos," the wounded man shouted at his partner and trained his gun on Mango to free him from her powerful hold.

Fearing Mango would be hurt, Brett instructed the pit bull to release the man and come to him. *"Pust,* Mango, *Pust. K noze."*

In a blur of white and tan, his dog raced to his side and behind the protective barrier of the island.

The two men, realizing their mission had failed, scurried back out through the broken remains of the door.

Brett zoomed toward the couch to make sure Anita hadn't been injured.

She cowered close to the floor, clutching the burner phone. She gazed up at him, eyes wide, her face white with fear. In a stuttering whisper, she said, "I—I—I c-c-called 911."

"You did good," he said, holstering his weapon, and held out a hand to help her up.

She grasped his hand and, once on her feet, launched herself into his arms. "You're okay," she said, hugging him hard.

"I am and so are you, thanks to Mango," he said, and at the mention of her name, the dog, who had followed him over, bumped their legs with her head.

He released Anita and bent to examine Mango, worried about the blows the intruder had inflicted. "You okay, girl?" he asked as he examined the pittie.

Mango sat and licked his hand as he ran it across her head.

Pounding on the front door had him back on his feet.

"Police. Open the door," someone shouted.

He hurried to the front door and peered through the peephole. Satisfied that it was the police, he opened the door and stepped back, hands raised as if in surrender so that they would see he was not reaching for the gun he had holstered at his side.

The cops rushed in, guns drawn. "Hands up. Keep them up there where we can see them," the one cop shouted. He planted a hand in the middle of Brett's chest and forced him back against the wall while his partner reached over and removed Brett's gun from the holster and tucked it into his waistband at the small of his back.

Mango, who had moved with him to the door, growled at the cop, forcing Brett to command the dog to sit. "*Sedni*, Mango. *Sedni*."

Anita shouted from across the width of the living room, "Stop. They're the good guys."

"I'm SBS K-9 Agent Brett Madison and this is my partner, Mango. If you let me put my hands down, I'll get my ID out of my wallet," Brett said calmly, trying to de-escalate the situation.

"Don't move," the cop said, training his gun from Brett's

head to Mango's as the dog sat beside him, growling. Ready to attack.

The other officer walked over to Anita. "Are you the one who called?"

ANITA NODDED, fearing for Brett and Mango. "They are agents for South Beach Security. Brett is my bodyguard and Mango, the dog, is his partner," she said, gesturing to the pit bull.

The officer narrowed his gaze, peered at her intently and, seemingly satisfied, turned to his partner and said, "You can stand down."

His partner hesitated, still eyeballing Brett, who was several inches taller and broader, as well as Mango. Both dangers if his partner was mistaken. But then the officer reluctantly complied and holstered his weapon.

"I'm guarding Ms. Reyes because she's an eyewitness to a murder. You can call Detectives Gonzalez and Williams at Miami Beach PD to confirm," Brett said.

Turning, he slowly reached for the wallet in his back pocket with one hand, the other still held up in surrender. Once he had the wallet, he finally removed a card that he handed the cop. "Or you can call Trey Gonzalez, who runs SBS," he added.

The officer took only a quick look at the card and glanced over to where his partner stood with her. "It looks legit, Sam."

Sam—Officer Monteiro, his badge read—nodded. "Can you tell us what happened?"

"Two men shot their way into the house," Anita said and pointed toward the shattered glass of the ruined sliding door.

"Mango was able to restrain one intruder, who dropped his gun," Brett said and gestured to the weapon sitting on the wooden floor. Anita noticed that there seemed to be some blood there as well.

"What about the blood?" the officer asked, also noticing it as he walked over to examine the scene, careful not to step on any possible evidence.

"The second intruder had on body armor. I had to shoot at his leg to take him down," Brett advised, then supplied physical descriptions of the two men and pressed on. "They ran once they heard the sirens, but they had to have left a trail to their transportation. Maybe our video cams or those of the neighbors might have more info."

"We'll secure the scene until the detectives arrive," Officer Monteiro said, then walked toward Brett and returned his weapon.

Brett had no sooner holstered it when his phone started ringing. "It's Trey," he said and walked over to Anita while placing the call on speaker. Despite his calm tone, his body vibrated with tension, and he raked his fingers through the short strands of his hair almost angrily.

"What's the sitch? Are you safe?" Trey asked.

"This is a soup sandwich," Brett said, words clipped and harsh.

At her puzzled gaze, he said, "Mission has gone all ways of wrong, but we're both okay. How did they know we were here?"

"We don't know. We're still working on the first leak," Trey said, the frustration obvious in his voice and the heavy sigh that drifted across the line.

"We're moving from here, Trey. Pronto."

"Detectives won't be happy if you run. They'll want to interview you," he said.

Brett shook his head sharply. "We've got to go before these guys can regroup. I know a place that should be safe, but I need wheels," he said and scrubbed his beard with one hand, his agitation clear.

"SBS K-9 Agents Perez and Rodriguez are closest to you. They can get there in less than fifteen minutes. Roni and Williams are also on their way to work with the local PD detectives," Trey advised.

Brett met her gaze, his brown gaze filled with steely determination. "Sorry, boss, but we're not going to wait around for them. Anita is not going to get killed on my watch."

A tense silence filled the air. "We're not going to let that happen. But we need to work with the police."

"Working with people we can't trust? I won't make that mistake again," Brett replied and shook his head, lips pursed. Every line of his body radiated fury that had nothing to do with what had just happened, Anita thought.

"You wait but get ready to go to your new location. There are burner phones in the desk drawer in the bedroom. Use them for all future communications. There's a pouch there also. Take it with you and use the cash inside for all purchases," Trey instructed.

Brett relaxed, but only a little. "Roger that, Trey."

He ended the call and slipped the phone into his jeans pocket. "Pack up your things so we can head to the new location once we're done with the detectives."

"Will that do any good?" Anita asked, worried that the new place wouldn't be any safer than where they had already been.

Brett laid a hand on her shoulder and squeezed. "Do you trust me, Anita?"

Trust him? The man who had broken her heart? But the image of him putting himself in harm's way to keep her safe just moments earlier immediately replaced those thoughts.

"I trust you," she said, and he shifted his hand, wrapped

his arm around her shoulders and drew her in to his strong and very capable embrace.

She wavered at first, but then relented, needing the security of his arms, fighting the rise of old emotions while at the same time telling herself he wasn't the same man she had once loved. He was harder now, not as easygoing as he had once been.

Whatever had happened before, what he clearly didn't want to happen again, had changed him.

When he shifted away slightly and met her gaze, his was dark, the melty chocolaty brown almost black. Troubled. "We need to get ready to run again."

She nodded. "I'll go pack."

BRETT WATCHED HER GO, muttered a curse and dragged a hand through his hair.

If not for Mango... I won't go there. I won't let that darkness claim me again.

He bent and rubbed the dog's ears and body, confirming yet again that the dog hadn't been seriously injured by the intruder's blows. "You're a good girl," he said, earning some doggy kisses in response.

But he had to get moving and grab what he needed to keep Anita safe.

Rushing back to his bedroom, he found the burner phones and pouch in the desk and a large empty duffel in the closet. He tucked one phone into his back pocket. The pouch and the rest of the phones went into the duffel along with the clothes Trey had bought for him.

Back in the kitchen area, he packed the laptop and filled a couple of reusable grocery bags with food, including Mango's kibble. They wouldn't be able to risk leaving the new location for supplies until he was confident they hadn't been followed.

Anita walked to meet him at the kitchen table, her things tossed into a plastic bag.

"You can put them in that duffel. There's plenty of room," he said, and she packed them as instructed.

"You've got company," the officer guarding the front door called out.

He peered past the cop to where his fellow K-9 agents Matt Perez and Natalie Rodriguez stood with their dogs, Butter, a Belgian Malinois, and Missy, a Labrador retriever.

Brett walked to the door to coordinate with his fellow agents while he waited for the detectives to arrive. As he reached them, Matt held up car keys, but as Brett went for them, Matt shifted the keys away and reminded, "Trey wants you to wait for the detectives. Full police cooperation."

"I know. I don't like it, but that's what the boss wants," Brett confirmed.

"Trey needs to keep things chill with the LEOs," Natalie said.

Brett understood. SBS often worked in connection with local law enforcement, and they had to keep a good working relationship with them. But that didn't change one very important thing on this assignment.

"I'm sure it's a cop who's leaking our safe house info."

Matt and Natalie shared a look, and then nodded in unison.

"We agree, but we cooperate for now while we work on this case," Natalie said, basically echoing what Matt and Trey had said earlier.

Brett looked away and shook his head. Blowing out an exasperated breath, he said, "We cooperate, but as soon as we're done, Anita and I are out of here."

"Agreed. You'll let Trey know where you're going?" Matt asked, gaze narrowed as he peered at Brett.

He nodded. "Trey and only Trey."

Natalie gestured to the driveway. "We'll secure this area, but after the detectives arrive, we'll see if they'll let us track your attacker's trail to where they had their getaway car."

"That sounds like a plan. Thanks," he said and went back inside to wait.

Wait and worry. Wait and fume about the leaks that were threatening Anita's life.

He more than most knew the danger of not knowing whom to trust. In Iraq his indecision had cost his squad two good soldiers and a young child's life as well. The memories of their deaths still haunted him. He wouldn't repeat that mistake again. Especially since it was Anita's life at stake. He gazed over to where she sat on the couch, waiting for the detectives to arrive.

Chapter Nine

He reminded her of a caged tiger at the zoo, pacing back and forth across the narrow width of the kitchen. It was as if he was trying to burn up the angry energy sizzling through him.

The two officers gave him plenty of room, as if sensing that he was on the knife's edge of keeping control, and it once again struck her just how different he was from the man she'd once loved.

That man was still there. She'd seen glimpses of him in the gentle way he'd been caring for her, from making an omelet to the way he'd held her, as if she was something precious.

But now a hard veneer made of danger and anger had slipped over him, two emotions she'd rarely seen from him before.

It made her wonder again what had caused the change and if it was for the better. Or maybe that facade was what he needed to work for SBS. She'd seen something similar in his boss. Hard and in control but also caring and protective, especially around his wife, Roni.

Brett met her gaze for the briefest moment, and she glimpsed the caring there, but also fear.

He hadn't wanted to wait, worried that every second they lingered at the no-longer safe house presented danger.

Luckily, the detectives for the local police force arrived

and peppered first Brett and then her with questions about the attack. Sometimes they asked the same thing in different ways, as if trying to trip them up, but they remained consistent even as she could feel Brett's rising anger, like lava getting ready to spew out of a volcano.

When he scrubbed his fingers across his hair for like the tenth time in the last ten minutes, she laid a hand on his arm to hopefully ratchet down his growing exasperation.

"I think that's about all the information we can provide, detectives. I'm sure Detectives Gonzalez and Williams can give you more details about this case once they arrive, so if you don't mind, we'll be going," she said in that sweet and very polite way her Miami mother had taught her.

And she didn't wait for their approval, knowing it was unlikely to come.

She just marched to where they had made a pile of their clothing and supplies, grabbed as many bags as she could and made a beeline for the front door.

Brett chuckled beneath his breath and followed her lead.

As they bolted past the officer stationed at the front door and rushed to where Natalie and Matt stood guard by their SUVs, he murmured, "That took *guts*, Anita."

"Why, thank you, Brett," she said with a laugh.

"You two good?" Matt asked, bewilderment on his features as Brett opened the back hatch and began loading the bags.

"Could be better, but we'll survive. Thanks for all your help," Brett said and shook his hand and Natalie's.

"Anytime. We kept the perimeter clear of any lookie-loos. Hopefully no one got any info they could use to track you," Natalie replied and quickly added, "As soon as Roni and her partner get here, we'll try to follow the blood trail to see what we can get on your attackers."

"Roger. Send that info when you can," Brett said and held the passenger door open for Anita to hop into the SUV.

He harnessed Mango into the back seat, got behind the wheel and plugged an address into the GPS.

"Where are we going?" she asked as he drove out of the development.

"A marine buddy has a place down in Key Largo. He's a skier so he's normally up north at this time of year and lets me use the place if I want to get away," he said and shot a quick look at her. "It should be safer than any police or SBS locations."

"Should be?" she repeated, not liking the uncertainty of those words.

His hands tightened on the wheel, knuckles white from the pressure he was exerting.

"Only Trey will have the address, so I know it won't get leaked."

"You don't think he'll tell Roni?" They were married after all, she thought.

BRETT PURSED HIS LIPS, giving it some consideration before he said, "I think they can separate business from the personal."

Or at least I hope so.

In the months he'd been working for Trey, he'd realized that SBS wasn't just a business, it was family as well. From the top down, the employees were all either family or an extended part of the Gonzalez clan. Even some recent clients had become relations by virtue of becoming involved with the SBS K-9 agents or Gonzalez family members.

That realization had him shooting a quick glance at Anita and wondering if somehow that would be possible for them.

Until he reminded himself that he had to keep this all business and avoid any distractions that could jeopardize her life.

He dragged his gaze away from her, giving his full attention to the road and keeping an eye out for anything out of the ordinary. Much as it had on the morning drive to the safe house, everything seemed in order. No one tailing them.

At least not physically.

With today's technologies, that was no longer necessary. Cell phones and tracking devices provided a digital trove of location information to those who knew how to collect that data.

SBS was always cautious about sweeping their vehicles to make sure they were clean. The burner phones also worked, although Trey, Anita and he had used their personal phones until their arrival at the Homestead location.

He was confident Sophie and Robbie, the tech geniuses at SBS, could easily use that phone data to know where they had been.

Could the bad guys be that sophisticated or was it a simple case of someone at the police department overhearing and leaking the information?

The simplest explanation, he reminded himself, only twice in one day?

The Aventura location could have been gleaned from discussions at the stationhouse, but Trey hadn't provided the Homestead address to anyone at the department, as far as he knew. Even if he had told Roni, Brett was sure she would have safeguarded it considering what had happened.

"What are you thinking?" Anita asked, and as he glanced over at her, she added, "I'm climbing the walls wondering why this is happening."

"Why is easy. You can ID a murderer, but like you, I'm also worried about how they could get the address for the SBS safe house."

Anita frowned and her head bobbled from side to side

as she considered his question. "You don't think it's a leak at the police department?" she asked, clearly picking up his vibes.

"I don't. Roni wouldn't share that with anyone," he said with a nod.

She firmed her lips and looked upward, thoughtful, and asked, "What about a tracker, like an AirTag or something like that?"

"SBS sweeps for trackers on their transportation. AirTag is possible, only we didn't bring anything with us where they could have slipped it and I think we would have noticed something in a pocket."

"That leaves the cell phones, right? Is it that easy? Could someone be tracking us now?" she asked and peered out the window, searching the road.

"We've shut down our phones and they'd have to have access to telephone company data. That normally takes a warrant—"

"Unless they have someone on the inside there as well," she jumped in.

He didn't discount that someone like Tony Hollywood, if that's who was behind the attacks, was capable of that. But he didn't think even Hollywood could get that info so quickly.

"It's possible, but I'm leaning toward a leak at the police department and I'm sure Roni has taken steps to plug that leak," he said, trying to sound more confident than he was feeling.

"You were always bad at poker," she teased with a laugh and shake of her head.

He couldn't deny that. It was why he'd always avoided playing cards with his marine buddies.

"I am bad at poker, but I have to have faith that Roni and the SBS team will have our backs."

TONY HOLLYWOOD WAS more pissed than Santiago Kennedy had ever seen.

Hollywood marched back and forth across the floor of the now-empty garage of his used car dealership.

He'd cleared it out the second that Santiago had limped in with Hollywood's useless nephew beside him, cradling his arm and whining like a little girl about how the pit bull had broken it.

"Shut up, Billy," Hollywood snapped and whirled on them. "I sent the two of you to clean up this mess and you've made it even worse," he screamed, face almost blue from his rage. Veins popped out along his forehead and the sides of his thick neck, worrying Santiago that the man would stroke out.

Hollywood was a powerful man, well over six feet with thickly muscled shoulders and a massive chest barely constrained by the expensive bespoke shirts and suits he liked to wear.

"It's broke, Tony. That dog broke it," Billy whined again.

Hollywood's temper finally erupted.

He backhanded Billy across the face, nearly knocking him out of his chair. The blow left a bright red mark and an angry scrape, courtesy of the large diamond-encrusted championship football ring Hollywood wore.

Tony told everyone he'd gotten it playing on his college football team. While Tony was certainly big enough to have been a linebacker, Santiago knew he'd taken the ring in exchange for not breaking a man's legs when he didn't pay his gambling debts.

"Do you two know what the felony murder rule is?" Hollywood said, then leaned down and got nose to nose with Santiago. "Do you?" he shouted.

Tony's spittle sprayed onto Santiago's face, but he didn't flinch or say a word. That would only make Tony even madder, if that was even possible.

At his silence, Tony straightened to his full height and dragged his fingers through the hard strands of his gelled hair.

"I sent you to find out where Manny put my money, not to kill him, Santiago," Tony said.

"He saw my face, Tony. I didn't have a choice," Santiago said.

A mistake.

Tony leaned down, grabbed hold of his injured leg and dug his fingers into the wound. Pain blasted through Santiago's brain, nearly making him faint. Dark swirls danced before his vision as Tony said, "That makes me part of the murder. That gets me life in prison unless you fix this."

"I'll fix it, Tony. I swear, I'll fix it," Santiago whined, hating that he was sounding too much like Tony's gutless nephew.

"Fix it. Get rid of the girl. Find my money," Tony said with a rough dig into his leg that nearly made him vomit.

He swallowed the bile down and nodded. "I will, Tony. I just need a few more days."

"Make it right and take this little coward to the doctor. That arm looks broken," Tony said with a sneer as he glanced at his sniveling nephew. With a final annoyed huff, Tony stormed from the garage and back into the dealership show-room.

Santiago looked over at Billy's arm. Maybe it *was* at an odd angle. And he had to have someone look at his leg anyway before they went after the girl again.

Only this time he'd take out that pit bull first, so he'd have no worries while he made the man sorry for the hole in his leg.

As for the woman, he'd have some fun with her before he killed her. Payback for making his mess-up even worse.

Wrong move, wrong timing, wrong everything, Santiago

thought as he slowly rose from the chair, wincing as pain shivered up his leg.

"Let's go, Billy. We've got to finish this so Tony won't finish us," he said and pounded the young man's back, part encouragement, part punishment.

Billy peered up at him, eyes wide with disbelief. "Finish me? I'm family," he whimpered and slowly got to his feet.

Santiago laughed and shook his head. "Tony's only family is money, Billy. Best you remember that," he said and limped toward the car they'd driven into the garage barely half an hour earlier after he'd called Tony to warn him about what had happened.

That's why the garage had been empty of the usual workers who'd be prepping and fixing the secondhand cars for the dealership Tony ran as a front for his assorted operations.

Operations Santiago knew a lot about. He'd made a point of learning and writing it all down. Insurance, he thought.

He might have made a mistake in taking out Ramirez, but he didn't intend to fry for it on Old Sparky.

Not alone, at least, he thought, and hopped back into the car to visit the doctor they used for situations just like this.

Once they were patched up, they'd find her, the man and his little dog, too, Santiago thought with a strangled laugh.

"What's so funny?" Billy asked.

"You. You're so funny," he said and finally drove out of the garage to finish what he'd started.

Chapter Ten

She hadn't thought it possible, but she'd fallen asleep and woken up to the views of wide-open expanses of water as Brett drove down South Dixie Highway on the way to his friend's home.

"Are we almost there?" she asked, voice husky from her short nap.

Brett smiled and shot a quick glance at her. "We're almost there. This is Barnes Sound and we'll hit Key Largo in a few miles. My friend's place is right near John Pennekamp Coral Reef State Park. Have you ever been there?"

He made it sound like he was a tour guide, and they were on vacation, but she guessed it was because he was trying not to worry her any more than she was already worried. Because of that, she said, "I've always wanted to go. I've heard there's some great snorkeling there."

"Glass-bottomed boats as well. Maybe after this is over..." His voice trailed off as even he must have realized how it sounded given their current situation.

"Maybe," she said meekly and gave her attention to the passing scenery, trying to distract herself from thoughts of the state of her life.

Water and more water. Greenery along the edges of the highway when it hit pockets of land. Every now and then she'd look back to see if anyone was following them. The highway rose over the water and then dipped down onto what she assumed was Key Largo.

More land and a highway with an assortment of businesses. Gas stations and stores catering to people who liked to scuba, snorkel or fish. The stores were fairly spread out on the road, with big patches of trees, palms and brush between them. Lots of boats, which made sense on what was a narrow spit of land surrounded by water. The Atlantic on one side and Florida Bay and the Gulf on the other.

The sign for the state park flew by and barely a few miles had passed when Brett turned off onto a small street barely wide enough for one car, much less two. A hodgepodge of houses, no two the same except for possibly the double-wide mobile homes here and there, lined the street.

Boats or boat trailers dotted the driveways of many of the homes. Front lawns struggling for life under the hot Florida sun and salt from the nearby waters were interspersed with homes where the owners had given up the fight and filled their front lawns with gravel or electric bright white shells. Overhead the fronds of palm trees swayed weakly with an offshore breeze, and holiday-loving owners had wrapped some of the trunks with Christmas lights.

She was sure that Brett, who'd grown up with snow and evergreens in New York, likely found that an incongruous picture, but having been raised in Miami, it was a familiar sight to her.

Several yards up, Brett pulled into a driveway much like many of the others, complete with an empty boat trailer. The stone crunched beneath the tires in front of the mobile home festooned with lights and a flat splash of color on the ground that she guessed might be an inflatable Santa.

"We're here," he said but held up his hand in a stop gesture. "Let me check it out first."

She waited as he exited the car and then released Mango from the back seat. Man and dog walked past a chain-link gate and approached the side door of the mobile home, where Brett punched in something on what she assumed was a digital lock.

Brett opened the door and called out, "Jake, you home?"

When there was no answer, he unclipped Mango's leash and signaled her to inspect the home.

Anita held her breath, nervous for the dog until Mango returned a few minutes later and sat at Brett's feet on the landing. Brett entered the home, hand cautiously on his holstered gun, but likewise exited a few minutes later and returned to the car.

"It's clear. Let's get settled and I'll call Trey and let him know we're good."

She wasn't sure *good* was the right word to use for their current situation. But they were alive, so she supposed that was as good as it got at that moment.

Nodding, she left the car and followed him to the back to grab their supplies. Together they entered the mobile home, which was surprisingly more spacious than she might have imagined.

The side door opened into a living room with two wing chairs, a coffee table, a couch and an entertainment center with a large-screen television. A breakfast bar with a seafoam-colored countertop separated that area from a galley kitchen with standard stainless-steel appliances and clean white cabinets.

A glass door off to the side of the living room/kitchen led to a deck. Opposite the breakfast island were a bistro table and two chairs.

"The bedrooms are down the hall that way," Brett said with a flip of his hand to the end of the room as she laid a bag with groceries on the kitchen counter. "You can take the main bedroom at the end," he added.

She grabbed the bag with the few clothes she had and walked down the hall, pausing to peer into the guest bathroom and first bedroom, a smallish room with a window and bunk beds for kids, she supposed.

Which made her ask, "Does your friend Jake have a family?"

Brett met her at the door, his body too close to hers in the narrow space of the hallway. "No, but his sister does. She sometimes comes to visit in the summer when the kids are off from school."

She hurried from that room to the next because being so close to him had her body responding in ways she didn't want.

That room was larger with a queen bed, nightstand, dresser and small desk all in white that looked like IKEA offerings. Above the desk was artwork of a beach scene, likewise mass-produced. But the room was happy thanks to the sunlight streaming in through the window beside the desk.

"I'll take this room," Brett said, and she supposed it was partly because they'd have to go past him to get to her in the last bedroom.

The main bedroom was much like Brett's with all-white furniture that gleamed from the sunlight flooding through the window.

She tossed the plastic bag with her "clothes" onto the bed, jammed her hand on her hips and whirled to face Brett, who stood at the door, nonchalantly leaning on the doorjamb.

"What do we do now?" she asked.

IF IT HAD been years earlier, the answer would have been easy.

He would have walked over, kissed her and in no time they would have been on that comfy-looking bed, making love.

Just the thought of it had him hardening, but that was then, and this was now, and things were totally different.

He jerked a thumb in the direction of the kitchen. "I'm going to text Trey and then scope out the deck and see if Jake's boat is there. It might come in handy."

Not that he wanted to make an escape by boat, but if he had to, he would. His dad and he would sometimes rent a boat at the Captree Boat Basin and head out to either the Great South Bay or the Atlantic. His father had always wanted to buy a boat or, as his mother had teased, a hole in the ocean you pour money into.

As Brett stepped out onto the tiny deck that somehow crammed in a small table and four chairs, he was surprised to see a very nice new Robalo 30-foot walk-around sitting on a boatlift by the dock on the canal behind the home. It had apparently replaced Jake's old fishing boat.

"Look at that, Mango," he said to the dog as she followed him out.

He whistled beneath his breath, wondering where Jake had gotten the money for such a luxury. From what he remembered of the catalogs his father always brought home, one as recently as his last Christmas trip home, a boat like this was easily over two hundred thousand dollars. Add several thousand for the power lift. It made no sense for a friend who often complained about being short on cash.

Jake's ears must have been burning since a spectral voice from the video camera by the back door said, "Dude, I thought someone broke in but then I saw it was you. Why aren't you answering your phone?"

"My phone broke. I have a new number. I'll send it to you," he replied into the speaker for the camera. He began to text Jake the number for the burner phone, but hesitated, well aware it might be a security breach. But he had trusted

Jake with his life in Iraq and he still trusted him, although the expensive boat was worrying.

He texted the number and his phone rang a second later. "Hey, Jake. Sorry for not letting you know in advance that I was borrowing your place."

"No problema, dude. I'm up at Lake Placid for a snow-boarding competition. Won't be back until the new year," Jake said, his voice barely audible over the noises in the background, a mix of bad bar music and boisterous shouts.

"Sounds like you're having fun," he said, keeping it chill to not tip Jake as to the actual reason for being there.

"A blast. YOLO, you know," his old friend replied.

"YOLO, *mano*. I love the new boat. When did you get that baby?" he asked, puzzled by how a friend who had only held intermittent jobs since leaving the Marines could afford it.

A long hesitation had the hackles on his neck rising. "You still there?" he pressed.

"Yeah, dude. I came into some money. That Camp Lejeune water settlement," Jake replied and for the first time ever, Brett wasn't buying it.

"I hope you and your family are okay, *mano*," he said, hoping they were all well and not suffering from the effects of the contaminated water at their old marine camp.

"We are. Nothing to worry about, dude. Enjoy yourself and have a Merry Christmas. I'll see you when I'm back in Miami," Jake said with forced merriment and hung up before Brett could ask him anything else.

For safety's sake, Brett shut off the phone to prevent anyone tracking that signal. He'd have to grab a different burner phone for future calls. He'd already texted Trey to let him know they were okay while Anita had been scoping out the bedrooms.

"Something wrong?" Anita asked as she stepped onto the deck and bent to rub Mango's head.

He could lie, but with their lives at stake, he didn't want a lie between them.

Motioning to the boat, he said, "That's a pricey toy."

"Boys with toys," Anita said with strangled laugh.

He nodded and rubbed two fingers together in a money gesture. "Yes, boys with toys, but Jake never had the cash for that kind of toy. He claims he got a Camp Lejeune settlement."

Anita narrowed her gaze and skipped it from him to the boat and back. "And you don't believe him?"

It was tough to say it about a man he'd trusted with his life on more than one occasion, but he didn't. "Jake's dad was a marine, too, and the family was stationed there when the water contamination occurred, so it's possible."

Anita digested that. "I hate to say it, but maybe SBS should check him out."

"Great minds think alike—"

"And fools seldom differ," she said, ending the quote for him.

"Better safe than sorry," he replied, dragging another rough laugh from her.

"We're just full of platitudes today, aren't we?" she said with a shake of her head, loosening a long lock of hair from the topknot she'd fashioned. It curled onto her forehead, and he reached over and tenderly tucked it back up the way he had so many times in the past.

"Thanks," she said and repeated the gesture, clearly uncomfortable with his touch.

It shouldn't have hurt, but it did. Still, he'd been the one to abandon her and couldn't blame her even as he told himself it had been for her own good.

Flipping his hand in the direction of the house, he said, "I'm going to take Mango for a walk and get the lay of the land. Please stay indoors."

THAT WOULD BE the safest thing for her to do, but Anita was tired of being cooped up in cars and houses. The inactivity provided too much time for bad thoughts to fester.

"I'd rather take the walk with you. I think I should know where to go, too, just in case."

He hesitated for a heartbeat, but then nodded. "It's a good idea."

Sweeping his hand toward the gate in the low railing that surrounded the deck, he invited her to walk with him and Mango in that direction.

With a few short steps, Anita unlatched the gate and stepped onto the cement path that ran behind all the houses and next to the docks where boats in all sizes, shapes and colors lined a canal.

The late-afternoon sun was still strong, glaring down onto the area. She shielded her eyes with her hand as Brett asked, "Do you know how to drive a boat?"

She nodded. "My father used to take us out sometimes on weekends. Every now and then he let me be the captain."

Brett pointed eastward along the water. "At the end of the canal, take a left and head straight to Blackwater Sound and the Intracoastal Waterway."

"Good to know," she said, although she hoped that this time they wouldn't have to worry about making an escape, especially by water. Even though she'd regularly boated with her dad and sister, the vastness of the ocean oftentimes made her feel uneasy. Too alone even when surrounded by her family.

"Exit to the street is right around that corner," he said and pointed to the far side of the mobile home.

He clipped the leash on Mango, and they walked around the corner to a narrow alley that ran between the two homes. A double set of stairs ran to the side door, one leading toward the driveway and the other toward the canal and dock.

Brett opened the gate to the chain-link fence that formed a barrier between the homes in the alley and secured the side-entrance area.

Her sneakers crunched on the uneven white stone blanketing a driveway barely long enough for their large SUV.

The home was just a couple of doors down from the corner and Brett gestured with his hand in that direction and explained how to get back to the Overseas Highway in case she needed to get away.

It struck her then that he was preparing for her to go it alone, only she had no plans of doing so.

"I'm not going anywhere without you," she said.

His face hardened into a look she'd never seen before. It was a stony, impenetrable face that spoke volumes as he glanced away before slowly meeting her gaze again. She knew what he would say, and it sent a sickly chill through her body, making her stomach churn.

"You may have to."

"I'm not going anywhere without you," she repeated and laid a hand on her belly to quell the upset there.

He firmed his lips, battling to stay silent, and reluctantly nodded. Reaching out, he cradled her cheek and she leaned into that embrace, drawing comfort from his touch.

"We go together," he said and shifted his hand to wrap it around her neck and draw her into his embrace.

Less than twenty-four hours earlier she would have protested the move, but not now. Not when it was possible that they might die if they couldn't stop the attacks. That he would be willing to give up his life to keep her safe.

As she stepped out of the embrace, wiping away unexpected tears, he kept an arm around her waist and she did the same, slipping her arm around his.

Much like he'd changed emotionally, he had changed physically as well.

He'd been fit as a soldier, but much like he'd become harder emotionally, his body had become harder as well. Leaner and more dangerous, but maybe that's what he needed in this new line of work.

Well, that and Mango, she thought as the dog loped beside him, tongue dangling from her mouth until the animal looked up at her and seemed to grin. Except she had seen what that mouth could do and was happy Mango was on their side.

It was quiet on the narrow streets as they walked, the only sounds that of the nearby oleanders and bushes rustling around them and an occasional boat engine in the distance. But as they walked the final block or two, the susurrus of passing cars intruded, warning they were close to the highway that ran from Key West all the way back up onto the mainland.

They turned and retraced their steps, stopping only to let Mango relieve herself.

It didn't take long to reach Jake's house again, but as he had before, Brett instructed her to stop by the gate while he made sure the area was still secure.

She held her breath, expectant, waiting for another attack, but seconds later Brett signaled to her that all was fine. She pushed through the gate and up the stairs into the home.

Inside the house, she flew into action, needing to stay busy to keep nasty thoughts from rooting in her brain.

Chapter Eleven

Brett watched Anita flit and flutter around the kitchen like a butterfly sampling nectar as she checked out the cupboards and fridge to see what was there.

She was already planning a menu, he could tell, and didn't interfere.

The planning would keep her busy and stop her from worrying.

What would keep him from worrying was knowing if they'd made any progress in identifying their suspect. Or maybe he should say suspects now that there were two of them working together.

Not wanting to add to Anita's worries, he walked to his bedroom and closed the door for privacy, but left it open just a gap so he could keep an ear open for any signs of trouble. When just the routine sound of pots and pans came, he called Trey.

"Good to hear from you, Brett. How's the place?" his boss asked.

"Safe. For now," Brett replied, that niggling worry about the boat ruining the peace he'd hoped to feel at Jake's place.

"What's the sitch?" Trey asked, picking up on his disquiet.

"Place is secure only… Could you do me a favor and check out something?" he said and when Trey agreed, he relayed the details about the boat, supposed settlement and Jake's real name and info. It made him feel guilty that he was doubting a friend, but he'd trusted the wrong person before with disastrous results. He refused to repeat that mistake.

"We can try to find out more," Trey confirmed.

"What about the leak? Any luck with that?"

"We've got the surveillance video from the back entrance at Miami Beach PD a short while ago. We're scanning it now," he said and quickly added, "The good news is that we think we've ID'd the initial suspect using facial recognition. I'll send you his info via email as well as several other photos for you to use in a photo lineup to show Anita."

Brett nodded. "Any connection to Hollywood?"

"Possibly. You'll see the rap sheet in the email. There's a major escalation from low-level bookmaking to assaults."

"You think he's been breaking legs for Hollywood?" Brett asked and blew out a rough breath, even more worried now that they had a more credible link to the mobster.

"Again, possibly. We may know more if the FBI ever gets back to us," Trey said, his tone filled with exasperation.

"Feds are slow-walking this. I guess they're worried the local LEOs are going to make their bust," Brett said, equally frustrated that the agents on the case would be more concerned with getting credit for the collar than keeping Anita safe.

Trey cursed the Feds and then quickly added, "We're going to get this guy. And his accomplice and Hollywood if we have to. Whatever it takes to keep you both safe."

"Agreed. Send me what you have—"

"I will. We'll have a video meeting at twenty hundred again, if that's good," Trey said.

With a shake of his head and rough laugh, Brett said, "I'll check my dance card and see if I'm free."

A troubled chuckle skipped across the phone before Trey signed off with, "Watch your six."

SANTIAGO SLOWED THE car they'd "stolen" from Hollywood's used car lot. If they got into trouble with it, they'd let Hollywood's manager know so he could report it missing to provide cover.

Police were still crawling all over the Homestead location. If Anita and the SBS agent were coming back here, it wouldn't be for some time.

"Why are we here?" Billy asked from beside him and gestured toward the house. His cast banged on the window, drawing the attention of an eagle-eyed cop at the curb, forcing Santiago to quickly drive away.

"You're a jerk," he said.

Billy glanced at him blankly and repeated his question. "Why? You think they'd be foolish enough to come back here?"

"Have you ever seen a rabbit on a trail when they're being hunted by a dog?" he asked.

Billy shook his head. "Do I look like I hunt rabbits?"

The Brooklyn was thick in his voice, picked up from his parents despite a lifetime in Miami.

Using one hand while keeping the other on the wheel, he mimicked Billy's accent as he said, "Rabbits will double back on a trail and wait for the dog to rush by, chasing the scent. As soon as the dog is far enough away, the rabbit will take off in the opposite direction."

"You think they're going to be rabbits and come back?" Billy said, eyes widening as the dim light bulb in his head went off as he finally understood.

"Maybe," Santiago said and pulled away to head back toward the Aventura location, another place they might rabbit to.

"What if they don't?" Billy pressed.

"If they don't, we'll find them some other way. Your uncle has a lot of connections," Santiago replied, thinking about the cop feeding them info as well as the many marks who owed Hollywood in one way or another.

A long silence followed, and Santiago could swear that he smelled wood burning. Flipping a quick glance in Billy's direction, the boy's troubled expression made his gut tighten with worry.

"What's up, Billy?"

Billy glanced at him and nervously plucked at a thread in a tear in his jeans. "Is it true what my uncle said? You know, about that rule thing?"

"The felony murder rule?" Santiago asked, just to make sure he was understanding Billy's concerns.

"Yeah, that thing," Billy said, sounding way younger than his twenty years.

Santiago understood his worry. Billy still had a lot of life to live and doing it behind bars was a scary thought.

Just as it was for him since he was only a decade older than Billy.

"It's true," he said, prompting Billy's immediate objection.

"But I didn't kill anyone. You shot Manny and the cops," he shouted, nervous sweat erupting on his upper lip as he pounded his uninjured hand on his thigh in agitation.

"It doesn't matter, Billy. You were there. You're as much a part of it as I am," he said steadily, trying to calm the increasingly agitated young man.

Waving his arms, his cast banging on the door and window again, Billy cried, "I won't go down for this. I won't. I didn't do it."

Billy was right that he hadn't pulled the trigger.

I did, and I'll be the one going to Old Sparky if Billy talks.

Which meant there was one more thing he had to do.

Like he'd thought before, Tony Hollywood only had one family: money.

He'd never miss a coward like Billy.

COOKING SOOTHED HER as it always did.

Since Brett had mentioned it, she busied herself making the *arroz con pollo* that he had said he loved while he worked at the nearby breakfast bar.

Much like he'd said he'd loved you, the little voice in her head chastised.

Trey had bought chicken breasts, which could get too dry, so she browned them quickly and removed them from the pot with the onions, peppers, garlic and pepperoni. She'd had to substitute pepperoni for the chorizo she normally used and hoped it wouldn't change the flavor too drastically.

She added the rice to coat it with the oil and keep the rice from clumping as it cooked.

Tomato sauce came next along with oregano, bay leaves, salt and pepper. She covered the Dutch oven and slipped it into the preheated oven. Once the rice was further along, she'd add the chicken breasts and finish the meal.

Which meant she had at least fifteen minutes or so before she had to do anything else.

Walking over to Brett, she swept a hand across his shoulders and asked, "Anything new?"

Beneath her hand his muscles tensed. "SBS has some photos of possible suspects. Want to take a look?"

His tension transferred itself to her.

I want to look, but then I don't want to also. What if it isn't him in the photos, but then what if it is?

"Yes, I want to see," she finally said and plopped onto the stool beside Brett.

Slightly turning the laptop in her direction, he brought up an array of photos. All of the men had comparable looks and hair. Anita scoured the assorted faces, worried that they all had such similar features, but there was one man who stuck out.

She pointed to his photo and said, "That's him. I'm sure that's him."

Brett nodded and enlarged the photo from the suspect's rap sheet.

Anita narrowed her gaze, inspecting the photo more carefully. The jaw was the same, but the hair was different. Longer. Darker she supposed, although with the buzz cut he now had, hair color was hard to tell. What cinched it for her were the eyes, those dark, almost soulless eyes, and the small scar beneath the one.

"That's definitely him."

Brett nodded and zoomed in to show his name. "Santiago Kennedy. Teen records are sealed, but he was arrested at twenty for bookmaking. Pled it down from a five-year stretch to two and got off in one for good behavior."

"Isn't there legal gambling in Florida? Why do people still use bookies?" she asked, surprised by that.

"Florida still has a lot of restrictions on sports gambling and bookies don't do a credit check because gamblers know what happens if you don't pay."

Like Manny had paid.

A frisson of fear skipped down her spine. She pointed to the laptop and asked, "Is that it? Is that all he's done?"

Brett shook his head. "There are later arrests. Mostly misdemeanor assault and battery arrests. In a few cases the victims recanted, probably worried about retribution or losing the use of their bookie."

"So he just walks the streets, a free man? Free to kill Manny and me? Free to shoot all those cops," she said, frustration giving rise to anger.

"Not once we're done with him. We will wrap up this case

so tight there will be no way for him to get free again," Brett said and placed an arm around her shoulders. Hugged her to him and dropped a kiss on her temple as he whispered, "We will get him."

"And his accomplice. But what about Tony Hollywood?" Anita asked, worried that there would be no safe place until they somehow had him in custody as well.

"If anyone can connect the dots to Hollywood, it's SBS." There was no hesitation in his voice, tempering her anger and frustration. Bringing some calm, especially as he said, "I smell something tasty. Is it what I think it is?"

She smiled and nodded. "It is. My way of saying thanks for everything."

Not that chicken and rice was any kind of payback for risking his life for her.

BRETT APPRECIATED THE gesture that could rouse so many memories. It had always been a special meal between them. And maybe it was time to put things to rights about what had happened so many years earlier.

"Thank you and… I know it's probably too late to say this, but I'm sorry for what happened between us. I truly am."

Her body did a little jump of surprise and then relaxed. "What did happen, Brett? Why did you ghost me?"

Thoughts whirled through his brain, so many, so quickly until he found himself blurting out, "Maybe because I felt like a ghost myself."

Her eyes opened wide with shock, and she tried to speak, her mouth opening and closing several times before she finally managed a stifled, "Why?"

Why? As if I haven't asked myself that hundreds, maybe thousands of times.

He shrugged and looked away, struggling to find the words as he had so many times before when others had asked. His commanding officer. A therapist. Trey, although he'd managed to unload some of it on his old friend because he had trusted him to understand.

She cradled his jaw and applied gentle pressure until he met her concerned gaze. "Why?" she repeated, patiently, like a parent coaxing a child to share a bad dream.

I only wish it had been a bad dream.

But like bad dreams that became less scary when you shared them, maybe it was time to let her in on what had happened.

"There was a young Muslim boy who used to hang out near our camp when we were deployed in Iraq. He was fascinated by my dog because some Muslim sects don't allow dogs as pets. They consider them unclean," he began, then paused to take a shaky breath before pressing on.

"I tried not to get involved with him, but he kept on tagging along and eventually he was a regular. He loved playing with Rin Tin Tin—"

"Rin Tin Tin? Really?" she said with a laugh.

He chuckled and shook his head. "Yeah, someone thought it would be funny for a German shepherd to be named Rin Tin Tin. Anyway, Yusef—that was the boy's name—asked to play with Rin—that's what I would call him—and I broke down and let him."

He had to stop then as the memories rose up, as powerful as the day it had happened. His chest tightened and his heart hammered so hard and fast it echoed in his ears. Sucking in a deep breath, he held it in, fighting for control.

Anita leaned toward him and laid a hand on his as it rested on the tabletop. "It's okay if you want to stop."

He released the breath in a steady, controlled stream and shook his head. "No, it's time. I want you to understand," he said and twined his fingers with hers.

"I'm here for you," she said, her gaze fixed on his face.

"Because we knew Yusef, trusted Yusef, we didn't think anything of it when he came into camp one morning."

Pausing, he looked away from her and forced himself to continue. "I should have seen something was off with him. I'm supposed to see things like that. Rin saw it. He was agitated, barking and jerking at his leash."

The images slammed into him almost as powerfully as the blast that day, stealing his breath. Tightening the muscles in his throat, choking him into silence.

The reassuring squeeze of Anita's hand on his provided welcome comfort and support. When he met her gaze, the understanding there nearly undid him. Somehow, he finished.

"The local ISIS group knew Yusef had access to the camp. They'd rigged him with a suicide vest filled with explosives. Punishment for us and him since he'd played with Rin."

"You can't blame yourself for what happened," she urged, her gaze sheened with tears, her voice thick with her own upset.

"I can. Like I said, I should have seen it. By the time I realized Rin had picked up on the explosives, it was too late. The blast tore through the camp, killing two members of my squad and injuring another half a dozen."

Chapter Twelve

"You and Rin? Were you hurt?" Anita asked, worried Brett would downplay his own wounds, both physical and emotional.

With a quick shrug and jerk of his head, he said, "We were luckier than most. Luckier than my two friends and Yusef. He was only ten. Those savages sacrificed a child."

She let that sink in and realized that he didn't really think he'd been lucky that day. That he carried the heavy burden of not only survivor's guilt, but also doubt about his instincts. About whom he could trust.

Maybe that was the emotional hardness she sensed. The wall he'd built around himself.

"Is that why you stopped writing and calling?" she asked.

He looked away again, but she cradled his jaw and urged him to face her. "Is it?" she pressed.

"What we had was…so special. After what happened, I didn't feel I deserved something like that. Something the two soldiers who'd died that day and Yusef would never get to have because of me," he said, his voice breaking with the emotion he was barely keeping in check.

Tapping his chest, directly over his heart, he said, "I couldn't trust myself not to make wrong choices again. Choices that hurt the people I care about. Like now. I can't let feelings get in the way of what I have to do. I have to stay focused."

Anita had never been a patient person, but cooking had taught her that very important virtue. You couldn't rush a dish if you wanted it to come out right.

Much like she couldn't rush this if she wanted him to be okay with his past. If she wanted things to be good between them.

After all, no matter his reasons, this man had left her without a word. And he wasn't the same man she'd once loved. He was different, and he was right that if they were going to get out of this situation alive, they couldn't let emotions distract them.

She dropped her hand from his face and untwined her fingers from his. "You're right. We need to keep level heads to finish this," she said, her voice as calm and supportive as she could muster.

He nodded and scrubbed his face with his hands. When he met her gaze again, the hard man was back. The stony look had returned and all emotion had been wrestled back inside.

For a moment she regretted that this man had reappeared, remembering the man she'd loved and who had emerged briefly to share his wounds.

But then the ding-ding-ding of the timer she'd set registered, calling her to action.

She shoved away from the table and back to the kitchen where she took out the Dutch oven, stirred the rice and nestled the chicken breasts in the rice to finish cooking.

At the breakfast bar, Brett had resumed work, his concentration on his laptop, although as she prepped the final toppings for the chicken and rice and an avocado salad, she caught him occasionally glancing in her direction. She told herself it wasn't longing she saw in that gaze. It was just worry about this case and their safety.

Armed with that conviction because it would protect her heart, she puttered around in the kitchen, cleaning and keeping busy until another timer warned dinner was ready.

Anita pulled the chicken and rice out of the oven and, satisfied it was finished, she called out to Brett, "I'm going to set the table."

He immediately closed the laptop and hopped up. "Let me do that. I'm sure you have things to finish."

She did and welcomed his assistance as he grabbed place mats from a nearby cabinet, cutlery from a drawer and napkins from a holder on the kitchen counter.

While he set the table, she spooned chicken and rice onto the plates and topped the servings with roasted red peppers she had made from a wrinkly pepper she had found wasting away in the fridge. Frozen sweet peas nuked in the microwave completed the dish.

She set those plates on the table, returned to the kitchen for the avocado salad and placed that on the table as well.

"There's some beer if you'd like, and it's not skunky. I used one of the bottles for the *arroz con pollo*," she said with a dip of her head in the direction of the fridge.

A BEER SOUNDS like heaven, Brett thought, and only one wouldn't affect his judgment in the event something happened tonight. Although he hoped for the first quiet night in days.

"Thanks. A beer would be great," he said and sat in front of a heaping plate of chicken and rice.

She set a beer in front of him and nervously wiped her hands on the apron she wore. "I normally would make *maduros* with this, but we didn't have any."

He loved sweet, ripe plantains, but understood their supplies were limited. "Maybe if things stay quiet, we can do some shopping tomorrow for food and clothing."

"That would be nice. I know Trey meant well, but something besides T-shirts and sweats would be good," she said with a half smile and tug at the oversize T-shirt she wore.

"I'll work it out with Trey," he said, and once she'd sat, he dug into the meal.

The flavors burst in his mouth, as delicious as he remembered. Maybe better, he thought and murmured in appreciation. "This is delicious."

"Thanks. I had to make do with what I had," she said, obviously uneasy as she picked at the meal she'd prepared.

"Well, you did good, Reyes. Real good," he teased and forked up a healthy portion of the chicken and rice.

HIS PRAISE LIGHTENED her mood, and they both must have been hungry since they ate in companionable silence. She was grateful for that because it kept away worry about the fact someone was trying to kill her as well as the conflicting emotions she had for Brett.

They finished the meal and cleaned up with little said, falling into the patterns they'd shared when they'd been together. After, he fed Mango, gave her fresh water and they took her for a quick walk.

Nightfall had come quickly in early December, but there was enough illumination on the street from the nearby homes, Christmas lights and scattered streetlamps. By the time they returned from the short walk, the puddled color that sprawled in the driveway by the mobile home had inflated. A large bare-chested Santa in board shorts, complete with a surfboard, greeted them upon their return.

"I gather Jake is quite a character," she said and chuckled.

"He is. You could always count on Jake to liven things up," he said and laughed, but then grew serious, his look severe and troubled.

She laid a hand on his arm. "I know you're bothered by that boat, but maybe there's a reasonable explanation."

"Maybe," he said and held up his hand to stay her entry as he went through the process that was becoming almost familiar by now. He entered through the side gate, opened the house and sent in Mango. Once Mango had given the "all clear," Brett signaled for Anita to follow.

Inside they each hurried to what had become their domains. Brett sat at the breakfast bar with the laptop, preparing for their upcoming meeting. She went to the kitchen to make coffee, expecting that it would be another late night.

By the time the coffee was sputtering in the espresso pot, Brett's laptop was chiming to warn it was time for their video meeting.

The television across the way from them snapped to life with the image of the SBS crew sitting around the table at their Brickell Avenue office. Roni and her partner were also there, faces solemn.

She worried whether that meant good or bad news but didn't press. They'd share when they were ready.

At the table, she set down the cups of coffee and took a spot beside Brett.

He mouthed a "thank you."

Trey began the meeting. "I'm sure Brett has shared the photo lineup with you," he said and displayed the array of photos she had seen earlier onto the screen. "Can you identify any of them as the man you saw the night Ramirez was murdered?"

Anita nodded and used the touch pad on the laptop to move the mouse until it rested on the photo she had picked out earlier.

"I'm sure that's the man," she said, and Trey returned the screen to the team. He handed Roni a piece of paper.

She nodded and said, "I hope this photo lineup will fly with the district attorney."

"Why wouldn't it?" Anita asked, puzzled.

"We would have preferred to do it ourselves, but there are exigent circumstances obviously. It would also be better if we could wait for the DNA analysis from the blood at the Homestead location," Roni said.

Williams quickly added, "Florida started collecting DNA in 2011 so Kennedy's DNA should be in the system because of his priors."

But DNA analysis could take time. *Time we don't have*, Brett thought.

"What about the leak? Trey mentioned earlier that you have video that might help?" he pressed.

Trey motioned for Sophie to take over, and a second later, a video popped up on the screen.

A uniformed officer, cap pulled low and his head tucked down, walked past the SBS SUV parked at the back entrance, paused and took a long look at the vehicle. He did another walk back and forth before entering the stationhouse again.

As he did so, he tipped his head down to avoid showing his face to the camera.

"We're working up his approximate size and weight so Roni and Heath can look through the database of officers at the stationhouse," Sophie said.

"How long will that take?" he pressed.

"Our end will be relatively quick thanks to John's super-computer, but the police analysis may take a little time since we can't access their database," Robbie advised.

Brett slumped back in his chair and released a frustrated sigh. "Doesn't seem like we have much."

Roni quickly countered with, "Actually, we think that

this officer memorized your license plate number in order to track you."

Anita leaned forward in interest and said, "Track us? With just the plate number?"

Roni and Williams shared an uneasy look and Williams finally explained, "PD has a number of automatic license plate readers in police cars as well as in static locations in Miami and along Route 1, which you took to reach Homestead. There's also a database of ALPRs from HOAs and other private places that feed info into a database we can access."

"And did someone access it?" Anita pushed.

"It will take time, but we're working to see who accessed the info," Roni confirmed with a tilt of her head.

Anita's rising tension coupled with his frustration seemed obvious since Trey said, "We're working this as fast as we can, Anita."

Brett believed that, but again, it was time they might not have if Hollywood and his crew had a say. Which made him ask, "What about Hollywood? Have you made a link to him?"

"Nothing yet, but we're—"

"Working on it," Anita finished, her irritation obvious.

"We are. Other than coincidence about the bookmaking and assaults, probably to secure payment of gambling debts, we don't have a direct link but we will," Trey confirmed, his tone brooking no disagreement. "If there's nothing else," he said.

Brett and Anita did a quick glance at each other and were clearly in silent agreement. "Nothing else. I'll keep working on whatever I can find out about our suspect," Brett said.

"We'll keep you advised as soon as we have more," Trey said and a second later the video feed ended.

Brett reached out and laid a hand on Anita's shoulder, squeezed lightly to offer reassurance. "I know it seems like there's not much progress, but you shouldn't worry."

She bit her lower lip and glanced away, but he didn't press. When she finally looked back, she said, "I'm worried about my business. My life." Pointing between the two of them, she said, "Us."

He wanted to say there was no "us" now, only it would be a lie. From the moment he'd laid eyes on her at the police station, all the old feelings and emotions had awoken. Denying them would be a lie and, as he'd thought before, he didn't want any lies between them.

Mimicking her gesture, he said, "This 'us' is complicated and dangerous right now, as we discussed."

She nodded, in agreement, and shifted the conversation to a safer topic. "Do you think I can call my sous-chef in the morning? My parents too?"

"As long as you use a burner phone. I'll get you one first thing tomorrow."

THE MORNING COULDN'T come fast enough as far as Anita was concerned.

Although she'd busied herself to keep distracted, with the meeting done and the evening looming large in front of her, it was impossible not to think about how her restaurant's lunch service had gone, whether the promised porterhouse steaks had arrived and how the dinner service was faring. By now it would be in full swing, and while she itched to call, waiting made sense.

She worried that even with a burner phone they'd be able to track them.

"Can you track a 'burner phone'?" she asked, using air quotes for emphasis.

Brett nodded. "You can track *any* phone. That's why we try to keep phone use to a minimum."

"And what about those APRs or whatever? Do you think they could have used that to track us to here?" she pressed.

Chapter Thirteen

"ALPRs," he corrected and jumped back on his laptop. "If they somehow grabbed Matt's license plate number, which I'm confident they didn't, they might be able to track it. There's a public site that may have more info," he said and popped up the video feed from the laptop to the television again.

Anita stood and walked closer to the television to get a better look as Brett typed in the zip code for Miami and chose a camera type. The website populated with a bunch of brown dots to show where various kinds of cameras were located. ALPRs, red light and speed cameras were all noted on the map.

"This is a crowd-sourced database so it relies on users providing this information," he said and used the mouse to move the map and display where ALPRs might have been on their route.

Relief flooded her as she realized the last location was in Homestead and the areas beyond that were clear of any readers until Big Pine Key, which she believed was quite a distance south of them.

"We're clear," she said with a happy sigh.

"Looks that way. Time for you to relax and get some rest.

If things have settled down in the morning, you can make your call and we'll take that drive for supplies."

"That sounds good. I'm going to shower," she said and jerked a thumb in the direction of the bedrooms.

A shower, together with the info they'd just uncovered, would help her relax.

"WHAT DO YOU mean Billy took off?" Tony Hollywood roared, fists clenched, face mottled with angry red and sickly white.

Santiago held his hands out in pleading. "He freaked out when you mentioned the felony murder rule. Started crying like a little baby about how he was too young to go to prison for life. He said he needed a refill for that stupid vape thing he's always sucking on and went into the store but never came out."

"Find him. Check with my sister. Billy was always a ma-ma's boy," Tony said and marched over. Jabbing a finger into Santiago's chest, so hard he was sure he'd have bruises, Tony said, "If he's a weak link, I need to know so we can deal with him."

"Deal with him? How?" Santiago asked, sure of what Tony would say, which was why he was surprised when his boss responded with, "Just find him and bring him here. I could always talk some sense into the kid. Besides, he's family."

Santiago cursed silently, hating that he'd been so wrong about what Tony would do to Billy, because if the truth came out...

"I'll find him, Tony. I'm sure he's just chilling somewhere and licking his wounds."

"What about the girl? Any news?" Tony asked, raising a hairy eyeball in a way that had Santiago sweating a bit.

"We lost them after they left Homestead, but I'm working

on it," he said, hoping his connection at the police station could point them in the right direction again.

Tony grunted. "Make it happen. Yesterday, Santiago. And find Billy before he does something stupid."

He nodded and rushed from the room, a streak of curses escaping him as he realized he was in deep trouble.

Family meant something to Tony. He'd made a big mistake and there was possibly only one way to rectify that error.

Find the girl before the police found Billy. Or what was left of him anyway.

BRETT HAD GROWN frustrated at the dead ends he'd been hitting for information on Tony Hollywood.

Sure, there were a bunch of news articles and reports on the mobster, but nothing that could link him to a low-level criminal like Santiago Kennedy.

Wanting a fresh set of eyes, he'd taken a break to shower, and come out to find Anita stretched out on the couch in a fresh T-shirt and sleeping shorts.

He needed time to think about all that was happening and what they had so far in the investigation and stepped out onto the small deck, with Mango at his side. The night was peaceful, the only sounds those of the palm fronds moving overhead, a distant set of wind chimes and the canal waters lapping up against the nearby wooden dock and bulkhead.

There were lights on here and there in the homes along the canal. Some people even had Christmas lights strung along their docks and boats. The reflections of the colors created a watercolor-like kaleidoscope on the surface of the canal.

A few houses down, a bright green light in the water highlighted the shadows of snook attracted by the glow so a fisherman might snag them for a meal.

He'd caught more than one himself when Jake and he had fished from this dock.

Jake.

He hadn't asked about his friend during the video meeting, thinking it had likely been too soon for Trey to have any info. Plus, he wanted to believe for as long as possible that he could trust Jake.

Mango nudged his leg and glanced up at him, eyes almost sad, as if she sensed Brett's upset.

He knelt and rubbed the dog's head and ears, accepted the doggy kisses some people he'd met would think of as impure. In his mind, nothing connected to love was impure, but to each their own.

"Let's do a last walk," he said, even if the walk only consisted of a quick check around the house and the immediate area.

Since it would be a short stroll, he didn't bother clipping a leash on Mango. He just stuffed a fresh poop bag into his pocket and, without a word, the dog heeled to his side, breaking their connection only long enough to relieve herself. Brett cleaned up the waste and deposited it in a trash can in the side yard.

Thankfully there was nothing to see in and around the perimeter of the house.

With it all quiet, he went back inside to find Anita asleep in front of the television. A gentle snore escaped her every now and then, signaling she was in deep sleep.

He'd wake her if he shut off the television. He only turned down the volume, so he'd be able to hear any abnormal noises. Returning to his laptop, he fired it up and got back to work, intending to search for anything he could find on Tony Hollywood or Santiago Kennedy.

Jake.

He hated that he had to add his friend to the mix, but he couldn't risk any surprises.

He made a hand gesture to Mango to take a spot by the

back door and the dog immediately obeyed, stretching out her tan-and-white body across the entrance. Her large, squarish head rested on her paws.

With Mango on guard, he gave his attention to the internet searches and found Kennedy on social media. More than once their suspect had bragged about his guns and connections but never mentioned Hollywood. It made him wonder why the posts with the weapons weren't flagged when so many other, less dangerous posts sometimes put a user in social media jail.

Brett took screenshots of the posts and saved the links to a list to share with Trey and the team. He suspected one of those guns could be the same make and caliber as the one used to shoot Ramirez and the police officers.

But as he was about to flip away from Kennedy's profile, something snagged his attention: a series of photos taken at a racetrack.

Checking the time stamps, he realized it was while the Paloma Challenge had been held. He screenshotted those and saved the links as well, and just to confirm, he pulled up photos of Waterside Park.

Bingo, he thought. The background in Kennedy's photo was Waterside Park, confirming that Kennedy had been at the racetrack at the same time as Ramirez.

Of course, that coincidence alone wasn't enough to say any wrongdoing had occurred at the track. Unless they could get more info, it was just coincidence.

The Feds might have more details, but clearly they didn't want to share. Keeping it to themselves could be about not having their case blown, but it could also be about not losing the collar of a high-profile criminal like Tony Hollywood to a bunch of local cops. Or SBS, for that matter.

Checking the dates on the races, he realized that a few months had gone by. Probably too long a time for anyone to be holding on to CCTV tapes, but you didn't have an event like that without plastering it all over social media to get the most bang for your buck. Not to mention local news stories as well.

Locating the page for the event, he scrolled through the photos leading up to the big occasion and then race day itself. Most of the photos were of the horses, jockeys and all the beautiful people and entertainers who would be there. Interspersed with them were a few screenshots of the crowd.

He zipped right past one crowd photo, but something called him back to it.

Was it just wishful thinking that the two people way in the back, in the fuzzy section of the photo, looked like Ramirez and Kennedy?

As he had before, he did a screenshot and saved the link. This time he also downloaded the photo since Kennedy had made his profile public. *Clearly not a rocket scientist*, he thought.

Brett's own page was limited to family and private because you never knew who might be trying to find you. Like now.

The resolution of the picture wasn't good to begin with, but he still tried to enhance the fuzzy section with his very basic photo editing software. That served to convince him that he wasn't imagining it.

It certainly looked like Ramirez and Kennedy although they were both wearing hats, which hid their hair and could alter their overall look.

Still, it was worth sending that info to Sophie and Robbie. If anyone could work magic on that blurry photo, it would be them.

Satisfied that he had added one more dot to connect

Ramirez's killer to Tony Hollywood, he did the one thing that he was dreading.

He pulled up Jake's social media and delved through all the posts and photos.

The latest ones confirmed that he wasn't lying about being in Lake Placid and a snowboarding competition. There was photo after photo of him with other snowboarders on the slopes. Some of Jake racing posted by the event organizers. Others with the groupies who tagged after a good-looking and charming guy like Jake.

He scrolled through the timeline, searching for anything about the boat.

Nothing.

That didn't make sense since most people who got their hands on a toy like that were likely to post photos of their new baby.

Unless you didn't want people to know, which seemed odd, especially for his friend.

Jake had always been someone who put everything out there. He'd never had anything to hide...until now.

He hadn't been wrong to think there had been hesitation when he'd asked Jake about the boat.

Growing suspicions curled their way around his gut, making him feel sick. Making him worry that he'd made a mistake again to trust his old friend.

It was that worry that drove him to pick up his phone to call Trey even though it was nearly midnight. But if he knew Trey, his friend and boss was probably still at work as well. Just in case, especially since Roni would likely be asleep, he texted him first.

You up?

Yes. Still at the office. Give me a minute. Roni's on my couch.

Because he also didn't want to wake Anita, he tiptoed to his bedroom and closed the door, but left it slightly ajar to listen for any issues.

"What's up?" Trey said after Brett answered.

"I may have found a connection between Ramirez and Kennedy. I emailed you a photo from the racetrack. I think it's them in the background."

"Good work. Every little piece of the puzzle helps," Trey said.

"What about the Feds? Still nothing?" Brett asked.

A rough sigh sputtered across the line. "Nada. They're not good at playing well with others."

"What about the cop in the video? Anything?" he pressed.

"Williams went back to the station with the info Sophie and Robbie provided about his physical description. Plus, Williams thought there was something familiar about the cop, so hopefully we'll know more soon," Trey advised, but Brett picked up something in his old friend's voice. Something that had nothing to do with the case.

"You good?" he asked, concerned about his friend.

"Roni isn't feeling well. It's why she didn't go back to the station with Williams," Trey replied.

Roni was the love of his life. He'd never expected to see that with a hard-ass like Trey, but Fate had apparently had other plans for his friend.

"Take care of her first, Trey. She and the baby are what's most important."

Another sigh filled the line. A tired one this time. "They are. I've got the others on double to get things moving. We'll work on that photo ASAP."

"Thanks, Trey. I'll keep on working on this, too," he said.

"I know you will," Trey replied and ended the call.

"Is everything okay?" Anita asked as she opened the door to the bedroom.

As Anita peered at him, Brett schooled his features, forcing away his fears about Roni but also about Anita and what he was feeling for her.

The devastation he'd feel if he somehow lost her after finding her once again.

Chapter Fourteen

Brett was standing in the room, his face in partial shadow from the dim light cast by a small bedside lamp. But despite that, it was impossible to miss the sorrow in his dark gaze as he said, "Trey is worried because Roni isn't feeling well."

"Is she going to be okay?" she asked, likewise worried because the woman was fairly far along in her pregnancy.

He did a quick jerk of his shoulders and ran his fingers across the short strands of his hair. "I hope so. She had some issues a few months ago but was doing better."

"Is she in the hospital?" she asked, and Brett quickly shook his head.

"Just resting at the SBS offices so maybe it's not all that serious."

"That's good news, I guess," she said and walked out of the room, Brett trailing behind her as she returned to the living room and plopped back onto the couch.

"We do have some good news," he said and explained the link he had discovered between Ramirez and Kennedy, as well as the possibility that they would soon have an ID for the cop who might be leaking information.

"That is definitely good news. I might just be able to sleep tonight," she said with a smile.

A half grin crept across Brett's full lips. A boyish grin that drove away the earlier sadness she had seen from his eyes.

"You were doing a pretty good job of sawing logs not that long ago," he teased, and the grin erupted into a full-fledged smile.

She wagged a finger back and forth in a shaming gesture. "You were a pretty good lumberjack yourself."

He jammed his hands on his hips, let out a whoop of a laugh, but then turned serious as Mango popped to her feet, faced the deck and growled.

Brett rushed toward the door and gestured for Anita to move behind him. As he walked toward the door, hand on his weapon, he turned and said to her, "Don't move from there."

With a hand gesture to Mango, he said, "*K noze*, Mango. *K noze*."

The dog instantly hugged Brett's side.

BRETT WENT TO the back door and peered through the glass.

A shadow on the dock. Moving slowly along the length of the boat.

There was little moonlight so Brett couldn't see his face until the person stepped toward the bow of the boat. A light on the deck shined on the man's face and Brett thought he recognized him as one of Jake's neighbors.

He opened the back door and stepped onto the deck, Mango plastered to his side.

"Is that you, Jim?" he called out, but never moved his hand away from his weapon.

"Brett?" the man responded and smiled. "I didn't know you were down. I was checking things out since I thought I saw someone here and knew Jake was away."

Brett relaxed and signaled Mango to lie down. After the dog had complied, Brett stepped down to the walkway to shake the man's hand. "Good to see you again, Jim."

"Same, Brett," he said and motioned to the boat. "She's a beauty, isn't she?"

"She is. My dad has been wishing for one for years. Jake is a lucky man," he said and ran a hand across the metal railing on the boat.

"I'll say. Imagine winning a cool million in the lottery," Jim said with a low whistle as he admired the boat.

"Wow, a million, huh?" he said, his gut twisting as he realized his friend had lied to him and possibly to his neighbor.

Jim nodded and smiled, but the smile dimmed as his gaze skipped down to the gun at Brett's hip and then back up to his face.

"Trouble?" Jim asked.

He remembered then that the neighbor was a retired police officer, which might work in his favor.

"Just came straight from work. I'm a K-9 agent for SBS in Miami," he said.

Jim's eagle-eyed officer's gaze skipped to Mango lying nearby. "Your partner, I assume."

With a dip of his head, Brett said, "Her name is Mango. She's a good partner."

"Good to hear. Well, it's late and now that I know everything's okay here, I'll go," Jim said.

As the man turned to walk back to his home, Brett said, "Thanks for keeping an eye on things for Jake. If you see anything out of line around here—"

"I'll let you know. Stay safe," Jim said and glanced back toward Jake's house, where Anita's silhouette was visible by the back door.

"Thanks, Jim." He waited on the dock until Jim had gone into his own home to click his tongue for Mango to follow him back into Jake's house.

"You know him?" Anita asked as he entered the living room.

Nodding, he said, "Jake's neighbor Jim. Retired cop who saw something here and decided to check it out. We're lucky to have cop's eyes next door."

"Cop's eyes? Is that a thing?" she asked and sat back down on the couch.

"Yeah, it is. They don't miss a thing. That's why he was out there, inspecting," he said, but then quickly blurted out, "Jim said Jake told him he won the lottery and that's how he bought the boat."

She sat silently for a long moment but plucked at the hem of her shorts nervously. "But Jake told you something different," she finally said.

"He did, and who knows what the truth really is," Brett said and wiped his face with his hands, his beard rasping with the action.

BRETT WAS CLEARLY troubled by his friend's lies, his gaze dark and filled with worry.

"Maybe there's nothing there. Maybe he just doesn't want people to know his business," Anita said, trying to make him feel better.

"Maybe. Hopefully Trey will be able to find out more," he said, then crossed his arms against his chest and rocked back and forth on his heels. "It's late. You should think about sawing some more logs," he said, obviously trying to lighten the mood.

She jumped to her feet and smoothed the fleece of the shorts with her hands. "I should. We have a big day tomorrow."

"Big day?" he asked, puzzled.

She laughed and tapped his flat midsection. "Shopping, big boy. Or did you forget what you said earlier?"

A chuckle burst from him, and he shook his head. "I remember. Get some sleep."

She walked over, rose on her tiptoes and kissed him. Just a quick, butterfly-light peck. And then another.

It just seemed so natural, so familiar as she leaned into him, and he wrapped an arm around her waist to hold her close. Dug his hand into her hair and undid the topknot she wore, letting her hair spill down.

He tangled his fingers in the strands and he almost groaned. "I always loved the feel of your hair in my hands. The smell of it. You still smell the same."

"You…do…too," she said in between kisses, savoring the masculine scent that had never left her brain. A fresh and citrusy cologne. Brett, all musky and male.

His aroma and the feel of his hard body, even harder now, tangled around her, urging her even closer. Calling her to rub her hips along his, against the obvious proof of his desire.

He groaned and cupped the back of her head, deepening his kiss. Dancing his tongue in to taste her before his body shook and he tempered the kisses and reluctantly shifted away.

"I want you, Anita. I can't deny that," he said and leaned his forehead against hers so that their gazes were eye level. "I've missed you forever, but now—"

"Isn't the right time for this. You've said that before," she reminded, and stepped away from him, arms wrapped around herself to keep it together.

She whirled on him, frustration and need fueling her anger. "I get it. You have responsibilities. You have to keep me safe, and I have a business to think about. One that consumes my entire life."

"You know that's right," he said, hands held out in pleading.

With an angry slash of her hand, she said, "Enough. I get it. But what if tonight is all the time we have left?"

She didn't wait for his reply. She bolted and raced to her bedroom, slammed the door shut. The loud thud of the door as it closed was somehow satisfying.

But the silence that followed...

She'd been alone for so long. Alone except for her business and chefs. The few men she'd given entry into her life had drifted in and out of it because she'd been too busy at work.

Too busy to have a life, but if she was honest with herself, staying busy had kept her from having time to think about the loneliness. To think about the one man whom she had never forgotten.

And now here he was because of the most unlikely of reasons.

Because someone was trying to kill her.

A frisson of fear skittered down her spine and drove away the anger, fear and need.

She wrapped her arms around herself and walked to the window. The night was still. Nothing moved outside except an occasional bubble and ripple in the waters of the canal. Fish, probably, she told herself.

Mango's growl sounded in the other room, causing Anita to pull back slightly from the window. A second later an odd-shaped silhouette came into view, and as the moonlight shone on it, she realized what it was.

A large green-and-fluorescent-orange iguana inched across the railing of the deck. With its long black-and-yellowish-banded tail, it had to be at least five feet long.

No threat. Not this time, anyway.

Luckily Mango was alert. Brett was lucky to have her. Anita was lucky to have both of them guarding her.

With that thought in mind, she told herself not to make Brett's life even harder than it was.

She'd stay away from him as he requested. For now. Maybe even for after.

He'd hurt her once before and she'd be a fool to let it happen again.

BRETT PACED BACK and forth across the narrow width of the living room, too awake after all that had happened.

Jim on the dock. The iguana.

Brett appreciated how alert Mango could be. It lifted a huge weight off his shoulders to know he had a second set of ears to help keep Anita safe.

Keeping Anita safe was the number one priority, which meant he had to stay focused.

He couldn't let their past relationship and lingering emotions take his focus off what was important.

With that in mind, he whipped out his phone to see if he had any text or email messages.

No texts but he had an email from Sophie forwarding the cleaned-up version of the photo he'd found online as well as other images that had been captured from the police station's CCTV footage.

The enhancement of the online photo confirmed that it was Ramirez and Santiago. And neither of the two men seemed happy.

If Santiago was one of Hollywood's goons and Ramirez owed the mobster money, it could explain what had happened the other night.

Which brought even greater worry. Would Hollywood keep on coming for Anita even if Santiago was caught?

He ran through all the permutations in his brain and decided Hollywood wouldn't come after Anita. It was way more likely he'd take out Santiago and his accomplice to avoid them spilling their guts to the police.

Unless Santiago and his accomplice got to Anita first. That was the real threat.

Opening the second email, he flipped through the images, scrutinizing them carefully to see if there was anything familiar about the officer. The man had hidden well, face always averted as he did Hollywood's dirty work.

Muttering a curse beneath his breath, he sat back down at the table and opened his laptop, but then shut it down. It was hours past midnight and even though he could function on only a few hours of sleep, he needed to get some rest to be alert.

The bed would be way more comfortable, but it was just too close to Anita.

And the two easiest entryways were visible from the living room and couch.

For safety's sake, he signaled Mango, walked her toward the front door and instructed her to guard the area. *"Pozor,"* he said and repeated it although the dog had so far proved to understand the command quite well.

Mango peered up at him and seemed to nod before splaying across the front door, head on her paws.

Satisfied, he returned to the living room and was about to sit when the need to see Anita was safe called him.

He walked to her door, leaned his ear close and listened. That soft snore confirmed she was asleep.

Opening the door a crack, he peered inside, worried about someone accessing the window.

All was good and he had no doubt that if Jake's neighbor Jim noticed anything, since Anita's bedroom was closest to the dock and Jim's home, he'd take action.

Satisfied that he could stand down for a few hours of sleep, he grabbed a pillow and blanket from his bedroom and settled in on the couch. Slipping his holster from his belt, he removed the gun and placed it within easy reach on the coffee table.

But as he lay there, a maelstrom of thoughts and images spun around his brain, making for an uneasy sleep.

His eyes had barely drifted shut when he noticed the lightening of the morning sky through the window. It bathed the room in shades of rosy gray and pale lavender.

A quick glance at his phone warned it was nearly seven. No new messages or texts. Regardless it was time to get up and get moving.

Shower first, he thought, rubbing his face and hair with his hand.

Mango was guarding the door, but she'd need to be walked soon. A quick peek into Anita's room confirmed she was still asleep, and he closed the door to avoid waking her.

Snagging a fresh shirt and underwear from his room, he showered and dressed in fresh clothes and his one pair of jeans. Hopefully he could buy another pair or two today.

Anita still hadn't stirred so he leashed Mango and walked her in the front yard and then did a loop around the house, making sure all was in order.

Nothing had changed since the night before, although he did notice the curtains on Jim's house shift as he walked along the dock. The old cop keeping watch.

When he returned to the house, the strong and welcoming smell of bacon filled the small space as he opened the door.

Anita. Cooking. The kitchen had always been her refuge and that hadn't changed.

But so much else had. Maybe too much.

Armed with that reality, he pushed into the kitchen.

Chapter Fifteen

She didn't register the footsteps until she sensed a presence behind her.

Granny fork raised like a weapon, heart hammering in her chest, she whirled, ready to defend herself.

"Brett. You scared the life out of me," she said and laid a hand on her chest to calm her racing heart.

"I'm sorry. I thought you heard Mango and me come in," he said and took a step back, hands raised as he gave her some space to recover.

She waved off his apology. "No, I'm sorry. Sometimes I get lost in my head when I'm cooking."

"It's why you're so good at what you do," he said with a smile and an appreciative dip of his head.

"Thanks. Breakfast will be ready soon. Coffee is already made," she said and tilted her head in the direction of the espresso pot.

"Can I get you some?" he asked as he walked over.

"No, thanks. I've already had a cup," she said, which was maybe why she was as jittery as she was.

She shouldn't have been that surprised when Brett had returned. She'd seen him walking Mango past her window when she'd woken and knew he wouldn't leave her alone.

She blamed the jitters on the coffee as she grabbed the

bagel from the toaster and split it between the two plates she'd warmed in the oven. A little Mornay sauce she'd made from the remains of a bar of cream cheese, butter and Swiss cheese slices went next. She topped the sauce with slices of crispy bacon and a little more cheese sauce.

Returning to the stove, she cracked the last two eggs from the fridge into the bacon grease and fried them, making sure the whites were tight, but the yolks stayed runny. Satisfied they were exactly right, she topped each of the towers of bagel, cheese sauce and bacon with a fried egg. She finished the dish with some salt and pepper.

"Wow. That looks and smells delicious," Brett said as she placed the plate in front of him.

"A fridge cleaner. There wasn't much in there and we've run through most of what we brought with us since we didn't take much," she said with a shrug, hoping the dish would satisfy a big man like Brett.

Brett broke into the egg and the yolk drizzled down, melding with the cheese sauce. He forked up a healthy portion, ate it and hummed in appreciation. "This is amazing. Really amazing," he said and dug into the meal.

His enjoyment of her food drove away the last of her jitters as well as misgivings about what had been a slapdash dish concocted from a hodgepodge of ingredients.

It awakened her own appetite, and she ate, pleased with the final product. "I could probably make you a real croque madame if we're able to do some shopping today."

He nodded. "I just want to check with the team. If they give the go-ahead, you can call your sous-chef and parents, and after we'll get supplies."

"Thanks for remembering about the call," she said, grateful for his understanding.

THERE WAS NOTHING he didn't remember about her, he thought, but didn't say.

"Let me clean up—"

She held her hand up to stop him. "I'll do it so you can make the call. Do anything else you have to."

"Roger that," he said and pushed away from the table, coffee cup in hand.

He dialed Trey and it rang a few times, which was unlike his friend. When he finally answered, he was out of breath, as if he'd been running.

"Sorry, but things are a little off the wall here this morning. Roni's in labor," Trey said.

"She's okay, right? Isn't it early?" he asked, worried since Trey had said she wasn't feeling well the night before.

"It's about a month early, but so far so good. Mia is taking over for me and can fill you in on what we've got so far," Trey said, barely audible over the noises in the background. Someone exhorting someone to breathe. A pained groan.

"Have to go," Trey said and ended the call.

"Is there a problem?" Anita asked and walked over, drying her hands on a kitchen towel.

"Roni's in labor. I have to call Mia for an update," he said and immediately dialed her number, then put the phone on speaker.

"*Buenos dias*, Brett," Mia said as she answered.

"Is it a good day, Mia?" he responded.

"It is. We've been able to identify the leak at the police station, but he's lawyered up," Mia advised.

"Wouldn't you? He's on the hook for those cops who were shot in Aventura," he said.

"Maybe more than that," Mia said with sigh.

"What do you mean?" Anita asked, obviously not liking what she was hearing.

He wasn't liking it, either, especially as Mia said, "Jogger saw a gator chomping on something this morning. Called the cops, who discovered the gator had an arm with a cast in its mouth."

"I'm not getting the connection to the case," Brett said, puzzled by this new development.

"When the coroner cut off the cast, he noticed there were some pretty serious bite marks, damage to the forearm muscles and a small fracture," Mia advised.

It all came together for Brett. "Damage like that which would occur if a pit bull was really holding on and shaking the man's arm. You think this is one of the people who attacked us in Homestead."

"I do and so does the coroner. He'd heard about the attack and put two and two together when he saw the injuries. He's taking DNA from the arm, but he's also taking DNA from the wound to confirm what kind of dog did the biting. If the victim has a record, we'll get a match on the DNA, and also from his fingerprints."

"Someone is tying up loose ends," Anita said in a small voice, clearly fearing she'd be next.

"He is, but we've plugged that leak. You're safe where you are," Mia said to calm her.

"But the cop isn't talking," Anita said, her confusion apparent.

"He isn't but once he hears there's a murder involved, he may want a plea deal, right?" Brett asked.

"Right. We've already reached out to our uncle in the DA's office to see how they can help get more info out of that cop with a plea deal," Mia confirmed.

"Are we safe enough for Anita to call her sous-chef and for us to get some supplies? We're running a little low," Brett said and glanced at Anita. Hopefulness filled her face, and as Mia acknowledged that it was clear for them to do that, a small smile slipped onto her features.

"Great. Keep us posted," he said.

Brett swiped to end the call and handed the phone to Anita. "Once you make this call, I'll burn this phone."

ANITA TOOK THE phone with shaky hands, almost dreading what she might hear from Melanie.

Her sous-chef answered on the first ring. "Anita?" she asked, a puzzled tone in her voice since she likely didn't recognize the number.

"Yes, it's me. I can't use my own phone. How are things?" she asked and braced herself for bad news.

"We miss you, but you trained us well. We got the steaks delivered as promised along with some extra filets to make up for it. We're all set for the next few days with the menu you left for us," Melanie advised, her voice relaxed, almost bordering on cheery.

But is it forced cheeriness?

"Are you sure, Melanie? I shouldn't be worried?" Anita urged, cell phone pressed so hard to her ear that her diamond stud dug into her flesh.

"I'm sure, Anita. Like I said, you trained us to handle things. Take care of things so you can come back quickly," Melanie said as someone called out to her.

"Chef, we need you here," one of her line chefs said.

"Don't worry, Chef," Melanie repeated and then the line went dead.

She dialed her parents next and it instantly went to voice mail. They had likely ignored the unfamiliar number. She left a detailed message and tried her best to tell them not to worry and that she was safe.

She handed the phone back to Brett, almost distractedly.

"It's all good, right?" he asked, ducking down so that he could read her face more clearly.

"It's all good," she repeated and actually believed it. Meeting his gaze, she said, "How about we do that shopping now."

TONY HOLLYWOOD'S FACE was buried in his hands, elbows braced on his desk, as Santiago limped into his office.

"What's up, boss?" he asked.

As Tony straightened, he could swear he saw the remnants of tears on his face and even though he knew the likely reason for it, he played stupid.

"Something wrong?"

"My sister called. The cops called to say Billy's dead. They found his arm—his freakin' arm—in a gator," Tony said and slammed his hands on the surface of the desk.

The sound was as loud as a gunshot, making him jump.

"I'm sorry, boss. What happened?" he said, feigning ignorance.

With speed he didn't think possible for a man of Tony's size, Tony rounded the corner, grabbed his throat and propelled him against the wall. He tightened his hold and lifted him off the ground, choking him.

"What happened to Billy?" Tony asked, nose to nose with him now that he had him half a foot in the air.

"Don't...know," he managed to squeak out with the little air he could breathe.

Tony tossed him away like a rag doll and, thanks to his injured leg, he crumpled to the ground.

Tony paced back and forth, raking a hand through his hair, muttering over and over as he did so. "He was family. My sister's heart is broken. He was her only child."

"I didn't do it," he lied, fearing that he'd underestimated Tony's love for his incompetent nephew.

Tony spun and cursed him out, veins bulging on his neck and forehead, angry red blossoming on his face.

"Liar. I should have you offed. You're nothing but a liability," he said with a toss of a hand in his direction.

"You should but you won't because you know I have insurance, don't you?" he said, pulling the ace card he had tucked up his sleeve.

Tony clenched his fists and shuffled his feet, almost like

a bull getting ready to charge, but then he stopped and stepped back.

"Get out of here. Find the girl. Finish her off," he said from behind gritted teeth.

Santiago eased his hands into his pockets, turned and sashayed away, a newfound sense of power flowing through his veins. But he couldn't be overconfident.

He'd misjudged Tony's reaction to Billy's death, but he hoped that in time Tony would realize that he'd done the right thing. Billy had been nothing but a liability. The weakest link in the chain leading to him and eventually to Tony.

Yeah, Tony would thank him one day, he thought, and headed out to his car.

Anita Reyes and the SBS K-9 agent had flown the coop, but his mole at the police station had been very helpful so far. He had hoped to end the problem in Aventura, but the SBS agents had been too quick thinking. And Billy and that damn dog had totally messed things up in Homestead.

He should have handled it by himself and from now on he would.

First step: see what his mole could tell him.

Chapter Sixteen

Brett hauled the half-a-dozen bags onto the kitchen counter. They landed with a resounding and very pleasing thunk. Anita followed him in carrying the packages with their new clothing, Mango at her side. She passed by the kitchen, probably to take the bags to their bedrooms, and Mango tagged along with her, carrying a small bag.

All the purchases were courtesy of the cash in the pouch Trey had instructed him to take from the desk drawer. Cash was king to avoid anyone tracking his credit card.

But to do that they had to know who he was, and it worried him that the mole at the police force might have overheard his name and shared it with Santiago and his cronies. Luckily, he'd never been one to overly share on social media.

But can you say the same for your friends? he thought as he unpacked the bags onto the counter.

That was especially worrisome considering Jake and the changing stories about the cash for the boat.

Not that he'd let on about those fears to Anita.

For the first time in the last two days, the worry had seemed to slip from her as they'd shopped. He hadn't wanted to bring her down by sharing his concerns.

She almost skipped back into the kitchen to help him unpack. Mango walked beside her but left her to drink some fresh water Brett had set out that morning.

"I put the bag with your things on your bed," she said.

"Thanks. Do you mind finishing up so I can check in with Mia and Trey?" he said and wiggled a burner phone in the air in emphasis.

"Go ahead. I can handle this."

He signaled Mango to guard the door and walked to his bedroom, wanting some privacy for the call.

Trey didn't answer and his gut knotted with fear.

It had been a few hours since they'd spoken. But labor could take that long, he told himself and dialed Mia.

She answered on the first ring. "How's Roni?" he asked, his best friend's very pregnant wife first and foremost in his mind.

"Still in labor. I spoke to Trey about an hour ago and everything seems to be going well," she said.

"That's good news. Any new developments?" he asked.

"Our suspect cop still isn't talking, but his lawyer is negotiating with my uncle on a plea deal. I'm no legal expert, but if it avoids having the felony murder rule apply, I think he'd be wise to take it," Mia replied, confidence ringing in her voice.

"Is it too soon for the DNA results on the gator victim?" he asked, aware that it sometimes took days or weeks depending on resources and backlogs.

"The coroner has a new rapid DNA test, but he's double-checking the results," she said, some of her earlier confidence fading.

He narrowed his gaze as he considered what might be wrong and said, "Is there a problem? Contamination maybe?"

A long pause and awkward cough was followed by, "Possibly. Police have an ID on the gator victim from the fingerprints. It's William Allen. Tony's nephew."

"Wow. Do you think Hollywood killed his own nephew?" he asked, shocked and yet not shocked. Ruthless mobsters like Hollywood had rubbed out family on more than one occasion.

"It gets more complicated than that. The blood from the suspect you shot and that from the gator victim show a familial connection," she explained.

"But the second Homestead attacker was probably Kennedy," Brett said and as his mind processed the new info, he added, "We have nothing that says he's related to Hollywood."

"You're right. If the second set of tests come back the same, we'll have to dig deeper into how that's possible," Mia said.

The sound of Anita putting things away in the kitchen ended. Her soft footfalls coming down the hall warned of her imminent arrival.

Since he didn't want to worry her, maybe it was time to wind down this conversation. But before he did so, he had one last question to ask.

"Have you been able to find out anything more about Jake and the boat?"

THE PHONE RANG and rang before going to voice mail.

It was the third time he'd tried to call his mole, but the third time hadn't been a charm.

His intuition warned that it wasn't a good thing that his cop wasn't answering.

He'd been compromised, which meant he wouldn't be getting more information from him.

But he wasn't the only mark tangled up with Hollywood. Santiago just had to pull the right strings to find someone who could give him the info he needed to find the chef and the SBS agent.

BRETT STOOD IN the middle of the room, head bent dejectedly. He scraped his hand across his short-cropped hair and said, "Yeah, I get it. I appreciate you working on that."

He ended the call and faced her with a forced smile. "No news on Roni. She's still in labor."

"What about the investigation? Anything?" she pressed.

"Cop still isn't talking, but Mia is confident they'll be able to work out a plea deal for his cooperation. They're double-checking the analysis. As for Jake, Trey and Mia's aunt, who's some hotshot lawyer, searched but couldn't find any evidence of Jake filing a Lejeune claim," he said. Every inch of his body communicated that not all was well with the case.

His upset transferred itself to her and she wrapped her arms around herself, trying to rein in fear and stay calm.

"What do we do now?" she asked.

"We keep on digging," he said and gestured toward the window in the room and the dock outside. "We start with that boat. Jake had to register it, and to do that he had to prove ownership. If we can find out who sold it to him, maybe they can tell us more about how he paid for it."

"You're still that worried about Jake?" she asked, trying to understand why he wouldn't trust an old friend, until she remembered.

"You're afraid to trust him because of what happened in Iraq," she said, then walked up to him and cradled his cheek. "It's okay to trust your friend."

He shook his head hard, dislodging her hand, and tapped his index finger against his chest. "Not when there are conflicting stories about how he bought a quarter-of-a-million-dollar boat. He told me it was a Lejeune settlement. Jim said it was a lottery win. The only likely reason to lie is because it's dirty money."

She couldn't argue with him about that. People lied when they had something to hide.

Nodding, she said, "Agreed. Where do we start?"

HER WORDS, her trust in him, relieved some of the concern that had twisted his gut into a knot during his conversation with Mia.

"We look up the address for the local DMV. They would have to issue the boat registration," he said, then slipped his hand into hers and gently urged her from the room and back out to the breakfast bar and his laptop.

Mango raised her head and peered at them as they entered, but otherwise didn't shift from her spot guarding the door.

It took only a few minutes to get an address, and armed with that and Mango, whom he leashed to take with them, they went outside so he could find the boat registration. He lowered the lift until the boat was low enough that he could climb aboard.

"Wait here," he said and handed Mango's leash to Anita.

He hopped on and immediately noticed the glove box in the boat's console. He popped it open and pulled out a plastic envelope that held an owner's manual and the boat registration. He examined the owner's manual, hoping that it might have the seller's name on it, but no luck. Same with the boat registration, which only had Jake's name on it.

Shoving the materials back into the envelope, he took them with him as he got off the boat. He slipped his hand into Anita's and signaled Mango to heel.

"Time to hit the DMV."

SANTIAGO HAD PULLED on more strings than he thought possible.

None had turned up any information that could lead him to where the chef and SBS agent might have gone.

Frustrated, he banged his palm on the steering wheel and wracked his brains for any other names, running through them until one suddenly came to him.

It would be a big ask and he might have to sacrifice the money owed to Hollywood to get the info, but it would be worth it.

Pulling a burner phone from his jacket pocket, he made the call.

LUCKILY, THE DMV office on the Overseas Highway was a short five-minute ride from Jake's house since there was barely an hour left before it closed. It was in a strip mall that held a large supermarket, clothing outlet, public library and an assortment of other stores.

At the late hour, there was little activity inside the DMV and a young woman at a window quickly flagged them to come over.

Brett turned on the charm since honey always caught more flies than vinegar.

"I was hoping you could help us out. My friend Jake Winston—"

"I know Jake well," she said, which came as no surprise to Brett.

The young woman—pretty, blonde and athletic from what was visible through the window—was totally Jake's type. Plus, the locals were a close-knit group from what he had seen in past visits with his friend.

"Jake and I were in the Marines together and I was hoping you could help me out with something," he said and gave her his most boyish grin.

"Like what?" she asked, puzzlement on her features.

Placing the boat registration in the window slot, he tapped it and said, "Would you have helped Jake register this boat?"

Her gaze narrowed, shifted from him to Anita and then

to Mango. "Is that a service dog?" she asked, her earlier friendliness dimming.

"Mango's my partner. I work with SBS. I'm not a cop, if that's what you're worried about. Jake is my best friend. I want to surprise him with something new for his boat," he said, and to prove it, he turned his left wrist over and shifted his watch so she could see the tattoo of the bulldog that he and all of his unit had gotten one drunken night.

The woman leaned forward, which gave him a clear view of her generous chest, but then she plopped back onto her high stool and smiled. "I helped Jake with the paperwork. He got the boat not far from here. Bob's Shipyard."

"Thanks. That's all I needed. I'll be sure to let Jake know you helped us," he said and gave her a little salute in thanks.

As they walked away from the window, Anita muttered under her breath, "Boy, can you turn on the charm."

He laughed and glanced in her direction. "You should know," he teased.

She stopped dead then and faced him, her gaze skipping all across his face. Pointing toward the DMV office, she said, "It was never fake with us the way it was in there."

He grew more serious and dipped his head in agreement. "It was never fake with you. Never," he said, cupped her cheek and leaned down to kiss her.

Chapter Seventeen

It was a kiss of promise and maybe possibly forgiveness for all that had gone wrong between them.

When he broke the kiss, he grinned, and it caused her heart to do a little flip-flop. She still wasn't immune to his charm. His real charm and not the act he had put on for Jake's fangirl in the DMV office.

Together, Mango comfortably at her side, they returned to their car. Brett harnessed Mango into the back seat, and once they were settled, Brett programmed the car for the ride to the boat dealer.

Bob's Shipyard was over half an hour away in Islamorada. As they passed multiple boat sale stores along the way, she said, "I wonder why he went that far to buy the boat."

Brett shrugged and it was clear he'd been wondering the same thing himself. "Maybe they were the only ones with the model he wanted."

"Or maybe Bob's Shipyard was the only place that wouldn't ask questions about how Jake was paying for it," she said.

Brett's lips tightened into a grimace, but he reluctantly nodded. "That's a very real possibility."

"But you don't want to believe there's anything criminal about how Jake got the money?" she pressed.

He bobbed his head, the movement stilted. Harsh. "I don't want to believe but it worries me. Jake didn't file a Lejeune settlement claim."

"Which leaves the lottery explanation," Anita said as Brett drove past yet another shipyard advertising boats for sale.

"Jake bought the boat a month ago. Florida keeps lottery winner names private for three months," Brett said, hands tight on the wheel.

She processed that info, trying to understand why Jake would lie about a settlement rather than tell Brett about the lottery win.

Brett must have been thinking the same thing since a second later he said, "Maybe he was worried I was going to hit him up for a loan. Some of our unit members have had a rough time. A couple are even homeless. Jake and I try to help when we can, but maybe he was worried people would come out of the woodwork once they found out about the lottery win."

"But he told Jim about it," Anita pushed.

Another shrug, followed by, "He didn't see Jim that way. As a taker."

She bit back that it meant Jake saw him as a taker because she didn't want to hurt him any more than he must be hurting.

Brett's comment created a pall in the vehicle that even Mango sensed since she sat up and whined.

Anita reached back and petted the pit bull, reassuring her that all was well. Mango licked her hand, dragging a laugh from her.

"Mango likes you," Brett said, watching the interaction in the rearview mirror.

"I'm glad," she said and rubbed the dog's ears and head again, earning another doggy kiss.

A ghost of a smile drifted across his lips. "I'm glad, too," he said and slowed the car.

She looked out the window and noticed the sign for Bob's Shipyard. Hopefully Brett would get the answers that confirmed his trust in his friend hadn't been misplaced.

SANTIAGO CURSED AS yet another online search came up blank for the SBS agent.

Brett Madison was the name that his contact at the FBI had provided.

Whoever he was, he had done an excellent job of scrubbing himself off the internet.

Either that or the SBS team had done it for him.

He pulled up the agency's website again and stared at the smiling faces of the Gonzalez family members who ran it.

Much like what had happened with Madison, there was little private info for the family members, except for Mia Gonzalez, now Mia Gonzalez Wilson.

Mia and her cousin Carolina had been top influencers before Mia had cut back on those activities to join her family's agency and marry John Wilson, a wealthy tech CEO.

There were hundreds of thousands of hits for Mia thanks to the successful business her cousin and she had run. He started reviewing them, but after scrolling through dozens of pages, he gave up on that angle because there were just too many articles, and most were about public events.

He went back to the website for the agency and tried to find out more about the acting head, Ramon Gonzalez III who was sometimes referred to as "Trey." Probably because he was the third Ramon.

Much as with the elusive Brett Madison, there was little confidential information online. But since Trey had been a detective on several high-profile cases, there were news articles galore. The only thing he could glean from them was Gonzalez's age and that he'd once been a marine.

Santiago closed his eyes, trying to remember what had happened in Homestead.

The dog attack on Billy.

Poor Billy, he thought for a fleeting moment.

The man commanding the dog in some foreign language.

A big man. Tall and broad-shouldered. Thickly muscled and hard-bodied and yet he had moved quickly. Decisively.

The way a soldier might.

That sent him down another rabbit hole, trying to locate any stories that might tie Gonzalez and Madison.

Well over an hour passed with nothing and his stomach grumbled, complaining that it was dinnertime.

He picked up his cell phone and ordered a Cubano, mango *batido* and *maduros* from a local place that had the best Cuban sandwiches and shakes.

Handheld food because he didn't intend to leave that computer until he had a clue as to where he would find the elusive Brett Madison and the chef who could send him to the electric chair.

THE NEWS CAME as they were driving back from the boat dealer.

After many long hours of labor, Roni had given birth to a baby girl they'd named Marielena after the two families' grandmothers.

"Roni and the baby are both doing well," Trey said.

Brett didn't miss the fatigue in his friend's voice. "How are you doing?"

"Exhausted," Trey admitted, but then quickly tacked on, "But I'm headed to the office now that I know Roni and the baby are fine."

He shared a look with Anita, who seemed to be totally

in sync with him. "Maybe you should stay with Roni and your new daughter."

"Roni understands. Believe me. She's already been on the phone with her partner," Trey said.

Brett hated to ask, but Trey had opened the door with his statement.

"Any news on the cop or the plea deal?"

"Williams told Roni that the plea deal was in place. Williams is in the interview room with him right now. As soon as I know more, I'll let you know," Trey said as the sound of voices nearby faded into silence when he apparently stepped out of the hospital.

"I have something to share as well. You may be able to take Jake off your plate. Jake's neighbor and the dealer he bought the boat from told us Jake won a big lottery prize a month ago. That's how he got the cash for the boat."

"We'll try to confirm that, but it seems like your gut wasn't wrong about going to Jake's," Trey replied, the subtext clear.

"I'm glad, too. We'll talk to you later," he said.

"Video call twenty-two hundred. Maybe we'll have more news by then."

"Roger," Brett said and ended the call.

"SEEMS LIKE GOOD news all around," Anita said, trying to understand why Brett didn't seem more excited about all the progress and his friend's happy event.

An abrupt nod was her only answer.

Brett did a quick glance at the cell phone. "It's well past dinnertime. I don't know about you, but I'm hungry."

In response her stomach did a little growl, dragging a chuckle from her. "I'm a mite peckish," she joked and covered her noisy belly with a hand.

"I think we can risk dinner out since things seem under

control for now," he said and executed a quick U-turn back toward Islamorada.

Barely five minutes later they were at a local restaurant that Anita recognized as an icon in the Keys. It had been around since the 1940s and was famous for its turtle chowder, classic Keys food and down-home dishes.

"I've heard about this place, but I've never been here," she said and shot a quick look back at Mango. "Will we able to bring Mango in?"

Brett tracked her gaze and shook his head. "I'm not sure, but probably not. Would you mind takeout and a picnic? It might be more secure to not let a lot of people see us as well."

"I'm game. Let's check out the menu online," she said, and within a few minutes they'd placed an order for conch fritters, turtle chowder and fresh-caught grilled wahoo and snapper. For Mango they added meat loaf with mashed potatoes, apparently a favorite of the pit bull.

They parked in front of the restaurant's patio with the colorful sea turtles where diners could wait for a table. Barely twenty minutes later, a server approached with a large shopping bag.

Brett stepped out to grab their order and slipped the bag into the back seat by Mango. Easing into the driver's seat again, he pulled out of the parking lot and turned onto the Old Highway. A few blocks up, another turn had them driving through a neighborhood of cinder block ranch homes on postage-stamp lots dotted with palm trees, crotons and other tropical plants and flowers.

They hadn't gone far when they reached a cul-de-sac with parking next to a beach access point.

Anita stepped out of the car and took hold of the bag with their food while Brett grabbed a blanket from the back of the car, unharnessed Mango and leashed her for the walk onto the beach. But as he did so, he peered around, clearly still vigilant despite his earlier comment that everything seemed to be under control for the moment.

"We're good to go," he said and together they walked down a path between some beachside houses and to the sand until they were several yards from the water, where Brett spread out the blanket for them to sit.

Once they were comfortably settled, Mango stretched out beside Brett on the blanket, they emptied the bag and spread the take-out dishes between them. Finding the conch fritters, they shared those first, laughing and talking as they ate.

It was easy for her mind and heart to drift back to when they used to date and how wonderful it had been between them. But every now and then, Brett would scan the area around them, reminding her that this wasn't just like it once was.

Someone was still trying to kill her, and it was only a matter of time before the peace they were feeling now would be shattered.

It dimmed her appetite, enough that Brett noticed she had stopped eating what was an absolutely wonderful grilled wahoo and started picking at it.

He offered her a smile and cradled her cheek. "It's going to be okay, Anita. Trust me."

She dropped her plastic fork onto her plate, shook her head and said, "Trust you? Seriously?"

His face hardened, confirming her shot had struck home on so many levels.

How could she trust a man who had ghosted her, but worse, trust a man who didn't trust himself?

She waited for an explosion of anger, almost welcoming it if it would clear the air around them.

But Brett only stared straight ahead, his body ramrod stiff, muscles tense. Hands taut on the plastic take-out tray with his meal.

In clipped tones, he said, "Yes, trust me. I would do anything to keep you safe."

As he finished, he slowly faced her, eyes blazing with emotion. "Anything, Anita. Don't doubt that."

She muttered a curse and looked away from that intense gaze because deep in her heart she didn't doubt him.

That almost scared her more.

"Don't die for me, Brett. Please don't," she said, aware that he wouldn't hesitate to do that. As both a soldier and SBS agent, Brett had committed to risk his life to protect others. That duty was as much a part of his DNA as the color of his hair and eyes.

Brett slipped an arm around her shoulders and drew her close. "It won't get to that, my love. It won't."

Throat tight with emotion, she said, "Promise me."

With a half smile on his face, he nodded and said, "I promise."

Mango, sensing the emotion and tension, popped away from her plate of food to stand before them, nose slathered with the remnants of meat loaf and mashed potatoes until her tongue swept out to lick them away.

It dragged laughs from them, ending the emotional moment and restoring the peace she had been feeling when they had first sat to eat.

Brett playfully bumped her shoulder with his and tossed Mango a bit of his fish that the dog snagged midair and gulped down in a single bite.

Their picnic finished with them feeding Mango the remnants of their meals. After packing their dishes and cutlery back into the bag, which Brett tossed into a nearby garbage can, they shook out the blanket, folded it and took Mango for a long walk along the beach. The dog needed the activity, but Anita did as well since she wasn't used to just sitting around.

As an executive chef, she spent her days at the market

scoping out the freshest ingredients for her restaurant's menu and then on her feet in the kitchen.

She welcomed the walk and the beauty of the beach at night since it had grown dark while they were eating.

A full moon scattered playful light on the surface of the water, making it glitter happily. Lights had snapped on in the homes along the beachfront, casting a warm, welcoming glow on the sand.

The slightest breeze stirred palm trees and the nearby bushes, making them crackle and rustle and prompting Brett to peer in their direction to make sure it was only the breeze and not more.

They reluctantly returned to the car for the trip to Jake's house, aware that Trey had scheduled a meeting for later that night.

The drive back was silent at first, but it was impossible for Anita not to notice that at one point Brett was nervously checking his rearview mirror, on high alert.

As he pulled into the right lane and slowed the car, he glanced at the mirror again and muttered a curse beneath his breath.

"Something wrong?" she asked just to make sure she was reading the signals right.

"Car has been on our tail for about two miles. Windows are too tinted to see who's driving," he said, and with a quick peek at the side mirror, he pulled back into the left lane and raced ahead, so rapidly it pushed her into her seat.

She flipped down the visor and opened the vanity mirror, noted the late model Mercedes sedan that did an exaggerated shift to the left lane, mimicking what Brett had done.

"The shooter at the police station was driving a Mercedes," she said, fear gripping her.

"I know," he said calmly and increased his speed, whipping around a slow-moving car in front of him, so quickly it tossed her from side to side.

He was speeding forward, but Fate intervened as the light just several yards away turned red and an oversize truck jack-rabbited into the intersection.

Brett swore and screeched to a halt to avoid a collision.

The Mercedes that had been tailing them pulled right up next to them at the light.

As the driver's side window on the Mercedes lowered, Brett swept his arm across her body and said, "Get down."

Chapter Eighteen

As soon as Anita hunkered down in the seat, Brett freed his gun from the holster and slid down the passenger side window.

To his surprise, an elderly woman, in her eighties if he had to guess, raised an arthritis-gnarled finger and with a quaver in her voice said, "My husband wants me to let you know your left taillight is broken."

Relief slammed through him, almost violently. He dipped his head, smiled and said, "Thank you, ma'am. I appreciate you letting me know."

Anita must have overheard since she sat up in her seat, her body trembling, a response to the initial adrenaline rush. She wrapped her arms around herself, apparently trying to rein in her fear.

He laid his hand on her shoulder and stroked it back and forth, trying to calm her. "It was just a helpful senior citizen."

Anita scoffed. "Helpful nearly got them shot. I saw you reach for your gun."

He couldn't deny it as he holstered the weapon and some-one honked from behind them, annoyed that the light had turned green and they weren't moving.

Driving forward, Brett traveled down the Overseas High-way until they reached the turn for the street that would take them to the almost serpentine labyrinth of roads along the man-made canals where Jake had his home.

He parked in the gravel driveway and raised his hand in a stop gesture to warn Anita to stay put until he made sure all was safe.

As he freed Mango from the back seat, he noticed a light snap on in the front room of Jim's home. A second later the curtain was drawn slightly away.

Jim checking up on who had arrived.

He waved at the man. The curtain drifted back into place and the light snapped off.

Brett examined the area all around. Quiet along the front of the home.

Walking with Mango to the side door, he let her sniff there for anything out of the ordinary, then walked to the back dock, where everything also seemed in order.

He unlocked the entrance and released Mango to inspect the area. A short while later, Mango returned to the front door and sat, confirming that it was okay for them to enter.

With a hand signal, he commanded Mango to heel, and they returned to the car for Anita.

"All clear," he said and helped her from the car.

Arm around her waist since she still seemed shaken by what had happened earlier, they walked to the side door, where he entered first and confirmed Mango's decision that it was safe. Satisfied, he opened the side door and held out a hand to invite her to come in.

She slipped her hand into his and walked in, but as she did so, she tucked herself against him and said, "Thank you. For everything."

He wanted to say that he was just doing his job, but Anita wasn't just a job. She could never be just that.

Hugging her tight, he bent his head and tucked it to hers, needing that connection. Wishing that they weren't in this situation so that they could rekindle the magic they'd once had, only they weren't those same people anymore.

He was a man with a lot of trust issues and baggage. She was a woman with her own life and a busy one at that.

"I wish…" she whispered against his ear, but stopped, as if knowing what he was thinking and the impossibility of not only the now but also the future.

"I wish, too, but if wishes were horses, beggars would ride," he said, repeating a phrase he'd heard the nuns in his Catholic elementary school utter whenever they'd long for a snow day.

Grudgingly they separated, hopes dashed.

With close to an hour before their big meeting, Anita excused herself to go unpack and wash the clothing they'd bought earlier that day.

He was too wired after the nonincident with the elderly couple, plus pit bulls were typically very active dogs. By now he would have normally walked or exercised Mango a few times, and as good as the dog had been, harnessed into the car or guarding the door, she needed more than the few walks she'd had. Even their earlier walk on the beach probably hadn't been enough.

Because of that, he headed to his bedroom and grabbed the tug toy and hard rubber ball he'd picked up while they'd been shopping.

Anita was at the end of the hall in the small laundry room, and he let her know he was going to exercise Mango.

"I'll meet you in a few minutes," she said.

With little space on the back deck or dock, he went behind his parked car and Jake's boat trailer to the narrow sliver of driveway that remained. There he unleashed Mango and tossed the ball.

The dog took off like a rocket, gravel flying up as she dug her powerful legs into the stone. She snagged the ball as it was still bouncing, whipped around and brought it back to drop it at his feet.

"Good girl," he said and rewarded her with a hearty rub of her squarish head and short pointy ears.

When Anita came out to join them, Mango raced to her and glued herself to her side until Anita bent and stroked her hands all along the pittie's glossy fur and muscular body. "I love you, too," she said, earning a doggy kiss.

Brett handed Anita the ball and for the next half hour or so they played with Mango, having her chase the ball and run through a number of the basic commands. He explained to Anita what each one meant and that he issued the commands in Czech.

"Why Czech?" she asked as he finally instructed the dog to heel so they could return inside for their meeting.

"So the crooks won't know what they mean and so Mango won't react to a commonly used word," he said, and after they entered, he locked up and instructed Mango to guard the back door since he'd have a clean line of sight to the side door from the breakfast bar.

As he had the night before, he powered up his laptop, sent the monitor image to the larger television screen and clicked on the link to join the video meeting.

The SBS crew, except for Roni, were gathered around the table with Roni's partner, Heath Williams, and Mia's husband, John Wilson.

"CONGRATULATIONS TO YOU and Roni, Trey," Anita said.

Deep smudges under his eyes, like swipes of charcoal on a drawing, and thick stubble darkened his otherwise handsome face, but a brilliant smile lit his aqua eyes.

"*Gracias*, Anita. I'm a lucky man. Marielena is a beauty," Trey said and popped up a picture of the new baby, which earned the requisite oohs and aahs from everyone.

"She is at that, Trey. Congrats," Brett said and for a second Anita thought she detected a wistful note in his tones, but then he was all action.

"I'm hoping for some good news."

Trey and Heath shared a look from across the table and Trey motioned for Heath to report.

"Our crooked cop agreed to a plea deal. He'll still do a good amount of time for the shootings of the two Aventura cops, but he won't get life for Billy Allen's murder," Heath advised.

"Have you found the rest of Billy in the gator?" Brett asked matter-of-factly.

Anita's stomach turned at the thought of what the gator had done to the man and Brett's seemingly uncaring tone. But then again, Billy had tried to kill them and Mango.

Heath nodded and continued. "Homestead police located his remains not far from where the jogger saw the gator with the arm. Coroner says COD was a bullet to the head," Heath said and mimicked a shot to the forehead.

Trey jumped in with, "Same caliber and make as with Ramirez and the stray bullets CSI dug out of the cabinets in Homestead. Ballistics should be able to confirm shortly if all those bullets came from the same gun."

She supposed that was some progress, not that it made her feel any more comfortable with her own situation.

"If I remember correctly, whoever shot Billy might be related to him?" Anita said, recalling something Mia had said the night before.

"Cousins, but what's more interesting is that the shooter is Tony Hollywood's son," Trey replied.

Brett shot a quick look at her, apparently as puzzled as she was since he asked, "Why is it interesting?"

"Because Tony Hollywood's one and only son is currently serving a five-year sentence for aggravated assault," Mia advised.

Anita processed that for a moment and shook her head. "Santiago Kennedy is Tony Hollywood's illegitimate child?"

"And now we have evidence also tying Kennedy to the assault on you in Homestead. Once ballistics confirms whether the bullets are the same, we've got him," Trey said.

"But not Hollywood," Anita said and pushed a stray lock of hair back from her face, feeling frustration despite all the progress that had been made.

Brett wrapped an arm around her shoulders, consoling her with a squeeze. "Once we get Kennedy, he may roll on Hollywood. But even if he doesn't, Hollywood is not going to come after you. There is nothing you know that can hurt Hollywood."

"Brett's right," Trey interjected. "The only person Hollywood should be worried about is Santiago Kennedy. He's the key in all this. He killed Ramirez and I'm sure that he killed Hollywood's nephew."

Everyone around the table nodded in agreement and then John Wilson piped in with, "I ran them through my program and the probability is almost one hundred percent that Kennedy killed both Ramirez and his cousin. But there is also a high probability that we won't get Kennedy alive."

"You think Hollywood is going to kill him?" Anita asked, thinking that the mobster had a lot to worry about with his illegitimate son.

Using his fingers, Wilson counted down the reasons. "One, Kennedy messed up with Ramirez. The program—and my gut—says he wasn't supposed to kill him, just scare him. Two, the nephew's murder. Three, the fear his wife will find out he fooled around. And finally, four, the fear Kennedy will spill his guts as part of a plea deal."

Trey had been nodding along as Wilson spoke and voiced

his agreement. "I don't need the program to tell me you're one hundred percent right, John. It's why we have to find Kennedy because he knows Anita is the final nail in the coffin to charging him with Ramirez's murder."

ANITA SHOOK BENEATH his arm at Trey's words.

Brett understood. She was more worried about being in the coffin than being the nail.

He leaned close and whispered in her ear, "We will get him."

She half glanced at him, eyes wide with fear. "But when, Brett. When?"

Her whispered words cut through the air and were picked up by the laptop mic, transmitting them to those seated at the SBS offices.

"Soon. We will have Kennedy soon," Trey promised, earning a chorus of assurances from those gathered around the table.

Buoyed by his colleagues, Brett nevertheless had concerns about one front. "What about the Feds? Still not cooperating?"

"Still not cooperating," Trey said, his annoyance obvious.

Roni's partner, Heath, tacked on, "But we're working on it."

He had to be satisfied with that, Brett supposed. "What are our next steps?"

Trey and Heath glanced at each other from across the table.

"We tie together the ballistics and get a BOLO out for Kennedy. Keep on working on the Feds," Heath said.

"SBS will work on finding out what we can about Kennedy's familial connection to Hollywood. Maybe there's something there that we can use," Trey said.

"Like where he might be hiding?" Anita asked, her body still trembling and tense beneath his arm.

Trey nodded. "Yes, like that. If we find his mother, we may be able to get info from her."

"We can work on that as well," Brett offered, his mind already racing on where he could search for that information.

"How long before they release Allen's body to his family?" Brett added, thinking that a visit to the funeral mass might also yield valuable insights.

"Not soon. They literally have to piece him together and search all those pieces for evidence. That's going to take time," Heath advised.

"Patience, Brett. I know you feel otherwise, but we've made a lot of progress," Trey shot back, testiness in his tone that made his baby sister, Mia, reach over and lay a hand on his forearm as it rested on the tabletop.

Trey shook his head and looked down, chastised. "As you can imagine, I've had a lot on my mind in the last twenty-four hours."

Although he hadn't said the words, the apology was apparent in his tone and the droop of his head. Brett accepted it and offered his own apology of sorts. "I get it. We've been kind of busy ourselves."

"Luckily, we do have some progress. I think you can rest a little easier tonight," Mia said, stepping in to be the mediator.

"Yes, we can. Maybe it's time we all got some rest," Trey said and rubbed his hands across the stubble on his face.

Brett nodded. "We'll check in tomorrow morning."

"Agreed. Ten hundred sharp," Trey said, and after a quick perusal of the table to see if anyone had anything to add, he ended the call.

"Can we rest easier tonight?" Anita asked, doubt alive in her voice.

Brett understood her concerns and they weren't just about

Hollywood and Kennedy. The tension had been building between them for days and the long night loomed large.

He had to do what he could to alleviate her fears and keep from doing something they might both regret.

Chapter Nineteen

Anita swiveled in her seat, wanting to make sure she didn't miss any nuance of Brett's response.

There was the slightest hesitation and furrow of his brow before he said, "We can. It's unlikely Kennedy knows where we are right now and considering what he's done—"

"You mean killing Hollywood's nephew, who is also his cousin?" she jumped in, needing to make sure she understood exactly what was happening.

"For starters. I'd put money on it that Hollywood sent Kennedy to collect a debt, not kill Ramirez. He's probably angry now that he's unlikely to get his money."

"Unless Ramirez's partner knows something he's not talking about. I got the sense that Manny and his partner, Kevin Marino, shared a lot," she said, recalling how close they'd seemed to be the many times she'd interacted with them.

Brett mulled over her comments and nodded. "The police have probably already talked to him, but maybe he'd share more if he wasn't worried about being arrested."

"It's worth investigating, right? That and Kennedy's mother. Who was she? Does Mrs. Hollywood know? I'd be royally pissed if my husband was cheating," she said, then frowned and shook her head. "Not to mention he had a child," she added.

"Any man who cheated on you would need his head examined," he said, a dangerous gleam in his gaze as he fixed it on her and reached up to stroke the back of his hand across her cheek.

"Leaving me isn't much better," she said, then covered his hand with hers and drew it away, but she didn't let go.

He nodded. "I left you. I think I left me as well. I'm not the same man. He's long gone."

Pain colored his words and his body, which sagged from the weight of it.

Squeezing his hand, she tempered her response. "He is, but the man I see here is honorable, brave and loving."

"Does that mean there's hope for us?" he asked, lifting an eyebrow in emphasis.

"Maybe," she said, needing honesty between them.

A smile filled with longing and hopefulness drifted across his lips.

With a final squeeze of his hand, she said, "What do we do now?"

SANTIAGO KEPT TO the shadows in the alley behind Marino's condo building. It had made sense to handle this first before searching for the woman and the SBS agent. If his research was on the money, they were hours away in the Keys.

As a light snapped on a few floors above, he leaped into action, pulling down the ladder for the fire escape and silently climbing until he reached the right condo. His injured leg protested the movement and he limped onto the last landing.

Flattening against the wall, he held his breath until he confirmed he hadn't been seen by Ramirez's partner, Marino, who had just entered the apartment. Sneaking a quick look, he noticed the man had poured himself a drink and sat at the small dining table close to the window. His back was to the window and his head was buried in his hands, as if he was crying.

Santiago scoffed at the man's show of emotion. *Weakling*, he thought.

He bent and tried the window.

Locked, but there was another window at the other end of the fire escape.

He hurried there, tried the window. Unlocked.

Smiling, he grabbed the frame to lift it, but a sudden knock on the condo door had Marino's head snapping up. The man wiped away the trails of tears, and disgust filled Santiago again at the man's weakness.

Marino hurried to the door and opened it, obviously surprised by guests, especially at such a late hour.

Santiago was surprised as well as he recognized Trey Gonzalez from the photos he'd found online. A woman was with him. His sister, Mia, he guessed. She didn't look like the party girl he'd seen in the photos on her social media, but there was no denying she was a beautiful woman. He'd have no issue with doing her before he killed her, he thought, but forced his thoughts away from that to what was happening in the condo.

Whatever the SBS duo said had Marino inviting them into the room. Ever the host, he must have offered them something, but the siblings waved him off.

Santiago couldn't hear from where he was standing but as the three moved to the table where Marino had been sitting earlier, he shifted to listen to their conversation.

Even though he was closer, the sound from the nearby street and the arrival of a garbage truck in the alley behind the building made it hard for him to hear everything. Only bits and pieces of their discussion drifted out, but it was enough to know they were pressing Marino about Ramirez.

Marino, who according to his police mole hadn't said a thing, was saying more now.

"Silent partner...struggle...pandemic."

He hadn't heard Hollywood's name yet but was sure it was coming.

He couldn't let that happen.

Whipping out his gun, he centered himself at the window and opened fire.

For the briefest moment, he squinted against the shattering glass.

A mistake.

Before he could shoot at Marino again, Trey had upended the table for protection and pulled both Marino and his sister behind it.

Stunned, he delayed another dangerous second.

Trey popped up from behind the protection of the table and fired.

The bullet slammed into the body armor beneath his guayabera, stealing his breath, but he forced himself to move.

Turning, he scrambled to the fire escape ladder and raced down, cursing as pain lanced through his leg.

"Call 911," Trey called out and, at the pounding above him, Santiago knew the SBS chief was giving chase.

He fired upward wildly and stumbled down the last few steps on the ladder.

His leg crumpled beneath him as he hit the ground, a lucky thing, otherwise Trey's shot from above might have struck home again.

Cradling an arm against his bruised ribs, he raced around the corner and onto Collins, dodging cars as he hurried across the street.

He didn't look back as he heard the screech of wheels, the crunch of metal and glass, and drivers cursing. His one hope was that Gonzalez was sandwiched between those crashed cars.

As he reached the BMW he had parked by Española Way, he risked a glance back.

No one was following.

Satisfied he was in the clear, he hopped into the BMW and sped off.

Chapter Twenty

Brett had barely laid his head on the couch pillow when his phone vibrated, rattling on the coffee table.

He snatched it up, not wanting to disturb Anita and disturbed enough himself since calls at this hour were never good.

Trey, he realized with a quick glance at the caller ID. He answered the video call.

Trey looked even more tired than before and his hair was disheveled, as if he'd repeatedly run his fingers through it.

"What's up, boss?" he whispered.

"Anita was on the money about Marino. He knew more than he was sharing with the police, but he's sharing now since someone tried to take him out less than an hour ago," Trey advised.

"Kennedy?" he asked, then popped off the couch and started pacing, waking Mango, who had been dozing by the front door. The pit bull popped up her head, instantly alert to the action, but seeing it was him, she laid her head back down on her paws.

"Kennedy. I got a look at him after he fired at Marino," Trey said, but Brett could tell there was more his friend and boss wasn't saying.

"Please tell me you didn't go after him," Brett pleaded, scared that Marielena would grow up without her father.

"I'm fine but Kennedy got away. CCTV tracked him to Española Way and a black BMW. Heath ran the plates, but the car was reported stolen just like the Mercedes he was driving earlier," Trey said with a rough sigh.

"Let me guess. Stolen from one of Hollywood's car lots," he said and angrily wagged his head.

"You got it. But Marino is talking, and Hollywood is definitely involved. Turns out he was a silent partner. Gave Ramirez and Marino a few million in exchange for access to the hotel and all its facilities. Probably to run his bookmaking and sell drugs. In addition, they were supposed to repay him, a million every year, but then the pandemic hit—"

"And all the best-laid plans fell apart," Brett finished for him.

Trey nodded. "Marino admitted that Kennedy had come around a time or two, asking about the money. Apparently, Hollywood thinks they're hiding the profits that should be repaid to him."

"We have our link," Brett considered and wiped a hand across his mouth. "Are you going to share this with the Feds?"

Trey smirked and laughed. "Do you think we should?"

Brett immediately shook his head. "Not unless it's going to be quid pro quo."

"I agree. They're keeping something from us, and we need to know what that is," Trey said and then looked across the room. A second later Mia walked into view and laid a hand on her brother's shoulder.

"I apologize but I'm taking *mi hermanito* home before he falls flat on his face," she said.

"Ten hundred sharp," Trey said as Mia's finger appeared on screen a second before the call ended.

Now that's real progress, he thought, grateful that Anita and he had shared her thoughts about Marino with his SBS colleagues.

And little by little, the case against Kennedy, and Hollywood as well, was getting stronger.

Which meant they were getting closer to ending the threat to Anita's safety.

He should have been happy about that, he thought as he softly padded down to her room and peeked in.

She was sound asleep in a tangle of sheets, her beautiful legs peeking out as she lay on her back. Her dark hair was free of the topknot she normally wore, a dark spill across the electric white of the sheets. Her hand lay outspread, palm open and wide next to her.

How many times had he come to her after a late shift on the base and found her like this. Slipped his hand into hers and woken her. Made love with her.

He hardened in the confines of his jeans and sucked in a breath to control his response.

That slightest noise woke her.

Her eyes fluttered open, and she seemed startled at first, but then relaxed as she realized it was him.

"Everything okay?" she asked and sat up slightly.

The blanket slipped down, exposing her upper body. The thin white fabric of the cheap pajamas did nothing to hide the generous globes of her breasts and darker areolas.

As she realized where his gaze had gone, her nipples tightened into hard points.

He forced himself not to remember how they'd tasted. How she'd moan…

"Everything's okay," he shot out and more calmly added, "You were right about Marino. He knew more than he was saying. Kennedy tried to shut him up, but luckily Trey was there."

Anita snatched the blanket back up in a stranglehold, a reaction to both his gaze and the news. "Trey wasn't hurt, was he?"

He shook his head. "Everyone is fine. They have Kennedy on CCTV fleeing the scene in a black BMW and Marino has implicated Hollywood. The noose is tightening so this will all be over soon," he said and in a softer, sadder tone, added, "You'll be home soon."

ANITA SHOULD HAVE been happy about that.

But she wasn't.

Being home again meant saying goodbye to Brett.

Or did it? she asked herself, her body humming with need from the hungry look he'd given her before he schooled his emotions and walked out the door.

Even now her insides vibrated and dampened as she remembered making love with him. She drifted her hand up over her breast, bit back a moan at the sensitivity of her tight nipples.

He'd always done this to her. Always roused this kind of passion.

Always satisfied as a lover, but as she'd painfully discovered, that alone hadn't been enough.

But as he'd said over and over, he was no longer the same man.

But was he a better man? A man who would stay? she asked herself as she willed passion to subside in her body so she could think clearly.

The answer came immediately.

Yes.

BRETT HAD BARELY settled onto the couch when he heard a footfall in the hallway.

He half rose on the couch and reached for his weapon, but immediately recognized Anita's silhouette in the dim light.

"What's wrong?" he asked and sat up.

She padded over and sat cross-legged on the couch beside him, looking slightly girlish with her loose hair cascading down onto her breasts.

Breasts he instantly pulled his gaze from to avoid an embarrassing reaction she would surely see.

"Earlier tonight you asked if there was hope for us and I said 'maybe.'"

Hopeful emotion choked his throat, making it impossible for him to speak. He tipped his head, urging her to continue.

"I was wrong," she said, making his heart plummet until she shifted and crawled into his lap.

She cupped his jaw and ran a finger across his thick, closely cropped beard. The sound rasped loudly in the quiet of night.

"Anita?" he asked but she laid an index finger across his lips.

"The past is…the past. The last few days…you've shown me what kind of man you've become, and while you're not perfect—"

"Ouch," he muttered against her finger.

"I'm not, either," she admitted with a siren's smile.

Being this close to her, with the woman he'd loved and wanted for so long, made it impossible to curb his need any longer. Especially as she snuggled close, bringing her warm center directly above his hardness.

He swept his hands to her hips to urge her even closer and she moaned and pressed herself to him.

"Brett," she rasped.

"I want you. I want this, whatever this is," he said, afraid to say the four-letter word he suspected she wanted to hear most.

"I'm a big girl. I'll take whatever this is," Anita said, then bent her head and kissed him.

Her consent released the hunger he'd been holding in check.

He ripped the thin cotton nightshirt from her body, exposing her to his gaze. Cradling her breast, he rubbed his thumb across her hard nipple and whispered, "You are so beautiful. More beautiful than I remembered."

She followed his lead, fumbling for a second before yanking his T-shirt away.

A shocked gasp filled the air and she gently, almost reverently, skipped her fingers across the silvery and hard ridges across his upper chest.

"Do they hurt?" she asked, voice tight with emotion.

He shook his head. "Not anymore."

IT WAS IMPOSSIBLE not to think about how he must have suffered, she thought as she traced the uneven ridges scattered across his upper body. Slightly lower there was a longer, smoother but clearly man-made scar. A physician's handiwork, and she shuddered at the thought that she might have lost him permanently so many years ago.

He tucked his thumb and forefinger beneath her chin and gently urged her gaze to his. She waited for him to say something. Anything. Instead, he just tenderly brushed back a lock of stray hair and kissed her.

A whisper-light kiss. An invitation and not a demand.

She accepted, opening her mouth to his. Dancing her tongue with his as he cradled her breast and teased the tip.

She wanted his mouth on her. Wanted him buried deep inside as she shifted her hips against him, and he groaned and pushed upward.

In the dance of partners familiar with each other, he cradled her breasts together and kissed her, shifting from one tip to the other, until he suckled on one and nearly sent her over the edge.

"Please, Brett," she keened, and he shot to his feet, cradling her against his chest.

At the front door, Mango jumped to her feet and growled, misunderstanding his action.

With a hand signal, he confirmed the command with, "*Lehni*, Mango. *Lehni*."

The dog hesitated but lay down.

"Good girl, Mango. *Pozor*," he said, commanding her to guard the door.

Mango settled in at the entrance, head on her paws.

He pushed forward to his bedroom, laid her on the bed and quickly stripped off his jeans. He slowed only long enough to remove his wallet and a condom he set on the nightstand.

As he climbed on the bed beside her, facing her, she once again explored his body, trailing her hand across his upper chest and down the long scar she hated seeing. She kept on going until she'd encircled him, and he sucked in a breath.

"You like?" she asked, feeling like a temptress.

He laughed and cupped her breast. Tweaked the hard nipple.

Now it was her turn to gasp as that tug ripped straight to her center.

"You like?" he teased, a boyish grin on his face before he bent and took the tip into his mouth.

When he sucked on it, she nearly lost it, but she bit her lip and cupped the back of his skull, urging him on while stroking him with her other hand.

The years of separation slipped away as they made love. Moves both familiar and yet also unexpected lifted desire to heights she hadn't experienced before until she was on the edge, barely hanging on.

He shifted inside her, driving her ever higher, and she called out his name, drawing his gaze to her face.

The words nearly slipped from her then. Nearly, but it was too soon. Too uncertain.

"It's okay, Anita. It's okay," he said as if aware of what she was keeping hidden, protected, deep in her heart.

But while the words wouldn't come, she splayed her hand over his heart and held on as he drove them ever higher until they both held their breath, poised on the precipice.

With one last stroke, he pushed them over and they fell together to the bed, joined. Wrapped in each other's arms.

Chapter Twenty-One

They woke tangled together, peaceful until Mango's growl had Brett flying from the bed naked.

He rushed to the coffee table and grabbed his gun as Mango rose and faced the front door, another low rumble coming from her throat.

Peering through the peephole, he realized it was Jake's neighbor and instructed Mango to sit down.

Tucking the gun behind him, he unlocked the door and opened it, staying behind it to hide his nudity.

"Mornin', Jim."

"Mornin', Brett. Sorry to wake you so early, but I thought you should know that I noticed a red Jeep driving by a few times. Seemed a little suspicious to me," the old man said.

Brett dipped his head in thanks, grateful for the retired cop's eagle eyes. "Any chance you have a video camera that might have picked it up?"

Jim shook his head. "Don't believe in all that new technology. I like my privacy," he said and, with a wave of his hand, turned and walked away.

Too bad, he thought.

It was also too bad that the video doorbell on Jake's house didn't face the street. At best the camera might have gotten only a sliver of anything passing by. Still, a sliver was better than nothing.

Since he'd helped Jake set up the camera and sometimes stayed there, he had access to the recorded videos.

Sure enough, the history showed that a red Jeep Wrangler had passed by the house in the early-morning hours. It had gone east, then west, then east again, toward the homes at the end of the canal. If it was just another neighbor, the car should be parked somewhere along this street or the perpendicular cul-de-sac at the end.

A quick walk with Mango would confirm that.

Anita slipped her arms around his waist, surprising him and making him jump.

He cursed and faced her. "You snuck up on me."

"You were lost in thought," she said and rose on tiptoe to brush a kiss on his lips, her naked body flush against his, rousing desire that he had to tamp down.

"Who was at the door?" she asked.

"Jim. It was nothing," he assured her and quickly tacked on, "We have a meeting in about an hour and I don't know about you, but I need some coffee and food." He rubbed his belly in emphasis.

She stroked the back of her hand across his stomach and laughed. "Man cannot live on love alone, right?"

The moment had been relatively lighthearted, but turned serious with what should have been playful words.

Stammering, he jerked his thumb in the direction of the kitchen. "How about I make some coffee while you shower—"

"And I'll cook breakfast while you clean up," she finished for him.

ANITA NODDED AND rushed off to shower. Alone. Thankfully.

Showering with Brett, which she'd done dozens of times in the past, would have been way too intimate now.

Way more intimate than what you already did all night long? the little voice in her head challenged, but she shushed it.

I won't apologize for having needs.

Needs? the voice chided but she ignored it and hurried into the shower. Washing quickly, she dried off and dashed to her bedroom to dress. She wouldn't have much time to make breakfast and clean up before the meeting with the rest of the SBS crew.

As she entered the kitchen, he handed her a mug. "I hope I got it right."

She sipped it, then nodded and smiled, pleased that he'd remembered how she took her coffee. "Perfect."

With that, he almost ran down the hall and her heart sank with the awkwardness between them this morning.

What did you expect? the annoying voice chimed in.

She ignored it, focusing on the delicious, perfectly made mug of coffee and the breakfast she had to prepare.

With the clock ticking away, she played it safe with blueberry pancakes, breakfast sausage and warm maple syrup. She normally wouldn't have bought the premade sausage, but she had remembered that Brett liked it and impulsively grabbed some while they'd been shopping.

Brett returned barely fifteen minutes later, dressed in khaki shorts and a pale yellow guayabera like those so many men wore in Miami. The pale color emphasized the cocoa brown of his beard, hair and eyes.

He went to the fridge and took out fresh food for Mango, dished it out and refilled her water bowl. He called the pit bull over, and Mango gobbled the food down so fast, Anita worried the dog might choke. But when she finished and drank deeply from the water bowl, she returned to her spot by the front door.

When Brett passed by her to grab place mats and cutlery, he laid a possessive hand at her waist and dropped a kiss on her cheek, alleviating some of the morning's earlier self-consciousness.

With a quick toss of the pan, she flipped the pancake, earning a "Show-off" from him.

She chuckled and winked. "Jealous much?"

He responded with a laugh and finished setting the bistro table as she placed a stack of pancakes on their plates and added the sausage. He took those over to the table while she poured warm maple syrup into a small jug for serving.

Because time was short, breakfast was relatively silent except for appreciative murmurs from Brett. When the plates were empty of everything but some scattered crumbs and a few drops of maple syrup, they worked together to clean and prepare for their meeting.

Barely five minutes later, they were staring at the SBS team.

"YOU LOOK A little better than you did last night," Brett said. The smudges beneath his friend's eyes were not as deep and his skin had a little more color.

"Some sleep and a visit to Roni and the baby this morning worked some magic," he said and, for good measure, shared a picture of mama and baby.

Everyone around the table responded with congrats again, but then Trey quickly turned the conversation over to Sophie and Robbie's report.

"As Trey advised, CCTV picked up on Kennedy's escape after he tried to kill Marino. The police sent us the footage and we were able to trace the passage of the vehicle using an assortment of traffic cameras and ALPRs. The BMW headed south. We lost it in the Homestead area," Sophie said, worry on her engaging features, so much like Trey's and Mia's that there was no denying they were cousins.

"You think he's headed here?" Brett pressed, brows rising in question.

"Possibly," Robbie advised and continued. "An ALPR at a traffic light last picked up the BMW on Route 1. There is a BOLO out for Kennedy and the vehicle so hopefully either a sharp-eyed officer or another ALPR will see it."

"But you're sure it was a black BMW?" he asked, mindful of what Jim had seen and the footage on Jake's doorbell video.

"Positive but be mindful Kennedy may have already dumped the Bimmer and secured another vehicle," Trey warned.

"Roger that. What about Marino and the Feds? Any progress?" he pushed.

"We're waiting for a complete report from Williams, but he texted to say that Marino has implicated both Kennedy and Hollywood in various crimes. As for the Feds, it seems there's been a change in their attitude, possibly because they don't want the local LEOs to get sole credit for apprehending a high-profile target like Hollywood," Trey said.

"Sounds good. Is it okay if I send you some footage from our video doorbell?" he asked.

"Something hinky?" Trey asked, espresso-colored brows furrowing.

"Maybe or it could be nothing. Jake's neighbor is a retired cop and noticed a suspicious red Jeep Wrangler. Our doorbell picked up the vehicle, but it's at a bad angle. I was hoping Sophie and Robbie could take a look."

"Send it over," Sophie immediately said.

"Will do," he confirmed.

Trey did a quick glance around the table to see if anyone else had anything to say and when all remained silent, he said, "We'll be in touch as soon as we have more."

When he ended the call, Anita leaned close and said, "Jim saw something?"

He didn't want to worry her, so he said, "It could just be a retired cop seeing things that aren't there."

"Or his expert eyes really picked up on something," she said and splayed her fingers on the countertop, as if trying to stabilize her world.

He laid his hand on hers and squeezed. "Let me send the video to Sophie and Robbie and see what they make of it."

Chapter Twenty-Two

Anita hoped that the SBS tech gurus would be able to allay their fears, but she was too anxious to just sit and wait for a reply.

Gesturing to Mango, she asked, "Is it time to take her for a walk?"

He nodded. "Now is a good time. That red Jeep headed toward the cul-de-sac at the end of the canal. Could just be someone heading home."

She hoped he was right and trusted that he would make the right decisions to keep her safe.

They walked to the front door, where he grabbed Mango's leash and clipped it on. He opened the door but said, "Hold on while I check."

He went ahead, Mango at his side, inspected the side and front yard and then doubled back to let her know it was clear.

Outside, they strolled to the street, still as quiet as it had been the day before. He assumed the position closest to the road, Mango between them, as they leisurely walked down the block, heading for the cul-de-sac to find the red Jeep, hopefully parked in front of the owner's home.

As they reached the end of the block, she peered down the street and pointed. "There it is," she said.

BRETT HAD SEEN the vehicle also. It was on the east side of the cul-de-sac in front of a small ranch-style home. Directly opposite that home was a row of tall, thick oleanders, flush with pink flowers, forming a dense border along another home's yard.

Too dense.

Someone could easily be hiding behind those bushes.

Because of that, he shifted to the other side of the street, the one where the Jeep was stationed, and directed Anita to the inside, away from the street and those possibly dangerous bushes.

He approached the Jeep, but nothing seemed out of order. For safety's sake, he snapped off a photo of the license plate so Sophie and Robbie could check to see who owned it.

Swiveling around, he inspected the area, but all was quiet.

Gesturing to the other end of the street, he said, "Let's finish our walk and get back to the house."

SANTIAGO CLIMBED OVER the short fence and hurried down the dock, working his way toward the house where he suspected Mr. Brett Madison was guarding the chef who could ID him.

After getting the name from his FBI contact, he'd searched the internet and, although Mr. Brett Madison had done an excellent job of scrubbing himself from most places, he'd found an article that the *Marine Corps Times* had done when several marine units had helped distribute food in the Philippines after a typhoon had caused extensive devastation.

He'd recognized Madison immediately, although he'd been several years younger. The photo had shown him, SBS Chief Trey Gonzalez and fellow marine Jacob Benjamin Anderson.

Jacob, apparently known as Jake to his friends, hadn't been as careful as Gonzalez and Madison.

Social media content galore and easily found via a free online phone book.

Just a few more houses, Santiago thought, but then he caught sight of the old man sitting on a lawn chair farther down the dock that ran behind the homes.

Even though he was older, the man was still in good shape. Whipcord lean muscles warned he'd put up quite a fight. Worse, he had that look about him. Either ex-cop or ex-military and he was directly in the way of him reaching his destination.

He could fight him or even just shoot him, but that would alert Madison to trouble.

That was the last thing he wanted to do. He needed the element of surprise if he was going to be able to overcome Madison and that powerful pit bull.

With a nonchalant wave at the man, he doubled back to where he'd parked the Jeep. He'd return later, when it was dark and easier to avoid prying eyes.

He hopped the fence again and raced across the last yard and around the thick row of oleanders.

As he slipped into the Jeep, he couldn't believe what he was seeing right in front of him.

Madison, the woman and that damn dog.

They were at the far end of the cul-de-sac and boxed in by cars on either side of the street.

Perfect, he thought, then started the car and gunned the engine.

Chapter Twenty-Three

Brett whirled around at the sound of the racing engine.

The Jeep was barreling toward them, but they were at the end of the street and cars lined either side, leaving no room for escape. But at their end of the block a wide swath of dock ran perpendicular to the street along the waters of another canal.

"Run," he said, urging Anita in the direction of the dock and scooping up Mango.

At the edge of the narrow dock, Anita hesitated.

He wrapped an arm around her and hauled her close as he jumped into the water.

SANTIAGO SCREECHED TO a stop, cursing and hitting the steering wheel in frustration as he watched the trio leap into the canal.

He raced out of the Jeep and ran to the edge of the dock, but he couldn't see them in the waters below.

That didn't stop him from opening fire into the canal.

He emptied his clip, but as people raced out of their homes, he couldn't linger.

He raced back to the Jeep, reversed down the block and, with a quick K-turn, sped away.

MANGO FOUGHT AGAINST HIM, clawing to be free of the water.

Anita started to rise, but he laid a hand on her shoulder and kept her down.

She looked at him, fearful eyes wide against the stinging seawater, and he gestured upward.

Above them bullets pierced the surface and flew downward, creating deadly trails in the water.

When the last of the bullets swam by, he pushed off the bottom and to the surface. Anita popped up next to him a second later.

He released Mango, who immediately began dog-paddling beside him as Brett searched for some way to reach the dock again.

Suddenly, Jim leaned over the edge of the dock and held out his hand. "Heard the commotion and came to help," he said.

Brett grabbed hold of Jim's hand and that of another neighbor who had also come to assist. The two men boosted him up easily and, in turn, he bent to lift Anita out of the water.

"You're not hurt, are you?" he asked, inspecting Anita as she stood beside him.

"I'm fine," she said.

Jim lifted Mango out of the water and deposited her on the dock.

The dog shook her body, sending water everywhere, and then immediately came to Brett's side and bumped his leg with her head, almost as if in apology.

Her thick nails had torn his shirt and raked deep scratches into his chest as she'd struggled against him underwater, fear gripping her.

"You're a good girl, Mango," he said and rubbed her head and ears.

The sound of approaching sirens perked up Mango's ears,

and barely a minute later, a squad car came around the corner and parked.

Brett had wanted to keep a low profile but clearly that would no longer be possible.

"Neighbors probably called 911," Jim said as he looked at the cruiser.

Brett nodded. His mind raced with all the possible things he could do to protect Anita now that this location was also blown.

One immediately came to mind. Turning to the old cop, he said, "Could you do me a favor?"

Jim bowed his head and said, "Sure. What is it?"

Not wanting others to overhear, he leaned close and whispered his request to the older man.

"Got it. I'll reach out to Jake and be waiting for you," he said and pushed off, hurrying past the police officer with a quick salute.

Anita stood shivering beside him, but a fifty-something female walked over and wrapped a beach towel around her. "Th-th-thank y-y-ou," Anita said past her chattering lips.

"No worries, honey. Keep it," the woman said and handed Brett another towel to dry down.

Not that it would take long. Even though it was December, the sun was strong and the day warm. Already in the low seventies, if he had to guess.

Anita's trembling was likely more from fear than cold.

He wrapped an arm around her and rubbed his hand up and down her side, offering support and reassurance as they answered the volley of questions the officer, a young Latino man named Hernandez, was asking.

Names, addresses and their business in the area. A description of the car, which also had Brett pulling out his cell phone to provide the license plate number. Officer Hernandez jotted it all down and was about to start asking even more questions when his radio chirped to life.

"Hernandez here," he said as he answered.

"Miami PD wants your report and said to release the victims ASAP," the dispatcher advised.

"10-4. We're done here anyway," Hernandez said and faced them.

"You heard. You're free to go. Do you need a ride?" he asked.

Brett flipped a hand in the direction of the street off the cul-de-sac. "We're just a few doors down."

The officer nodded and headed to his patrol car while Anita, Mango and he rushed down the block. But the officer, obviously aware that this was an unusual and dangerous situation, followed them in his cruiser and parked in front of Jake's house.

Brett walked Anita toward the entrance of the side yard and door and said, "Wait here."

Hurrying back to the cruiser, he leaned down and said, "This guy won't hesitate to shoot, so stay vigilant."

The young officer nodded. "10-4. Do you need an escort to somewhere else?"

Brett peered toward the SUV in the driveway. He had no doubt it had already been compromised by Kennedy noting the plate number. They had no idea how many dirty cops Kennedy had in his pocket who would use the ALPRs to track their travel.

He shook his head. "We're going to stay here for now," he said, even though he had no plans to do that.

"I'll be sure to drive past here often while I'm on patrol," he said.

"That would be appreciated," Brett said and tapped his hand on the window frame to let the officer know he was good to go.

Hands on hips, he watched the officer drive away, did another quick look around the property and then walked with Mango back toward the side yard and door.

As he had so many times before, he opened the door and sent Mango ahead to scope out the house.

Not that he expected Kennedy to have lingered there after trying to run them down.

But he had no doubt Kennedy would be back, which meant they had to be on the move as soon as possible.

Inside, he turned to Anita, who stood in the dining room, shaking even with the towel and her arms wrapped around herself.

He laid a hand on her shoulder and cupped her cheek. Leaning down so she couldn't avoid his gaze, he said, "It's going to be okay. Take a warm shower and pack up your things. We'll be on the move as soon as I talk to Trey."

She nodded and walked down the hall, and he pulled out a fresh burner phone and called Trey.

"Are you all okay?" Trey asked, clearly having been filled in by MPD.

"Pretty much," Brett said and peered at the angry scrapes on his chest that were stinging from the salt water in the canal.

Trey released a colorful stream of curses about the state of things and Brett had to agree. "Yes, it's totally messed up. We can't stay here, it's compromised."

"I agree. I'm looking for another place for you—"

"No need, Trey. I have an idea," he said and relayed the plan that had occurred to him.

"Unorthodox, but it makes sense," Trey said with a low whistle.

"How did he find us? I thought you had plugged the leak at PD," Brett pressed, angry that another location had been compromised.

"I don't know but I have my suspicions, particularly since the FBI is finally involved in this," his friend said.

"You think the leak is there?" Brett asked, not that the FBI agents were so far beyond reproach.

"Possibly. Williams, Roni and I are going to speak with the lead Fed. Alone. In the meantime, go ahead with your plan. I'll reach out to you later once we've finished," Trey said.

"Roger that," he said and ended the call.

THE SHOWER HAD helped immensely to chase away the fear of the moment and the salt water of the canal.

And as she'd shoved her meager belongings into a plastic bag, anger replaced fear. Determination replaced worry.

She marched out to the dining room where Brett had just finished his call.

"What can I do?" she asked, chin tilted up defiantly.

But as Trey turned in her direction, she gasped and walked over to him to gently brush aside the torn fabric of his shirt. "Oh my god. We need to tend to those," she said, shocked by the deep, angry scratches on his chest.

"Mango panicked underwater, but I couldn't let her stay on the dock. Kennedy would have shot her," he said in explanation.

Anita bobbed her head in agreement. "I get it. Why don't you shower, and after, I'll get those cleaned and bandaged."

"Thanks. We're leaving here. Would you mind packing up our food supplies? Nothing too perishable."

"I'll get them ready," she said and hurried to do as he asked, mentally preparing a menu from the foods they had and which would keep for a few days.

She carefully packed things away and then returned to her bathroom and searched the cabinet for disinfectant, antibiotic ointment, gauze and tape.

Brett exited his bedroom bare-chested and wearing un-buttoned jeans that hung loose on his lean hips, toweling dry his high-and-tight hair.

Lord, but he was gorgeous, even with his warrior's scars.

Her heart pounded with need, but also that fear again that she'd almost lost him forever.

Juggling the items to tend to the scratches, she said, "Why don't you sit on the couch."

When he did so, legs splayed wide, she slipped between his powerful thighs and sat opposite him on the coffee table. She laid out her first aid supplies, applied disinfectant to some gauze and swiped it across the scratches to clean them.

His muscles jumped beneath her ministrations, but he didn't move otherwise.

With fresh gauze, she applied the antibiotic ointment and then taped more gauze in place over the scratches.

"Did you pack up?" he asked when she'd finished, and he offered her a hand up from the coffee table.

She motioned to the assortment of bags on the floor by the kitchen counter. "All ready to go."

He smiled, waggled his head and said, "I'll be back."

He sauntered down the hall, popped into his bedroom and exited a second later, shrugging on a fresh guayabera, the duffel with his clothes in hand.

When he reached her, he stuffed her clothes into the duffel and slung it on his shoulder. After, he filled his hands with a number of the bags she'd packed and she did the same, grabbing as many as she could. Mango helped out as well, picking up a smaller bag with her mouth.

She followed Brett to the back door, where he paused and peered out.

Looking back at her, he said, "We're good to go."

Chapter Twenty-Four

When they stepped outside, she realized Jim was by their dock, a shotgun cradled in his arms. The boat that had previously been high up on the lift had been lowered into the water, where it bobbed gently in the canal.

"Was Jake cool with us taking the boat?" He'd asked Jim to call his friend for permission to use the boat and, if it was okay, prep it.

"He is," Jim said with a dip of his head.

"Thanks, Jim," Brett said and clapped Jim on the back.

The older man nodded and handed him the shotgun. "You might need this," he said and added, "Put a box of shells in the console glove box."

"Thanks again. I truly appreciate it," he said and shook the other man's hand. It was then he noticed the Semper Fi tattooed on the man's forearm.

"Anything for a fellow marine," he said, then turned to Anita and jabbed a finger in her direction.

"You take care of him and you," Jim said with another determined point.

"Good man," she said and watched him walk away in the direction of his house.

"Yes, he is," Brett agreed, then laid his bags on the deck and gently placed the shotgun against the nearest console on the boat. He turned, reached across for her bags and put them on the deck of the boat as well. Finished loading the bags, he asked, "Did you take Mango's food also?"

"Of course. I would never forget Mango," she said and kneeled to pet the dog, who had been patiently sitting on the dock beside her.

Smiling, he held out a hand to help her onto the boat. She stumbled a little as the boat rocked and laid a hand over her stomach, as if a little nauseous already.

"It'll be better once we move. There is a sleeping area, galley and head down below," he said and opened the cockpit door, familiar with the boat from his father's catalogs and having rented similar vessels.

"I'll get these supplies put away," she said, then grabbed some of the bags and disappeared through the opening to belowdecks.

Brett picked up the shotgun and placed it at the cockpit door, just in case. He checked the console for the shells and, satisfied they were in easy reach, stowed his gun there as well to keep it dry but easily accessible. He hopped back onto the dock and signaled Mango to heel as he returned to Jake's house and went into a pantry where he had noticed a big-box-store-sized package of bottled water.

He hoisted that in one hand, locked up the house and returned to the boat.

Mango didn't follow him down, remaining on the dock, where she paced almost nervously. Unusual for the normally fearless dog, and he wondered if she was associating the boat and nearby waters with the scary moments she had experienced not that long ago.

"Come on, Mango. *Kemne*," he urged, instructing her to come onto the boat. She hesitated and he repeated the command. *"Kemne."*

This time she finally hopped up and over the side, her feet

skidding on the smooth surface amidships as she landed on the deck.

"Good girl," he said and stroked her head. He caught sight of a familiar package through the thin plastic bag, reached in and took out Mango's treats. He handed her one and further reinforced her behavior with another rub of her head.

"Lehni," he instructed, and she immediately lay down, sprawling in the middle of the deck. He was grateful for her quick response because he had to be able to rely on her following her commands without hesitation.

He snatched up the last of the bags and took them down to the galley, where Anita was unpacking and stowing items in the cabinets. She turned as he entered and said, "The fridge isn't working."

Nodding, he said, "It probably needs the engine running or a solar panel for power. We'll figure it out once we're underway."

He returned topside for the bottled water, brought it down to her and then went back up to untie the boat.

Anita came up then. "I'll get the bumpers," she said, reminding him that she'd sometimes gone boating with her father.

"Thanks," he said, and as he maneuvered away from the dock, she pulled up the bumpers that protected the boat from dock damage and stowed them beneath the seats at the stern.

She stepped over Mango, who hadn't moved, and joined him at the console.

Laying a hand on his shoulder, she asked, "Where are we going?"

"Jake and I used to go fishing in this area and sometimes stay overnight. There's an anchorage spot near Islamorada and Shell Key that's perfect for tonight," he said, carefully steering the boat to the end of their canal. He turned away from the spot where they'd had to jump into the water.

He cruised wide past that area slowly, keeping an eye out for anything untoward, and caught sight of a police cruiser doing a K-turn on that block.

Officer Hernandez, patrolling as he'd promised.

Brett drove ahead sluggishly, aware of the no-wake zone in the canal area, but as soon as he cleared the last bit of canal, he pushed the boat to its top speed, heading for the Atlantic Intracoastal Waterway and Cowpens Cut. That channel would let them navigate down the Intracoastal and to the familiar spot where they could anchor. Maybe even fish for dinner.

He kept an eye on the boat's radar to make sure he was avoiding any of the shallow shoals or reefs in the area.

"You seem comfortable with this," she said and slipped onto the seat opposite him. Surprisingly, Mango hopped up into her lap, dragging a laugh from her.

"You are so not a lapdog," she said as Mango insinuated herself into the tight space between Anita and the padded console in front of her.

"Mango. Get down. *Lehni*," he called out, but the dog remained in Anita's lap, worrying him, but he didn't press since it seemed to reassure Anita.

"IT'S OKAY. REALLY. She's not too heavy," Anita said and rubbed the dog's head as she sat there, tongue lolling out of her mouth. A cooling breeze bathed them as the boat moved along, and Anita raised her head to catch the air, much like Mango was doing.

If she hadn't been on the run for her life, she might have appreciated the lovely views of the bright cerulean waters, darker in spots from the reefs below, or the lush, verdant foliage and expensive homes along the shore.

It didn't take long to reach what she supposed was Cowpens Cut.

Mangrove and underbrush marked the edges of the narrow strait while channel markers warned of the depth in the center.

Blue-green waters also identified the navigable areas in the middle while white sand was visible beneath the shallow waters along the edges of the cut.

It was a short trip through the area, and once he'd cleared it, Brett increased the boat's speed, following the buoys and channel markers that identified the path for the Intracoastal Waterway.

"That's Plantation Key over there," Brett said and gestured eastward to a larger collection of homes and land along the spit of sand and highway that made up the Keys.

"Will it take long to reach Islamorada?" she asked, unfamiliar with these waters. When she'd gone out with her father, they'd stayed in Biscayne Bay.

"Not long. We should be there in about an hour. Once we get there, we'll anchor and see if there are solar panels we can set up to power the fridge, appliances and the lights for tonight," he said, his gaze constantly traveling along the route and also peering back, making sure all was good.

"What about Trey? Can we reach him out here?" she asked, worried about cell reception, not that they were all that far from land.

"We have service where we anchor even though it's not all that close to shore. I'll call as soon as we're anchored and set up for power."

As PROMISED, it wasn't long before they had reached their destination.

In one of the storage areas, Brett located solar panels and cables that connected to a battery array on the boat. In a second area along the hull of the boat, he found rods, reels and Jake's tackle box, filled with lures and other necessities.

He quickly set up the solar panels and plugged them in to power the appliances and provide light at night. Once he'd done that, he pulled out the rods, reels and tackle box and brought them to a bait station at the stern.

"I thought we might fish for our meal," he said, thinking that the task would also distract Anita from thinking about what had happened just hours earlier.

He was about to help her assemble the tackle, but she went into action without hesitation. "This is old hat to me. My *papi* didn't cut me and my sister any slack when we went fishing."

"Good to know. Since you can handle that, I'm going to call Trey," he said, then pulled out the burner phone and walked around the cockpit area to the bow of the boat. He climbed up onto the seats there and perused the area, vigilant for any danger.

There were several pleasure craft out on the waters, but none seemed to be heading in their direction. Feeling secure, he dialed Trey.

"Have you anchored?" he asked as soon as he answered.

"We have. Everything seems secure for now," Brett advised and did another slow swivel to scope out the area around Shell Key.

"Good. We spoke to the FBI agent handling the Hollywood investigation. He admitted that they'd suspected they had a leak on their team since Hollywood kept slipping through their fingers every time they got close," Trey advised.

Brett blew out a breath, shook his head and drove a hand through his hair. "Is that why they didn't want to cooperate?"

"Yes. They were afraid the leak could compromise our investigation, which had made more progress than theirs," his friend reported.

"And now? Why the change in their attitude?" Brett wondered. He hopped off the seat cushion and walked back to the stern, where Anita had their poles all set to go.

He sauntered to her and said, "I'm putting the phone on speaker."

"Great," Trey said and continued with his report. "The FBI had their suspicions on who the leak was and, with all that was happening, upped their surveillance. That caught one of their agents sending your name to what turned out to be a burner phone. The agent confessed that he had sent it to Kennedy."

"And Kennedy somehow connected me to Jake? Is that possible?" he asked.

"I doubted it, too, but I put Sophie and Robbie on it, and they instantly got a hit in a marines newsletter that's also posted online. Jake, you and me were identified in the photo and Jake's info—"

"Is readily available online," Brett finished for him.

"What do we do now?" Anita asked. He noticed the worry lines across her forehead.

An awkward silence followed until Trey said, "The accused FBI agent lawyered up, but he's willing to assist us in exchange for a lighter sentence. We're working on a plan to draw out Kennedy."

Brett didn't like the sound of that at all. "Draw out. Like in a trap?" he asked just to confirm.

That long, pregnant hesitation came again. "Yes, as in a trap."

"And we're the bait?" Anita shot out, obviously understanding exactly what they were planning.

"I'm not a fan of this, either, but it's local cops and the FBI in charge and making the decisions. But I'm not going to hang you out to dry. I'll call in Matt, Natalie and their canines, as well as several of our other agents, to safeguard you," Trey said, his conviction clear.

Brett and Anita gazed at each other, and as one they nodded, trusting Trey. "Whatever you need so we can close this case and Anita can get back to her life," Brett said.

"I'll call at 0900 with an update," Trey said before disconnecting.

Chapter Twenty-Five

Anita didn't know why the thought of returning to her old life saddened her, but she bit her lip and fought off that emotion.

When the call ended, Brett powered down the phone and laid a hand on her shoulder. "Trey will keep his promise. You'll be home soon. Back at the restaurant and with your family well before Christmas."

She forced a smile and bobbed her head up. "I know. It's just that…"

She couldn't finish. Stepping against him, she leaned into this comforting strength. He was like the proverbial oak, strong and steady, but also flexible enough to move as he'd had to with each challenge that had arisen.

He wrapped his arms around her and rocked her gently, comforting her, murmuring over and over that she would be fine. That everything would turn out okay.

She made herself believe that. Repeated it to herself as she stepped away and picked up a rod to distract herself from everything that was happening.

"We have a few hours before it gets dark. Should be enough time to catch something. We usually have luck in this area," Brett said and took hold of the second reel.

Since it seemed like he wanted to keep things chill, she asked, "What do you normally catch here?"

"Snapper, hogfish or snook. Sometimes mahi-mahi," he said.

"All good-eating fish," she said. She reeled in some line and, after releasing the bale arm, did an overhead cast that sent the lure flying out into the waters.

"Good cast. Your *papi* taught you well," he said and playfully clapped her on the back.

"He'd be happy to hear you say that," she said, not intending to return things to serious mode and yet that's where it went.

After a long moment during which Brett cast out his line, he said, "I'd like to meet your *papi* someday. Your *mami*. Maybe your *hermanita*, too. Are you the oldest?"

"I am," she said, but couldn't risk a look at him, afraid of what she might see. Instead, she reeled in her line slowly, hoping for a bite. Anything to keep from looking over at him. To keep it from getting more personal.

She was about to give up on a bite and reel the line in more quickly, but a sharp tug followed by a second stronger hit had her instinctively jerking the rod back to hopefully set the hook.

It worked.

Suddenly a fish came flying out of the water, battling against being hooked. The powerful surge of its leap nearly unbalanced her, but Brett was immediately there, his big body behind her. Hands at her waist to help steady her.

"It's a big tarpon," he said, laughter and surprise in his voice.

Tarpons were known for the fight they put up, Anita knew. Her father had snagged one many years earlier and had spent some time working the fish up to the boat, battling the many leaps and runs the fish had made.

Today was no different.

Over and over the silvery body of the tarpon shot out of

the water, leaping and thrashing, its large scales flashing silver in the sunshine. A rattling noise from the fish's gills escaped with each leap.

Mango, hearing the commotion, had hopped up and placed her front legs on the edges of the stern, watching the leaps and the two of them battling to bring in the big fish.

Anita's arms ached from fighting the jerk and tug of the line and the constant reeling. Sweat dripped down her back and her legs ached, but she had Brett's support behind her, urging her on until she was finally able to reel the tired fish close.

They leaned over to examine the tarpon as it rested on the surface behind the boat, sucking in air through its big mouth, a trait unique to the almost prehistoric fish.

"I'm guessing it's about thirty inches long," Brett said with a low whistle, then whipped out his phone, turned it on and snapped a photo.

At her puzzled look, he said, "So you can show your dad. Tarpon are catch-and-release only."

The catch-and-release made sense. A beautiful warrior like this deserved to go free, she thought.

Just like you have to let Brett go? the little voice in her head challenged.

This investigation may have hooked him into being with her, but she had no doubt that Brett was free to make his own decisions, much like she was.

Brett bent and gently worked the lure out of the tarpon's mouth. He cradled it gently in the water, letting it rest and recover in his hands after the ferocious fight. As soon as the fish seemed to have more energy, he released the tarpon and it slowly swam off, silvery body gliding along the surface for a few feet until it dived and became a dark blue blur speeding away underwater.

Body trembling from the fight, she sat down on one of the

cushioned seats behind the console. "I'm beat," she said and wiped some sweat from her brow with the back of her arm.

Brett nodded and smiled. "Understandable. I guess it's up to me to catch our supper," he said and cast out his line.

Mango had remained by the stern, but seemingly bored with what was happening, the pit bull lay down by her feet.

Anita bent and stroked the dog's body, and Mango rolled over to present her belly for a rub. She did, giving her a good massage with both hands. But as she did so, it occurred to her that they had no way to walk the pit bull.

Rising, she strode to Brett's side, careful to avoid the line as he cast. Watching him from the side of her eye, she asked, "How will we walk Mango?"

Brett risked a quick glance back at the pittie, who had risen to watch them as they stood at the stern. "She's trained to go on command. I'll take her up front to relieve herself. Mind taking the rod?"

"Sure," she said and accepted the rod while Brett went below and came back with a plastic bag and some paper towels.

"*Kemne*, Mango," he said and swayed his palm toward him in command.

Mango immediately obeyed, following him toward the bow.

A tug on her line dragged Anita's attention back to fishing.

She tried to set the hook, and when she had a stronger tug and slight run on the line, she knew she had possibly snared dinner. Not a tarpon, she could tell from the way the fish stayed underwater, fighting against the line.

When Brett returned with Mango barely a few minutes later, she handed him the rod, too tired to finish hauling in the fish.

Mango and she stood at the stern and watched Brett work the line, slowly maneuvering the fish closer and closer until he finally brought it to the stern. He leaned over, hooked his fingers into the fish's gills and hauled it onboard.

"Lane snapper, luckily. We're out of season for red snapper," he said as the nice-sized fish flopped around on the floor of the boat.

"Excellent eating. Do you want to prep it or should I?" she asked, but even as she said it, the loud sound of an engine approaching had them both turning.

A Boston Whaler headed straight for them at breakneck speed.

Chapter Twenty-Six

Brett swept his arm in front of Anita and urged her behind him. "Go below," he said, unsure whether the approaching boat was friend or foe.

As Anita hurried away, he slowly backed toward the cockpit door as well to grab the shotgun.

But as he reached for it, the Boston Whaler slowed. As it did so, the bow dipped slightly, allowing him to see the khaki-clad person at the wheel, wearing a familiar drab green baseball cap and black life vest.

Trusting his gut that it really was a game warden patrol boat, he walked back toward the stern of the boat, waiting for the other vessel to pull closer.

The craft slowed and tossed out large white bumpers to protect the two boats from bashing into each other. As they did so, he caught sight of two game wardens, one at the wheel and another at the stern. A large gold star in a circle with the FWC's name sat on a large green vertical stripe on the side of the boat along with the words "Florida Wildlife Commission State Law Enforcement."

"Mind us seeing what you have there?" the officer at the stern asked.

"Feel free," Brett said and waved at the officer to come aboard.

The FWC warden did just that, agilely hopping from his boat to theirs.

"Nice-looking snapper," the warden said, hands on his hips.

"A keeper from what I can see," Brett said with a bob of his head.

The officer nodded in agreement. "It is. You have your license with you?"

Brett reached into the back pocket of his shorts, took out his wallet and eased out the colorful, credit-card-style fishing license. He handed it to the game warden, who reviewed it and said, "Looks like we're all good. You plan on anchoring here overnight?"

"We do. Just taking a few days off," he said.

The warden narrowed his gaze, peered around the boat and noticed the shotgun by the cockpit door. It had him laying a hand on the weapon on his belt as he said, "Do you have a license for that?"

Brett nodded and pulled out both his concealed carry license and an SBS business card, still damp from the unexpected swim he'd taken earlier that day. He handed them to the warden.

"SBS agent, huh? On the job?" the warden asked and returned the documents.

Shaking his head, Brett said, "Just a few days off from work. Shotgun is for protection. I know this area is pretty safe, but I don't like taking chances."

Seemingly satisfied, the other man did a little wave and said, "Enjoy the snapper. My wife makes it oreganata-style and it's delicious."

The other man hopped onto the gunwales and then across into the Boston Whaler. As his partner, a blonde warden, started up the engines and pulled away, the man hauled in the big white bumpers and waved again.

Brett breathed a sigh of relief, picked up the snapper and removed the hook.

Anita popped out from below, walked over to him and, with a laugh, said, "His wife is right. Oreganata-style would be a good way to cook this."

With a chuckle, Brett nodded. "I'll get it scaled and clean. Do you want me to filet it?" he asked.

"If you don't mind. I'm going to cook up some sides," she said, then turned and went back below.

On the portside of the boat was a bait prep station with a freshwater hose and an assortment of knives and pliers he could use to prepare the filets. Jake had clearly spared no expense when he had equipped his boat.

As he tossed the scales, bones and scraps into the water, an assortment of fish came up to feed. At one point a small blacktip shark swam by to eat the scraps and one of the smaller fish.

The circle of life, Brett thought.

It had him looking back toward the cockpit and wondering about his life.

Anita had never responded to his less-than-subtle probing about meeting her family, but then again, what did he expect?

He wasn't the man she had fallen in love with nearly a decade earlier. The man who had ghosted her because he had lost faith in himself.

But Trey and this assignment had forced him to believe in himself. To trust his gut to do what was right.

And what was right was to finally admit that he still loved her. That he could be the man for her.

If she wanted him, that was. If she was willing to let him into her very busy life. A life she'd worked so hard to build for herself.

But he could handle that. Handle giving her the space she

needed because he would need space at times as well if he was going to be a reliable SBS K-9 agent.

Armed with that, he scooped up the filets and whistled to Mango to follow him below.

IT HAD TAKEN Anita some time to familiarize herself with the galley kitchen tucked amidships in the bow, almost directly in front of the cockpit area.

There was one small electric burner and a combo toaster/microwave oven. Beneath them, the fridge was gratefully chilling now that they'd set up the solar panels. To the side was a circular sink and faucet. She'd been careful when using the water, unsure of just how much the boat stored for cooking and washing. But they also had the bottled water just in case.

In the deeper, V-shaped portion of the bow, a comfy-looking padded bench wrapped around the area with a trapezium-shaped table at the center. She hadn't seen any kind of sleeping area except for a small nook to one side. She assumed the table and cushions would do double duty later that night.

The snapper was baking, as the warden had suggested, in the oven. Brett had brought it down earlier but then gone back up to clean up and secure the fishing equipment.

The flavorful aromas of toasty breadcrumbs, garlic and lemon with the subtler sweeter scents of the snapper filled the bow as she stirred a pseudo rice pilaf, a mix of butter, garlic, onion and chicken broth. She had lacked the orzo to make it a real pilaf.

Already resting on the dining table was a plate of roasted asparagus dressed with a simple vinaigrette.

Simple being the key because of the minimal ingredients onboard and the single burner.

It was a real challenge to her normal cooking style, but maybe that was a good thing.

Sometimes she got too caught up in fancy and forgot what was really important.

Like tasty meals made from simple ingredients.

Brett poked his head through the cockpit door. "Permission to come down, Captain," he teased.

She laughed and waved him in. "Permission granted."

It was a tight squeeze past her into the table area as he came down the spiral steps from above, Mango awkwardly hopping from one step to the other. Once he was there, he lifted the cushions to check what was beneath them.

He came up with a bottle of wine that he waggled in the air. "I assume white? Jake has a nice stash in there. Sheets and pillows, too."

"White would be nice," she said, and he tucked it into the fridge.

"Hopefully it will cool down a little," he said, then came up behind her and laid a hand on her waist as he watched her cook.

It was a familiar stance. He'd done it often when they'd been together, always seemingly fascinated by how she created while at the stove.

"Smells good. Looks great," he said. He dropped a kiss on the side of her face and then worked on feeding Mango, spilling out kibble and fresh water into the bowls they'd brought with them.

After, and with nothing to do, he sat at the table and Mango settled at his feet, content now that she'd been fed.

With a side-eyed glance, Anita watched him turn on the burner phone. His fingers flew over the keys and then stilled. His gaze narrowed and his lips thinned into a knife-sharp slash. Another flurry of texting followed until he stopped and powered down the phone again.

"Nothing new?" she asked and stirred, worried about what he might say.

"Police and FBI are still working out the details of the trap. We'll know more in the morning."

The morning. Nearly a dozen hours away, she thought and peered out through the small oval window. Dusk had arrived and night would come quickly, before six at this time of year.

A lot of time for them to be alone together in that confined area.

Memories of the night before flamed to life. She couldn't deny wanting that. Wanting him, but once again she told herself that passion alone wasn't enough.

Because of that, as she stirred the pilaf, she shot him a half glance and said, "It might be nice if you met my parents and sister. Papi might be a little gruff. He probably still remembers how you broke my heart."

"I didn't want to," he said, his tone soft, almost pained. "I didn't think you'd want to be with me the way I was."

"I know," she said, then grabbed plates from one of the cubbyholes above the stove and spooned pilaf onto them.

She grabbed pot holders and opened the oven. Satisfied the snapper was ready, she pulled out the pan onto a trivet on the granite countertop. With a long spatula, she lifted the snapper from the pan and laid a filet on each plate beside the pilaf.

She took a few steps to the table, placed a dish before Brett and sat opposite him.

He thanked her, rose and went to the fridge, where he grabbed the wine, twisted off the cap and served it.

His pour was substantially smaller, she realized as he returned with the glasses.

At her questioning glance, he said, "I feel like celebrating, but have to stay sharp."

Smiling, she lifted her glass, and he did the same as she

toasted with, "To the tarpon catch, which my dad wouldn't believe without your photo, the snapper and, more importantly, being alive."

He added, "And second chances."

She couldn't disagree. Nodding, she clinked her glass against his and said, "To second chances."

Dinner passed without much talk, both of them seemingly lost in their thoughts and the scrumptious food.

"This is absolutely delicious," he said as he forked up the last bits of his fish and rice, leaving such a clean plate it didn't seem to need any washing.

Humbled by his praise, she said, "Or maybe you're hungry because we haven't eaten in hours."

He pointed his index finger down at the plate. "No way. This gets five out of five stars in the Madison review of restaurants," he teased.

The heat of a flush swept across her cheeks. "High praise. Thank you," she said, then rose and grabbed her plate, but he stayed her hand.

"You cooked so I'll clean. Why don't you grab another glass of wine and get some fresh air on the foredeck?" he said as he piled all the plates together.

It had been getting a little warm belowdecks. "Will you join me?" she asked, her emotions in turmoil.

She wanted to explore what was happening with him especially since no matter what Brett said, this might be the only time they'd have to be together.

She didn't want to die without experiencing his loving once again.

Chapter Twenty-Seven

Brett nodded. "I won't be long."

He waited until she climbed the tiny, twisty stairs up into the cockpit area. Seconds later he heard her footfall above him as her shadow passed by the porthole in the middle of the ceiling and she settled into the cushions above the bow.

Knowing the clock was ticking between them in so many ways, he hurried in cleaning and drying the dinnerware, pots and pans, and making sure everything was shipshape. Satisfied, he headed above deck, signaling Mango to follow him up.

Anita was lying across the cushions on one side of the foredeck, her head resting along the edge of the gunwale, her gaze focused on the stars that had flared to life with the coming of night.

They weren't all that far from civilization but remote enough that there was little light pollution, making the celestial bodies brilliant against the inky night sky since the moon hadn't risen yet.

He mimicked her posture, stretching out as best he could against the cushions, his long legs hanging over at the end of them. With a click of his tongue, he instructed Mango to lie down and she immediately settled in the middle of the deck.

Gesturing with his hand up at the night sky, he said, "That's Jupiter. The big one."

"Is that Orion over there?" Anita asked, pointing to the telltale belt of three stars that identified that constellation.

"It is," he said, but then silence reigned as they enjoyed the cooler night air and quiet.

There was little movement on the water where they had moored, the boat remaining fairly still on the surface.

He'd left only one small lamp on in the deck below to conserve their power and it cast muted light up through the porthole. But with no moonlight for hours, he had to snap on more lights to warn other boats of their position.

Returning to the cockpit area, he searched beneath the cushions and dug out an anchor light that he snapped into place at the stern and turned on. It cast a glow all around, alerting others to stay clear.

"Bright," Anita said as she came up behind him and stroked a hand down his back.

"Safety," he said and dipped his head in the direction of the cockpit door. "Why don't you head belowdecks. I'll take care of Mango and be down in a second."

She nodded and walked away.

Mango must have followed her aft and now sat at his feet, looking up at him almost accusingly.

Did Mango have a clue what he wanted to do with Anita once they were belowdecks?

"Don't give me that look," he muttered, then grabbed a fresh plastic bag and paper towels from beneath a cushion and set them up at one corner of the stern.

"Hovno," he commanded and pointed at the bag and towels.

Mango hesitated, worrying him. He needed Mango to listen to his commands without fail if they were going to protect Anita.

He repeated the instruction with more urgency, and to his relief, Mango immediately complied. Cleaning up the waste, he stuffed it into a garbage bag beneath one of the cushions and headed to the door of the cockpit.

Mango followed but he raised his hand, palm open and outward, to stop the pit bull.

"Pozor," he said, and without delay, Mango settled herself across the width of the opening.

"Good girl," he said and rubbed her head and fed her a treat.

Closing the cockpit door, he carefully navigated the steps down in the near dark.

Anita had figured out how to convert the dining area for sleeping. Cushions now ran from one side of the bow to the other and she had spread out sheets and pillows on them. She had also opened the four small oval windows and the porthole above, letting the cooler night air sweep through where she lay in the middle of the makeshift bed.

But there was also a narrow sleeping nook to one side of the galley. He flipped a hand in its direction. "I can bunk there if you want."

THIS WAS THE MOMENT, Anita thought.

"I don't want. I want you here. With me," she said, then lay down on the cushions and pulled off her cotton nightshirt, baring her body to him.

He jerked his shirt over his head and tossed it aside. Then he kicked off his boat shoes and hopped around as he slipped off his shorts and briefs before crawling onto the bed with her.

The space was narrow, not that they needed space as they spooned together and made love like there had never been any hurt in the past, but also like they weren't sure of any joy for the future.

He worshipped her with his mouth and hands, exploring every inch of her until she was shaking and pleading with him to take her.

Leaving only long enough to grab a condom and roll it on, he laid a knee on the cushion and, like a big cat, prowled over and slipped between her thighs. But he hesitated and in the dim light of the cabin, it was almost impossible to see his face.

She rose on an elbow, needing to see his face. Needing to know what he was feeling at that exact moment.

She knew even before he said the words.

"I love you, Anita. I've never stopped loving you," he said and cradled her cheek.

"I love you, too, Brett. I loved the man you were, but I love the man you've become even more."

She kissed him, taking his groan of relief deep inside. Taking him deep into her body as he began the rhythm of their loving. He shifted over and over, dropping kisses on her lips and body as he moved, lifting her ever higher until she could no longer refuse giving him everything.

ANITA ARCHED BENEATH HIM, driving him ever deeper, and he lost it.

A harsh breath left him as he climaxed, but he didn't move, riding the wave of their mutual release as long as he could. Even then, he gently lowered himself to her side and laid an arm around her waist.

"I love you," he said again, just to be sure she had no doubt about it.

"I know," she teased, then ran her hand across his arm and turned to face him. The smile on her face was bright even in the murkiness of the night.

"I love you, too," she said.

A sharp breeze swept through the cabin, rousing goose

bumps on her skin and making her shiver. He used that opportunity to ease a sheet over her and excuse himself to clean up in the head just off the galley.

When he returned, she had closed her eyes, but sleepily opened them and smiled again before sadness crept into her gaze, turning the green so deep it looked black.

She didn't have to say why. "Don't worry about tomorrow. No matter what, Mango and I will protect you."

"But at what cost?" she said in a strangled voice and laid a hand over his heart. Then she skimmed that hand over the bandages on his chest and the older, scattered shrapnel scars.

He covered his hand with hers and brought it back over his heart. "After what happened, I sometimes felt I didn't deserve to live. I even sometimes didn't care whether I lived or died, but I care now. A lot. There's nothing I won't do so we can be together."

She shifted closer and twined their legs together. Kissing him, she said, "That's what worries me. I want to be safe, but I want you to be safe, too."

He raked back a lock of her hair that had fallen forward. "Trust me," he said, and as she leaned forward to kiss him again, relaxed her body into his, he realized that she did.

She trusted him with her body. With her heart. With her life.

He would guard all three with everything he had no matter what tomorrow brought.

Chapter Twenty-Eight

They woke well before the sun had risen and made love again.

She cooked breakfast just as the first rays of sun, a blurry blend of pinks and purples, filtered through the windows.

They ate and since the tide was so far out, Brett slung Mango over his shoulders so they could walk to a small nearby cay and let Mango relieve herself and run loose. Brett found a piece of driftwood and played fetch with the pit for well over half an hour, exercising her after the day spent cooped up on the boat.

Soon, however, the tide started coming in and reality drifted in with it, she thought.

Brett scooped up Mango again, struggling slightly with the pit bull's weight and the deeper water. Mango seemed skittish, probably recalling what had happened the day before.

Fortunately, they were able to board Jake's boat without any problems.

But once onboard, Anita felt like a caged animal, anxiously awaiting the moment when Trey would call.

Like her, Brett nervously paced back and forth across the stern, constantly checking his watch.

The sun rose, bringing heat in the early morning.

She sat beneath the canopy protecting the console area,

trying to stay cool. Telling herself the damp sweat across her body was from the ever-rising temperature and not fear.

It seemed like hours and yet it had barely been twenty minutes since they'd come onboard. Brett powered up the phone and it rang.

"Any progress?" he asked, put the phone on speaker and walked back to where she sat.

"Police and FBI have a plan. They want you to come to the Miami Beach Marina on Alton Road," Trey said, and it was obvious from his tone that he was less than happy with the plan.

"That's a busy marina," Brett said, apparently well familiar with it.

"It is, but they're making arrangements for you to come into the slips by the watersports and parasailing companies," he said.

"That's a pretty exposed area. There's the causeway and at least two parking lots nearby. Perfect spots for a shooter," Brett countered.

"It is, which is why we're working up our own plan to protect you. Do you have your laptop?" Trey asked.

"I do. I should be able to use this phone as a hot spot," he advised, worry about the plan overriding concerns about someone tracking the phone.

"Law enforcement wants you at the dock at thirteen hundred, but I think we have enough time to have a meeting," Trey responded, and from the background, someone called out to him.

"We do have time. It should only take a little over two hours to get there," Brett advised.

"Roger. Give us an hour at most," Trey said and ended the call.

She'd been staring back and forth from the phone to Brett's face, trying to read what he was thinking and feeling.

"You're really worried," she said because it was so obvious from the deep ridges across his forehead and the frown lines bracketing his mouth.

He nodded and ran a hand across the short strands of hair at the top of his head. "Like I told Trey, that area is really exposed. We'd be close to a walkway along the edge of the marina. Anyone could take potshots at us from the causeway or parking lots and then hop into a car and speed off."

She stroked a hand across his arm, trying to reassure him. "What can *we* do?"

BRETT'S MIND HAD been running through possibilities as Trey had been speaking, imagining the area at the marina that he knew quite well.

When he had first arrived in Miami so many months earlier, he had used to rent WaveRunners there before he had reconnected with Jake and visited him down on Key Largo instead.

"Let me show you the area so you're familiar with it," he said and hopped down the stairs belowdecks to where he'd stowed his things.

He pulled out his laptop and went back on deck. He placed the computer on the free space of the passenger console, powered it up and turned on the phone's hot spot. It took a few seconds for the laptop to connect to the wireless, but as soon as it did, he pulled up a satellite view of the area to show Anita the layout of the marina and the nearby elements.

Running his fingers along the screen, he pointed out the areas he thought would be the riskiest. "If I pull in here, you'll be exposed. Anyone in these parking lots or the causeway will have a shot and easy escape."

ANITA TRACKED BRETT'S FINGER, understanding his concerns. Unless he reversed the boat into a slip, a possibly time-consuming maneuver, she'd be a sitting duck if she was above board.

"Someone can shoot at me from all these areas," she said, motioning to the locations with her index finger.

"Nothing about Kennedy says *sniper*, so I'd rule out the far parking lot. Causeway is possibly too exposed. There's nowhere to hide," Brett advised, but then quickly tacked on, "My money is on that walkway and the ground level of that parking lot."

She agreed, which made her say, "I think you're right. I could hide belowdecks, but if I do—"

"We might not draw him out. He's not likely to shoot at you once you're surrounded by the police and FBI. He wants to do it before," he said and waggled his head, obviously unsettled.

"I have to be where he can see me," she said, willing to take the risk if it would bring an end to the nightmare.

He encircled her shoulder with his hand and drew her close. "I don't want you hurt. There has to be another way."

She shook her head and laughed harshly. "I could wear a disguise. Maybe one of those fake noses with the glasses and moustache," she kidded.

Brett's eyes opened wide, and she could swear she saw the light bulb pop up over his head.

"It's not a bad idea."

IT HAD TAKEN him almost all night and multiple calls to reach his informant at the FBI.

He had worried that the man wouldn't come through for him, but he had finally answered as Santiago had been picking up a *café con leche* and Cuban toast at a small breakfast shop in a strip mall not far from Jake's home.

"*Mano*, why are you avoiding me?" he asked, trying for a friendly tone and not the worry twisting his gut into knots.

In a low whisper, the man said, "Things are moving quickly here. They plan on bringing the woman in today."

"Where?" he asked and sipped on the coffee, wincing as the heat of it burned his tongue.

His informant hesitated, making Santiago worry that the man was going to burn him as well, but then he said, "I need to know this is it. If I give you this info—"

"You're paid in full," he said, because if he didn't finish this woman and maybe Marino as well, Hollywood was going to finish him.

"They're on a boat and coming into the Miami Beach Marina," the FBI agent said and continued laying out the details of the plan for bringing in the chef and the SBS agent.

Santiago listened carefully, logging all the info into his brain while planning what he would do at the same time.

After the man hung up, he considered what he'd heard and finalized his plan.

Surprise, firepower and speed.

That would be the key to ending this disaster.

BRETT NAVIGATED PAST Key Biscayne, steering toward the Bay Bridge in the Rickenbacker Causeway. Once he cleared the bridge, he'd head toward Fisher Island and work his way into the Government Cut to reach the marina just as planned.

The boat's radio crackled, snapping to life, and Trey's voice erupted across the line. "We're in place," he said.

"Roger that. We're on schedule. Any luck with the search warrant at Kennedy's place?" Trey had mentioned in an earlier call that a judge had finally felt they had enough evidence thanks to the DNA match from the blood at the Homestead location.

"Police executed the warrant this morning. His mom wasn't surprised that the police were knocking on her door.

We expect them to bring us some of his clothing in about twenty minutes so we can confirm it's him," Trey said.

Brett bit back a curse. "That's cutting it close, *mano*."

"I know, *mano*. I know," Trey said wearily.

"I'll radio as soon as I'm closer," he said and replaced the handset on the console hook.

He thrust forward, catching sight of the luxury buildings on Fisher Island and the ferry that carried residents to the exclusive enclave.

Slowing, he made sure he was clear of any other boats or the large ocean cruise ships that also used the man-made channel. Satisfied the way was clear, he gunned the engine, aware they had a schedule to keep.

Heart pounding, hands gripping the steering wheel so tightly they cramped, he searched the area, keen eyes taking in the boats parked in the marina slips. Everything from immense multimillion-dollar cabin cruisers to small fishing boats. People walked here and there on the docks, worrying him.

Kennedy could be one of those people as well.

As he passed the last few docks for the marina, he throttled down the engine and radioed Trey. "I'm here. Heading toward the watersports dock."

"Roger. Matt and Natalie have the sample. They're searching the ground floor of that parking lot right now."

Little consolation, Brett thought. It might be way too late already.

They would be sitting ducks as he pulled into the slip, especially since the police and FBI agents would not jump into action until they had a clear view of Kennedy.

If he even decided to show up.

But Wilson's program had predicted he would, and Trey had reached out to his psychologist brother, Ricky, whose profile of Kennedy warned he was a loose cannon and probably fearless of what might happen to him. Ricky had agreed with Wilson's program.

Brett couldn't disagree. Anyone who would knowingly take out Hollywood's nephew, and his own cousin, was reckless.

But that kind of reckless came with a price.

He hoped one of the many agents supposedly stationed in and around the marina would be able to either take him down or take him into custody.

Turning to the starboard side, he navigated into the gap for the last slips next to the floating docks for the WaveRunners and other personal watercraft.

This is it. This is when it'll happen, he thought and risked a quick last glance at the console seat opposite him.

Chapter Twenty-Nine

As he turned starboard again, motion on the walkway caught his attention.

Kennedy in full body armor. Agents racing from all over, but all too far to make a difference.

Bullets sprayed across the side of the boat, shattering the windscreen and pinging against the metal railings and hull.

Brett released the wheel and hit the deck, swiping the throttle on the way down to kill the engine.

A surprising pause came in the shooting. Metal clacking was followed by a loud stream of Spanish curses.

Brett jumped to his feet, pointed at land and shouted, *"Vpred. Útok."*

Mango leaped from the boat and at Kennedy, a white-and-tan missile flying through the air.

To protect her, Brett fired at the other man, who seemed to be struggling with the magazine on the assault rifle.

The bullet struck his shoulder, and he staggered back.

Mango latched onto his right arm and thrashed her head until he dropped the weapon.

Kennedy was screaming and trying to dislodge the pit bull as Brett leaped from the boat, ran down the dock and launched himself at Kennedy, tackling him to the ground.

"*Pust*, Mango. *Pust*," he said so the dog would release his hold.

Mango instantly complied and Brett flipped Kennedy onto his stomach and placed a knee in the middle of his back to hold him down as an assortment of agents swarmed around them, including Trey and his fellow K-9 agents, Matt and Natalie.

Trey helped him to his feet, but as he looked toward the boat, he cursed. "Anita. *Dios*, Anita," he said and was about to race to the dock when Brett laid a hand on his arm.

"It's okay, Trey," he said and faced the boat where Anita slumped on the console seat.

"What do you mean it's okay?" Trey shouted, almost frantic.

"Anita, you can come out now," Brett called out and headed back onto the boat to help Anita from belowdecks.

Trey hurried over with the other SBS K-9 agents as well as several other SBS personnel, local law enforcement and some suits he assumed were the Feds.

ANITA SHAKILY CLIMBED the stairs to the deck, heart hammering and a sick feeling in her gut, especially as she looked at "herself" on the console seat.

A number of bullets had torn through the dummy they had assembled in secret.

Fake Anita had been fashioned from some boat cushions, Anita's clothes and handfuls of dry seaweed ribbons Brett had gathered that morning to make fake hair held in place by a baseball cap. Foam guts spilled from the body, a reminder of how deadly the shots might have been if she had been sitting there.

She quickly examined Brett, who had been exposed to the gunfire, shifting her hands across his chest and arms as she searched for any injuries.

He grasped her hands and held them tenderly. "I'm okay."

"Mango?" she said and peered toward the dock where the pit bull sat beside her K-9 counterparts, tongue hanging from her mouth. Not a scratch on her apparently.

Relief washed through her, making her knees weak.

As she started to crumple, Brett hugged an arm around her waist and offered support.

She glanced up at him and smiled. "Thanks."

"Ms. Reyes," said one of the suits as he dipped his head in greeting and approached the boat. "I'm Special Agent Santoro. We'd like to have a word with you."

"She's not going anywhere without me," Brett said.

The FBI agent hesitated, but recognizing that Brett was serious, he said, "If you both wouldn't mind coming with us to the police station." He gestured to the dock, inviting them to deboard and follow him.

Trey laid a hand on her shoulder. "I'll have Aunt Elena meet you there in case you need assistance."

"Thanks, Trey," Brett said and glanced at her intently. "Are you ready to go?"

Anita nodded and accepted the FBI agent's assistance onto the dock. But once she was there, she turned and examined the beautiful new boat, now pockmarked with ugly bullet holes. The windscreen lay in ruined shards on the deck. A side window had also been blown out.

She glanced at Brett and then at Trey. "I think you owe your friend a new boat."

WHEN THEY ARRIVED at the Miami Beach police station, Detective Williams was waiting there along with Roni and Trey's aunt, a respected trial attorney. Tia Elena had married Trey's father's brother. Tio Jose was a member of the Miami district attorney's office and the man who had helped them negotiate the plea deal with the crooked cop.

They greeted Roni effusively, happy to see her. "Isn't it too soon after the baby?" Brett asked, worried that she was pushing herself before she was ready.

Roni smiled, a tired smile that spoke volumes about the demands of tending to a newborn. "I'm just here for the interview and the lineup. I had to be here for that," she said.

Brett understood. It was a huge collar to not only get Kennedy but also possibly a mobster like Tony Hollywood.

Special Agent Santoro had been waiting patiently as they exchanged niceties, but clearly wasn't happy with the delay and the presence of Elena Gonzalez.

As Trey's aunt introduced herself to the FBI agent, he said, "There's really no reason for you to be here. Ms. Reyes isn't a suspect."

Elena nodded. "I know, but we want to make sure everything is done properly so that both Kennedy and Hollywood don't have any cracks to crawl through. Ms. Reyes needs closure so she can get on with her life."

Brett had been standing next to Anita, a hand on her shoulder, offering support. She jumped with Elena's words and softly said, "I need to get on with my life."

After she said that, she shot a quick look up in his direction and smiled, offering hope that her life would be one spent with him.

Agent Santoro's lips thinned into a line of displeasure. "Let's get going, then."

They walked toward one of the police interrogation rooms, but when they reached it, the FBI agent barred his entry with a beefy arm.

"You'll have to wait outside," he said and then eyeballed Roni and Williams. "I assume you two will tape this for us?"

"We'll be in the viewing room. Brett can join us there," Roni said and directed him to a door several feet away from the interrogation room.

He walked with Roni and her partner to the viewing room and was about to enter when he turned and locked his gaze with Anita's. He mouthed, "You'll be fine."

She offered him a weak smile, nodded and entered the room.

WHAT SEEMED LIKE hours dragged by as she answered questions for Santoro and his partner, who had walked into the interrogation room right after Trey's tia Elena and she had entered.

She was grateful for Elena, whose steady presence and gentle encouragement buoyed her flagging energy and patience. She wanted all this over. She wanted to get back to her restaurant. She wanted to get back to Brett.

When the interrogation finished, they took her to another room with a large two-way mirror that faced a narrow space. A lineup room, she realized from the true crime shows she watched. The far wall of that space had horizontal lines that marked off the height of the men who marched into the room.

"I'll be waiting outside," Elena said and squeezed Anita's shoulder in reassurance.

The door closed behind Elena, leaving her alone with Agent Santoro. A few seconds later, six men walked into the lineup room. They were all dressed similarly and of like height, race and weight. Once they were in the room, Santoro had them step to the left and then to the right before facing forward again.

"Can you identify the man who shot Manuel Ramirez? Take your time," he said.

Because of his admonition, Anita examined each man carefully even though she had recognized Kennedy right away. Slowly drifting her gaze over each face, she finally said, "It's the third man from the left. That's the man I saw that night."

"Are you sure?" Santoro asked.

Anita nodded. "I'm sure."

With a wave of his hand, Santoro directed her out of the room. Not only was Elena there, but she had also been joined by Roni, Williams and Brett.

She immediately went to Brett's side and slipped her hands into his. "I'm ready to go."

Turning, she looked at the FBI agent and said, "Are we done now?"

Santoro peered at her and then Roni and Williams. "We're done...for now. We may have more questions for you."

Relief swept through her until Roni asked, "What about Hollywood? When do we pull him in?"

Agent Santoro clearly didn't like being challenged by Roni. "As soon as *we* finish with Kennedy. His lawyer has already offered to flip on Hollywood to avoid the death penalty," he said, his tone as biting as a great white shark.

Roni wasn't backing down. She walked up to the much taller and broader agent and rose up on her tiptoes until she was almost nose to nose with him. "You button this up and keep Anita out of Hollywood's business. She has nothing to do with that."

She appreciated Roni's defense, worried that this wouldn't be over if Hollywood thought she was a threat to his freedom in any way.

"I got it, Detective. Your friend doesn't need to worry about Hollywood or Kennedy," Santoro said.

Brett slipped an arm around her waist and said, "We'll get going, then. I'm sure Anita wants to check in with her restaurant and her parents, and get some rest."

At Santoro's nod, she thanked Elena for her help and hugged Roni, embracing the other woman hard since she imagined it had taken a lot for her to leave her newborn to come to the station. She shook hands with Williams, Santoro and his partner, and then Brett was there again, his arm around her waist as he guided her out of the station and out to the large plaza in front of the building.

The FBI agents had driven them to the station in one of their vehicles, but it would be an easy enough walk to her restaurant and then her condo, although her things, including her pocketbook and keys, were still on the boat.

"What now?" she asked, looking around and wondering what to do about so many things.

He cradled her cheek and smiled wistfully. "What do you want to do now?"

Pushing away a lock of hair that had come loose of her topknot, she shook her head, confused about almost everything except one thing.

"I want to be with you. I love you, Brett. I want a life with you."

His smile broadened and he wrapped his arms around her waist and drew her close for a deep kiss.

When they finally broke apart, he said, "I love you, too, Anita. I want a life with you, too, but there's one thing I want right now."

Puzzled, she narrowed her gaze, wondering what it was, especially seeing the gleam in his dark eyes, so reminiscent of the young man she had fallen in love with so many years earlier.

"What is that?" she asked.

He spread the fingers of one hand wide across his stomach and, with a broad smile on his face, said, "A nice big bowl of your famous chicken and rice. With chorizo this time. Do you think you can do that?"

She stopped, faced him and cupped his face in her hands. Rising on her tiptoes, she brushed a kiss on his lips and said, "I can do that today and forever."

He chuckled. "I might get a little tired of chicken and rice forever, but I'll never get tired of you," he said and deepened the kiss until a rough cough broke them apart.

Trey was standing there holding her pocketbook and a set of car keys, which he handed to Brett.

Eyeballing them, he said, "I guess things are good between you two?"

Brett smiled and said, "Never been better."

He tugged her hand, leading her in the direction of the SBS SUV sitting at the curb, and as she hurried there with him, eager to get to her restaurant and the after, she couldn't argue with him.

They'd faced death multiple times and now it was time to live, Brett at her side. Forever. Nothing could ever be better than that.

* * * * *

COLTON'S K-9
RESCUE

COLLEEN THOMPSON

To all the dogs who fill our lives with love, warmth and loyalty…but especially to those occasional rapscallions who arrive on the scene to keep us on our toes and season our days with a ration of laughter.

Chapter One

Breeze ruffling his shaggy, dark-brown hair, Malcolm Colton adjusted his cap and zipped the collar of his tactical all-weather jacket higher as the wind shifted and the fine mist turned to drizzle. If Pacer, his K-9 search-and-rescue partner—and often, his only reason for getting out of bed these past three years—felt the deepening chill through his thick coat and working vest, he gave no indication. The red-and-black German shepherd mix, whose DNA contained just enough hound to make his ears floppy and his nose exquisite, was far too intent on dragging Malcolm to follow the scent trail he'd picked up, several miles from the area where the task force had previously chased.

This unsanctioned mission had come courtesy of a new tip from a citizen. It was a tip that Malcolm had risked everything—including his future volunteering with Owl Creek, Idaho Search and Rescue—to pursue on his own after shutting off his phone and disabling his GPS tracker so no one would have any way to find him. He felt even worse about lying to his family, telling his dad over their morning coffee that he was making the two-hour drive to Boise to meet up with a friend for the weekend. "If you can spare me on the ranch for a couple days, that is," he'd added, as if his father hadn't been practically begging him to take time for a getaway since the tragic drowning of Malcolm's fiancée three years earlier.

Beaming over the rim of his mug, Buck Colton had nodded his approval and reached over to scrub Pacer's thick ruff affectionately with his free hand. "Don't you worry, son. The ranch can spare you for a few days, especially with Greg and Wade both here to help me. And you know I'll have fun spoiling your buddy while you're gone—if he's not too busy playing with Betty Jane to give me the time of day." He chuckled warmly at the reference to the way his cousin Wade's dog and Pacer would wrestle when both K-9s were off duty.

"Oh, I'm taking Pacer with me," Malcolm had told him, racking his brain to come up with a reason that would throw off any suspicion about the dangerous idea that had taken root in his mind. "This friend of mine is quite the fan of animals, and to be honest, she's asked specifically if she could meet him."

Laughing, his dad—who was currently head-over-heels in love and convinced that everyone else should be—set down his mug and clapped Malcolm on the shoulder. "You sly dog, you! So, who's the lucky woman? And how long have you been hiding this big news from me?"

"This is exactly the reason I didn't tell you, Dad. It's still early days and very casual, so I don't need you making a huge deal of this. Or telling anyone else in the family before I'm ready. Got it?"

His father mimed locking his mouth and tossing away the key, a gesture so totally unlike him that Malcolm chuckled and shook his head remembering it now. Still, he felt another surge of guilt for getting the man's hopes up, because every time Malcolm so much as thought of putting himself out there in the dating world again, he broke out in a cold sweat, remembering the moment he'd finally caught the eye of one of the EMTs who'd been working frantically to revive Kate beside Blackbird Lake that horrendous August day. Remembering the bitter truth he'd seen there as he'd listened to the other Dowling sister screaming.

He still heard those heartrending screams in his nightmares. Screams forever etched into his memory.

Malcolm staggered to a stop as Pacer abruptly pulled up short, raising his head and sniffing the breeze deeply. A trailing rather than a tracking dog, he didn't follow the footprints of the criminal who was their quarry—which was a damned good thing since Malcolm hadn't spotted any in the hard-packed, rocky ground at this elevation. Instead, the well-trained K-9 sought out the scent cones that floated in the air or attached to items their quarry brushed against, such as vegetation or rocky outcrops.

Jerking his head sharply to the right, Pacer barked and lunged again, indicating that he'd caught another strong whiff of the scent matching that of the old T-shirt belonging to the subject. Thinking of where the item had been collected and the damage the man had done to Malcolm's family had him telling himself that *nobody* got to cause his loved ones so much pain and then use the cover of some freak storm to disappear forever. Because at this point, Malcolm cared far less about his own personal safety—this storm and Markus Acker's track record of putting Coltons in the ground be damned—than he did about ending the nightmare that had held his family in its grip for far too long now.

As Pacer led the way, Malcolm kept his bearings using various trails they crossed in the normally popular recreational area. They crested a hill, and the sight of a familiar ridgeline had him catching his breath, though it hurt like hell to remember those vibrant, sky-blue days when he and Kate had hiked out from her family's ski cabin, one of the many in the area, to enjoy the scenery. With the cold rain pattering down around him, he could almost hear the echo of lost laughter among the rocks and trees. Could almost see the tears gleaming in Kate's beautiful gray eyes as she had clapped her hands together, saying, "Of course I'll marry you! Even if you hadn't adopted the most adorable puppy in all Idaho, can't you see I'm absolutely crazy about you, Malcolm? And you know how much I love your family."

Shoving aside the painful memory, Malcolm reached up to switch on his headlamp against an afternoon that had grown as dark as that day had been brilliant. Driven by a bitter wind, the rain blew straight into his face. Half blinded by the worsening conditions—the very reason that Ajay Wright, the officer in charge of the SAR operation, had ordered the team to hold off instead of heading out here—Malcolm missed seeing a hole underfoot and yelped as he found himself unexpectedly hurtling forward.

Throwing out his hands to save his face, he heard the crack before he felt it when the two outermost fingers of his left hand caught a small rock and snapped back sharply.

"It's okay, boy," he told Pacer, who had circled back and shoved his face directly into Malcolm's, his deep brown eyes worried. "I'll be fine."

Apparently not buying it, Pacer whined and snuffled and licked at Malcolm's face, warm breath pluming in the chilly air around them.

"I'd be a lot more flattered by your concern," said Malcolm, "if I didn't know you're just eager to go find yourself a bad man."

Pacer barked loudly, bouncing on his front paws, reminding Malcolm never to use the word *find* unless he was well and truly ready to get moving.

"Sorry, boy. Give me a minute. Settle," Malcolm said, before testing his injury by carefully flexing the hand—which turned out to be an even worse idea. Once he'd finished seeing stars at the agony arcing across his knuckles and letting fly with a curse, he slipped off his backpack and fished out the first aid kit he had brought along.

With the rain growing even colder by the minute, he quickly abandoned thoughts of attempting to immobilize the hand, figuring he'd only make a mess of the bandage trying to wrap it under these conditions. Instead, he swallowed a couple of ibuprofen with some water, hoping the pills would at least delay the pain and swelling—because there was no way in the world he was turning on his phone to beg for help after disobeying orders.

Not as long as his dog, his legs, and his right hand were all working—and he had the pistol he'd brought along in case he unexpectedly found himself face-to-face with Acker.

Soon, he and Pacer were on their way again, Malcolm's effort to tune out the ache in his hand aided by his need to concentrate on where he put his feet next on the steep uphill incline. But between the heavy run-off and the encroaching darkness, he was quickly forced to rely on Pacer's superior senses to guide them safely through the intensifying storm.

Just as he was beginning to worry this had all been a fool's errand, they emerged near a gravel road, where Pacer wagged excitedly as he sniffed a clump of weeds. He looked up at Malcolm, his brown eyes smiling before he gave a hound-like howl of pure joy. His entire body vibrating with anticipation, he charged off barking, head held low.

"That's a boy. I'm coming," Malcolm said, practically tripping over his own feet in his effort to respond to the pulling. But as they began passing ski cabins, many already closed up with the recent spring thaw, he began to wonder if it was possible that his dog was following not his nose, but a memory from when he was last here as a tiny pup.

Surely, he can't recall that far back. He has to be on Acker's scent. Look at him.

But as Pacer unerringly continued heading in an undeniably familiar direction, he asked himself if it was possible that, of all the places Markus could have decided to hole up to ride out this weather, he could have really chosen, by pure coincidence, the one spot that Pacer had visited before.

"Ridiculous," Malcolm muttered as they turned up the long, tree-lined driveway.

Though he saw no sign of a vehicle, he knew one could be parked either behind the cabin or inside the small, detached garage. As he and Pacer started up the evergreen-studded slope, he soon made out the warm yellow glow of the lights in the single-story log dwelling's windows. With the wind making the steady rain feel even colder, that familiar light carried him back in time, promising comfort and welcome. He pictured Kate, her beautiful face illuminated by her phone as she checked her schedule at the clinic or shot a quick text to her writer sister down in Palm Springs. Or maybe Kate was curled up in her favorite overstuffed chair by the living room picture window, watching the rain fall over the valley. The same valley where, on a clear day, one could plainly see the shimmering sapphire eye of the same lake destined to take her life in one cruel blink.

Jolted back to reality, Malcolm cursed his foolishness. Painful as it was, she was three-and-a-half years gone now, and if he didn't want to join her before his time had come, he had damned well better pay attention. Because between his dog's behavior, the lights, and what he'd almost swear was the scent of something warm and fragrant cooking, he was 100 percent certain that there was someone in this house now.

And that someone might very well be Markus Acker, who, already alerted by Pacer's ruckus and his own headlamp, might be taking aim from some unseen position. Or were they still too distant?

Eager to improve their odds, Malcolm switched off his light and gave the command, "Hush," before shortening Pacer's lead to allow for better control.

His K-9 whined in protest, the hound in him wanting his say about the importance of his mission, but with a few freeze-dried chicken treats Malcolm had brought along as bribes, he was able to convince his partner to keep his peace.

With only the steady patter of cold rain for company, they continued toward a back patio dimly illuminated by rectangles of soft interior light spilling out from the panes of the rear door's windows. The real question was, had Markus's path led him up those porch steps, where he'd forced entry through that same door? Or had he bypassed the cabin, perhaps to hide out as close as the garage downslope to the rear?

Crouching low, Malcolm pressed forward, his heart pounding as he strained to hear another door or window opening. As they reached the bottom of the three porch steps, a loud crack—what he took for gunfire—had him shouting in alarm, nearly jumping out of his skin.

He felt like a damned fool when a bright flash lit the sky at the same moment before thunder pealed again.

Legs shaking like a newborn foal's, he grabbed the handrail and let out a curse before quietly reassuring Pacer—who seemed uncharacteristically jittery as well. "It's only a lightning strike, boy. We're going to be all right."

"You're right about the lightning," said a female voice, positioned just behind him. A voice with a volume and a confidence that carried over the fury of the storm. "But as for the question of whether you're *really* all right, that very much depends on whether you make any sudden moves. And on whether you keep a firm grip on your animal as well."

"Owl Creek Search and Rescue," Malcolm identified himself and Pacer, his heart pounding at the clear warning in her words. "And I swear to you, we're here looking for a wanted criminal who may be in the area and not to do you any har—"

"Malcolm?"

The astonishment ripping through that single word stripped away the threatening tone, allowing him to hear something impossibly familiar. Something he'd thought lost forever, causing him to spin around to face the woman who was already lowering the handgun she'd been aiming at him...

The same woman whose limp body he himself had pulled too late from the lake more than three years before. He saw that his fiancée's once chin-length blond hair now nearly reached the shoulders of the old, green fatigue sweater she wore with a pair of jeans that molded to her slim form. She seemed oddly tall as well, but maybe that was because his perspective was off, shifting as he backpedaled to avoid the gun, the raw shame, and this impossible hallucination.

His feet tangled with the dog's lead, drawing a pained yelp as he stepped on Pacer's paw. Instinctively reacting but already off-balance, Malcolm ended up sprawling on his back.

In the next bright flash that followed, he found himself staring up not at a ghost, as his shell-shocked mind first thought, but what he'd belatedly realized was a damned *ghostwriter* instead.

Chapter Two

It struck Giselle Dowling like a body blow, having the man who had played a starring role in so many of her nightmares invade her sanctuary.

Yet in that split-second of strobe-lit illumination, she saw the emotions parade across her sister's fiancé's face: the pain and confusion quickly giving way to horror and revulsion.

So it's the same for him, she barely had time to think before more thunder rumbled, so close and so deafening she felt its vibration in her sternum. Or maybe that was only the pounding of her heart.

Whichever it might be, she was darn well freezing out here, and quickly getting soaked since she'd grabbed her grandfather's old revolver and run outside without a jacket when her cell phone pinged an alert activated by one of the outdoor security cameras. She'd initially assumed it was a bear making a nuisance of itself, since the animals occasionally came looking for an easy snack this time of year after emerging from hibernation. Normally, she would have simply grabbed the air horn she kept to run off the hairy intruders. But one glance at the man-and-dog-shaped silhouettes on her screen had had her running for the gun.

Surely, what he'd said couldn't be right, could it?

"You're tracking a wanted criminal?" Shaking her head,

she tried—and failed—to make sense of what he'd told her. "You're definitely the first trespasser my security cameras have picked up on. Maybe you're a little lost? Or was the temptation to check out the old place while you were in the neighborhood simply too much for you?"

"You can't honestly think I'd willingly get within ten miles of this place if I had any choice in the matter," he fired back, looking and sounding outraged by her suggestion. "Anyway, why aren't you back hobnobbing with your rich celebrity clients and those air-kissing suck-ups you hang out with back in Palm Springs? I heard you sold this place three years ago. Couldn't wait to put the bad memories as far behind you as possible."

Using the gun, she gestured shakily toward the house. "If we have to t-talk about this, can't we d-do it inside?" she began, her teeth chattering. "I can't imagine your team wouldn't want you seeking shelter, at least until this lightning passes anyway, right?"

He hesitated before gesturing toward her gun. "I'll make you a deal. I'll come in if you quit waving that thing around like some maniac. And then maybe we can check that camera footage? You have a way to do that, don't you?"

Lowering her weapon, she nodded. "Sure—and there's no need to be so dramatic. I wasn't even pointing at you that time."

But when she reached down to grasp his hand, he jerked it back with a pained grunt.

"You're injured?" she asked, alarmed as his dog sprang between them, hackles rising, as it eyed her with obvious suspicion.

Wincing in answer, he told his dog, "Settle down, boy. It's okay."

"Sorry if I hurt you." As she wiped the cold rain from her face, she realized that she meant it. Though his presence was an almost unbearable reminder of the most traumatic moments of her life, seeing him in pain only turned up the volume on her own discomfort.

Help him, Zella, her sister insisted. Giselle felt lightheaded for a moment, her eyes stinging because it had been so long since she'd even thought about the childhood nickname, much less heard Kate's voice, so clearly that she might have been standing right beside her.

Using his apparently uninjured right hand, Malcolm awkwardly pushed himself to his feet, his expression unsettled as his gaze swept over Giselle's hair, her eyes, her clothing. As if he were cataloging the differences between her and the woman she had once been—the one who'd put a premium on things like manicures, makeup and fashion. "Believe me, an aching hand's the least of my worries at the moment."

Shaking off her dizziness, Giselle motioned for him to follow her, taking him around to the side door that led to a combination mudroom/laundry area with the same golden-brown split log interior walls as the remainder of the cabin. Once inside, she laid the pistol on top of the dryer before opening a dark-green cabinet to grab a stack of folded towels.

"Here you go, for yourself and your hairy friend there," she said, passing him a few.

When the top towel tumbled to the floor, she said, "Let me help you with that."

"I can manage," he said, a bit brusquely. "You're dripping wet yourself, and I can see you shivering. Whoa there, buddy."

"Ugh!" She turned away, raising an arm uselessly as the big shepherd shook himself, showering her—and most of the room—with mud and cold droplets.

"Sorry," Malcolm struggled to cover the animal, who ducked the end of the towel before snatching it in his teeth and giving it a playful shake. "Pacer, knock it off."

"Wait a minute." As the dog relinquished his prize, she dried her face. "*Pacer?* You aren't telling me this is really the same sweet pup from back when—when I came out to visit Kate after you had just adopted..." The rest caught in her throat as she recalled the sounds of her big sister's laughter and the happy puppy yips of a rousing game of keep-away.

Malcolm's green eyes warmed, some of the tension easing in a face she had to acknowledge was still as handsome as ever in his mid-thirties, despite the addition of what looked like a few days' worth of dark stubble and the lines of tension etched across his forehead. "It's him, all right. Pacer in the flesh."

Giselle wrapped herself in the thick blue towel she'd been using and kicked off sodden sneakers to slip her cold feet into a pair of dry, lined moccasins she kept stashed beneath a bench. "He was mostly all floppy ears and fluff back then. But now, just look at him." She gestured toward the logo on Pacer's vest. "An actual search and rescue dog."

"A trailing dog, specifically—and a damned fine one." She heard the pride in Malcolm's voice as he squatted to dry his K-9 partner. "But you haven't told me how—and *why*—you're here and not back in the desert dressed to the nines and lunching with your social-climbing friends."

She scowled but stopped short of defending her Palm Springs crowd, since none of them had checked in on her in ages—or even returned her last few texts since word had gotten out about the implosion of her professional reputation. Banishing the traitors from her mind, she sighed. "After the—after the services"— she still couldn't say the word *funeral* in reference to her sister without her throat closing up—"I packed up a few things and went back to work."

"I know you had that major deadline coming." The window behind him flashing bright with lightning, Malcolm shook his head, his tone hinting that he still disapproved of how quickly she had fled her hometown.

Recalling how alien it had felt to her, with every last member of her family gone, she swallowed past a painful lump in her throat. "After losing both my sister and my boyfriend—"

"I'd argue that the latter was no great loss," he said angrily. "If it weren't for that irresponsible son of a bitch…"

Her cheeks burned. "Did you know that Kyle *died* last year? I heard he was killed in an auto-pedestrian accident. Hit after stumbling drunk into the street following an evening of heavy partying in Vegas."

"So your old boyfriend never *did* learn to watch for traffic," Malcolm said, his judgment as harsh as his anger was enduring. "Or when it was important to stay sober."

"Doesn't sound that way," she murmured, too ashamed of having been involved with such a person, however briefly— and of having been so utterly oblivious as to the potential consequences of the always charming, witty, and well-dressed Kyle's chronic lack of accountability—and tolerance for boredom—to do anything but quickly change the subject. "As I was saying, after everything that happened, I figured I'd be better off throwing myself back into my work—and there was a lot riding on that project for the other parties involved as well."

"So in other words, you were under pressure to fulfill your obligations," he guessed.

"That was certainly part of it," she admitted. "But then the buyer's financing on this place fell through at the eleventh hour."

"So what did you do then?"

She shrugged. "Asked my real estate agent to put the cabin back on the market so I'd never have to face those memories again." *And my guilt*, she wanted to add but didn't, unable to imagine ever again drawing a breath free of its crushing weight.

"That's understandable," he said, coming to his feet, "and I want you to know how damned sorry I am..."

As caught up as she was in her explanation, his words barely registered. "But the problems just kept coming," she continued. "Issues with the foundation and then the cabin's plumbing, which shorted out the old electrical wiring as well. By the time it was all fixed, interest rates had skyrocketed."

Malcolm blotted his face with another towel. "So you couldn't sell the place?"

She threw her hands up before admitting, "I'm sure I eventually could have, but the bigger problem was I couldn't sell *myself* any longer on glamorizing the escapades of some rich, entitled musical 'genius' even more famous for his appalling treatment of everyone around him—especially the women—than what some consider talent."

"Wait a minute," he said. "Don't tell me your big ghost-writing job involved that singularly named guy with all the lawsuits people can't seem to stop talking about? As if I could care less about his latest awards-show meltdown or which famous friend's wife he's sleeping with this week."

"The very one, I'm afraid." The one good thing about being blackballed from New York to Hollywood was that confidentiality agreements no longer really applied. "Or at least it was before I walked out on him—because every second I spent catering to Nico's ridiculous whims or dodging his tantrums, every hour I wasted trying to humanize that absolute *polyp* on the colon of humanity, the more upset I became that someone as kind and sweet as Kate could be gone while someone so horrible keeps right on hurting people."

"You're absolutely right. It *isn't* fair she's gone," Malcolm agreed, his face stretching into a pained-looking grimace. Then one side of his mouth twitched, amusement sparking in his green eyes. "But did I just hear you call Nico a *polyp* on the colon of humanity?"

"You'd have been treated to a lot worse, I'm afraid, if you'd been around before I ran out on him." Her stomach tightened as she recalled the incident that resulted in the destruction of a reputation that had made her one of the most sought-after younger ghostwriters in the country.

"Surely, it was provoked," Malcolm said.

She waved it off. "What *he* did isn't the point. What matters is that after I went nuclear the way I did—I couldn't get work ghosting for a D-list cartoon spokes-animal, let alone a celebrity of the caliber I'd spent years working with before this happened. And I needed a place to lie low and lick my wounds—to write about the only person whose life story I still care enough about to put to paper."

"You mean you've been writing about *Kate*?"

"Trying to," she admitted, knowing it wasn't talking about Kate's *life* but her death instead that was the problem. Or the enormity of Giselle's own role in it.

"But how can you bear being here alone, with all these memories of your family? That has to be so—"

Glimpsing the concern in his face, she turned away as images tumbled through her memory. *A flash of sunlight off a steel blade, a coil of long, blond hair wrapped like a tentacle around a towrope in the water. The hair she'd once taken so much pride in, dragging her into the blue depths...*

She felt her shoulders stiffen, along with her resolve. "Maybe at some point." She was barely conscious of reaching behind herself to touch the tip of a finger across the faint, horizontal scar on her lower neck, one barely hidden by her hair. "I realized it was no more than I had coming. Now let's get you out of that wet hat and coat so I can take a look at your hand."

Shaking his head, he said, "Hold on a minute. *What* did

you say? Why on earth would you imagine *you* deserved to suffer?"

"Didn't you want to check that camera footage?" Giselle rushed to say, hating the rising note of panic she heard in her own voice. "Make sure that criminal you've been tracking isn't right here after all?"

"Of course I do, but—"

"I'll pull up the cameras' live feed on my computer in the second bedroom—I've shoved a little worktable into one corner for a makeshift office. If you need any help figuring it out, I'll be in the kitchen."

She then turned and fled the room—leaving the question he had asked her still hanging in the air.

Chapter Three

Malcolm stared after Giselle's retreating form, a hollow opening in the pit of his stomach as he realized that Kate's death had impacted far more than her ability to work. He tried telling himself that his responsibility to her ended with the need to warn her about the dangerous fugitive on the loose in these mountains, but seeing the contrast between her current misery and the confidence and spirit she'd once embodied hit him far harder than he would have imagined. He told himself he only cared for Kate's sake, knowing how painful she would have found seeing her beloved younger sister struggling instead of moving forward with her life.

Reminded of his own inadequacies in that department, he removed his hat and jacket, along with Pacer's vest, before drying himself and his dog as best he could, a slow and clumsy process with his throbbing hand.

After finishing, he hurried down the hallway in his socked feet, Pacer close behind him. Anxious as he was to check Giselle's computer for any evidence that Markus had set foot on the property, Malcolm hesitated outside the bedroom doorway, steeling himself before stepping into the space that Giselle and Kate had shared as children. Though the bunk-beds they had slept in had long since been replaced with a desk and pullout sofa, the room still felt haunted by the distant past, its walls adorned with framed photos of the two blond sisters growing up. Other pictures featured the grandparents who had raised them, and still others, the young parents who'd fallen victim to an avalanche while skiing in these mountains when Giselle was still an infant and Kate was attending preschool.

Wondering how Giselle could even think of writing among so many ghosts, he averted his eyes before seating himself at her computer. When he touched the mouse, a split-screen popped up on the monitor, showing a live feed featuring three views and one blanked-out spot in the lower right-hand corner.

As the rain outside beat against the windows, he spent the next twenty minutes playing with the settings and clicking through recorded footage until Giselle tapped at the doorframe and stepped into the room. To his profound relief, he saw that she'd changed out of the cozy, forest green sweatshirt he'd immediately recognized as one of Kate's old cabin favorites and into a dry, navy sweater she'd paired with a pair of dark-gray joggers.

"So how're things going? Did you spot anybody out there?" she asked.

As she reached to pet Pacer, who had gotten up to greet her, the angle of her shoulder—or perhaps it was the way her wheat-colored hair swung forward—had his brain's warning lights all flashing. Internal sirens blared out the name of the woman he should be married to, perhaps even starting a family with, by this time. Yet when Giselle glanced up at him a moment later, she shifted back into herself again, leaving him scrambling to push back grief's shadow, to anchor himself to the present.

"No," he said, raising his voice to speak over the rumbling of thunder. "I haven't seen any sign of an intruder. But did you know you have a camera out?"

"Let me guess." She padded over to the desk. "The garage again, right?"

Pointing out the screen's blank quadrant, he concentrated on keeping both his voice and his hand from shaking. "So you've been having trouble with it lately?"

"Something's chewed through the wiring out there a couple of times, beginning last summer. I tell myself it's squirrels or chipmunks. But my neighbor's been suggesting I might want to adopt a mouser from the shelter—or invest in traps and peanut butter." She made a face, nose crinkling in distaste at the thought.

"I'll want to go check things out just to be sure," he said. "It should be easy enough to tell the difference between a gnawed wire and a cut one, if that's what we're dealing with."

"Knock yourself out. I'm pretty sure those rodents don't have scissors, though."

"I'd love for you to be right," he said, turning in his seat to look up at her, "but we can't discount that scent trail Pacer and I tracked up here. Makes me wonder if your vehicle's still really in your garage."

"Oh, I'm sure it's still there," Giselle said. "I have one of those antitheft apps hooked up to my car alarm. My cell phone would be wailing if someone tampered with it."

"You use a car alarm way up here?" he asked, somehow surprised, since people tended to be casual about such things in this lightly populated vacation area.

She shrugged. "I had a car stolen once, back when I lived in California."

"I'd forgotten that little red convertible you used to drive."

She grimaced. "Well, I definitely haven't, so I take reasonable precautions, the same way as I lock my doors and use security cameras to help keep an eye out on the property."

"Makes perfect sense," he said, "especially since you're so far from anyone you can call for help way up here."

"I take care of myself these days," she said, a bitter edge to her voice, "so, please, don't ever feel obligated to come running to my rescue. Not again…"

"Is that what you believe you are to me," he asked, hurt by the stinging tone of her rejection, "just some kind of… *obligation*?"

"What else am I supposed to think, when you came out of your way to head over here to warn me about some supposed danger?"

"Like I said before, it *wasn't* out of my way. Pacer led me here, on the scent, and I figured it would be a new homeowner." Pushing back from the desk, he stood to face her. "Someone *grateful* to be warned that a desperate fugitive might be on the property."

"I *do* appreciate the warning. Please don't get me wrong. It's just that—" Her shoulders drooped. "It's just that seeing you again here, I'm afraid it's…it's…more root canal than roller coaster."

He frowned. "Root canal, huh?"

"Don't take it personally," she said, a plea in her blue eyes.

"Only if you won't when I tell you it's the same for me," he admitted.

"That's definitely understandable," she conceded. "But this criminal you and your dog were following, he's definitely not here."

"Not that we can see now, maybe, but I'll still need to check your garage to be certain."

"Can't that at least wait until this weather's passed? This storm sounds like it's getting worse." She looked toward the window, where lightning flickered, and an intensifying rain pummeled the glass.

"I'm not trying to frighten you unnecessarily, but this fugitive I'm tracking's no garden-variety criminal. Markus Acker's smart enough to elude authorities and smooth enough to con followers into willingly signing over all their assets. But when push comes to shove, he'll take out anybody who gets in his way."

"So he's killed before, you're saying?"

Malcolm felt a coldness unfurl deep within his chest. "He was behind my uncle Robert's death last June."

"I'm *so* sorry," she said, her beautiful eyes brimming with compassion.

"And only two weeks ago, he shot my mother dead as well."

"You—your *mother*?" She reached out, her hand skimming the surface of his upper arm before pulling away as if she'd accidentally touched hot metal.

He shook his head, "We'd been estranged for decades."

"Kate mentioned that she left your father and you and your siblings a long time ago and that during most of your childhood, there was no contact. That must have been so difficult."

"My mother wasn't exactly a blameless victim of Acker's, either," Malcolm said grimly. "She'd gotten herself caught up in his cult, to the point where she was possibly tied up in what happened to my uncle Robert and some scheme to get my family's money."

"In some ways, I imagine that's even worse," Giselle said, sounding sympathetic, "grieving someone when your relationship's been so…complicated."

"I couldn't even really call it a relationship. But that still doesn't mean I'm about to let Acker get away with the hell he's put my family through this past year. Or use the cover of this storm to disappear. It's why I couldn't sit around and wait out this weather so the rest of the team could join me before I—"

"Wait a minute," Giselle said. "You mean to tell me you came up here all *alone*, without permission?"

"I had to. Don't you see? I couldn't allow him the chance to go on as if my family's suffering meant nothing and start up his same scam elsewhere, the way he has before. If that happens, before you know it, he'll be brainwashing and fleecing other people—until he's backed into another corner and starts killing once again."

"And you really think this man could be hiding in my garage?" she asked, a look of horror coming over her as if the personal threat had for the first time become real to her.

He considered for a moment before answering, "To be honest, I'd be surprised at this point. Pacer here can't help barking when he's on a scent trail, and I'm sure Acker would be listening for dogs."

"I imagine he might've heard us talking outside, too," she said.

Malcolm nodded. "Unless I miss my guess, he'll be trying to put as much distance as he can between us in the hopes that this storm will give him the cover he needs to shake off his pursuit. Only I can't let that happen, so I'll need to get going while you pack your things to head down—"

"Pack up to head down where?" she asked, sounding bewildered.

"You can't possibly stay here on your own now. Not with a desperate murderer on the loose."

"Are you serious?" She shook her head. "I'm not leaving my home, especially not in this awful weather. I'll just keep my doors locked and my gun handy."

"No, please," he said, sensing that despite her talk of taking care of herself, she would be no match for a remorseless and experienced killer like Acker. "Just drive slowly and carefully and head down to the ranch. We have plenty of room there, and we'd be glad to have you as our guest until Markus is—"

"Didn't you hear me? I said I'll be fine right here. Just

check my garage to make sure he's off my property and
I'll stay—"

"You can't."

"Stop it right now, Malcolm," she said sharply.

"Stop what?"

"Acting as if Kate left you in charge of my life somehow."

"I'm not trying to be in charge of you, I swear it," he said.
"But I can't help remembering how much you meant to her.
I'm absolutely certain she'd never want you to be here alone
under these circumstances."

"You—you *really* want me to be okay, Malcolm?" As a
fresh tear trailed down her cheek, Giselle ran a hand beneath
the fringe of blond hair near her lower nape, not far from the
spot where he'd once sawed through her tangled locks to save
her life. "Then the minute that it's safe to, you can go back
to your manhunt. Go back to your life and leave me here to
mine, *please*. Because I never asked to see you. Never asked
to and hope to heaven that I never will again."

As Giselle started to walk out of the room, a blinding flash
lit up the window, followed by a booming thunderclap that
had her jumping in response. The computer chirped in protest, and she turned back in time to see its screen go blank
as the lights died.

The house's interior went deathly quiet, the storm outside
sounding even fiercer against the sudden hush.

"I suppose I should've seen that coming," she said, hugging herself and rubbing at the rising gooseflesh on her arms.
"At least I have surge protectors to keep my electronics from
getting fried."

"Do you have a good flashlight?" Malcolm asked.

"In the kitchen, with my lanterns."

As she headed in that direction, his footsteps came immediately behind her. Despite the fact that only moments

before, she'd wanted nothing more than to see the back of him forever, she felt a certain comfort in his presence now, with the fiercest storm she'd heard in years lashing the cabin's exterior.

"Oof, watch yourself there, Pacer," Malcolm said, stepping around his dog.

"Is he afraid of storms?" Giselle asked.

"Pacer would scent-trail through a hurricane. He's probably just anxious to get back out there and back to work."

"You can't be thinking of going back out in that now, though, are you?" she asked, feeling anxious at the thought. "As bad as it sounds, you could be electrocuted."

Malcolm frowned. "You're probably right. We'd be better off waiting out the worst of the storm here—that is, if we wouldn't be too much in your way."

Guilt twisted inside her as she grabbed a flashlight from the drawer and passed it to him. "Listen, what I said before— I'm sorry for the way it came out. It's just that—"

He waved off the apology. "Don't worry about it. I can't imagine I would've taken it any better if some walking root canal had turned up on my doorstep, either."

The laughter that bubbled up—a little rusty from disuse—surprised her. Still, she kept her focus on the match she'd just pulled out and struck.

After using it to light a lantern from a shelf lined with glass jars filled with canned fruits and vegetables, she said, "Please, stay until it's safe again. I'll even feed you. There's plenty here." She gestured toward the soup and the loaf of bread she'd pulled from the oven just prior to his arrival. "If Pacer can have a little sourdough and soup, I'll fix him up a bowl, too."

"He'll be better off sticking with the food I brought along for him, but I'd definitely love to have some. Thanks," Malcolm said. "I'd better go wash up first, though, and maybe try to wrap this hand of mine before it swells any worse."

"Why didn't you say something sooner?" she asked. "Let me help you with that before we eat."

"You don't have to—"

"Please," she said. "Allow me the illusion of feeling like living up here like a hermit hasn't turned me into a completely awful person."

"You're not an awful person," he protested.

She snorted. "High praise indeed, for someone who could barely tolerate me even when I *did* have social graces."

"Barely tolerate you? What in the world ever gave you that idea?"

"Oh, come on," she said. "You might've loved my sister too much not to rub it in her face, but you clearly were less than thrilled whenever I came to stay for the weekend."

"If I ever for a second made you feel anything less than welcome around Kate and me, I apologize," he said, though the flickering light from the lantern made it hard to read his expression.

"It wasn't that you were ever rude. I mean, you always went through all the motions," she assured him. "It's just a vibe that I got, when Kate and I—"

"—Stayed up all night chattering about the old days or any celebrity gossip she could squeeze out of you so she could share it with her work friends?"

"I imagine we both got carried away and left you out of our conversations sometimes," Giselle said, thinking back on it and frowning. "And I know I liked to tease you sometimes. Maybe a little too mercilessly, on occasion, about your moo-cow wrangling?"

"Ranching," he corrected before shaking his head. "And seriously, after growing up surrounded by three take-no-prisoners siblings and a bunch of cousins, did you really expect

me to be impressed with that kind of weak sauce razzing, Miss Green Cuisine?"

"Oh, wait a minute," she said. "We're getting warmer now, aren't we? Back in those days, when I was still so new to it, I expended a lot of energy trying to convince people to come over to the veggie side with me. If I was ever obnoxious about your carnivorous ways, I *sincerely* apologize."

"I honestly don't remember you ever being *that* bad."

"High praise indeed," she joked. "But I know I kind of could be. I'm embarrassed now even thinking back on it."

"We all have our regrets. And mine's getting a little jealous of how much attention my fiancée gave her little sister every time the three of us all got together, when all I wanted was to enjoy some time alone with her. Just thinking back on *that* now makes me feel a little childish."

She shook her head. "I'll admit that I sometimes felt the same way, when she'd go on about how incredible it was, what the two of you had together, and how excited she was to spend the rest of her life with you. I used to worry she'd forget all about me, especially once the two of you got busy raising your own…"

Seeing grief twist his expression, she used the distraction of another growl of thunder as an excuse to change the subject. "Come on. Let's head to the bathroom and look for those first aid supplies to take care of your hand."

"Sure thing. You lie down and stay here, Pacer," Malcolm said.

Lifting the lantern carefully, Giselle led Malcolm down the hall and entered the room ahead of him. Once she'd taken an elastic bandage, antibiotic ointment, and fresh towels out of the closet and set the lantern in front of the mirror, she grew uncomfortably aware of how tight the space was with the two of them both standing in it.

But considering how long she'd been living alone, she reminded herself that being squeezed into such a tight space with anyone was bound to feel claustrophobic to her.

"May I take a look?" she asked him.

Grimacing, he laid down the lit flashlight before hesitantly extending his left hand. "Careful—it's the knuckles where the pain's worst."

"From the looks of this, I'm not surprised." She grimaced in sympathy at the deepening browns and purples of fresh bruising. "Can you turn it over—this way?" Touching him gingerly, she caught his sharp intake of breath as he moved his swollen hand.

"When I fell, I caught a rock and bent those last two fingers halfway back to my wrist."

"That looks super-painful," she said.

"Is that your professional opinion?"

"As an unemployed ghostwriter? Sure, for whatever *that's* worth. But if I were you, I'd get to a real expert with it as soon as you're able because it sure looks like you could have some kind of fracture or dislocation."

"I've seen enough of those kinds of injuries on the ranch that I wouldn't bet against it."

"Okay, then," she said. "If I'm remembering from way back in my first aid classes in school, we'll want to wrap it in a compression bandage and maybe elevate it with some ice to help reduce the swelling. And I have some over-the-counter pain tablets you can take, too."

"Thanks, but the bandage will do for now," he said, pushing up his sleeve. "I've already taken a couple ibuprofen out on the trail. And I'll want to try washing some of this mud off before we wrap it."

Once he'd cleaned up, she helped him gently blot the injured arm dry and wind the bandage around his hand and forearm to immobilize it. With the sounds of the raging storm outside, she felt as if they'd been dropped into the distant past and imagined that as soon as she finished helping him, they'd go out and find Kate in the kitchen, putting the finishing touches on a dinner the three of them would share.

But the sadness in his green eyes, when she caught him looking at her for just a moment in the mirror, reminded her those days were as irretrievable as her own dreams of happiness.

"That isn't too tight, is it?" she asked as she finished with the bandage.

"Actually, you're pretty good at this," he said.

She dredged up a half smile. "Kate used to insist on practicing on me when she was still in nursing school, so I couldn't help picking up a few things."

He nodded. "Well, I really appreciate the TLC. And the offer of dinner, too."

"You do realize I may have given up the lectures, but I still don't eat—"

"—Anything that had a mother. How could I forget?" He flashed a grin. "But meatless or not, whatever you've been cooking smells amazing. And besides, I'm almost hungry enough to choke down…a tofu smoothie." He made a face.

"As entertaining as it might be to make you put your money where your mouth is, that's not on tonight's menu. But let's go check out what is."

Some time later, as Malcolm used the heel of the sourdough to sop up the last of the vegetable stew from the bowl, she raised her voice to be heard above the storm to ask, "Another helping?"

He shook his head. "Thanks, but I really should've stopped already. Would have, except I can't say when I've enjoyed a meal so much. Meatless or not."

"All that trekking through the mountains probably worked up quite an appetite," she said, waving off the praise.

"Pacer and I both burned off some serious calories out

there." He glanced toward his dog, who was picking distractedly at a bowl of the food Malcolm had put down for him. "But don't sell your cooking short. Or your company."

She laughed, "My company? You're full of something other than the stew. We've hardly managed two words since we sat down together."

"It's been a little noisy for much conversation," he said. "But I really need to talk to you. Seriously, Giselle, about evacuation. With the power out, especially, it doesn't feel safe leaving you way out here on your own."

She shook her head. "I have a portable generator. I'll go get it out of the garage as soon as the storm dies down and you've checked for boogeymen. We have outages up here all the time. It's made me very self-reliant."

"Enough to handle Markus Acker if he comes back this way?"

She shrugged. "I guess I'll find out, if the situation arises."

Malcolm stared at her as if she'd lost her mind, causing her to add, "Don't look at me like that. You already said he's most likely moved on."

"Are you really willing to gamble with your life that I'm right?"

"It's *my* life," she reminded him.

"So why do I care more than you do about what happens to it?" he demanded, leaving her too stunned to answer. When she left the statement unchallenged, he pressed harder, saying, "That's it, isn't it? You've lost your sister and you've lost your way, so now you're not sure it's worth the bother of fighting for the life Kate would've given anything to still have."

"Stop it, Malcolm—just *stop*," she said sharply, her eyes gleaming. "If you'd really wanted Kate, you should've let go the moment you realized it was me instead of her you grabbed when my hand managed to break the water's surface. You should've left me there and gone and found her. Because I've wished every single day since then that you had."

Chapter Four

Malcolm's stomach pitched, his mind reeling with the horrifying realization that Giselle *knew*. She understood that despite the fact that once he had shouted back over his shoulder for Kyle—that useless piece of garbage—to dial 9-1-1 and get in the damned water with a life ring to help him, that there had been a moment after he'd spotted her that he'd been certain it *was* Kate he'd caught hold of, recognizing the deep purple of her bikini as she'd struggled beneath the surface.

An instant later, the horror of the tangled hair—far too much of it hopelessly trapping her head beneath the surface—had reminded him how Giselle had borrowed her sister's swimsuit after forgetting to pack her own for this trip.... And in that single, shocking instant, to his utter shame, he'd been tempted to let go of Kate's annoying younger sibling and swim on, to pretend he'd never made the contact, or even seen her struggling.

Still, it haunted him, the knowledge that if he had done so, no one would have ever been the wiser and Kate would likely be alive. But when he'd looked down through a foot of water to see the primal terror in Giselle's face, he'd only tightened his grip on her instead. And ducked his head beneath the water to share with her the breath from his own lungs...

"There's fault enough to go around in what happened that day, but as far as I can figure, none of it was yours," Malcolm told her. "I wasn't lying back then when I told the sheriff's investigators, when I told *you*, I caught a glimpse of Kate floating in her life vest as I was struggling to help you." He would never forget his last sidelong look at the woman he'd loved with all his heart, not as long as he lived. Nor would he forgive himself for not making damned well certain that Kyle had been coherent enough to act on his shouted order to go see to her safety. "But she was slumped like she was dazed or something. Still, she seemed safe enough for the moment that I thought there was time to save you—or that help would come to—"

He remembered looking back at that same spot on the water, as he had finally lifted Giselle, who was choking and gagging—and bleeding from the back of her neck, where he'd nicked her with his knife while sawing away her hair—to the surface. Remembered his heart's deep dive when he had spotted his fiancée's life vest floating on its own.

"It was *never* your fault," Giselle insisted, tears now streaming down her face. "*I* was the one who distracted you when she needed you. The one who thought that *Kyle* was a good idea."

"We've all had lapses when it comes to dating," he said. "It doesn't mean you should beat yourself up for it for the rest of your life on account of—"

He was interrupted by the sound of an old-fashioned landline ringing, jarringly loud inside the darkened house, despite the noise of the storm outside. As Giselle moved toward where the black corded phone was sitting on its own small table, he warned, "You might not want to do that. Those wires can conduct lightning."

"It'll be Claudette from up the mountain. She's the only one who ever calls on this line, and with this storm…"

Malcolm was surprised to hear the elderly widow was still living on her own in the rustic cabin farther up the mountain. She and her late husband had lived there full-time since Giselle and Kate had both been small. Though he'd never met her personally, Kate had sometimes dropped in to check on her grandmother's onetime friend or gift her a small care package of items she'd picked up from the pharmacy or grocery store in town.

Giselle lifted the receiver. "Claudette, are you all right?"

Even from where Malcolm stood, he caught the terrified shriek that had Giselle wincing and pulling the phone back from her ear.

"Please, I'm listening, and I have help right here with me to come if you need us." Giselle caught Malcolm's eye. "But I need to know exactly what's wrong. What's happening right now at your place?"

As the woman spoke, Giselle's face paled and her eyes grew rounder. "I need you to stop for a moment. Listen to me, please. *Let* him break into the garage. Forget about the Bronco. Just keep your doors locked and stay out of sight inside your cabin. I've just been told there's a dangerous criminal on the loose—and—Claudette, no—"

Giselle shook her head as her neighbor continued speaking. "That old SUV can be replaced, but you cannot—"

"Tell her I'll be right there. I'll borrow your car and head straight to her," Malcolm said, his heart a wild drumbeat in his ears to think that he was so close to finally stopping the man who'd inflicted so much pain on his family.

Though he dimly remembered what he'd told Giselle— and what he'd promised *himself*—about calling the authorities rather than attempting to confront Markus on his own, Malcolm realized that, with another woman's life imminently at risk, there was no longer any question that he had to personally act.

"I'm coming with you," Giselle insisted, before once more speaking into the phone. "Did you hear that, Claudette? My Kate's fiancé—he's a dog handler with Search and Rescue—is coming with me. We're on our way. And no, this fugitive who's trying to break into your garage isn't there to bother your chickens, no matter how special they are. So please stop worrying about them and keep yourself safe right now."

Giselle frowning, nodded, before her expression softened. "No—you listen to me, *please*. I think it's wonderful that you have that rifle. But I just want you to hold onto it right where you are in case he tries breaking through your locked doors to get inside the house. Do not, under any circumstances, go outside with it—*Hello?* Can you still hear me?"

After tapping at the phone a few times, Giselle shook her head, tears in her eyes as she looked up at Malcolm. "I thought she'd just hung up, but the line's dead."

"Forget the phone," he told her. "We need to get over there, right now."

"Just let me get my bag and gun," she said over her shoulder as she hurried toward the mudroom to grab her boots and jacket as well.

"I'm not sure your coming is a great idea," he said. "Maybe you could stay and try contacting the authorities on your cell."

"I'm not sure if you know Claudette—"

"Only by reputation. Kate said she wasn't much on strangers, especially of the male persuasion."

Giselle nodded. "That's Claudette, all right. Only now, she's older, even harder of hearing, and just about impossible to reason with when something gets her riled. And she's plenty upset right now, seeing what she called 'some wet and filthy vagabond' trying to pry his way into her car shed."

"Did I hear you say she has a Bronco?" Malcolm picked up Pacer's harness.

"The thing's ancient, but it still runs great," Giselle balanced on one foot to shove the other into a boot. "My point, though, was that Claudette not only won't listen to a stranger in her current state of mind, she might even be a hazard. She keeps a .22 rifle to safeguard her chickens."

"She did seem pretty preoccupied with them," he said as he knelt down to get Pacer situated.

"She brings me eggs, so I hear a lot about those fancy poultry shows she used to take their ancestors to back when she got out more."

He rose and accepted his jacket as she passed it to him. "I guess everybody needs something to love to keep them going." He glanced down at Pacer, reminded anew of what a critical lifeline the bond between them had provided for him.

"Maybe," Giselle said. "But as far as Claudette goes, you'll need me with you to make sure she understands that you're there to help keep her and the things that she holds dear safe. Otherwise, she could decide you're just as dangerous as one of the hungry foxes or weasels she's always watching out for—and leave you just as dead as any bullet from Markus Acker's gun."

AFTER RUNNING THROUGH the rain to her garage, Giselle climbed behind the wheel of her red Crosstrek as Malcolm loaded Pacer into the rear seat before getting in beside her.

As she strapped in and fired up the engine, she said, "Before Claudette started in about her chickens, she mentioned that since she keeps the shed locked, her Bronco's keys were in there, in the ignition."

"So in other words, if he does break in, he'll be gone in a flash," Malcolm reached inside the pocket of his jacket. "Let me try 9-1-1, see if we can get some backup to meet us up here. And maybe they can put up roadblocks to keep him from making it over to the interstate."

He turned on his phone as Giselle backed out of the garage. "No signal," he said as she started up the hill. "Mind if I try yours instead?"

She shook her head. "In all the rush, I'm afraid I left it back inside. That was stupid."

"It doesn't matter," Malcolm told her. "It'll more than likely be using the same cell tower as mine is. Storm's probably knocked out all service."

"So we're completely on our own," she said. As they turned onto the road, lightning pulsed overhead, and the heavy rain renewed its assault. "Just what we needed."

"If you need to stay inside the car at Claudette's, I'll certainly understand."

"I didn't come with you to hide." Hearing the sharpness in her own voice, Giselle blew out a breath. "I'm only nervous, that's all."

"Just try not to accidentally shoot anybody you don't mean to with that old revolver of yours," Malcolm warned.

"You don't have to worry about that." She slowed to make a sharp right. "After my grandfather passed away, Grandma decided she didn't care for having a loaded weapon around the cabin."

Malcolm's head whipped around to stare at her. "Wait a second. Are you seriously telling me that gun—the same gun you *pointed* at me earlier—isn't even *loaded*?"

She shrugged. "Not the last time I checked. And I have no idea when I last saw that box of ammo."

"So you were just bluffing me before? Do you know how incredibly dangerous that is? How foolish, to threaten an unknown intruder the way you did me with a weapon when you're not even certain of its status? Which means, I'm sure, it hasn't been cleaned or tested since your grandfather, who's been gone for, what, fifteen years, at least?"

Irritated by the judgment in his voice, she blasted back,

"There's no need to lose your mind about it. I only had the gun as a deterrent, that's all. I was never going to hurt anyone."

He shook his head. "But what if it hadn't been me, Giselle? What then? Because if Markus had seen the useless thing and perceived you as a threat, he would've shot you down without a moment's hesitation."

Feeling her face heat, she said, "You know, I've done just fine on my own up here for three years without you mansplaining my survival for me."

"If you can't see the difference between mansplaining and discussing reasonable precautions when we're on our way to confront a man who meets the textbook definition of a serial killer, you ought to be *really* grateful I'm here to point out the difference."

As the rain intensified, her grip on the wheel tightened. "When this is over, I hope you'll remind me to throw you and your ego a parade."

"This isn't about my ego. It's your total disregard for your own safety."

After flipping on her high-beam headlights, she pointed out a gap between a large pine tree and a boulder just ahead. "If you could quit talking about yourself for one minute, we're almost there."

Tapping the brakes, she turned left. An instant later, she shrieked as the Subaru came face-to-face with a far larger vehicle barreling directly toward them on the steep and narrow, deeply eroded drive as it slewed around a sharp curve.

When the thirty-year-old Bronco failed to slow, Giselle jerked the wheel to the right to avoid smashing into it head-on. But as deeply rutted as the drive was from years of prior rain events, the Crosstrek's right-hand wheels immediately ran up the side of the mud-and-stone cut.

As the Bronco blasted past them, she heard the shriek of

metal as the side-view mirror was shorn off. But her startled gasp almost instantly gave way to the blood-freezing conviction that they would flip over as the Subaru's right side continued its climb.

"No, no, *no!*" Giselle cried out, before jerking the wheel back to the left. At the same instant, a portion of the rain-saturated slope collapsed beneath the vehicle's weight. Malcolm shouted in alarm at the same time as Pacer yelped from the rear seat.

Somehow, the Crosstrek skidded and bounced down on all four wheels before Giselle hit the brakes. By some miracle of physics she would never understand, the Subaru squelched to a stop in the low center of the drive, which had become a chute for the rainwater pouring down it.

"You—are you okay?" Malcolm asked, as she sat in stunned silence, shaking visibly.

"I—I'm fine, b-but—" she stammered, shaking her head before asking an incredulous, "—how on earth are we *alive*?!"

"WE CAN WASTE time later debating over whether you're the world's best driver or its worst one," Malcolm said, his pumping heart still in his throat and his gut still somewhere on the floorboards. Relieved when a quick glance told him that Pacer, too, appeared unharmed, he returned his attention to Giselle. "For now, I'm more concerned with whether you saw which way Acker went after he left here."

She shook her head. "All I saw were the Bronco's headlights—and my life flashing before my eyes. But there's really only one way he could've gone. This road dead ends in less than thirty yards if you try to take it any higher. So he must be heading down the mountain—and back toward the state highway."

Realizing she was right, Malcolm nodded before he noticed the rising water level. "We need to get out of this gully quickly before the engine floods out and we end up drowning in this mud. But before we go after Acker, we have to make sure your neighbor's safe."

"You don't think he could've *taken* her?" Giselle asked, recovering from her shock enough to resume driving. "You didn't see her inside of the Bronco, did you?"

Malcolm thought back before shaking his head. "I couldn't see anything but headlights. But at this point, there's not much I'd put past him. Not even dragging an elderly woman to a couple of ATMs and forcing her to max out her daily withdrawals before he dumps her somewhere."

Giselle shuddered. "You don't think he'd—that he'd really kill her after taking her money, do you?"

Malcolm couldn't bring himself to say what he was thinking, so instead he deflected. "Let's just hope she listened to your excellent advice and stayed safe inside her house."

As they approached the front of a snug-looking cedar cabin with a steeply pitched green roof and matching shutters, Giselle pointed toward the open front door. "I hope that just means she ran to check her little flock after he took off with her Bronco."

"I'll head down and check the outbuildings," he said. "Meanwhile, why don't you go to the house first and call for her before you move in my direction? That way, if she's in there calling the authorities or maybe hiding somewhere upstairs, she'll hear a friendly voice and know it's safe to come out of hiding."

Though Giselle had at first looked poised to argue—perhaps about his idea of splitting up—she instead hesitated and then nodded. "I guess that makes sense. All right."

"Then I'll meet you and Pacer out in that little blue barn, where she keeps her chickens." She pointed out one of a pair of outbuildings a short distance behind the cabin, one of which—the weathered gray shed he presumed had held the Bronco, had its door standing wide open.

"All right. I'll start there," he said before bailing out of the passenger side. Once he'd unloaded Pacer, he looked back at Giselle over the roof of the Crosstrek. "Just be careful to announce yourself at every step, in case Claudette's inclined to shoot first and ask questions second."

Nodding, Giselle said, "As an armed male and a stranger, I'd definitely be more concerned about your safety than mine."

"I'll definitely keep that in mind."

As Pacer led him toward the two outbuildings, the dog's left ear—the only one he was able to raise at all—sprang to attention, quivering at its tip before he gave a plaintive whine.

"What do you hear, boy?" Malcolm asked him, eyeing the large open door of the gray shed that must have been the outbuilding where the old Bronco had been stowed.

Sniffing the air, Pacer tugged him in that direction rather than toward the little blue barn. After a few steps forward, Malcolm paused and, taking his own advice, called and identified himself before adding: "Miss Claudette, I'm the friend Giselle mentioned on the phone. She's checking inside your house right now. We've come to help you. Can you hear me?"

After waiting in silence with the rain splashing down into growing puddles, he tried again. "Can anybody hear me?"

Once more, he heard no human answer.

Praying he would find her there, he broke into a run... and stopped, spotting a bloody handprint on the white trim of the blue door.

Chapter Five

Giselle was more than willing to run through heavy rain to meet Malcolm out at the barn after discovering the house was empty. But when she opened the door, flash after flash of lightning lit up the sky, and she gaped at the rare sight of hail clattering down, striking against the ground, the cabin, and the glass and sheet metal of her Subaru. Ranging from the diameter of dimes to quarters, the icy chunks bounced off every surface they struck and quickly began to accumulate in low spots.

She startled at a splintering sound, as a large window to the left of the doorway where she was standing cracked diagonally. When the swirling wind snapped off a pair of treetops in the yard and sucked them up into the sky, she fought to push the door closed for her own safety.

Worried that might not be enough to keep her safe, she then ducked inside the shelter of an interior bathroom—the cabin's one windowless room—question after question spinning through her mind. Had Malcolm found Claudette, and if so, what was her condition? And would they and Pacer all be safe from the storm's fury, perhaps inside the barn? She wondered, too, had what she'd just witnessed happening with those two treetops been the prelude to a tornado that would flatten everything around her—including both outbuildings and perhaps even this cabin?

But instead of the rushing, train-like sound so many news reports had led her to expect, the rattling of the hailstones and the howling of the winds died down over a course of several minutes that felt as long as hours. When she finally dared to peek outside again, she found that the lightning, too, had subsided.

Not surprised to find Claudette's landline still dead when she checked it, she headed back outside, where she felt a hot rush of relief to see both outbuildings and the trees nearest to them all remained undamaged. When her gaze strayed to her red Crosstrek, however, her jaw dropped, seeing that one of the treetops had come down across the SUV's now-mashed hood and shattered windshield. What sheet metal remained visible was a moonscape of hail damage.

"Wow..." Unnerved by the fact that she and Malcolm had been sitting in that vehicle only minutes before its destruction, she breathed a silent prayer that both he and Claudette were safe and pulled up her jacket's hood against the rain. Jogging toward the barn, she avoided low spots where some of hailstones had piled up and shouted, "Malcolm? Are you all right?"

He appeared in the doorway, his green eyes somber. "I'm fine—and relieved as hell to see that you're in one piece, too—"

She flung her arms around his neck, giving him a quick hug before she could think better of it. Withdrawing almost as swiftly, she said, "In a lot better shape than my poor car."

"Your car?" Sounding thoroughly distracted, he barely glanced in its direction.

She felt a quick jab of annoyance, imagining he'd been bothered by a hug that had been nothing but a reflex. "Just look at the poor thing. It's pulverized," gesturing toward the

Subaru, until something red against the white-trimmed blue doorframe caught the corner of her eye. "Wait—is that…is that *blood* right there?"

She turned enough to realize it wasn't a smudge so much as a…

Oh, no…

"I'm almost positive it is, so please don't touch that—" His palms rose. "Giselle, you should stay back. There's no need for you to see her."

"You mean Claudette's inside there? You mean she's—? She's *hurt*?" Giselle craned her neck to see past him. Surely, if her elderly neighbor was injured, she would need the reassurance of a friendly face, someone she knew well to help her. "Please, let me go to her. She needs me."

Malcolm shook his head, his broad shoulders filling the doorway and Pacer whining near his feet. But Malcolm's voice was gentle as he laid one big hand on her upper arm. "I'm sorry, Giselle. Very sorry. But I'm afraid that she no longer does."

Beneath the weight of his hand, her shoulder quivered. "Then she's—you're saying that she's…?"

"Gone, I'm afraid. I'm so sorry."

"No. That can't be right." She shook her head emphatically, her throat too tight. "Please tell me you're—"

"I found her in here just before the hail started," he continued, his gaze regretful. "Judging from this handprint, I'm guessing she was shot confronting him at the shed before she ran inside here, injured. Then she fell and—and most likely bled out in front of her hens' enclosure."

"I—I wonder—do you think she suffered…?" Giselle's vision blurred at the thought of the neighbor she thought of as a last, tenuous link with her childhood dying such a cruel and lonely death.

Malcolm's strong arms closed around her. As he pulled

her to his chest, her stomach flipped with the memory of the last time he had held her like this. Only that time, they had both been sobbing, their hearts both shattered beyond repair when they'd learned that Kate was gone.

Because you stopped to save me. Do you despise me for delaying you for those critical few minutes half as much as I've come to hate myself?

"I'm so sorry, Giselle." Malcolm stroked her shaking shoulders. "I can't say for certain, of course, but considering that it appears to be a chest wound and judging by how much blood is pooled around her, I believe she would have lost consciousness very quickly. So I can't think she was aware for more than a matter of seconds before—"

"I so hope that you're right," she said, grasping at that lifeline, "and that she didn't—she didn't have time to feel too much pain or be too frightened..."

Malcolm gave her a clean bandana from his pocket, which she used to wipe her tears. Peering over his shoulder, she caught a glimpse of her neighbor, lying prone, one frail arm thrown out before her in the straw. As Malcolm had warned Giselle, a shockingly large, deep-crimson circle had ponded around her chest and torso.

"Oh, no—no, Claudette," Giselle choked out, feeling something break inside her.

"Let's get you away from this." With a nod and a light touch, he directed her attention toward a wired enclosure, where a dozen hens crowned with the feathery white bonnets that marked their breed scratched and pecked about their enclosure looking for unclaimed morsels.

"That's it," he told her, his words as soothing as the steadying hand he kept on her shoulder. "Keep watch over this peaceful little world that she created, that she loved. Not a sight she'd never want remembered."

"But she—I need to—"

"Shh. Right now, you don't *need* to do anything but keep on breathing," he said. "Right after the worst of the storm passed, I managed to get a couple of calls out, and help is on the way."

Her hand found Pacer, who had maneuvered himself to offer comfort. She stroked the shepherd mix's broad, warm head and thick ruff as she looked up at Malcolm. "The police are coming?"

"Police, an ambulance—and most likely more rescue people than we'll know what to do with," he assured her, his voice the one point of calm amid the maelstrom of emotion threatening to tear her into pieces.

"But what good can any of them possibly do at this point?" she asked, fresh tears streaming as the reality of the situation struck her. "They'll be as useless to her as they were for Kate."

"It's true, they won't be able to bring Claudette back at this point. You and I both know that no one has that power. But they'll do the same as Liam, Ajay, Fletcher, and so many others on the law enforcement joint task force have been working to do for my uncle, my mother, and all of Acker's other victims and bring her the justice she deserves. That, and to see that Acker's stopped before he gets the chance to add even more names to the list of lives that he's destroyed."

"He *has* to be stopped," she insisted, her red-rimmed eyes burning with the light of a fierce determination, "because it's absolutely clear that anyone who could do this kind of thing is nothing but pure evil. Evil in the flesh."

Chapter Six

Disturbed to see how pale Giselle was looking, Malcolm suggested that she wait inside Claudette's house, away from the body and out of the weather. But because he needed to be certain they wouldn't be disturbing a portion of the crime scene, he asked her, "You didn't find any signs in there of a break-in or a struggle inside, did you?"

"Everything looked neat enough in there," she said, "except the .22 rifle I mentioned earlier was missing from its rack. Did you notice, does she still have that with her?"

"I didn't see it out here. She could've dropped it by the shed when she was hit or somewhere near there. I'll take a look, but I'm betting we won't find it at all."

Giselle frowned. "Then you think Acker's taken it?"

"It's hard to imagine Markus would miss the chance to add another loaded weapon to his arsenal," Malcolm said grimly.

"As if he wasn't already dangerous enough."

"We can only hope this weather was as hard on his stolen ride as it was on yours." Malcolm nodded in the direction of the Crosstrek. "I'm afraid that if he makes it to the interstate, he's going to be a heck of a lot harder to catch than if they can keep him contained within this general area."

"I can't help fantasizing about this storm sending another

of those flying trees down from the sky to squash him like a roach inside that stolen Bronco," Giselle said.

"I'd definitely spring for popcorn and two tickets to *that* movie," Malcolm said, though in his heart he knew that getting rid of someone as smart and adaptable as Acker was highly unlikely to be so simple.

"While I'm inside," Giselle said, "should I be looking for the Bronco's plate number or anything like that for the police?"

"That'll all be in the state's system, so they should be able to pull it up with their computers. But if Claudette has any next of kin—"

"I know there's no one local, but she did mention a niece on the East Coast that she was fond of."

"If you see an address book, maybe you can find this niece's contact information."

"Should I—should I—try to reach out and tell her that her aunt's…?" Giselle asked, running her hands through Pacer's fur.

"Oh, no." Taking her hand in his, he noticed how very cold it had gone. "Definitely leave the notification to the police. And before you worry about any of it, I want you to make yourself a cup of tea if Claudette has it. You still drink tea, don't you?"

She nodded.

"And why don't you take Pacer inside the house with you as well? Let him keep you company for a while," he suggested.

"You're sure you won't need him to work?"

"Not for a while, I don't think. Besides, he's been pretty much glued to you since you came out here." He glanced down at his dog, who was smiling in open-mouthed canine bliss as she rubbed his ear. "If I were the sensitive sort, I might have to dock his pay a biscuit or two for his disloyalty. Though I really can't fault him for his good taste."

"Thanks, Malcolm. As terrible as this is, it's a relief to have you to help me through it—especially after I practically chewed your head off earlier."

Her eyes brimmed with regret. But when she stopped petting Pacer to give Malcolm another quick embrace—the second time she'd done so—it took him by surprise. Reminding himself that they'd just survived an ordeal that would have shaken anyone to their foundations, he told himself that he had no business feeling any different about that hug than he would have had it come from any female friend or family member.

Except it wasn't what he felt at all, and it didn't sit well with him. Being anywhere near her didn't sit well, making him uncomfortable in ways he'd rather not delve into too deeply. But her expectant look reminded him she still awaited his response.

"So, neither of us was a pleasant surprise for the other today when I showed up on your doorstep," he acknowledged. "But moving past that, I'm seriously relieved to see you're safe and sound. I'm absolutely certain Markus came *right* past your cabin before he headed up to find your neighbor. He might've just as easily stopped and killed *you* for your SUV instead."

For one horrifying instant, he pictured her body lying in a pool of blood rather than Claudette's.

Laying a hand over her chest, Giselle drew a deep breath, a flush suffusing her face. "And once more I'm left knowing that my survival may have cost the life of someone I cared for."

"You can't blame yourself for things outside of your control," he told her, only to see she'd stepped away to gesture toward the open barn doorway.

"Look at that," she said. "A break in the rain at last. Pacer and I had better run inside while we can manage it without getting soaked."

Noting how quickly she had changed the subject of the guilt she carried, he made a mental note to try again to talk to her about it another time. Nodding toward the darkening sky, he said, "Go on ahead, then. I'll check in with you soon."

She'd been inside only a few minutes when a familiar blue Jeep Wrangler Rubicon pulled up. Moments later, Ajay Wright jumped out. Though he was dressed for search and rescue fieldwork—and the weather—rather than in his police uniform, there was nothing informal about the intense expression on his face as he approached, with his SAR-trained yellow Lab, Pumpkin, trotting at his side.

Malcolm didn't look away, knowing he deserved the royal chewing out he was about to get for disobeying a directive issued for everyone's safety. But as Ajay drew nearer, he saw that the lines etched into his warm brown brow were those of concern rather than anger, and his grip, when he grasped Malcolm's forearm, was that of a friend, not an accuser.

"Before I see this body you've called in, I need to know if you're okay," Ajay said.

"I'll be just fine. I'm—"

"The minute I heard that half-baked story about you running off to see some girlfriend no one had never heard of, I knew damned well *exactly* the kind of stunt you'd pulled. I even knew the reason, considering how upset you were about my decision—a decision I made along with Liam Hill and the whole damn task force—to hold off on the search until we had both the conditions and the manpower in place to assure everybody's safety."

"I'm sorry," Malcolm told him. "Sorry I questioned your professional judgment and even sorrier I took off on my own to do this. But at the moment, I couldn't think of anything but Acker laughing at everything he's put my family through while he runs off to start his murderous cycle all over again someplace else."

Ajay regarded him, the intensity of his golden-brown gaze softening a fraction. "I've known you for quite some time now, and you've always been so reliable, so focused on doing the right thing for others, that it's easy to forget you're carrying some pretty heavy baggage of your own. It's only been, what, three-and-a-half years since your fiancée's passing, hasn't it? Maybe that, in combination with these latest losses—"

"Listen, Ajay, I know how close you and my sister are, but whatever Lizzy's telling you, I'm not looking for any excuses for my actions."

"It's a damned good thing," Ajay said bluntly. "Because there's *no* excuse good enough to make up for shutting off your GPS tracker and leaving me scared spitless I'd end up having to explain to the woman I love how I'd missed the signs her brother was about to go rogue and get his fool self killed."

Malcolm winced, realizing he shouldn't be surprised that his father had broadcast the news of Malcolm's "secret rendezvous" far and wide the second he was out of sight. Buck had been practically giddy since he and Malcolm's Aunt Jenny had found themselves in a relationship. After Jenny's husband Robert passed away a while back, she realized Buck was the person who had truly loved her for years. And it was only natural that Lizzy would have mentioned it to Ajay, especially considering Malcolm's recent—and very firm—insistence that he had zero interest in meeting one of her single friends for coffee *just to see how things might go.*

Nodding toward Giselle's wrecked Subaru, Malcolm said, "It's clear to me now that coming up here in this weather was the wrong move—and risking your safety by running off the way I did was a worse one, so whatever your decision, I'm prepared to accept the consequences."

"I'm glad to hear that, Malcolm, because until I feel confident that you're thinking like a team member again instead of a lone wolf with no regard for personal safety, your only involvement with SAR is to be at Crosswinds, assisting Sebastian and Della with that latest batch of pups that they're training."

Malcolm's pride stung at the thought of being relegated to puppy duty, of all things. The headstrong younger man he'd once been wanted to argue the decision, to shout at Ajay that he needed to continue his involvement with the hunt for his uncle's and his mother's murderer with one of the best trailing dogs on the team. But he saw Ajay watching him, waiting to see if he was really man enough to accept the consequences he'd more than earned without balking.

Nodding, Malcolm drew a deep breath. "Whatever you need from me is fine."

Ajay nodded. "*Good*, because right now, there's a victim deserving of my full attention and a task force I need to help coordinate so we can get this perpetrator into custody as soon as possible. Do we understand each other?"

"Absolutely, we do," Malcolm said, understanding that it could take some time to repair the damage he'd done to their relationship—if it could be repaired at all. But there was little time to worry over such things, as Ajay kept him busy answering questions about what had happened as he headed into the barn to do his initial assessment of the victim and scene.

When an SUV with law enforcement markings and an ambulance pulled up, Ajay poked his head outside again and told Malcolm, "While you're waiting, I want you to have the EMTs check out that hand I've noticed you've been keeping out of my sight."

"It'll be fine," Malcolm said, amazed that he had even noticed the bandage.

"No, Malcolm. You'll get yourself checked out, now," Ajay said, more firmly. "You're part of a team. And a team sees to members who are hurting so they'll be prepared to serve the mission together at some point in the future. Do we understand each other?"

"Absolutely," Malcolm answered, grateful that despite the hell he'd just put Ajay through, the man cared enough about his welfare to give him hope that what amounted to a suspension from real search-and-rescue work wouldn't last forever.

After getting his hand rewrapped by the EMT, who advised him to visit the emergency clinic in town for X-rays and further evaluation as soon as he was able, Malcolm spotted Giselle walking toward him, her eyes puffy and red-rimmed. Seeing him, Pacer trotted ahead of her to greet him.

"He started whining at the door when he spotted the other dog out here," she said by way of explanation.

"Probably figured he was missing out on some action," Malcolm said as he rubbed his dog's ears.

"He's not the only one," Giselle admitted as Ajay stepped out of the barn and joined them.

Malcolm was quick to launch into introductions. "Giselle Dowling, this is Lieutenant Ajay Wright. He's coordinating Owl Creek Search and Rescue and also co-directing the task force in charge of the manhunt for Markus Acker. Claudette Hogan was Giselle's family friend and neighbor."

"I'm so sorry we're meeting under such circumstances," Ajay told her. "My condolences on your loss."

"It doesn't—it doesn't seem possible it's real." Her voice thickened as she brought her hand to her mouth. "I keep hoping I'll wake up from this. But it's not a nightmare, is it?"

Malcolm laid a hand on her shoulder as Ajay said, "I can't change what's happened, I'm afraid, but I can promise you, my colleagues and I are already taking steps to bring the person responsible to justice. Liam Hill, my colleague from the FBI, is working out of our command post in Owl Creek, coordinating checkpoints along the only two routes leading out of this immediate area and putting out a statewide BOLO on the Bronco registered in your neighbor's name, just in case the suspect has somehow managed to slip past our net."

"Surely, you know you're chasing Markus Acker?" Giselle asked, sounding confused.

"We certainly believe that to be the case," Ajay said, "but since Malcolm tells me that neither of you saw him face-to-face, we don't yet have confirmation."

"Assuming it really *is* him, though," she said, clearly unwilling to consider any other possibility, "do you think it's likely he's already left the area?"

"What with all the downed trees around this elevation—" Ajay gestured toward the Subaru "—I have serious doubts about him getting very far. Even if he could escape, I have to suspect there's some reason he's been lingering close to this area so long in the first place."

"Like what?" Malcolm asked.

"The general thinking on the task force has been that he's holed up in some unoccupied ski cabin he's broken into, using it as an easy source of shelter and supplies. But either he's run low or something's forced him to move on for some reason. Or possibly he has some new plan in mind."

"Have you come up with any theories on what that might be?" Malcolm asked.

"Presuming he sticks with his usual M.O., he's going to need funding to reestablish his cult in a new location and start recruiting and fleecing some new converts. Or he may try to reconnect with past followers still willing to help him."

"Who could possibly want anything to do with him now?"

Giselle asked. "Surely, everyone's seen on the news how he's been exposed as a swindler and a killer."

Ajay explained, "Acker had them so twisted inside-out with all that happy-family garbage he was selling them that at least some might still be vulnerable enough to fall for it again, regardless of how badly he abused them."

She shook her head. "I'm not sure whether that's more sad or sick."

"There's room enough for both, I'd say. We've been trying to reach out to as many as we can, offering them some incentives to give us a call instead of helping him in case he does reach out—everything from offers of counseling and job placement assistance to information about the reward fund that's been set up for anyone offering help resulting in Acker's apprehension."

"You really think one of those ex-cult types would rat out their former guru?" Malcolm asked him.

"Money talks," Ajay said. "Especially when it's paired with a firm reminder of the penalties for aiding and abetting someone fleeing multiple murder charges. Or maybe a dirty, desperate Markus Acker will have broken down too badly to lay on the same charm he once did with them."

Malcolm could picture the well-dressed, fit, articulate man—so used to adulation by his followers—now spitting mad at having been reduced by circumstances. "I can imagine that seeing him in that state could finally open some eyes."

"Which once again leaves him on the run, on his own and strapped for money. And with absolutely nothing to lose since he knows he'll never breathe air as a free man again if he's caught."

"Does this have anything to do with that text that Lizzy sent out last week warning everyone in the family that we should all take extra precautions until he's been captured?"

Ajay nodded. "I'm sure it does. I've warned her that with Acker on the move, this could be the most dangerous time for everyone in your family since he's already zeroed in on them as a potential source of wealth. Plus, there's a history between Marcus and the Coltons."

Malcolm felt an icy chill cleave through him as his thoughts went to his loved ones, from the oldest to the very youngest and most vulnerable members of his extended family. "You really think he'd have the guts to make another run at any of us at this point? With the task force closing in on him and everyone well aware by now what he's capable of, the idea seems almost suicidal."

"If he were a normal person, I'd tell you you're absolutely right," Ajay said, "but Acker's desperate—and enough of a narcissist to imagine he's capable of making one more end run around us."

"I'll get the word out about what's happened up here today," Malcolm said, "and make sure everyone in the family understands that he's definitely mobile as well."

"That's a good idea, but I need to review today's chain of events with both of you before you leave here for the ranch— or at least that's where I presume you'll be going, Malcolm."

"I'm hoping that we both will," Malcolm was quick to say, glancing at Giselle. "We have plenty of space for guests there, and with Markus armed and on the loose—"

She shook her head. "I wouldn't want to intrude on your family."

"Don't be ridiculous. You wouldn't be intruding," Malcolm told her. "And we both know there's no way that staying in your cabin is a reasonable option, especially now that you're cut off without transportation."

"You would be awfully vulnerable alone up here," Ajay agreed.

"And the phones have been in and out, too," Malcolm

added. "So unless you'd rather contend with having Pacer and me camped out on your porch every single night for the duration to stand guard over you—"

She rolled her eyes at the suggestion. "That won't be necessary, Malcolm. I'll take advantage of your hospitality—but only until either Acker is in custody or I've had the chance to make arrangements for a rental car and lodging."

"For what it's worth," Ajay told her, "I think you've made a very wise decision."

"I'm not sure I had another choice," she said, "unless I wanted to deal with Malcolm and Pacer staking out my doorstep morning, noon, and night. I'd definitely never get any writing done then."

"So now we're pretending you were doing loads *without* me?" Malcolm fired back.

She sent a look in Malcolm's direction that convinced him to drop the subject.

After briefly excusing himself to speak to Fletcher and two other officers who'd arrived about evidence collection, Ajay returned and asked Malcolm and Giselle to join him inside of Claudette's cabin, where he planned to record their statements using his phone.

Once Ajay had asked the last of his questions, Giselle walked over to the kitchen counter, where she picked up an address book. Passing it to where he stood with Malcolm beside the small table where they'd all been seated, she said, "I found this earlier in Claudette's sewing room. Her niece's name is Lorna Hunnicutt. She lives in Massachusetts."

"So this Lorna is the only family?"

Giselle nodded. "Unless you count that little flock of hers. I know they're only chickens, but Claudette—she loved them."

Malcolm grabbed some tissues from a console adorned with poultry-themed trophies and photographs of a smiling, younger Claudette holding various chickens with long blue ribbons. Passing the box to Giselle, he said, "Don't you worry about those hens. If Ajay and the niece have no objections, my dad knows a nice retired couple who keep farm animals, mostly minis, around to keep their grandkids happy. I'm betting they'd love to add Claudette's little flock to their menagerie. That way, you'd never have to worry about them ending up in anybody's stewpot."

"I'd appreciate you seeing to that," Ajay said. "As soon as we're finished processing the scene, I'll give you a heads-up so you can come remove them from the property. In the meantime, I'll be sure they're taken care of."

"Thank you both so much," Giselle said. "And I can help you collect them later, Malcolm."

With her SUV undrivable, Ajay asked Malcolm for his truck keys and assigned a junior officer to retrieve the pickup from the trailhead where he'd spotted it earlier. Turning to Giselle, he added, "That way, you can make a quick stop by your place to pick up whatever you'll need for your stay at the ranch. I'd definitely like to see both of you off the road before full dark."

Malcolm and Giselle shared a look. In her eyes, he saw the realization that even on the run from the authorities, the armed and dangerous Markus Acker had the potential to pose a threat to them on these lonely, unlit roads.

A SHORT TIME LATER, Ajay excused himself to step inside of Claudette's sewing room, where he said he planned to contact her niece.

Giselle shook her head as he closed the door behind him. "What a terrible part of his job that must be, notifying people with such awful news. I don't know how he does it."

"He's a good man," Malcolm told her, as he headed for the

small living area with Giselle following. "He's been amazing for Lizzy, too."

"He's seeing your sister?" Giselle took a seat on a striped sofa draped with a fringed blanket. "Is it serious?"

Malcolm chose a sturdy-looking chair that faced her. "I'm sure it is. They're great together. As hellacious as this past year has been, I can't tell you that no good has come of it. My cousin, Fletcher—you may have seen him outside—has come back to work as a detective here in town, and his sister Frannie—"

"Isn't she the one who's into books?" Despite her sadness, Giselle felt a smile tug at her lips. "I remember we had that in common."

Nodding, he said, "She owns Book Mark It, the local bookstore and café. You'd love the place. But she has another project going now as well." His green eyes warmed with pleasure. "She and her husband, Dante, are expecting their first child soon."

"I'm so glad to hear it," she said. "After your losses, Coltons deserve something to celebrate, and what could be more wonderful than welcoming a new life?"

"Is that—is that something you've ever imagined for yourself, having a family of your own someday?"

She was quick to shake her head. "Maybe at one time I thought that way, in some distant sort of future. But now?" The scoffing noise she made was tinged with bitterness. "How can I imagine moving on now, writing a new chapter of my story that Kate can't ever be a part of?"

Malcolm's forehead creased. "She'll always be a part of you. Of both of us. And I know she wouldn't want to see you stuck forever, holed up in that old cabin like some recluse."

"Is this your way of telling me that *you've* come unstuck, Malcolm?" she challenged. "That you're out there enjoying a healthy social life—or going out with any women since the accident?" Hoping she was wrong, she added. "Or maybe by this time you've moved on to something more serious? After all, it *has* been more than three years."

He shook his head, "No. I—no," he stammered. "And I can't imagine five years or ten or a lifetime making any difference. No one else will ever…could ever hope to compare to—"

"Malcolm," Ajay said, as he came down the hall, his phone in his hand.

"Did you reach Claudette's niece?" Giselle asked.

"I've left a message for her to call me, but I'm afraid that something else has come up." Once more, Ajay's attention turned to Malcolm. "It's about your truck, over at the trailhead. I've heard from the officer I sent to retrieve it from the scenic overlook where I spotted it parked earlier, above the lake."

"Was there some sort of problem?" Malcolm asked.

"She's telling me it's missing from the lot."

"The three-year-old silver RAM? You're sure you have her looking in the right spot?"

Ajay nodded, his expression grim. "I am—especially since she's just discovered Claudette Hogan's wrecked Bronco. Looks like Markus must've rolled it off the hillside into some heavy timber."

"Guess he figured it would be too hot, after murdering the owner," Malcolm said. "But why steal *my* truck?

"Most likely, it was the only vehicle left up there in this weather. You didn't keep a magnetic key box on it, did you? In case of a lock-out?"

Malcolm sighed. "I thought I had it hidden well enough, but yeah. I lost my keys a couple of years back while I was out doing SAR work, and it turned out to be a huge, expensive hassle to replace them."

"Thought I remembered you mentioning something

about that at one time," Ajay said. "Anyway, I'm sorry about your truck."

"Don't be. It's all on me, the way I figure—Claudette's death, the loss of my pickup. If I had only listened to you and waited until tomorrow to head out with the team, we could've counted on support from the whole task force, just the way you said."

Giselle shook her head before reaching out to touch his hand. "Claudette's death is a tragedy, but it happened because of Markus Acker's choices, Malcolm. Not yours or mine. He's the one who pulled that trigger."

"She's right about that," Ajay insisted. "And as furious as I've been with you all day—mostly because I couldn't quit worrying about breaking the news of your death to your family—your actions today may have kept us from losing whatever momentum we'd gained after that hiker called the tip line about spotting a man matching Acker's description in this vicinity. As much as I hate to admit it, you and I both know this kind of rain would have obliterated any scent trail. So let's not waste any more time or energy on self-recrimination. All right?"

With that, he offered Malcolm his right hand.

Malcolm hesitated. "I don't suppose this gets me out of puppy duty over at Crosswinds, does it?"

"I don't know, man. Does it change any part of that GPS-tracker stunt of yours?" Ajay asked. "And anyway, *who* doesn't like puppies?"

"*I* like puppies," Giselle murmured as she stroked Pacer's shoulder.

"That's not the issue, and you know it," Malcolm said as he shook Ajay's hand. "But I'll quit complaining and take my medicine."

Giselle felt a knot inside her loosen as some of the tension between the two men eased.

"And while you do," Ajay said, "All the members of the task force and I will be doing every single thing possible to run Acker to ground and bring him in, I swear it. And if I have a single thing to say about it, we're going to do it before he has the chance to take another life."

Chapter Seven

The stormy afternoon's gloom had given way to a deeper evening darkness by the time that Ajay was able to spare an officer to drive Giselle, Malcolm, and Pacer back to the ranch, following a brief stop at Giselle's cabin.

"Don't worry too much about forgetting something," Malcolm said as she looked through her closet. "We can always stop back tomorrow to pick up anything else you need."

But as she rode with him in the rear seat of the police SUV, however, she couldn't help picturing herself walking back inside of the blue barn, looking down at the blood-matted straw where she had last seen Claudette's body.

Giselle's stomach turned, her heart fluttering. She turned to hide her face, her shallow breaths steaming the police SUV's side window as light raindrops pattered down against it. Seeming to sense her mounting distress, Pacer, who was resting on the floorboard, shifted his position to lick and nuzzle her hand.

"You okay?" Malcolm asked her.

"Just thinking about having to return there," she said, her voice sounding thin and reedy in her own ears. "After what happened—what we saw inside."

"I know it's hard," Malcolm said, "but I want you to try right now to focus on your breathing for me. Pay attention to letting the air out—all of it. That's good. Then allow your-self a moment before you fill your lungs again completely…"

For the next portion of their journey, he helped her cen-ter on that one thing: breathing, reminding her that she was safe with him. At first, she had a hard time focusing, wor-ried that the officer transporting them might be listening and judging her for not doing a better job of holding herself together. Gradually, however, Malcolm's quiet, steady tone captured her full attention, until she felt the tension drain-ing from her body.

Exhausted from all the nervous energy that had been coursing through her, she eventually found her eyes grow-ing heavy as she threaded her fingers through the fur of Pacer's warm ruff. The next thing that she knew, Malcolm touched her elbow, waking her.

"I hate to disturb you," he said, "but we're just driving up to the ranch's main house and I didn't figure you'd like your first meeting with my father and anybody else who might be up this late to be slung over my shoulder while I hauled you inside like a sack of feed."

"Um, definitely not." Straightening, she yawned. "But you've probably forgotten, I *have* met your father. And most of your siblings and your cousins, too, at that big engagement cookout celebration your dad hosted for you and Kate here."

He smiled. "And that wasn't enough to scare you off?"

"Far from it," she said, remembering how she'd originally rolled her eyes at the idea of a family living surrounded by their crops and livestock in a home that Kate had described as a custom big red barn. "I was totally charmed. I remem-ber how your sister had just finished updating the space. Everything was so fresh and modern."

"Lizzy hasn't lived out here on the ranch for some time, but she still loves nothing more than when Dad sets her loose with a budget and a mission to spruce things up and bring us up to date."

"It wasn't only your home, though, that impressed me. Everyone was so friendly and fun to be around that day." Giselle smiled at the memory. "And they all kept gushing about how excited they were to have my sister joining the family. I'm sure you remember how much they adored her…" She tipped her hand in an awkward gesture. "But that was Kate—wherever she went. She had an energy people were drawn to."

Nodding, he glanced out the window as they rolled up to the house, but not before she glimpsed the pain in his eyes at the reminder of the treasure he had lost.

Once they had both thanked the officer for taking the time to bring them here, Giselle and Malcolm headed for a side door, where someone had left a light on. With Pacer beside them, Malcolm carried his backpack over his shoulder while Giselle slung her tote and overnight bag over her arm and walked with him through what was now only a fine mist.

As they reached the sheltered porch, she stopped short, putting her bags down on a bench beside the porch. "Before we go inside and face your family—"

"It'll probably only be my dad at this hour, unless my aunt Jenny's visiting. They've been seeing each other for a while now."

"His brother's widow?" Wincing, she said. "Sorry—I know that came out sounding as if I'm judging, but I suppose it's only natural that they might comfort each other."

"Don't be sorry. It's definitely taken a little getting used to for a lot of people. But my aunt and uncle Robert hadn't really been close for years before his death, and Mama Jen and my dad… My siblings and I all grew up thinking of our aunt Jenny as a second mother, since she helped with us so much after our own mom ditched us. They genuinely care about each other and make each other very happy."

"Then that's all that really matters, isn't it?" Giselle said quickly. "And what I'd *wanted* to say—before I put my foot in my mouth, at least, was thank you, for helping me before."

"For helping you?" He shook his head.

"The way you helped me get a handle on my breathing in the police cruiser, slowing me down so I could catch hold of my emotions. It really—it made a difference for me."

He nodded. "I could tell by the way you dropped off right afterward. You were clearly so worn down by everything you'd been thinking and feeling, you didn't have enough energy left to stay awake."

"You've been there, too, haven't you?" she asked quietly.

He hesitated, studying her for a long moment before admitting, "All too often, especially in that first year or two after the accident. I'd have these—I guess you'd call them episodes, where I'd find myself right back there, living through what happened. But I expect you'd know something about those, too, considering that we were both there."

Her heart bumped at her sternum, her mouth drying in an instant. "I—I definitely do know. It's funny...how I used to...used to imagine that a person...would have to be asleep to have night terrors."

He nodded, their gazes coming together, holding. She saw the sadness in them and heard his hard swallow before he spoke again.

"Ranchers are doers. We aren't talkers. So I threw myself into the things that needed doing around here on the ranch. And then there was the SAR volunteer work and the training. But it wasn't helping, not enough...because the better part of me was still back out on that lake."

In her mind's eye, she saw the diamond pattern of the water sparkling. Pictured the red speedboat—the one that was never identified afterward, despite extensive efforts by investigators and the Colton family's offer of a large cash reward for information—racing for the towrope. Saw Kate's head turn, in that last split second, the white of her teeth flashing with a scream that Giselle's memory had mercifully muted...

"My father came across me one day," Malcolm told her, turning to peer into the mist-softened darkness, "out in the working barn, messing with my lariat sort of idly when I figured there was no one else around. Only somehow that loop ended up sailing up across the top of one of the rafters—"

"You weren't planning to...?" she asked, a bright line of alarm cutting through the past like the sharp corner of a razor dragged across soft flesh at the deadly image of the dangling noose that took shape in her mind.

He shook his head and then sighed. "I can't honestly tell you *what* I was thinking because I don't rightly remember. I only know that my dad says he saw a blankness in my eyes that day when he spotted me. It must've scared the devil out of him, because as allergic as he's been his whole life to talking seriously about things like a person's feelings or, worse yet, mental health, he made a bunch of calls and pulled some serious strings. Never mentioned a single word about it to any of my siblings, as far as I know, but he got me into some intensive sessions starting that very afternoon."

A warm tide of relief spilled through her. "So you got the help you needed?"

"I got some valuable first aid—and eventually, what you might call a sort of toolkit with some techniques to help me break myself free when I start to spiral. I won't lie and tell you that it's filled in the giant crater that day on the lake left in my heart. But so far, it's kept me right here with my family—and this guy—" He reached down, to rub his dog's ears, "where I'm needed."

"That has to be nice, to know there's someone who still needs you," she said.

"You have a hell of a lot more to offer than you imagine," he assured her.

She made a scoffing sound. "Thanks for the vote of confidence, but I'm not really sure what anybody'd want from a washed-up ghostwriter whose social skills have dried up with her income."

"Don't you worry, Giselle," he said, reaching out to touch the side of her arm. "I'm pretty sure I've got some ideas for you on that front."

"As much as I appreciate your trusting me with your story—and your tip about the breathing techniques—I'm not looking to be anybody's pity project," she told him as she jerked her arm away. "Especially not somebody who can't help but remind me of the worst moments of my life."

MALCOLM TRIED TO continue the conversation, but Giselle only shook her head. Before he could think of anything more to change her mind, Pacer lunged toward a rattling at the door a moment before it opened.

"I thought I heard voices out here," said Malcolm's father, who was—Malcolm was grateful to see—still dressed in a pair of jeans and sweatshirt, though his silver-tinged brown hair was mussed as if he'd been relaxing with some TV. Quickly raking it back into some semblance of order, Buck Colton—a tall and hearty-looking man who remained fit from years of ranch work—frowned at Malcolm, his deeply tanned face crinkling. "I didn't realize you'd be back tonight, son—or bringing home a guest."

"You remember Giselle Dowling, don't you, Dad?" asked Malcolm. "You met her a few years back, at the party for Kate's and my engage—"

His father speared him with a shocked look. "You're dating Kate's *sister*?"

"Dating?" Giselle erupted, shaking her head with her eyes flared in what looked like horror. "No! It's bad enough I'm being forced to—absolutely not."

Malcolm felt himself wince down to the subatomic level as he realized the misunderstanding was entirely his fault. "Listen, Dad, what I told you earlier, about visiting a woman I've been seeing in Boise for the weekend. That was actually just a cover story."

"A cover for what? Spill it, son."

"Why?" Malcolm asked irritably. "So you can blab it to the entire family, the way you told everyone that I was seeing someone after I asked you to keep it quiet?"

His father frowned and waved off his complaint. "Serves you right for getting an old man's hopes up, however you want to sugarcoat it. So, are you going to tell me what this is all about or not?"

"Pacer and I took a little trip on our own to the mountains above the lake," Malcolm explained, "to try to pick up Acker's trail before the storm could wash it out."

His father stiffened. "So you lied to me and went off on your own to risk your neck? Do you have any idea what it would do to me, or to this family, if you'd ended up getting yourself hurt or worse out there? I thought we'd been through this before and you were past this sort of nonsense."

"It's not anything like that, Dad. I promise you it isn't," Malcolm said, shaking his head as he held his father's gaze. "I had no intention of getting myself killed. I only wanted to finally put an end to this hold Markus Acker's had on our family once and for all."

"All on your own, instead of acting as part of a team, like anybody with some damned sense?"

Malcolm grimaced before waving off the criticism. "You

can save the lecture about my impatience. I've already heard enough from Ajay. And Pacer and I *did* hit on Markus's trail, which we ended up following past the Dowlings' old family ski cabin, where I found Giselle living on her own."

For the first time, his father stopped and truly seemed to look at her. "That's odd. I understood that you've been out in California all this time. Writing those stories for the stars your sister was so proud of."

"I'm afraid I can't seem to make myself care about their dramas any longer," Giselle confessed, sounding defeated by the admission.

"Well, I never *could* see what was so interesting about them, so join the club," Buck said almost cheerfully before waving them both after him deeper into the entryway. "Why don't you come on inside with me? Could I get you something? A drink? A sandwich, or I've got a real nice lasagna that my Jenny brought by earlier. I could heat it up for you if you're up for a late dinner? If you don't mind my saying so, you two look like you've had quite the day."

Giselle started to demur, but Malcolm said, "I'll warm myself up some of that lasagna in a little bit, Dad, but I can make you something meat-free, Giselle. You do eat eggs, right? Or how about a cheese sandwich with some fresh lettuce and tomato?"

"As much as I appreciate the offer, I'm too exhausted to think about eating right now," she said, leading him to notice that she was looking somewhat pale. "Maybe just some water."

His father hurried off to the kitchen before returning with a full glass, sparkling with ice. Beckoning them both into the great room, he looked from her shaking hands, as she accepted his offering, to Malcolm, once they were all seated.

"Well, son?" his father asked, handing him a beer, the top

already popped off. "You going to fill me in? Did you ever find any sign of Markus?"

"About the time I reached Giselle's place, the storm's full fury hit." Malcolm raised the temptingly cold beer before setting it down again on the table at his elbow without drinking any of it.

"Thank goodness you were someplace safe, at least," his father said before nodding toward Malcolm's bandaged hand. "But what happened there?"

"A minor fall. I'll go and get it looked at tomorrow. But unfortunately, after leaving Giselle's property, Acker encountered one of her older neighbors."

"Claudette Hogan," Giselle supplied, her voice thick with emotion. "He—he murdered her. An old friend of my grandmother's..."

"I'm so sorry—and so damned furious. Forgive my language, but that sorry excuse for a man should have been put in prison—or put down like a mad dog—months ago." Malcolm's father leapt up from the recliner where he'd been seated, his big fists knotting in impotent frustration as he paced the room. "First, he took my brother, and then he—how many others have to die or have their lives turned upside-down before he's finally stopped?"

"I know, Dad. I know," Malcolm said, feeling utterly undone by his father's grief as he, too, stood. "It's why I had to try to find him. I couldn't bear to let it go on any longer. But now he's killed another woman, and he has my truck to get around in."

"Your truck?"

"It's my own fault, I'm afraid. But both Ajay and I agreed that there was no way Giselle should stay alone up there so close to where the murder took place, not knowing if Acker might still be holed up somewhere nearby for some reason."

"No, of course not," his father said, giving her a sympathetic look. "Heaven only knows we have plenty of extra room here."

"I won't impose on you long," she said. "In the morning, I'll start looking for someplace else to—"

"You couldn't impose if you wanted to, young lady," Buck Colton insisted, his rich voice resonating in the high-ceiled great-room. "As far as I'm concerned, you're practically family. You know, we all thought the world of Kate, and she'd tell anyone who'd listen about her little sister. She was so proud of you. You know that, don't you? Not just of what you did and the people you rubbed shoulders with, but who you are inside."

"Th-thank you for that." Rising from her seat, Giselle stared at him, her eyes shimmering with moisture.

Malcolm's father surprised him by going to her and, without a moment's hesitation, enfolding her in one of the same dad hugs he might have given Lizzy.

But Giselle stiffened in response, clearly unused to anyone making such an assumption about her state of mind. Before Malcolm could warn his dad to back off and give her space, however, she crumpled against him, responding exactly as his sister might have. And sure enough, his father signaled for Malcolm to pass over the box of tissues, reassuring her in that way of his that had so often made him and his siblings believe that, despite whatever seemingly impossible odds were stacked against them, tomorrow might somehow turn out to be a better day.

Chapter Eight

Lying low didn't come easily for Markus Acker. By nature, he was a man who preferred getting out and interacting with his fellow humans, using the gifts he had been given, namely patience, intelligence, and cunning, to transform himself into whatever it took to convince the gullible to devote themselves body and soul—and bank accounts—to his needs.

Only upon the rarest of occasions, such as when his greed outstripped his caution, would Markus resort to riskier measures. Regrettably, in recent months, several such incidents had led to certain acts. Acts resulting in a string of deaths that law enforcement had eventually linked to him, just as he was certain that they soon would today's.

Markus didn't have it in him to regret the resulting fatalities themselves. After all, who was he to know how much longer any of the lives he'd terminated—he thought again of that frail-looking, pathetic woman, her hair more white than gray—would have lasted anyway, or whether any of his "victims" had been especially happy? What he *did* regret was that these so-called "murders" had forced him to abandon the comfortable life he'd worked so hard to build and hide out like some filthy desperado, sleeping in a musty cabin and surviving on old canned goods.

The thought was especially maddening since he'd been so

close to reaching his very own Wilderness Chapel of Contemplation. Located on one of the small, wooded islands a short distance off the southern shoreline of Blackbird Lake, the spartan chapel was, by design, neither connected to the grid nor a place of creature comfort. Yet the moss-covered hillside structure was at least stocked with the basic necessities of life. And more importantly, Markus suspected that the last penitent he'd sent there—to contemplate the wisdom of questioning one of his directives—would still be waiting faithfully, completely unaware of recent events and eager for his chance to do whatever was necessary to once more regain favor...

But Markus had opted against that choice for now, fearing that the authorities might have somehow permeated the layers of false entities he'd used to hide his ownership and set up some sort of remote surveillance. Instead, he'd broken into a seemingly abandoned cabin, where he'd bided his time for two long weeks. He might have remained there for a little longer, but earlier that day, two powerfully built men wearing flannels, jeans, and work boots had shown up towing a trailer loaded with the kind of heavy equipment that made it clear they'd come to do extensive property cleanup. With his supplies dwindling and the two men looking too capable to risk taking on single-handedly, Markus had hurriedly shoved what he had into his backpack and slipped out the back way undetected in the hope of finding a better place to wait for the authorities to decide that he must have long since moved on already.

Yet even though he'd finally secured himself a decent vehicle, leaving the Owl Creek area wasn't something he was prepared to do. Instead, he had to find a way to recover what he rightfully had coming to him, what he desperately needed if he didn't want to waste years building himself back up from absolutely nothing.

He still felt hurt and angry, recalling the betrayal that had ended with Jessie Colton, who had vowed so many times that her true loyalty was to him rather than the wealthy family she had turned her back on. She'd even gone so far as to unwittingly assist him with a scheme to defraud them in the past. What he'd imagined to be his perfect control, however, had shattered the moment she'd chosen to catch one of the bullets he had meant for her daughter and her lover, who'd been scheming to bring down everything he'd spent years building.

His lingering rage over her betrayal, however, had little to do with any real attachment he'd felt for the woman he'd planned all along to abandon once she had served her purpose. Instead, he'd been furious to have been cut off from access to the small go-bag he'd hidden inside one of her most prized possessions, which contained not only the money he'd intended to use to escape the country, but his most precious asset as well. Unlike the poorer quality, easily discernable fake he'd had made for Jessie, his own nearly undetectable falsified passport was his only ticket to starting afresh in a civilized overseas destination. Once there, he would be free to access the offshore accounts where he'd put away the bulk of what he'd stolen from the trusting zealots who'd so foolishly signed over their investments, inheritances, and retirement accounts to his "ministry" over the years.

The real question was, how could he gain access to the home he and Jessie had once shared—*her* home—to retrieve the go-bag from the hiding place he was praying the authorities had missed in any search they may have conducted? Was it possible that his secret remained in place, just waiting for him to reclaim it—or could Jessie's heirs have already begun the process of removing their mother's old furnishings, perhaps inadvertently carrying out his treasure along with them?

Alarming as the thought was, Markus vowed to do whatever it took to find out—and gain the cooperation of any Colton that might be needed. After all, for a man already wanted for as many serious crimes as he was, why pause at something as inconsequential as kidnapping and another paltry murder?

As MALCOLM STOOD drinking coffee at the kitchen counter the following morning, the phone in his back pocket started buzzing. Hoping for an update from Ajay or any one of his relations or SAR teammates who might be involved with the hunt for Acker, he frowned seeing Sebastian Cross's name flash across the screen.

It wasn't that Malcolm didn't have a great deal of respect for the founder of Crosswinds Training, where Malcolm had spent so much time putting the broken pieces of his shattered soul back together while learning about trailing with Pacer. Still, he'd hoped to have a few days' grace before Sebastian called in the puppy training chit that Ajay had evidently already handed to him.

Dredging up some semblance of manners, Malcolm mumbled a good morning and asked after Sebastian's fiancée Ruby—who was one of Malcolm's favorite cousins—and their infant son.

"Ruby's great, and Sawyer's an amazing kid," Sebastian said, boasting. "What a set of lungs that boy has, even at two a.m."

"I have to wonder if Ruby's as enthusiastic about that part as you are," Malcolm said, grinning at the image of Sebastian, with his shaggy blond hair, lumberjack's build, and beard, as doting partner and father.

"She was *very* enthusiastic when I took him for a drive last night and let her get some extra shut-eye."

"I'll bet she was, especially when she had to get up early

to open her vet clinic. So what can I do for you this morning?" As if Malcolm couldn't guess.

"Heard you and Pacer had a pretty rough day yesterday."

"So you've spoken to Ajay?"

"Lizzy called Ruby to warn her about Markus and give us an update," Sebastian said. "And then Ajay texted me something about you getting injured."

"I'm going to need to have my left hand x-rayed, but I doubt it'll slow me down much."

"I understand you had a brush with Acker, too. And lost your truck as well. Tough break," Sebastian said, sounding genuinely sympathetic.

Malcolm stalked toward a window overlooking the paddock where his big buckskin quarter horse, Sundance, grazed near the fence line next to a pinto mare named Ivy. "Not nearly as bad for me as the poor, innocent woman who caught Acker's bullet."

"I was sorry to hear that. Did you know her?"

"Not personally," Malcolm said, "but she was a friend and neighbor of Kate's and Giselle's. I ran into Giselle while Pacer and I were working the scent, and we—we discovered the victim together."

"I'm sorry," Sebastian told him. "I remember Giselle Dowling a little, back from when we went to school together—and I understand she's suffered a lot of losses over the years."

"Yeah. She's completely on her own now," Malcolm explained, "so she's staying at my family's ranch until it's safe for her to go back up to that cabin."

"Sounds like a really good idea until Acker's in custody. Your sister said she's warning everybody in the family that he's on the move in your truck."

"I'm glad to hear that Lizzy's got that covered," Malcolm said.

"So if you're feeling up to it later, with your hand and all," Sebastian said, "I was wondering if you might swing by Crosswinds this afternoon. I've got somebody here who wants to meet with you."

"Let me guess, there's a problem child among your current crop of pups who could use my special one-on-one attention."

"I'm definitely hoping you can help us salvage the time and training we've already put into this one, but I wouldn't call so early about just that."

Hearing something in his voice, Malcolm set his mug down on the counter. "What's going on, Sebastian? Have you heard something about the search for Markus that I haven't?"

"Nothing except that they're still looking high and low. It's something else. I almost hate to bring this up, with everything your family's had going on this past year, but I knew you wouldn't appreciate being blindsided."

Malcolm felt himself tense. "Come on and spit it out, man. Just tell me what's up."

"It's about that flyer you've had posted on the back bulletin board at Crosswinds these past few years—the one offering a reward for information on the red boat that caused the accident."

Recognizing the bitter taste of disappointment, Malcolm let him in on the reality he'd been living with for years now. "If someone's come to you with information, I need to warn you. I'm still getting calls on those flyers a few times a month. Some of the callers mean well, even when it turns out the boats they're describing aren't remotely similar to the one I had drawn up for that graphic we used. Others are just tragedy junkies who get some kind of sick pleasure trying to pry details about Kate's death out of me."

"Why didn't you tell anyone you've been dealing with that

garbage? A few of us could've helped you screen the calls, saved you a whole lot of pain and aggravation—"

"This was my responsibility, my fiancée, and I wasn't about to pawn it off on anybody else. I couldn't," Malcolm explained. "What if I did and someone who hadn't been there missed some critical clue that I would've known was legit?"

"I see what you mean," Sebastian said. "Still, I'm sorry you've had to deal with clueless and insensitive callers."

"Those haven't been nearly as bad as the scammers, once word got out about the reward my family was offering. After that, so-called tips starting flooding in from everywhere— wild stories meant to cash in."

"That's terrible, but I'm positive that what I heard yesterday is no scammer," Sebastian told him. "Just hear me out."

"I'm listening."

"Have you met Kelsie over here yet? She's this teenager we've had working part-time at Crosswinds, mostly just kennel cleaning and dog-walking for the moment, but the kid's got aspirations."

"The girl with the reddish-blond hair," Malcolm said, recalling a freckled face and friendly smile. "Seems like a good kid."

"She is, but the sorry excuse for a car she drives is broken down again this week, so she's been begging rides from family members. Her uncle stopped by yesterday afternoon to say hello and to thank me for giving her the job. Apparently, it's been a lot of help after a bad stretch she went through after losing her best friend to cancer last year."

"That's damned rough."

"It surely is. But anyway, the moment the uncle spotted your flyer hanging on our bulletin board, the guy did a double take and walked straight over to tap at it, saying he'd seen that boat that very day. A customer had trailered it to his shop. Did I mention Kelsie's uncle is a boat mechanic at a repair shop over in Hadley?" Sebastian said, naming a small town about thirty miles north of Blackbird Lake.

"You did not," Malcolm said, his mouth going bone dry.

"He told me this customer had bought the boat from a storage facility that auctioned the contents of a unit after the rent hadn't been paid in quite some time."

"So *that's* what happened to the boat," Malcolm blurted, his heart accelerating. "The son of a bitch driving it crossed the county line to put it into storage. To deliberately hide it because he absolutely *knew* that he'd sent the raft with Kate and Giselle on it flying."

"It sure as hell sounds that way to me," Sebastian said. "I want you to know Kelsie's uncle took the flyer and headed to the sheriff's office to report that the boat's in his shop now."

"Where's this shop exactly?" Malcolm asked.

"Do you think you should wait until you hear from the investigators, man? You wouldn't want to do anything to possibly compromise their investigation, would you? Or what if your showing up somehow tipped off the boat's original owners and led them to move it somewhere else—or maybe even try to do something more drastic like destroy it? You don't want to mess things up now, when we've got the first real lead we've had in more than three years."

With adrenaline's drumbeat in his skull, it was hard to think straight, but Malcolm heard some sense in what Sebastian was saying.

"No, I don't," Malcolm said, "but I won't sit around and wait forever for the sheriff's department investigators to pick up the phone and call me, either. I'm heading straight over there this morning to find out what they're doing to track down the men who were in the boat that day."

Sebastian waited a beat before saying, "You probably aren't going to want to hear this, but at the risk of hacking you off, I'm going to offer you a little friendly advice right now."

"If you're going to counsel patience, I've been waiting for more than three years already, watching that department kick the case from a retiring detective with one foot out the door, who could barely be bothered to check out the local marinas, to a rookie detective who started out sounding determined but eventually quit returning any of my calls."

"I can only imagine how frustrating that must have been."

"Frustrating's not the half of it," Malcolm said. "But I only made things worse when I tried asking Ajay to give Danvers, the detective working on the accident investigation, a call. You know, to offer any assistance that the Owl Creek police could give with the investigation."

"I take it that didn't help."

"Made things even worse, in fact," Malcolm explained. "The sheriff, apparently, is super-sensitive to jurisdictional boundaries. He didn't at all appreciate an outside agency trying to muscle in on his turf."

"I can't imagine how aggravating all this must have been," Sebastian said. "But still, for right now, I'd advise taking a couple of deep breaths and going to get your hand seen to. Then swing by here if you're up for it, and we can work on smoothing the rough edges off this wild bunch of puppies I've got—especially this wrecking ball of a ringleader who keeps getting everyone into trouble. You can even bring Giselle along if you'd like."

"Why do I get the feeling you're just trying to distract me?"

"Because you need to give this detective half a chance to check out this fresh lead before you go charging and put him on the defensive again. Otherwise, you and I both know the case may end up getting pushed back again—or maybe not happening at all."

"Fine. I'll give Detective Danvers *one* day," Malcolm agreed, seeing the sense of what he was saying. "But if I don't hear from him by tomorrow morning, then he's definitely going to have me breathing down his neck."

AFTER CAREFULLY STICKING to the most obscure back roads to navigate his way there, Markus passed by the late Jessie Colton's home several times to assure himself that all the neighbors and their children had left for work or school for the day. He was doubly grateful to spot no new signs on the house's front lawn boasting of a new security system, either, and best of all, no parked vehicles to give any indication that anyone might be present. Still, he remained wary, checking for any bowls and toys that might indicate the presence of a dog, which would require elimination. Once he'd satisfied himself that none was present, he hopped the solid stockade-style back fence from the next street over and then attempted to peer through several rear windows to get a look inside the house.

But it was little use, since someone had taken care to close every window covering, making it impossible to peer inside. Could it have been the authorities, after ripping out the false bottom panel he'd built up underneath his one-time lover's supposedly valuable antique Victrola record player?

Telling himself he was being paranoid, Markus went to the back door. Someone had replaced the old lock, making short work of Acker's plan to fish out the hidden spare key from its fake rock in the garden. Annoyed, he ended up smashing a rear window panel instead before carefully reaching for the latch inside and letting himself in that way.

For the first few minutes he stood listening, his blood rushing as he worried that he'd made so much noise, it was possible that someone he'd missed might have heard it and called in a report. Deciding his best chance would be to get in and out of the house quickly, he began to look around at cardboard boxes stacked around the kitchen counters. Most bore labels such as "Kitchen Utensils—Women's Shelter" or "Food Bank—Canned Goods," though someone had already removed the table and chairs from the small dinette area.

His gut churning, he headed for the family room. There, he spotted more boxes, where a sofa, television, and a pair of end tables had once been, though the leather recliner and coffee table remained in place. Praying that the Coltons hadn't given away the Victrola as well, he remembered how Jessie had always insisted the thing was practically an heirloom and assured himself that not even a family with Colton money would simply toss a valuable antique without a second thought. Still, he sprinted for the bedroom, his lungs burning with panic as he raced up the stairs…

Only to find the record player long gone…along with his traveling money and his precious passport.

Shouting with rage, he assured himself that he would make them *all* pay unless he could quickly find some way to retrieve it. And he would damned well see that they paid interest on the pain and suffering they'd cost him.

DRESSED FOR THE day in a pair of joggers and a casual turquoise top, Giselle followed the smell of coffee downstairs to find Malcolm in the kitchen a few minutes after eight, his back to her as he stood over a cutting board covered with fruit at the oversized kitchen island. But his knife was idle as he gazed out the nearest window—staring out into the middle distance. Probably brooding over whatever Markus Acker might be up to, Giselle imagined, or his own failure to find and stop the man before he'd killed again.

Deciding not to start the day by bringing up a sore subject, she simply greeted him. "Good morning."

Malcolm turned and smiled at her, freshly shaven and

wearing a dark gray Henley and faded jeans that fit his tall, lean body all too well. "Morning. You're up a lot earlier than I expected. I always remember you sleeping in until all hours when you came to visit Kate."

"That was mostly because of our marathon late-night gab sessions." Giselle smiled wistfully, thinking she'd give anything to experience such bliss again. "Besides, after sleeping in that dark cave of my cabin bedroom for so long, that eastward-facing guest suite and this beautiful, bright sunshine definitely woke me up this morning."

"Guess I should've shown you how to close those automated curtains last night."

"And miss the sight of all those gorgeous horses and cows grazing and one of the cowboys riding out at dawn? No, thanks," she said, smiling.

Humor sparked in Malcolm's green eyes. "So you're into cowboys these days, are you?"

"Purely from an aesthetic standpoint, so don't get any weird ideas involving awkward introductions to your ranch's hired hands."

"We have a strict policy against the harassment of our employees anyway, miss," he told her with a tip of an imaginary Stetson, "so I'm afraid you're out of luck there."

When she laughed at his delivery, he said, "All kidding aside, I hope you're feeling a bit better this morning."

She nodded. "As unreal as everything that happened still seems, a shower and a good night's sleep certainly have me feeling a lot more human, thanks."

"You'll feel better still once we've gotten some caffeine and breakfast in you. Let me start the kettle for you first…" He walked over to the stove and turned on a burner underneath.

"Thanks."

"No problem. And I've been cutting up some apples and

berries to go with the yogurt and muffins we had on hand, if that sounds like something you might like for breakfast. Or I could whip up a veggie omelet for you. It'd just take me a few minutes."

She raised a hand. "Honestly, Malcolm, I stopped listening after *muffins*. Although the fruit and tea sound good, too. Will your dad be joining us as well?"

"He's off breaking the news to Aunt Jenny in person about this latest murder. But the truth is, those two can barely seem to stay apart these days."

"And you're okay with this?"

"How could I not be? My brothers and my sister and I were all so little when our mother left us high and dry, but my father was the best single parent and role model you can imagine. And as much as I always liked Uncle Robert, Mama Jen deserved a man who truly appreciated her. Someone who'd never dream of sneaking around behind her back with her selfish sister…"

"Are you telling me that your uncle Robert and your mom were…*involved* back in the day?" Giselle made a face at the idea of such a horrible betrayal.

Malcolm nodded. "We've only recently learned that after my mother left my family, she moved to a nearby town and secretly gave birth to two children fathered by my uncle."

"So you're telling me that you and your cousins have a couple of half-siblings that you knew nothing about? Have you had any contact?"

"We *did* meet after Uncle Robert's death—and to everyone's surprise, both Nate and Sarah are amazing people. We now consider them our sister and brother and look forward to getting to know them even better."

"That's wonderful, and I'm very happy your father and your aunt have each other to help them cope with whatever feelings that must've brought up."

"So am I, but enough with the family history for now. What kind of tea would you like?" He showed her several boxes from a cupboard.

"Ooh, that Irish breakfast tea, please," she said, "maybe with a little honey in it, if you have some."

He pulled out a bag and dropped it in a mug for her before pouring the steaming water over it. "You've got it. I'll just finish putting the fruit onto our breakfast tray, and we can sit right here and eat at these barstools if you're okay with casual dining. Otherwise, we can go into the dining—"

"Oh, please," Giselle said. "After eating on my own in my cabin for the better part of three years. I'd happily have my breakfast sitting on the floor."

"I'm sure Pacer would be *very* enthusiastic about that idea." Malcolm nodded toward the dog, who had planted himself in the spot with the best view of the food Malcolm had been preparing. "But if you want a real shot at your muffin, I'd definitely suggest the counter."

Giselle hadn't been eating long before she noticed that Malcolm was mainly just sipping at his coffee while barely picking at his food.

"When I came out here," she said, "I couldn't help noticing how worried you looked. And now—" She gestured to his nearly untouched plate. "This isn't like you. Has that hand gotten worse this morning?"

"It's definitely bruised and swollen enough that I still plan on going to the Express Medical Clinic to get it checked out, but after keeping it wrapped and elevated and icing it off and on last night, the pain's not bad at all."

"So what's bothering you, then?" She shook her head. "You haven't gotten bad news, have you? Acker hasn't hurt anyone else, has he?"

"No, thank goodness it's not that. But I've had a couple of calls before you got up, starting with my cousin, Fletcher Colton."

"I remember you mentioning he was at Claudette's yesterday." She shook her head. "But I don't believe I've actually met him."

"He was with the Boise Police Department back around the time Kate and I became engaged, so you probably wouldn't have run into him back in the day, either. That's a shame because he's a great guy. Practically another brother to me."

"I've heard you say the same about more than one of your cousins, you know—except for the women, who are all 'practically sisters,'" she teased.

"We did all grow up thick as thieves," he admitted, "but that doesn't make it any less true. But getting back to Fletcher, he came home from Boise last year and was hired on by the Owl Creek PD as lead detective. I'm not sure how he pulled that off, considering that his father was one of Acker's victims, but somehow, Fletcher talked his way onto the joint task force."

"He sounds like one very determined person."

"He's definitely that when he sets his sights on a goal," Malcolm agreed. "And right now, nothing's more important to him than hunting down the man who's caused our family so much pain, which—" He drew an audible breath before grimacing "—he's told me in no uncertain terms I'm to leave to the professionals from now on so they won't end up having to waste their time running to my rescue."

Giselle couldn't help but smile. "I'm liking him already. So did he share any updates on what's going on with the search for Acker?"

Malcolm nodded. "Unfortunately, there's been no sign of either him or my stolen truck so far, so they figure he's most likely found himself another vacation place to break into in the area."

"Or is it possible that Acker's gone back to wherever he might've been hiding before he headed toward my place earlier?" she asked. "After all, he did manage to hang out someplace for two weeks undetected, so it must have been pretty well hidden."

"I'm sure the task force will be considering all possibilities. They've put a statewide BOLO out on my truck, alerting every law enforcement agency that the driver's armed and dangerous. They're also bringing in extra manpower for door-to-door checks of as many properties in the general area as they can."

"I only hope the searchers stay safe," she said.

"That makes two of us," Malcolm agreed. "But as Fletcher reminded me, this is what law enforcement trains for, so now's the time for us to sit back and leave them to it."

Peering at him curiously, Giselle said, "You mentioned that you'd gotten more than one call. Was the other anything important?"

"I...ah...it was just Sebastian Cross, the owner of Crosswinds, wondering when I could come help out with that litter he's been training."

"I didn't realize that's Sebastian's place. I remember him from back in high school," she said, momentarily distracted from his hesitation by old memories. "He was a good guy, from what I can recall."

"Still is—and part of the family now, too, since he's engaged to my cousin, Ruby. They have a baby boy as well."

"Is there anyone in or around Owl Creek your family *doesn't* claim as a relation?" she asked. "At this rate, you'll need to book the football stadium for your family reunions."

Laughing he said, "I'm sure it seems that way at times. And anyway, Sebastian remembered you as well. In fact, he mentioned that you'd be welcome to come with me today if you'd like, while we work with the puppies."

"That sounds like fun, thanks," she said, flashing a quick smile before zeroing in on his odd behavior. "But I can't help suspecting that's not what has you sitting here brooding over a plateful of delicious food.... Is there something else, Malcolm?"

"Don't you think I have enough to worry about, between Markus being out there doing heaven knows what in my truck and my status with the SAR team now being in question?" He frowned, his gaze avoiding hers. "Add to that, my aching hand, and maybe I've got more on my mind than eating."

"You're sure there wasn't something else? Something it might help to talk out?" she said, unable to recall the last time she'd seen him so grumpy. "Because, if you're conflicted about hosting me here like this, without Kate around to act as a buffer..."

Tossing his unused napkin over his food like a white flag, he stood to stare down at her. "Why on earth would you think that? I invited you here, didn't I?"

"Yes, but you probably felt obligated because of the circumstances. But now, perhaps, it feels awkward."

"The only thing that's awkward is you picking apart my eating habits," he insisted. "I'm *fine* with having you around. Stay as long as you like."

She felt her brows rise. "And I thought *my* social skills were rusty."

"You're absolutely..." He gusted out a sigh. "You're right. I'm being an idiot—not to mention a terrible host. I didn't mean to make you feel unwelcome."

"So why *did* you, then?" she demanded.

He drew an audible breath. "Because about an hour ago, I found out that someone might have found the boat."

She blinked reflexively. "What boat? Wait. You don't mean the...?"

"The *red* boat," he said, pausing to let the significance sink in. "It hasn't been confirmed yet, but apparently, it's been hidden away for years, inside a storage container north of the county line. After the bill went unpaid for some time, however, it was purchased by a bidder who took it to a marina for a tune-up. The boat mechanic ran across one of my flyers and reported it last night."

"The boat that killed Kate..." Giselle's mouth went so dry, she could barely get the words out. "Why didn't you tell me right away?"

He shook his head. "I'm still trying to wrap my brain around it. Plus, Sebastian—he's the one who told me—talked me into promising to give the sheriff's department detective on the case some time to investigate before immediately jumping down their throats and demanding information."

"That—that actually makes sense," she said. "But this— don't you see what this could mean? We could actually end up learning who the driver was—maybe even seeing him charged with leaving the scene—or even—"

"Don't, please. This was exactly why I didn't want to tell you." Malcolm shook his head. "I didn't want to get you too excited for something that might never happen."

"What do you mean, *too* excited?" She stared at him. "This could be it, Malcolm. What I've dreamed about forever—justice for my sister."

"The only real justice would be in giving her—and all of us—our lives back."

"Believe me, I'm as painfully aware of that as you are," she said. "But I can't—*we* can't—have that, so we'll have to focus on seeing the person responsible for hitting us held accountable for the damage he did. Making him face up to what he cost us after slithering away and hiding for all these years."

"Then we'll do our very best to move the authorities in that direction. But don't be shocked if we encounter some major disappointments along the way."

"Considering what we've both lived through during the past few years," Giselle said, "disappointments are nothing we can't handle. Especially now that we have real hope that someone might finally be named, in a court of law, the responsible party in Kate's death. Someone who can shoulder a portion of the blame we've been spending these past few years heaping on ourselves."

Chapter Nine

Later that morning, as they waited for his X-rays to be read at the minor emergency center, Malcolm peered over at Giselle, who was wrapping up yet another phone call with a representative from her insurance company, and wondered if she'd been right. Had it only been the sheriff department's failure to name anyone who might be legally held accountable that had left each of them trapped in a prison of self-blame for so long?

Malcolm had to admit that, for a long time, he'd harbored resentment against Giselle as well for bringing along her useless boyfriend Kyle on that visit, especially after she'd returned to her life as if nothing had happened. Realizing now how incredibly wrong he'd been about that, however, made it impossible to hold onto any trace of that anger any longer. Instead, he felt only compassion—along with a tenderness he'd never seen coming and a bone-deep desire to protect her from further pain.

Easy there, he thought, warning himself that whatever he was feeling was less about Giselle herself—as beautiful, bright, and appealing as she was—than the many small ways in which she reminded him of her sister. *You're only missing Kate, that's all.* And as for why his thoughts kept returning to the way it had felt to hold and comfort Giselle, or how he couldn't quit thinking about those two quick squeezes she had given him, he vowed that the last thing he was going to do was embarrass her—or disgrace himself—by treating her as a substitute for the only woman that he wanted.

He waited for her to finish her call before asking, "Any news about your car?"

She nodded. "They're going to need me to go back to take a bunch of photos from all different angles for their app and then input the vehicle identification number. But according to the person I spoke to, as soon as I've done that, the process should go quite smoothly, and I should receive a payout for the claim—assuming they decide the vehicle is totaled."

"Considering what it looked like, I can't imagine any other outcome."

"The woman on the phone said that if my description was even close to accurate, she had no doubt I'd have my payout in four to six weeks."

"I guess you'll need to start thinking about a replacement vehicle, then."

"Oh, joy," she said grimly. "Car shopping."

"That bad, eh?"

She rolled her eyes. "You try doing it while female. Some of those salespeople are still living in the Stone Age. Last time, I ended up going through four dealerships before I finally found one who deserved my business."

"I could go with you this time to run interference," he said. "I actually kind of enjoy the whole horse-trading aspect."

"As much as I appreciate the offer," she said, splashes of color coming to her cheeks, "what does cowering behind some random man teach these people about how to earn the business of all the women who are coming in there to make their own financial decisions?"

"So I'm some random man now?" he asked, biting back a smile as he called her on it.

"Not to me you aren't, but as far as those jokers are con-cerned," she said before frowning and shaking her head. "The point is, I'd rather walk out on those who refuse to treat me with respect or give me what my research has told me is a fair price. Then I'll call their managers and let them know exactly why they've lost my business after I've closed a deal elsewhere."

"It's good to hear you sounding like yourself again," he said honestly.

She shook her head. "How do you mean?"

"Yesterday, I have to admit you had me worried. Wor-ried you'd forgotten how to stand up and fight for the kind of life that you deserve."

"I believe it's possible that I had, at least a little," she con-ceded, her expression growing somber. "But sitting in that cabin blaming myself for everything and beating my head against the wall hasn't changed anything in more than three years, so maybe it's time I tried a new approach."

Before he could offer to help in any way he could, she turned her head toward the sound of approaching footsteps. Dr. Herrera, who'd examined him earlier, was back, looking eager to discuss Malcolm's imaging results.

Giselle rose, saying, "I'll give you two some privacy."

"You're fine staying," Malcolm said. Turning to look at the older woman to make sure that she'd heard, he added, "I take it you have the report back on my hand?"

Dr. Herrera nodded. "The news is just as I suspected. You have a fracture near the knuckle with some ligament involvement."

"Is that serious?" he asked.

"An orthopedist will need to monitor your healing and see that you complete the correct exercises to restore full mobility, but I don't see any reason to believe you shouldn't have a complete recovery."

"That's good to hear." Malcolm felt relief wash over him.

"Meanwhile, I'm going to give you an immobilizer splint that will protect your fingers, hand, and wrist, so you should be able to stay active, with some reasonable care," she said. "I'm also sending you home with printed instructions for managing any pain and swelling, along with a prescription for a painkiller to have available should you need it."

A short time later, they left the clinic, his left hand feeling stiff and awkward—but reasonably comfortable—inside of the well-padded splint.

After a quick stop by the pharmacy to drop off his prescription—though he suspected he might not end up needing anything stronger than the over-the-counter medication he'd been using so far—Malcolm climbed back behind the wheel of a dark-blue pickup that bore white door decals marking it as ranch property. "What do you think? Shall we run up to take those photos of your SUV so we can get the clock ticking on your insurance claim?"

"Do you think it's safe to go back up there?" she asked.

"I can't imagine Acker having any reason to return there, of all places, since he'd have to figure law enforcement would be thickest around a place where he committed a murder only yesterday."

"I suppose that's true," she said, still sounding uncertain.

"I'll go ahead and text Ajay, though, just to make sure they've finished processing any evidence." Malcolm pulled out his cell.

When Ajay didn't immediately respond, Malcolm told himself not to take it personally. "He's probably swamped right now—or maybe even catching a few hours of shut-eye if he ended up working through the night."

"The pictures can wait for now. Let's distract ourselves with something else, then," Giselle suggested before her blue eyes brightened. "I vote for puppies."

He couldn't help but smile. "Why am I not surprised?"

"I mean, unless you're not feeling up to it…with your poor hand…" she added.

"I'm fine, and I'll tell you what. I'll make you a deal. How about we grab a quick lunch first at one of these places around here?"

"I could go for a veggie burger," she said, "but only if you'll let me steal half of your fries."

"You've got yourself a deal." He smiled, recalling how Kate would often say the same thing. "Afterward, we'll grab my prescription and then drive out to Crosswinds. That way, we'll already be most of the way to the lake, if Ajay gives us the go-ahead on the photos."

"Either way, I'll get to hang out with some *puppies*," Giselle practically sang, "so consider me all-in."

Located on a beautiful, fenced property overlooking the mountains along a private road that bore his family's name, Sebastian Cross's Crosswinds Training facility consisted of a neatly painted kennel building, along with outdoor training and play areas. After saying hello to Malcolm, the tall and bearded Sebastian turned a welcoming smile on Giselle. "It's great seeing you again after all these years. My fiancée is one of your biggest fans."

Assuming he was merely being polite, Giselle nodded. "That's kind of her to say."

"Seriously. I'm not just blowing smoke here," Sebastian said, brushing longish, dark-blond hair from his eyes. "If I could talk you into signing one of her copies that I managed to sneak off her bookshelf before you leave today, it would earn me some very serious rewards."

Giselle flashed a smile. "Anything for the man who controls access to the puppies."

Malcolm chuckled. "I tried telling her we're here to work with them and not just to play and cuddle."

"Come on, Mal," Sebastian scolded him. "You know we always turn them out ahead of their training session to blow off a bit of steam before we get them started so they can give us their full focus. A few minutes of fun surely isn't going to determine which of our potential future detection dogs will make the cut."

"Sure, make *me* out to be the bad guy," Malcolm said. "But don't complain when she's lining them up for belly rubs and using her phone to order them all matching sweaters. She's already got my Pacer half-convinced to forget about the search-and-rescue business and start a new life as her personal lapdog."

Sebastian laughed. "There's not a chance in the world you could ever keep that workaholic dog of yours from trailing."

"You talked about the puppies making the cut," Giselle said to Sebastian. "Do you mean to say that not all of them can be taught to do what they're bred for?"

"They can all be *taught*, but unfortunately, not every one of them will necessarily have the temperament or develop their skills sufficiently to measure up to our professional standards."

"So then what happens to them?" she asked, hoping they didn't end up in some scary animal shelter.

"Since they've already had so much training time invested in them to get to the point where they are, we first reach out to other programs where we feel their individual skills and energies might be a good fit. For example, right now, out of the litter of eight we're working with, I see three that probably won't be suitable for scent detection."

"That many?" she asked.

"Considering how high Crosswinds' standards are, a pass

rate of greater than fifty percent would be exceptional," Malcolm assured her.

Nodding in agreement, Sebastian explained, "Two of the others have qualities that I believe could make them excellent candidates to become service dogs for the hearing impaired, so I'm going to have them evaluated by a partner program to see if they'd be interested in continuing their training."

"And the third?"

When Sebastian hesitated, Malcolm said, "They can't all be rock stars."

"But if anybody can keep this hot mess of a puppy from washing out completely, I have faith that Malcolm here can help me do it," Sebastian told her. "This guy's definitely the Goofball Puppy Whisperer."

Looking around, she asked, "So when do I get to meet these pups? Those aren't any of them, are they?" She pointed out a trio of fawn to reddish-brown colored dogs with a shepherd look to them who were romping and wrestling around one fenced area.

"Oh, no. Those big fellows—they're Belgian Malinois— are just having a little free time after their last training session. Let me go put them up. Then I'll bring out the Puppy Pack."

"Sounds good," Malcolm said, turning to Giselle as Sebastian walked off and whistled for the big dogs, who instantly responded to his signal.

"Wow," she said. "Those dogs are beautiful, but a little intimidating when they turn and run straight toward a person."

"They're a little intense for the average person but amazingly driven and focused when they're given a job to do," he said. "But don't worry. The puppies we'll be working with are a whole lot smaller."

"I assumed they'd be larger breeds as well, like these dogs or Pacer."

"Most people think of big dogs when they imagine working dogs," Malcolm said. "But in some cases, there are advantages to using smaller, less intimidating breeds in public-facing settings like airports and other transportation hubs. What really matters is that the animal is highly responsive to training and has a great nose. That's why, in this particular instance, Sebastian decided to try—"

"Oh, my goodness!" she laughed as a wagging, low-to-the-ground tricolor blur of motion raced and tumbled over each other as they entered the play area. Just about the cutest blur of motion she had ever seen. "Are those..." She leaned forward, trying to focus on the flopping, reddish-brown ears "...beagle babies?"

As he led her toward the gate so they could step into the enclosure, he said, "They're a little older than they look—about five months now—because they're on the smaller side, even for beagles. And wait'll you get a load of the runt. Livewire that she is, she's extra-tiny."

"So which one is she?" Giselle asked as Malcolm opened the gate and quickly ushered her inside before stepping in behind her and closing off the potential escape route.

It turned out to be a good thing that he moved quickly, because the moment the pups noticed their arrival, they stampeded in Giselle and Malcolm's direction, their tails wagging and their small brown faces split with adorable white blazes and happy beagle grins.

Laughing as she bent to greet them, Giselle offered pets and sweet talk in equal measure and noticed that Malcolm, too, could not resist the young dogs' joyous greetings. But after briefly indulging them, Malcolm began asking them to sit in a semicircle around him, praising them lavishly as first two of the pups, then five, and finally all seven obeyed his verbal command.

"Good dogs, every one of you," he told them. "So where's your naughty sister?"

"I've given the wrecking ball a few minutes of one-on-one. Now let's see what you can do with her," called Sebastian from outside of the gate. A moment later a red-and-white-colored puppy charged in. Despite the fact that she was only two-thirds the size of the smallest of the other pups, she moved as if it she had been supercharged, a snapping, yapping dervish of pure energy who leapt onto the backs of or plowed into one sibling after another.

The result was pandemonium, as the puppies immediately forgot the humans and turned their attention to defending themselves against the onslaught. Clearly realizing that his only hope was in corralling the troublemaker, Malcolm used a firm voice to command, "Scarlett, *sit*," slapping the side of his leg in an attempt to garner her attention.

When she paid him no heed, he ducked down as she raced past and reached to scoop her up. He nearly had her, but the splint on his left hand made him awkward enough that she was able to wriggle free and stir up her littermates once more.

Still at the gate, Sebastian began removing the other pups singly and in pairs, giving Malcolm a chance to focus on the disruptive element and motion for Giselle to step to one side. As the overly excited Scarlett continued to feed off the energy she'd set into motion, Giselle wondered how the pup might respond to the opposite approach.

As Sebastian removed the last of the other puppies, Giselle sat down on the ground, drawing her knees up and casually draping her arms around her bent legs. Immediately intrigued, Scarlett came racing toward her barking.

"Good instinct," Malcolm called over. "But now, *don't* give her attention. No pets, no voice, no eye contact. Not until she chills out and shows us the calm energy we're after."

It took at least twenty minutes, by Giselle's reckoning, a period during which she repeatedly, gently deflected the pup's repeated attempts to engage her with nips and yips and pitiful whining. When she started with the play bows, flattening her white forelegs to the ground while wriggling her behind in the air and imploring with a pair of liquid brown eyes, Giselle felt her resolve weaken.

"Look at her," she said, deciding Malcolm was being a little too hard-hearted. "She's only a baby who needs love and understanding."

"Hold your position," he advised, "please. I know she's pulling out all the stops, but trust me, what she needs even more than coddling is to make the connection between calm, settled energy and achieving the kind of bond she really longs for. Otherwise, she's not only facing being bounced out of the scent dog training program here but an altogether uncertain future."

"What do you mean?"

"I mean that whether it's in some sort of working environment or even a pet home, nobody wants the kind of dog who constantly creates disruptions, much less bites, scratches, and jumps onto people and other animals in order to get her way. And Sebastian's absolutely committed to making certain that no animal that comes into his program ever ends up with an unhappy outcome."

Giselle nodded, steeling her resolve. "All right, then. You've convinced me."

"Don't worry," Malcolm said. "Under all that beagle stubbornness, I'm convinced that there's a very bright mind working. Since she seems particularly interested in you— it's not unusual for dogs to be especially drawn to women— and what she's doing isn't working, I'm betting she'll come up with the solution pretty soon. Either that, or finally wear herself out."

Sure enough, it was only a few minutes later that Scarlett heaved a long-suffering sigh and plopped herself down a few inches from Giselle's leg, panting rapidly.

"Can I pet her *now*?" Giselle asked.

"Give her just a little while longer to relax," Malcolm said. "Otherwise, she'll just jump back up and hype herself up again."

When the panting finally stopped and Scarlett closed her eyes, Malcolm quietly instructed, "Now, try to keep everything as low-key as you can. Your voice, your movements, and especially your touch, because we don't want to overstimulate her. Try speaking to her first and then maybe allowing the side of your leg to come into contact with her shoulder."

Giselle did as he suggested and felt something inside her unfurl as, instead of jumping up and biting at her hands or running around wildly, Scarlett slowly raised a foreleg, clearly indicating her hopes that Giselle might favor her with a scratch.

Instead of giving in, Giselle said softly, "You really *want* to be a good girl, don't you? You just happen to be wired a little differently, aren't you?"

Scarlett slowly lowered her leg, seeming content to simply watch Giselle's mouth as she spoke.

Taking this as a step in the right direction, Giselle reached out to stroke her blaze-marked head and shoulder a few times, her heart melting when the whip-like white-tipped tail began to slowly wag.

Malcolm smiled. "*Very* well done. Now, let's find out if she remembers anything of the basics that her puppy raiser and Sebastian have tried to teach her."

They continued working with her for a session that seemed to fly, a period during which Scarlett continued to gravitate toward Giselle, following a few, but not nearly all the commands Malcolm suggested. With Malcolm, however, she did far worse, no matter how soothingly he tried to speak or how he attempted to lower himself to her level.

When Sebastian came back to ask for his assessment, Malcolm gestured toward the young dog, who was calmly maintaining a sit position and allowing Giselle to stroke her head.

"I think there's a great dog behind all her outbursts," he said, "but maybe not a working dog. I'm not sure she'll ever have that kind of discipline and focus. She could still have a wonderful life as a loving pet if she can learn to control her impulses, though."

When Sebastian nodded, Malcolm continued, "Scarlett needs intensive one-on-one work—preferably with Della, since her response to Giselle makes it clear she'll do far better with a female trainer."

"I've noticed, too, that she does better in sessions with Della," Sebastian said, "but as busy as we are right now around here, I'm afraid that extensive one-on-one time with only her isn't really feasible. Not when I have a target date to finish training the rest of the litter—*if* I can keep Scarlett from undoing all our hard work."

Malcolm shook his head. "Maybe the best thing you can do then is remove her from the premises. Let me take her to the ranch with me."

"I thought you said that she needed a female trainer."

Tipping a hand toward Giselle and Scarlett, Malcolm said, "I realize she's no Della, but look at her. The woman's clearly a born puppy whisperer. And with a little guidance from me…"

"What's this?" asked Giselle, her blue eyes wide and her expression dubious as she looked up sharply. "Just what is it you're getting me into, Malcolm?"

Grinning, he assured her, "I promise you, you'll thank me later."

"But just in case you don't," Sebastian said, "can I get you to sign that book for Ruby *before* you leave with your new charge?"

Chapter Ten

As Malcolm carried the kennel and other supplies Sebastian was sending with them to the pickup, he glanced over at Giselle, who was having difficulty getting Scarlett to walk correctly on the leash without leaping up and biting it or rolling onto her back and kicking her feet every which way.

"I know she's a handful," he said, "but try not to give her enough slack to let her get away with that. If you shorten up your lead—"

"I'll *try*," Giselle said.

Distracted by movement from across the lot, Scarlett threw her head back and gave a single *barroo* of a bark, greeting the slim, teenaged girl who came running toward them with a bag of kibble in her arms, her long, strawberry-blond braid bouncing along her back.

"Sebastian asked me to let you know you should continue feeding her this special puppy formula," Kelsie said as Scarlett's entire red-and-white body wagged in excitement to see her. "And, I know this is going to sound silly—"

Glancing at Malcolm, the girl blushed so deeply that her freckles appeared to vanish "—since I've seen you here before and know that you probably know more than I ever will about training dogs like her, but she really seems to like it when I sing to her."

Giselle smiled warmly. "It makes perfect sense to me and helps to explain why she likes females so much. You've been giving her extra attention, haven't you?"

Kelsie nodded at her. "After I overheard Sebastian and Della talking about how she might be an early cut from the program, I was afraid something bad might happen to her, so whenever I could, I rushed to finish up my regular duties and pulled her out to try to see if loving on her a little extra might help. That wasn't the wrong thing, was it? I didn't end up messing her up so she's being permanently kicked out of Crosswinds, did I? Because I love what I do here, but if I hurt Scarlett, I'll tell Sebastian right now that I'm quitting."

"Hold on—please," Malcolm urged her. "I'm sure Sebastian and Della would both be glad to hear you've taken some initiative, although I'd suggest that you try talking to one of them about *how* they'd like you to reinforce what it is they're doing next time. I know that Sebastian in particular has mentioned thinking that you have potential for working with the dogs."

"Really?" she asked, her brown eyes shining. "You're not just saying that to be nice?"

Meeting her gaze directly, he said, "I promise I'd never lie about something so important. Here, let me put up this crate and take that dog food off your hands."

"Let me get that," Giselle said, nodding to indicate his hand in its brace before stepping in to help him fold down the truck's rear seat and place the crate and food inside.

"That's not necessary, but—"

"No, I've got it," she insisted, passing him Scarlett's lead.

While Giselle loaded the wiggly pup a couple of minutes later, Kelsie lingered outside the truck for a moment, her expression serious.

"Is there something else?" he asked her.

She nervously fiddled with the frizzed end of her braid,

her expression serious. "I just wanted to tell you I'm really sorry, Mr. Colton. Sorry if my uncle Larry finding that red boat brought up a lot of bad memories for you. I know— I know how bad it hurts losing someone important to you, and I..." She sniffled. "I wanted you to know I'm thinking about you and the family and all, because it *really* stinks."

"Yes, it very much does," said Giselle, who had reappeared beside him. "Kate Dowling was my big sister...and I'm very sorry to hear you've suffered a recent loss as well."

"Oh, wow. That's rough. And, thanks," Kelsie said.

"And thank *you* and especially your uncle," Malcolm insisted, "for coming forward with the information he has. I can't tell you what a relief it is to have some hope after all this time that the case might finally be solved."

Kelsie nodded. "I really hope it works out. Um, my uncle says that if you want to get the straight scoop, to go ahead and call him." She passed Malcolm a business card featuring a boat overlaid with the image of a wrench and a couple of incidental grimy thumbprints. Printed below the name Larry Willets was the name, address, and phone number of Creekside Marine in Hadley along with the promise of *honest work at a fair price.* "He said that anything he tells the cops, you deserve to know as well."

"That's very..." Malcolm hesitated a beat before deciding on the right word. "I appreciate the offer." He slipped the card into his wallet before they said goodbye to Kelsie after promising to take good care of Scarlett at the ranch.

Once he and Giselle had the pup loaded and themselves in the truck as well, Malcolm pulled his cell from his pocket to see if Ajay had gotten around to responding to his earlier text message.

Nodding toward Kelsie, who was heading back inside the kennel, Giselle said, "Her uncle sounds like a pretty good guy—especially because I know how hard it's been getting any information out of the sheriff's office. I've barely been able to get the detective assigned to Kate's case to return any of my calls these past couple of years, either, and believe me, it hasn't been for lack of trying."

Malcolm lowered his phone. "Part of that may be my fault." He told her about asking Ajay to offer police support with the investigation and the sheriff taking immediate offense.

"Sounds like someone's awfully territorial," she said.

"Yeah. But I'm afraid my actions may've really messed things up there."

She grimaced, shaking her head before reaching out to touch his arm. "But if there's one thing we should both know by now, it's that second-guessing our past choices changes nothing. As of today, we finally have a fresh lead. *And* someone who's offered to discuss it with us, whether or not the authorities choose to play nice."

"We need to keep in mind, though, this boat mechanic's not necessarily offering his help out of the goodness of his heart," Malcolm warned her.

She shook her head. "I don't understand what you mean."

"I *mean* that Mr. *Honest Work for a Fair Price* has seen my flyer. The one promising a reward for information leading to the arrest of the responsible party," Malcolm said pointedly.

"So what if he has?" She shrugged. "You haven't decided that you don't want to pay it now, have you? Because if the money's an issue, I'll be glad to pitch in—or even foot the bill myself, if that's the sticking point. Justice for Kate would be worth anything."

Shaking his head, he said, "The money is not the issue. It's the ugly lies, the sick scams. You have no idea how many I've fielded. Dozens of them—Hundreds, maybe, some of them so twisted and revolting that I thank God you've been spared them."

"Wait, what do you mean?"

He made a face. "Suffice it to say that once the wrong crowd decides it might be profitable to exploit someone's family tragedy, they can be disgustingly inventive when it comes to cruelty."

"Oh, Malcolm, that's *terrible*," Giselle said, her voice faltering.

"It's all right. I've gotten used to—"

"You should never have had to. It's absolutely *not* right for a bunch of creeps and losers to treat any grieving person, especially someone as kind and courageous as you are, like that," she insisted, a fierceness sparking in her blue eyes that made her more beautiful than ever. "So I take it you're not going to reach out to Kelsie's uncle, are you?"

He shook his head. "Let's give Detective Danvers a reasonable chance to look into who put this boat into storage and see if he can track down the culprit first."

"I understand your concerns about maybe being scammed again. Truly I do," she said, even as a note of impatience crept into her voice. "But as far as I can tell, that guy hasn't exactly been a ball of fire up to this point."

"True, which is why I was very tempted to go get up in his face right away myself and demand that he actually *do* something. But this may be the first solid lead he's gotten on the case, so Sebastian's right. We need to at least give him half a chance to run with it before we do something that might end up putting him and the whole department back on the defensive."

She frowned before blowing out a breath. "I guess I can see the sense in that. But we've already been waiting *so* long. *Kate's* been waiting…for any kind of justice."

Seeing the tears clumping her beautiful, long lashes and

hearing the all too familiar anguish in her voice, Malcolm couldn't resist the impulse to reach over to catch her hand in his. Giving it a squeeze, he pulled it to his mouth and tenderly placed a kiss atop her knuckles. "Kate's at peace now, Giselle. And I believe she'd want us to try to somehow find the same."

She blinked hard, avoiding eye contact as she stiffly withdrew her hand before scooting back over and buckling herself into her seatbelt. After an awkward silence, she said in a strained voice, "So, are we heading straight back to the ranch now? Or should we see if we can get those photos of my SUV first, while we're this close to the mountains?"

Realizing how uncomfortable he'd clearly made her, he mentally kicked himself for getting so personal with her. What the hell had he been thinking, kissing her hand like some cut-rate Romeo? Would she imagine he hoped to take advantage of the situation—or worse yet, that he was thinking of her as some sort of *replacement* for the sister she was still grieving every bit as much as he was?

Sick with regret, he allowed the awkward change of subject drop and quickly checked his messages. "Ajay says his team's finished at Claudette's, so we're welcome to go over there and get those pictures. We can look in on the chickens, too, but one of my brothers and I will come back later to get them, after my dad's spoken to the folks I have in mind to adopt them."

"That sounds perfect, thanks," she said as he put the truck into gear and pulled out of the lot.

"And I'm sure Scarlett won't mind taking a little detour up there," Malcolm said. "We'll try to keep the trip as short as possible."

"Believe me, after what happened yesterday, I'm in no mood to linger."

"If it makes you feel any safer," Malcolm said, "when

he spoke to me earlier, Fletcher made me promise that I wouldn't drive around unarmed until the task force has Acker in custody."

"Let's hope they're closing in on him as we speak—a good, safe distance from where we'll be," she said as Malcolm turned in the direction of the mountains.

As they reached the recreational area, they passed several marked law enforcement units from various agencies before they were stopped at a checkpoint where two state police officers briefly asked their destination while subtly peeking inside the vehicle through their lowered window.

Once they'd continued on their way, Giselle said, "Maybe we should've waited to drive up here. All I can think of right now is driving up to Claudette's yesterday in the rain, almost running into Acker head-on—and that awful scene in the barn..."

"Would you prefer I turn around?" Malcolm asked her. "If you want, I could take you back to the ranch and drive out later, or even tomorrow to take some photos for you. Just tell me what you need, and we could transfer them to your phone."

She sighed and shook her head. "As nice as it is of you to make the offer, we're almost there now. And in spite of the awful memories, I can't imagine anyplace less likely for Markus to return to, so let's just go and get this over with."

"If you're sure..."

"I am," she said, sounding determined.

"Then we'll get our errands taken care of and be on our way back home in no time. After that, you'll have nothing to worry about but getting Scarlett settled in and shopping for your next set of wheels," he said, hoping to redirect her thoughts.

"Have you thought about another vehicle for yourself?" she asked.

"To tell you the truth, it hadn't even occurred to me. I suppose I'll need to report the truck's theft to my insurance company as well."

"I'm crossing my fingers that you'll get lucky, and the police will find it soon, and in one piece."

As they reached Claudette's property, he steered carefully to avoid the ruts left by the emergency vehicles that had come through since yesterday. "I appreciate the thought, but honestly, I'd trade that truck and a whole lot more if I could only know that Markus Acker could never hurt anyone again."

"As my grandmother would've put it, 'from your lips to God's ears,'" Giselle responded, her words so solemn that they might have been a prayer.

Once Malcolm had parked the truck, he headed off to see to the chickens while Giselle went to the wrecked Subaru, her phone already in hand as she prepared to deal with her insurance. By the time he spotted her slipping the phone back inside her pocket about ten minutes later, Malcolm had finished up in the barn and was walking Scarlett on her lead outside the structure, where he'd been allowing her to sniff after small creatures among the debris blown down by the storm.

"Chickens seem okay?" Giselle asked as she walked over to join them.

"As far as I can tell, they're doing just fine. At least, they're eating and drinking—and I even spied a few fresh eggs in their nest boxes."

"Claudette would be so relieved they weren't too traumatized by—by everything they witnessed yesterday."

Since Malcolm had never given much thought to the emotional range of poultry, he was relieved when Scarlett introduced a change of subject, straining at her collar and barking when something rustled in the underbrush.

Pointing out a squirrel running up a tree trunk, he told the pup, "You keep that up, and I'm sure that pesky fuzz-ball will surrender."

As Scarlett settled, her tail wagging, Giselle smiled. "She seems so much more relaxed out here than she was at the kennel. Inclined to settle down when you speak to her."

"Probably overstimulated at Crosswinds, considering the amount of activity and all her siblings to distract her. I have the feeling she's going to flourish in a more natural environment where less is happening."

"Enough to eventually get back on track to become a working dog?"

"I don't see it for her, since those environments would hold so many more distractions."

"So what'll happen to her?"

"There are always people willing to take on dogs who've been given extensive basic training, even if they didn't score high enough to make the grade as professional K-9s. Sebastian has a list of prescreened potential pet adopters interested in career-change dogs. Some of those folks have been waiting to get one of Crosswinds' program candidates for years."

"Oh, I see," she said. "Then I guess I'd better be extra careful with her—not that I wasn't always going to be, of course."

He shook his head. "I don't understand."

She shrugged. "Not to let myself get too attached, I mean. She really *is* adorable, and I was kind of thinking, if she were about to become homeless, maybe I would volunteer…since we seem to get along so well. But it was a silly idea. Please forget that I said anything."

"There's nothing silly about it," he said. "It's obvious that you're even more in love with dogs than Kate was."

"I'm sure she told you about the spaniels our grandparents had back when we were growing up. They were the sweetest."

He nodded. "She did. And I'm sure you'd make an incredibly devoted owner. We could always talk to Sebastian about getting you signed up for his wait list. I'd been thinking of suggesting it to you myself, almost from the moment I saw how you were with Pacer." *And how untethered and unhappy you seemed on your own, up at the cabin. Just the way that I was.* But he knew better than to voice that thought.

"I don't know," she said, shaking her head. "Like you mentioned before, that could take years, and who knows where I might be by then or what I might be doing for work and whether it will involve the kind of extensive travel I did while I was ghostwriting for celebrities?"

"Do you really see yourself going back to that profession? Would you even want to?"

"I'd definitely like to go back into some kind of writing. But not the kind I did before—if anyone would even have me after Nico finally ticked me off enough that I deleted scores of hours of recorded interviews and destroyed hundreds of pages of work product."

Catching something in her voice, Malcolm abruptly stopped walking Scarlett to turn and fix a serious look on her. "What exactly did he *do* to you? Because Kate shared some of the stories you told her over the years about wild celebrity behavior you've put up with."

Shaking her head, she said, "To be fair, most of my clients were absolute dreams to work with. Some of them still send me gifts from time to time and reach out to see how I am—even after hearing how my agent dropped me."

"But there *were* definitely a few jerks mixed in there," he reminded her.

"The word 'jerk' doesn't begin to touch on Nico's conduct," she admitted.

"So I ask again," Malcolm said, "what did this guy do—other than trashing your career?"

"Actually, *I* did that part all on my own."

"But why? Tell me, did he…touch you, Giselle?" At the thought of it, Malcolm wanted to track down the musician, cut through his phalanx of steroid-pumped bodyguards, and knock the sneering grin off that famous face of his for daring to cause her a moment's grief.

But once more, she shook her head. "Not me, no. He limited his gross behavior around me to allowing his male parts to hang out of his silk robe while I was interviewing him about his disgusting exploits, no matter how many times I asked him to cover himself or walked out of the room on his exhibitionism. Which, I have to tell you, was not nearly as impressive as he seems to imagine."

"That still doesn't make it right."

"*He's* not right," she said. "But anybody who hasn't been in a cave for the past ten years knows this guy's greatest joy in life, probably even greater than creating music, comes out of shocking and outraging people. Besides, I'd beaten out a *lot* of other ghostwriters to get this gig and was going to be very well compensated for my labor—so I was willing to overlook a certain level of discomfort, the way that everyone always ends up excusing Nico."

"So what was it then that finally pushed you over the edge?" Malcolm had to know.

She heaved a sigh. "There had been this big mentorship competition for young musicians, and the girl who won it was only fifteen. And a very *young* fifteen, if you know what I'm saying, like it was obvious that she'd been pretty sheltered. Still, she was unbelievably gifted in her own right, someone I'd bet anything will make a huge splash in the industry with her ability to spin out these original songs that have a person leaning in to catch not only every note but every breath between them."

"Don't tell me he was flashing his 'assets' around her as well," Malcolm said.

"At first, it seemed like he was actually behaving better. But Cami Carlson—that's the girl's name—idolized him to such a huge extent, his attention was like a drug to her. And I could see that he—that utter piece of filth—meant to take advantage of that beautiful, sweet child."

Malcolm's contempt for the man went white-hot. "Didn't she have a parent with her, watching over, someone you could warn?"

"If you could call him that. I know that stage mothers get a bad rap, but this 'manager-daddy'—" She angrily sketched out air quotes with her fingers "—had nothing but dollar signs where his protective instincts should've been. When I tried to have a private word with him, he only accused me of being jealous and told me not to do anything to sabotage his daughter's shot at making it big."

"Some father." Malcolm made a scoffing sound. "So what about Nico? Did you confront him?"

"I went to his handlers first to see if maybe I could generate some interest in getting them to run interference. But all those little toadies did was rat me out to the man himself. Predictably, Nico came absolutely unglued, shouting at the top of his lungs and throwing things—he smashed his second-best guitar that day—while accusing me of violating his trust to undermine him with his team and Cami's father. He was completely out of control, saying he had no idea how he could trust me with his story any longer."

Seeing the tears in her eyes, Malcolm asked, "Were you frightened of him, physically?"

"I was far more frightened by how close I came to begging for his forgiveness. To saying whatever it took to save my job—and the career I'd work so hard to build—to placate that vile piece of filth. And I might have done it, too, the way that everybody always has for him, if I hadn't spotted Cami leaving his bedroom at that moment, wrapped in nothing but a sheet."

His stomach turned. "That poor kid. So what did you do?"

"What else? I went with the nuclear option. I left that night and reported what I'd seen to investigators at the local police department. But, in the end, nothing happened, with Cami and her father denying it and everyone from Nico's camp calling me a disgruntled ex-employee—a woman half-deranged by grief for her drowned sister—and threatening to sue me into oblivion if I ever breathed a word of it in public."

"Those sons of—" He ground his teeth in frustration. "No wonder you destroyed the damned work product."

"I *had* to," she insisted. "Otherwise, they could've re-edited and used what I'd done to make that—that disgusting *pedophile* out to be some rules-flaunting rock 'n' roll hero for the ages. And I knew that Nico would never have the patience to sit through all those hours of interviews with anyone else again."

"That was damned brave of you," Malcolm said, looking at her with renewed admiration, "facing down a monster like that."

"It all would've been for nothing if I hadn't tracked down Cami's mother—who actually *does* care about her child's welfare, thank goodness."

"So I take it she had something to say about her daughter's 'opportunity'?" Malcolm asked.

"Apparently, she showed up on site, immediately realized Cami was lying about what she was getting out of her mentorship and told the girl she could come back in a few years and teach Nico a few lessons of her own about being a *real* professional in the industry. The kind of lessons she wouldn't have to learn on her back."

"Glad to hear that mama came through," he said.

Giselle nodded. "Then she packed up Cami into her minivan and drove away, leaving her husband with his jaw unhinged—along with the news that she was filing for divorce and full custody of his meal ticket. And she'd hired a real shark of a lawyer."

Stepping in closer, Malcolm laid a hand on Giselle's shoulder and looked her in the eyes, "I hope you realize that what you did *saved* that girl, whether or not she appreciated it at the moment."

"Considering the horrible names she called me, she most definitely did *not*," Giselle insisted. "But let's hope that three years maturity, her mother's influence, and going viral this past year with the song she recorded for the soundtrack of that blockbuster movie have shifted her perspective. It may've taken her longer than she'd hoped, but she's definitely made it to the bigtime now."

"Well, whether or not Cami *ever* appreciates the sacrifice you made for her—and how amazing you really are—I certainly do," he told her. "Maybe for the first time ever."

"Thanks for the reminder," she said. "Living up here in these mountains..." Closing her eyes for a moment, she lifted her face toward the azure dome of the sky and took a deep breath "...I'd almost forgotten that there was anything to me at all other than the things I've failed at."

Seized by an undeniable impulse, he took a step closer to pull her into his arms. But instead of pushing away, as he'd more than half expected, she squeezed him tightly back, as if she was holding on to him for dear life.

"When I'm listening to you, I don't hear *any* kind of failure, Giselle," he insisted. "I hear a beautiful, bold, and compassionate woman who's handled more grief than anybody ever should have, completely without support. But you have my word that that part of your life's all over now."

She pulled back enough to look up at him, her eyes damp with tears. An instant later, she was pushing herself up onto her toes and pulling his head down toward hers. Draping her arms over his shoulders, she sealed her lips to his. The shock of their contact shook him to his foundations, barriers he'd imagined built to withstand eternity collapsing like sandcastles overtaken by the tide. In that moment, he was overwhelmed with an awareness of her trembling eagerness, with the heat surging through him as they stood entwined together, with the pulsing roar of his own blood rushing through his body.

Needing more of her, he deepened the kiss, forgetting where he was and why, only hours before, he had sworn never to do this very thing when he'd recognized the first stirrings of a powerful attraction to her.

All too abruptly, she broke off the kiss, leaving him bereft until she caught his gaze with a shy, sidelong glance and captured his hand in hers. When she guided it to her chest, her lips drifting to his neck, he cupped the softness of her breast and squeezed it, his mind filling with temptations, each more erotic than the next.

He had no idea how far things might have gone right there, but an angry yap of protest and a hard tug at his lower leg finally drew his attention, causing him to look down at Scarlett, who had managed to wrap her lead around his ankles. Frustrated with her inability to free herself, she was growing frantic, chewing at the lead itself.

Drawing a deep breath, he said to Giselle, "Let me—I'm sorry, but I need to take care of this. She's pretty upset."

As he bent to gently pull the portion of the lead she'd been chewing from her mouth, he reassured the pup, "There you go, Scarlett. Sorry I messed up and forgot about you down there for a few minutes."

"No, *I'm* the one who's messed up," Giselle insisted, looking deeply shaken. "*Really* messed up, standing right out here in front of all of creation trying to seduce my sister's fiancé where my friend was murdered only yesterday. What kind of monster even *does* a thing like that?

"Not a monster, Giselle. A human being," he said gently, "with a perfectly natural need for connection." He picked up Scarlett, who seemed to need the reassurance of an ear scratch, and, on instinct, offered her to Giselle. "Or just a woman who's sensed that I'm finally seeing who you really are—for the first time ever. Or maybe it's you who's changed."

"I've changed, all right," she said, voice shaking, "if I've turned into the kind of woman who could jump from spending all my energy trying to figure out how to *honor* the sister who died in my place three years ago to the person who would make a move on her fiancé the first chance I get."

Too upset to take the pup, she turned and rushed back toward the pickup, leaving him one last glimpse of her tear-stained face.

Chapter Eleven

Markus Acker's gut turned to ice water when he saw sunlight gleaming off an approaching vehicle's windshield through the screen of trees that shielded his stolen truck from view. He was already on edge, worried that the two workmen who had evidently packed up after yesterday's storm hit would soon return to collect the tools and trailer they'd left behind outside his previous hideout—and even more anxious after hearing what had sounded like police sirens in the vicinity earlier.

If he'd had any choice in the matter, he never would have risked returning here, so close to the scene of the killing he'd committed. But this morning, he'd discovered, in a moment that still broke him out in a cold sweat to think of, that the little notepad he kept, containing all of his offshore account information, was missing.

With sickening clarity, it had come to him that it must have somehow fallen from his backpack when he'd been rummaging for a flashlight or his multi-tool when he'd first broken into the pitch-black cabin.

Immediately realizing that without the notepad, he'd be permanently cut off from his substantial nest egg, he'd had no choice but to return for it, no matter the risk—or who he had to kill to get it. When he'd discovered the property unoccupied and the notebook exactly where he'd expected it might be, he'd broken down for the first time in his long ordeal, sobbing with relief. But that relief had been tempered with a desperation to get away before he could be discovered.

As he eased slightly forward now, Markus saw that the vehicle he'd spotted wasn't law enforcement as he'd feared. But the dark-blue pickup did bear some sort of white logo on the driver's side door—a logo he realized with a start as it came closer—belonged to the Colton Ranch.

As the truck passed Markus's position, he struggled to get a good look at the vehicle's occupants. A glare prevented him from making out the passenger, but behind the wheel he glimpsed a dark-haired male in his mid-thirties.

"A damned Colton—has to be," he said aloud. But could this one lead him to the Victrola that held the go-bag containing his money and the ever-so-precious passport?

He decided that for now, he would attempt to follow and keep watch on the truck from a safe distance, to get a better idea of who he might be dealing with and whether he and his companion might somehow be taken by surprise. As Markus slowly pulled out, he hung well back. He needed time to come up with a solid plan for ending his time as a fugitive from justice—a plan that he admitted to himself might very well end with at least one additional Colton in the cemetery.

As GISELLE AND Malcolm left the recreational area, silence crowded into the space between them, crowded into the space inside of Giselle's lungs until, finally, she felt she'd die if she didn't shatter its suffocating spell.

"Once we get back to the ranch," she finally told him, "I'll start making calls. Line up a rental car for starters. Then I'll find another place to stay until this manhunt's over, because I can't be with you at the ranch any longer. I'm sorry, but... I need some space right now to wrap my head around what happened. And to make absolute certain that I *never* make the same mistake again."

Malcolm glanced her way, his Colton-green eyes both sad and thoughtful. "I'm sorry to tell you this, Giselle—and even sorrier if I somehow misread your intentions when you kissed me—but as far as I'm concerned, it was the furthest thing from a mistake I can imagine. For the first time in forever, I feel like some part me that's been all bent up and off-kilter has finally dropped back into its track again and started running smooth and easy."

"But don't you understand? It wasn't *me* that you were thinking of. It couldn't have been."

"Hold on, please," he said. "Just give me a chance to finish speaking, and I won't ask any more of you. I swear it."

She leaned back against the headrest, pinching the bridge of her nose against an encroaching headache, before deciding she owed him at least that much. "Go on."

"I was thinking of *you* and you alone—the woman who'd risked her career, and possibly even her physical safety, with that entitled child predator you were working with on behalf of the well-being of a young girl. It's *you* I've been seeing in a new light—but I can also see the way this is tearing you apart, too." He paused a moment before adding, "And I won't allow that. I can't."

Confused, she said, "I'm not sure what you think you're going to do to stop it."

"How about taking a giant step backward in our relationship and forgetting about what happened today? Being the friend you obviously need instead of trying to become something it's clear that you can't handle?" he asked, a suggestion that took her utterly aback.

Before she could tell him that there was no way she could forget something as cataclysmic as that kiss had felt, he rushed to speak again, sounding almost desperate. "And let's definitely forget, too, the part about you heading off someplace you wouldn't be able to take Scarlett. Because we both know the ranch is the best place for you to build the kind of bond with her that I believe would truly benefit you both. Plus, to be a little selfish here, it'd keep me from losing touch with you again...maybe forever this time. Because I feel like, even aside from what just happened, there's something between us—a connection that's worth preserving. Don't you?"

As one of the two vehicles she'd noticed a distance behind them came up rapidly on their rear bumper, Malcolm slowed and waved the car's driver, who was clearly in a hurry, past them.

"We—we certainly both loved Kate," she agreed. "But part of loving her, for me, means understanding boundaries. Especially those that would amount to a betrayal of her memory."

She jerked her head, startled when the phone Malcolm had left in the console started ringing.

Malcolm frowned down at the screen. "I'm sorry. But this is Kelsie's uncle."

"You should see what he wants," she said, wondering why the finder of the red boat would be calling Malcolm.

Malcolm pulled over onto the wooded shoulder and made sure that she saw him hit the speakerphone icon before he connected. "This is Malcolm Colton."

"Larry Willets over at Creekside Marine, up the way in Hadley. Got your number over at Crosswinds when I dropped my niece off. You know Kelsie, I understand?"

"Terrific kid. Hard worker," Malcolm said, the set of his jaw saying he hadn't yet decided whether the same could be said of her relation. "I'm told that you stopped by the sheriff's office yesterday—or maybe it was this morning? About a boat that showed up at your shop."

"Is that what you heard?" Willets asked him, before his tone and volume abruptly changed, rising to a level of hostility that had Giselle's stomach pitching. "That what *you* told somebody, Colton? Because I *don't* like being threatened. And I especially don't appreciate it when my family's brought into the mix."

"Threatened?" Malcolm's bewilderment was unmistakable. "Who on earth's been threatening you?"

"I figured maybe you could be the one to tell me, since Sebastian said that, other than you, he hasn't mentioned our conversation to another living soul. Yet whoever this fella is callin' my shop over here from a blocked number, disguisin' his voice and threatening me by name, sayin' he'll come after me and that niece of mine if I say another word to anybody in a uniform."

"First of all," Malcolm said, "I can't imagine why you'd think I of all people would want to threaten you for giving me the best damned news I've had in ages. Do you know how long I've been trying to drum up information on that boat you've got there—assuming it's the right one?"

"It *has* to be," Willets said. "Why else would the fact that it's suddenly turned up cause this kind of trouble? And whatever you had printed on that flyer, how am I to know that really wasn't all for show? Maybe you didn't really *want* the damned thing found in the first place? Who's to say you weren't even somehow involved in this whole thing from the get-go?"

"What the actual—?" Malcolm demanded, his volume rising as he jerked forward in his seatbelt harness so abruptly that it snapped tight. "Are you honestly suggesting *I* had something to do with hiding that boat myself—or with my fiancée's *death*? Because I haven't found a need to go and physically stomp a mud hole in a man in my entire adult life, but for either one of those two lies, I'm of a mind to make an exception right this minute. And I promise you, you won't have to wonder for a second who's doing the stomping or worry about anybody in your family, either. Just what's left of you when I'm finished rearranging your skeletal structure. You hear me?"

Giselle sat frozen in the seat beside him, shaken to realize that the same Malcolm whom Kate had once joked was so even-tempered that he was impossible to pick a fight with had absolutely meant his threat of violence.

"So you're saying that it *wasn't* you, callin' me this mornin'?" Willets stammered over the phone.

"Glad you're finally putting two-and-two together," Malcolm said dryly. "But in case you have some further issue, I have a woman friend right next to me—my late fiancée's *sister*—who can verify that I've been with her all morning and haven't touched my phone. And if that's not good enough, you can—"

"No, no. I have to believe that that wasn't the reaction of a guilty man. And for what it's worth, I'm sorry," Willets said. "I was wound up pretty tight myself, on account of that caller bringin' Kelsie into his threats. I have to say, I prefer your brand of intimidation." With a low chuckle, he added. "The part about rearrangin' my skeletal structure was a nice touch, by the way. I'll have to remember that one in the future."

To Giselle's surprise, Malcolm laughed at that. "Feel free. I stole that one from my younger brother—or maybe it was one of my cousins. So I take it that you visited with Detective Danvers last night?"

"He'd left for the day already. But there was this lady sitting next to his desk there, dark-haired lady with a real nice set of—"

"Just get on with it," Malcolm said, cutting an apologetic look toward Giselle, who rolled her eyes in response.

"Anyway, she said her name was Rudolph. You know, like the reindeer?"

Giselle presumed that he meant Detective Danvers' partner, Ariana Rodolfo. Over the past couple of years, Giselle had gotten through to her on a few occasions and found her to be refreshingly honest, at least, about the realities of her sister's case.

"I assure you," she'd confided, her voice steeped with regret, "it's not for lack of effort put in. I was assigned to take a fresh look at all the cold cases and personally ran down every lead imaginable after I first came on with this department. But at a certain point, you run out of leads to explore. Out of everything except newer cases, each one with its own victim, along with family members desperate for answers."

"So my sister's file gets shut back inside a drawer somewhere, or wherever it is things go to be forgotten?" Giselle had accused, her pain and frustration spilling over into what she'd understood, even at the time, was pointless anger.

"I won't forget her," Detective Rodolfo had insisted. And though that vow was far more than she had ever gotten out of Detective Danvers, Giselle had been too frustrated to thank her or even to say goodbye before abruptly disconnecting.

"Rudolf-o, Rudolph—same difference," Larry Willets said now, responding to Malcolm's correction on his pronunciation of the detective's name over the speakerphone. "Whatever her name, she seemed pretty interested as she took my information and copied the photos I'd brought of the boat from my phone."

"What photos were those?" Malcolm asked him.

"She especially seemed keen on the ones where you could see where somebody'd scraped off the registration and the Hull ID numbers. Trailer tags were missing, too."

"So you're saying there's no way to trace this speedboat back to its original owner?"

"I'm sayin' that was damned well somebody's *intention*. Except they missed that scrap of paper I pulled out from between a couple of the seat cushions this morning," Willets boasted. "And who knows. Maybe the deputies'll come up with more, once they tow the boat off and take it into evidence this afternoon."

At the mention of that slip of paper, Malcolm's eyes had gone wide, finding Giselle's at the same moment that she reached over to squeeze his arm.

"So what, exactly, was on that paper?" Malcolm asked him, making what Giselle could tell was an effort to disguise his level of interest.

"Hard to say. Might've been a receipt or bill of sale at one time," Willets said, "but the thing's in such rough shape— like maybe it had been water-damaged and then dried all crumpled. When I tried to straighten it to take a picture with my cell phone, it started falling apart."

"Could you—would you mind sending me that cell phone photo you took of it?"

"No offense, Colton, but yeah, I would. If I had the sense I was born with, I wouldn't have run my mouth to you about it in the first place. You know, considerin' I still don't know who called to threaten me. If neither you nor Sebastian mentioned that I went to the cops to anybody—"

"What about your niece?" Malcolm asked him. "Kelsie could've said something to a friend, who brought it up to the wrong person."

"Now you're accusin' Kelsie of making trouble?"

"I'm sure she would never intentionally do that, but kids do talk. Or maybe someone from the sheriff's department mentioned this break in the case while in a coffee shop or somewhere else where it could've been overheard by someone with ties to whoever wanted that boat to stay hidden—"

"Listen, I've gotta go now. My boss—the boss is signaling for me to get back to workin' for a living."

"Is everything all right there, Mr. Willets?" Malcolm asked him, the concern in his voice telling Giselle he'd picked up on the same sudden tension she'd heard come into the mechanic's voice.

"Uh...yeah, sure, right as rain," Willets said. "See you tonight at dinner, darlin'."

The call disconnected, and Malcolm turned to look at her, his face lined with a mixture of confusion and concern. "You heard that, too, right? The strain in his voice? And what he just called me?"

"I'd swear he sounded scared," she said, goosebumps rising along her arms. "That man's in some kind of trouble. Should we call 9-1-1?"

"And tell them what, exactly? That we got spooked by Willets's tone—or that a boat mechanic called me 'darlin'?"

Giselle made a face. "I see your point. But what else is there? Try calling him back?"

"I seriously doubt he'd answer." Malcolm checked his mirrors before putting the truck into gear and pulling back onto the road. "We can get there in about twenty minutes, if I step on the gas. Meanwhile, you need to try calling Detective Rodolfo, or maybe Danvers."

She gave an irritated huff. "That guy ignores my calls on a good day."

"Whoever you can reach is fine, as long as it's someone that'll help stop this new evidence from possibly disappearing—and maybe keep Willets alive."

AFTER LEAVING A voicemail and two frantic texts when Ariana Rodolfo didn't answer, Giselle decided to try one more time before giving up the effort.

On this attempt, however, the sheriff's department deputy detective finally picked up. "I'm seriously beginning to regret ever giving you my cell number," she said, sounding unmistakably irritated. "When I don't answer you, it's because I'm *busy*. It's definitely not because I want my phone blown up with a bunch of messages and texts about some supposed 'life or death' drama while I'm running down an important lead."

"But I meant the 'life or death' part *literally*! I'm almost positive that someone's just walked into Creekside Marine to silence Larry Willets," Giselle said, desperate to finally be heard. "I just heard him tell Malcolm Colton over the phone that he's received multiple threats this morning related to speaking to you regarding the red boat someone brought into his shop."

"Oh, he reached out to *you* to say that, did he? Instead of, say, calling the sheriff's department?" Rodolfo sounded more suspicious than she did alarmed.

"He seemed to have some crazy idea that maybe Malcolm wouldn't *want* the boat found for some reason, not that it made a lot of sense to me," Giselle said. "But once Malcolm set him straight, he—"

"Went on to try his hand at whatever new game he's decided to try out?" the detective suggested. "I have Detective Danvers here with me right now, Ms. Dowling. I want you to know that at this very moment he's calling Mr. Willets to put your mind at ease. But while my partner's reaching out, let me inform you that Mr. Willets has a—a history with law enforcement that's given us both some reason to wonder if his story might not be exactly what he's representing."

"I'm sorry—what are you saying?" Giselle asked, cutting a quick glance toward Malcolm and wishing that she'd thought, as he had earlier, to put the call on speaker.

"He was a guest of the county a couple of times where he lived prior to this one about fifteen years back," the detective said. "Theft of materials from a jobsite where he worked and what looks to have been a bar fight…"

"Just because he did a little jail time during his younger years doesn't mean he's not entitled to protection now, though, does it?" Giselle asked her. "Because I'm telling you, this guy sounded terrified to both of us. And he said he'd found something that sounded like it might be written evidence, way down in the boat's seat cushions."

"Hold on just a second, could you?" Rodolfo said before muting the call.

While waiting for her to come back on the line, Giselle said to Malcolm, "I'm on hold, but it kind of sounds like she thinks Willets could be playing us. Apparently, the guy's had a couple of jail stints in his past. Nothing major-sounding, but…"

"Maybe she got a cop's gut feeling that something wasn't right when he came in to report the boat to her yesterday." Malcolm sounded a great deal less certain of the situation himself.

Before Giselle could respond, Rodolfo came back on the line. "Willets isn't answering the cell number he gave me," she said, "and Detective Danvers wasn't able to raise anyone at the main number for Creekside Marine, either. But at the moment, the two of us are right in the middle of following up on a time-sensitive lead related to this same case, so he's calling over to dispatch in Hobarth County—since Hadley's outside our jurisdiction—to send a unit to do a welfare check as soon as they have a deputy available."

"Right away, then?" Giselle pressed, unable to forget the fear she'd heard in the boat mechanic's voice.

"I'm sure they'll get to it as soon as they're able," the deputy answered carefully, "depending on their manpower situation."

"Which means that Willets could be a dead man by the

time anybody bothers," Giselle said, her mind filling with images of Claudette lying face down in a pool of blood.

"Or more likely," Rodolfo countered, "he might instead be sitting around wondering why we weren't gullible enough to cross county lines to come running in response to that tempting bait he's dangled."

"I'm sure that, as someone in law enforcement," Giselle said, "you must find it aggravating, even embarrassing, to go running in response to people's cries for help, only to find that you've been manipulated for whatever reason. But let me tell you how *I* felt yesterday when my neighbor called me for help and we *didn't* make it to her before she fell victim to a murderous fugitive from justice. A man still on the run today."

"I'm terribly sorry you were affected by that tragedy," the detective said, sounding genuinely regretful. "Of course, we're well aware of yesterday's homicide in the ski resort area and the ongoing manhunt, but I see no reason why Markus Acker would have any interest in either Larry Willets or a boat that may have been involved in your sister's death more than three years ago. Do *you*, Ms. Dowling?"

"I'm not trying to say this *is* in any way connected," Giselle said. "I only meant that I can't bear the idea of arriving too late to help again and possibly finding another body. Can't you understand that?"

Detective Rodolfo paused for a beat before demanding, "Wait a second. Are you telling me that you're on your way over to Creekside Marine right now?"

"Yes, Malcolm and I are heading over there together," Giselle said, glancing over to see him focused on the curving county road that tightly hugged a tree-clad hillside. The same route that she had for so long gone out of her way to avoid since it ran so close to the lake. Realizing it was far too late to turn around now—even if she knew that any dread she felt about the view soon to open up below them was worth the extra time a detour would add to their route—she fought back her nausea.

"I'll tell you what," Detective Rodolfo said over the roaring in Giselle's ears. "I'll make sure we communicate the urgency of this situation and ask, as a matter of professional courtesy, that a deputy be sent out to check on Mr. Willets right away. In the meantime, I need the two of you to turn around and go home—or *anywhere* but the vicinity of Creekside Marine in Hadley. Do you understand me?"

"I do, but—" Giselle began as they rounded the curve and the vast blue expanse of Blackbird Lake stole the breath from her lungs. Though the only signs of life were the silhouettes of a few birds bobbing on the sparkling blue surface about seventy yards below, Giselle's memory supplied a vivid summer scene alive with canoes and kayaks, anglers fishing in the shallows, personal watercraft, and swimmers in life jackets. And a pair of happy blond sisters—the one with far longer hair wearing a borrowed, deep purple bikini—laughing together aboard an inflatable raft being towed toward an unstoppable disaster.

"Ms. Dowling, are you still there?" the detective repeated, her voice floating in as if from a vast distance. "If you can hear me, please confirm that you're listening to reason here, for your own safety, if nothing else."

"Our—our *safety*?" Giselle stammered, blinking away the threat of tears as the past evaporated. "So you think I could be right about Larry Willets possibly being in danger?"

"Giselle?" Malcolm said, his forehead lined with worry as he glanced her way.

She gestured for him to wait a moment as the detective continued speaking.

"I'm certainly not ruling out the possibility," Rodolfo said, "any more than I am that you could be walking into some sort of shakedown he's cooked up looking for a reward for his assistance. Just give Hobarth County's deputy the chance to find out, and I promise you, as soon as possible, I'll personally get back to you and Mr. Colton with a full update on what's happening."

In the background of the call, Giselle heard what sounded like Detective Danvers urgently reminding his partner, *"We can't wait any longer—not if we hope to catch up with this suspect today."*

Coming back on the line, Rodolfo said, "I really have to go now, but we'll be in touch."

Once the detective ended the call, Giselle told Malcolm, "We need to get off this road and turn around. Detective Rodolfo doesn't want us going anywhere near Willets."

"Because she doesn't trust him?" Malcolm asked, switching on his right turn indicator to leave the road.

"She seemed uncertain whether he's trying to set us up or might really be in trouble. But whichever it is, I'm sure she'd rather have a deputy figure it out than have two civilians walk into the middle of it," Giselle said, feeling suddenly off-kilter as the turnoff narrowed, leading them down out of the mountains and closer to the lake. "But she—she d-did—she promised to keep us informed on whatever's ha-happening…"

"You haven't been this close to the water *since*, have you?" he asked gently as they rolled up to a stop sign.

She shook her head, her throat too tight to speak, her chest filled with the nearness of the lake whose presence she felt in her tingling nerve endings but could no longer see, thanks to the angle of the road and the screen of trees, partly leafed out with spring greenery, across the street.

As he waited for a couple of vehicles to come through the intersection, Malcolm said, "It really got to me, too, the first time I came this close. Let me turn the truck around up in this little park over to the right here. Then, I promise you, we'll get back on the road to the ranch again. Sound good to you?"

"The—the ranch will be fine for now," she managed, her breath catching as he pulled out and began driving toward a small park. Not the same park where the rescuers had brought an unresponsive Kate to continue attempting to resuscitate her shockingly pale and inert form. That had been miles to the north, near the edge of the ski basin. But at her first glimpse of the railings along the sidewalk, the benches, and even the empty parking spaces in front of a walkway along the lakeshore, Giselle cried out, their similar design elements sending her spiraling back to that desperate August day.

"Please stop! I have to—" She clawed to remove her seatbelt as a hot ball of nausea rose inside her, her awareness crowded with the inescapable images, the sounds and smells and textures surrounding the unimaginable price of her own survival.

Malcolm hit the brakes. "Are you all—"

But she was already flinging the door open and exiting the pickup. She only made it a few steps before her stomach made good on its threat.

After she was finished, she moved away and started walking. Feeling too raw to face conversation, she headed for the sidewalk, thinking that if she could just stand there for a minute and look out at the water, maybe she could find the peace and contentment she'd once felt each time she'd gazed out across its surface.

Yet she lasted only seconds before she had to turn away, screwing her eyes shut against the horrific images that assaulted her, one after another until her tears flowed freely. Eventually, she heard approaching footsteps, followed by the sound of Scarlett's whimpering before Malcolm softly shushed her.

"Not right now, girl," he gently told the pup. "She needs a little space. And how about some of this water bottle?"

Nodding, Giselle did her best to wipe away her tears, more than a little embarrassed by her meltdown but needing to rinse her mouth too much to turn down the offer.

"Here you go." He handed her both the container and a few of the fast-food napkins from the truck. "I figured maybe you could use these, too."

"Thanks," she said. "I—I'm sorry to have behaved like that. It's just that—sometimes I'm right back there. Trapped beneath the surface. Or in the boat, watching you do CPR before the first responders got there..."

She began to turn toward the low rumble of another vehicle pulling into the parking lot, but the engine shut down before coming any closer, and Malcolm was already shaking his head in response to what she'd said.

"If there's one person on the planet you *never* have to explain to, it's definitely me," he told her, his own expression haunted. "After what happened, I got rid of my own boat as fast as I could—practically gave the thing away because I couldn't bear the thought of ever having anyone else's life in my hands that way again."

Giselle cracked open the cap of the bottle she was holding. "For the first full year I lived in the cabin, I kept the big picture window covered because I couldn't even bear looking out at the lake from that distance. If the darkness hadn't gotten to me, I'd probably still have it covered up." Holding up the water bottle, she added, "Excuse me for a moment, please."

Walking away from him, she cleaned herself up as best she could. After depositing the sodden napkins in a nearby trashcan, she came back to see Scarlett wagging her tail as she stared up her, her sweet brown eyes pleading for attention.

Giselle knelt down to cuddle her and then surprised herself by laughing as she fended off the pup's attempts to cover her with kisses. Grinning, Giselle said, "Okay, now. That's enough. Blech, let's keep that floppy ear out of my mouth, too!"

Smiling, Malcolm offered his right hand and helped her back to her feet while keeping a firm grip on the leash. "She could definitely use some work on her manners..."

"No doubt about that, but at least she's got me laughing again, even here. So maybe you were right, about my needing her."

"It *has* been known to happen. My being right, that is," he said. "If you just give me the chance."

Catching a low rumble in his voice that put her to mind of the sort of shared intimacies she had no business thinking of, she stole a peek at him. And the look he slanted down at her had her all too aware of how close they were standing. In his eyes, she saw a depth of feeling she had never once glimpsed in any of the men she'd dated. In that moment she knew, with a certainty she could never recall feeling in her life, that if there was ever anything she needed—whether it was next week or twenty years from now—he would always be the one person she could pick up the phone to call.

When he stepped back, opening a respectful space between them, she knew as well that he was also the one man who would never ask anything of her in return.

At the thought, she realized it was the reason that once all of this was over, she needed to permanently lose Malcolm Colton's number. Because keeping in contact with a man she knew had feelings for her that she could never allow herself to reciprocate—no matter what some traitorous corner of her heart might want—would be not only wrong but unkind, and he'd already lost enough to the cruel waters of this lake.

From somewhere not too far off, she heard the solid *chunk* of a vehicle's door closing. In nearly any other setting, such a normally innocuous sound—a sound she'd heard in parking lots thousands of times in her life before—would have gone unnoticed. But this time, a pinprick of alarm pierced her awareness.

A split-second later, she found herself spinning around, as her mind clicked onto a detail that hadn't registered on a conscious level. The vehicle she'd spotted out of the corner of her eye when she had turned to wipe her face a couple of minutes earlier had not been just any vehicle, but a silver pickup matching the description of Malcolm's missing truck.

On turning, however, the first thing she caught sight of was not the pickup, parked about thirty yards away, but instead the middle-aged man in a hooded gray jacket who'd left it and was sprinting toward them, both hands rising together as he aimed a—

"Gun! Behind you!" she shrieked, her cry so loud that a phalanx of ducks floating on the water nearby took to the air, quacking in alarm.

"Get down!" Malcolm shouted as he scooped up Scarlett—who gave a startled yelp—and, rather than following his advice to her, raced for the cab of the ranch truck they'd been driving.

Having dropped flat to her stomach, Giselle stared in disbelief, certain for one shocking moment that the very man she'd been so certain she could count on was about to drive off and leave her to what had to be Markus Acker. But before she could recover, Malcolm burst back out of the pickup. Only this time, instead of the beagle, he was holding his pistol in his uninjured hand.

And unlike the man she assumed to be Acker, Malcolm

didn't hesitate an instant before squeezing off three shots in quick succession.

With a shout of either surprise or pain, Acker swerved abruptly and then fell to the ground—perhaps only tripping in his haste, considering how quickly he rolled and sprang back to his feet. He'd clearly thought better of his charge, however, for he turned tail and made for the stolen pickup.

Malcolm, who'd been aiming to fire again, lowered his weapon, grimacing in her direction. "I may not have the stomach to shoot a man in the back, but I can't just let him get away. You coming, or should I call someone to come pick you up?"

She ran to the passenger door and flung it open, clambering inside to find Scarlett standing on the front passenger-side floorboard, shaking.

"It's all right, girl," Giselle said, bending low to try to soothe her as she pulled herself into the seat and Malcolm dropped the truck into reverse. "She's really frightened, Malcolm. Should I hold her in my lap to calm her?"

"No, try to keep her on the floor for now," he said, "and keep your head low if you can, too, because I have no idea what he's going to do when I go after him."

"Should I call 9-1-1, or would you rather try to reach Ajay?"

"Nine-one-one will be quicker, but you'd better buckle up first. Looks like he's on the move."

Giselle sat up to fasten her lap and shoulder harness, glancing nervously in the direction of the silver pickup as it snapped into place. As the silver truck started rolling, Malcolm backed out and then hit the gas, running the four-wheel-drive ranch truck over a concrete bumper through a grassy border between the parking lot and an area containing playground equipment.

Rattled by the rough ride—and the realization that instead of following from a safe distance as she'd expected, Malcolm was trying to cut off Acker's escape from the lot— Giselle sat bolt upright to brace herself. "Are you trying to get us killed? *Wait*—"

She snapped her jaw shut as the silver RAM braked hard and an arm was thrust out through its window. Not only an arm but a long, straight shape that she didn't recognize until the first bullet pierced their windshield and foam exploded from the headrest right beside her neck.

Chapter Twelve

If Malcolm lived to be a hundred, he knew that he would never forget the abject terror of Giselle's scream. Sick with the certainty that she'd been struck, he wrenched the wheel to the right, causing the truck's back end to spin around, exposing himself to danger but protecting her from the next shots he heard thwacking against sheet metal on his side.

Desperate to get them out of range, he mashed down on the accelerator. As the pickup leapt forward, the side window right behind him shattered, prompting an even shriller cry from Giselle.

A moment later, the silver RAM squealed out of the lot, prompting a screech of tires and the blare of a horn from what Malcolm saw was a large school bus full of what looked to be elementary children whose driver had been forced to brake hard to avoid a collision.

As desperately as Malcolm wanted to give chase, the sight of those kids, along with the sound of Giselle's sobbing, drove home the dangers of continuing to escalate this situation instead of calling in the professional law enforcement officers who were trained to deal with it with a reasonable degree of safety. With Giselle's earlier question—*Are you trying to get us killed?*—still ringing in his ears, he looked over at her, meaning to reassure her that he'd come to his senses.

That was when he saw the blood staining her sleeve, deep-red blood oozing out from beneath her right hand where she had it clasped over her upper left arm.

Heart dropping, he blurted, "You—you're hit?! Oh, Giselle! Oh, no. This is all my—I'm so sorry."

"Is—is there a—a cloth? A rag or towel or something I—can..." She looked around frantically.

Putting the truck in park, Malcolm got out and went around to her side but forced himself to check the back seat first, looking for any sort of cloth she could use to put direct pressure on the wound.

Not finding anything suitable, he peeled off his jacket and then stripped off his long-sleeved T-shirt. He wadded it up before opening her door. "Best I could do," he said, thrusting it at her.

Pale as Giselle was, her tear-stained blue eyes widened at the sight of his bare chest. "I—um—what're you—"

"Press this against your wound," he said, sparing a glance at Scarlett, who was crouched trembling on the floorboard but appeared physically unharmed. "But first, can you let me take a quick look."

Giselle was shaking as she nodded mutely and lifted her right hand off her blood-soaked upper left sleeve. He grimaced, seeing the slash-like tear in the fabric above a two-inch gouge across the surface of her flesh. Blood flowed from it unabated, but when he pulled her forward—causing her to cry out in pain, he was relieved beyond measure not to see a larger exit wound hidden on the rear side of her body.

As he leaned her back again, he said, "I'm sorry for moving you. I'm sure you're hurting. And I need you to keep as much pressure on it as you can stand," he said. "But the good news is, it looks like a graze wound, so I'm almost positive there's no bullet in you."

"*Good* news? You know what, Malcolm?" she shouted, angry tears streaming from her red-rimmed eyes. "Markus Acker, the man who *murdered* my friend only yesterday, just left one bullet in my headrest and another slicing through my flesh! Because *you* totally lost sight of everything except your need to take down the man who's hurt your family!"

The truth of her words hit him like a gut punch. "You're absolutely right, and I'm so sorry you're hurt. But I need to call 9-1-1 now, to get help on the way for you and report what's happened so the *right* people can catch Acker."

EVEN AS GISELLE was lighting into Malcolm, she suspected she wasn't being fair, not when she'd willingly chosen to join him in the truck after he'd told her he was going after Markus. But with adrenaline shuddering through her system, the sight and smell and stickiness of her own blood turning her stomach to an oily pool, and her arm pulsating with an electric-hot pain, she couldn't keep the anger from her voice.

By the time he'd finished with his call and then placed Scarlett in her kennel after giving the pup some gentle re-assurance, Giselle turned to Malcolm as he climbed back behind the wheel. "Sorry I yelled at you," she said, her own voice soundly oddly distant to her. "I'm just—I'm a little freaked out, that's all."

"As you have every right to be. And you're hardly the first person I've upset lately with my actions where Markus is concerned." Looking stricken, he shook his head. "I don't like letting down the people I care for like this, and know-ing that I've gotten you injured—"

"I'm—I'll be just…fine once I…" she began, meaning to reassure him she was okay. Or trying to before a wave of fatigue swamped her, and oily black blobs began to crowd into her vision.

"Hey there. You still with me?" Malcolm asked her, an urgency firming his voice as his hand squeezed her forearm.

She realized only then that her eyes had rolled back and closed as she leaned back against the headrest. She only wanted to shut out the sight of the blood for a few moments. To eclipse the memory of how it had the power to form small lakes when spilled from its proper vessel.

"Giselle," Malcolm repeated, fear piercing his voice this time. "Giselle, *please*. You have to—"

"Ow!" she said, her eyes flaring wide when he applied firm pressure to the wound on her upper arm. "That *hurts*, Malcolm!"

"Sorry if that's painful," he told her, though what she saw written in his face as he slowly came into focus looked more like relief than regret. "But after you passed out, I had to apply pressure to help control the blood loss. If that bullet nicked a major vessel... Wait a minute. Are those sirens?"

Straining, she nodded. "Yes, I think so." She wasn't sure she did, though, over the roaring in her ears.

"Let's cross our fingers that at least one will be the EMTs. You aren't hurting anywhere else, are you? Any other place I might have missed?"

She shook her head, an act she instantly regretted as the truck's interior did a slow spin around her. "No, but..."

She closed her eyes to stop the carousel.

"But what? Please talk to me," he pressed.

"I'm probably..." she murmured, but her voice strengthened as she put together the pieces of the puzzle. "Have them—have them check my blood...when they transport me..."

"What about your blood, Giselle? Is there something—

can you look at me a moment, tell me—is there some kind of medical condition you haven't mentioned to me?"

Hearing the panic in his voice, she fought to open her eyes again, to try to alleviate his worry. "N-not that big a—" A wave of nausea. "Check the hemo—"

"You're not telling me that you're a bleeder, are you? That you have hemophilia?"

She tried to tell him that he had it wrong, that the last thing she intended to do was to die here, so near the same lake that had claimed her sister. But before she could explain, the roaring in her ears merged with the black blobs and she sank into unconsciousness once more.

DESPITE THE NUMBER of task-force-affiliated law enforcement personnel who'd been entering and exiting the small park, Malcolm's full attention was glued to the receding ambulance. Though Giselle had been conscious and speaking to the EMTs when she had been loaded and no sirens had been switched on, he had a leaden lump in his gut nonetheless watching the flashing emergency lights as the unit headed off toward the nearest hospital in Conners, a somewhat larger community about a forty-minute drive from Owl Creek.

"I understand how worried you must be," said Owl Creek PD's lead detective, Fletcher Colton. With his athletic build, dark brown hair, and green eyes, he bore more than a passing resemblance to Malcolm himself, though the recent Boise transplant was a few years younger and had a squarer jaw and broader forehead. "But I've seen enough gunshot wounds in my career to tell you what the EMTs won't. She's going to be okay."

"She might've seemed a whole lot better before they took off, but after watching her pass out twice already..." Malcolm shook his head, zipping his jacket a little higher since he'd given his shirt up to stanch Giselle's wound. "I've answered enough questions for the moment. As soon as Greg makes it here to give this pup a lift back to the ranch for me, I need to get to the hospital to make sure they run tests on Giselle's blood. And make certain she doesn't take another bad turn."

When he started digging in his pocket for his truck keys, Scarlett tilted her head to look up at him from the end of her lead.

Fletcher laid a hand on his shoulder. "Sorry, Malcolm, but I can't let you go anywhere quite yet. For one thing, I don't want to answer to Ajay about why I didn't finish getting your truck processed for evidence. And anyway, if you haven't noticed, your left rear tire's flat."

Malcolm looked over and cursed, seeing that one of Acker's bullets must have punctured it. "I can have it changed in no time."

"You can hold on until we're finished here. Then I promise you, I'll take you over to Conners myself, where you'll see they've been busy checking her bloodwork and stitching up that little graze wound so she'll be ready to go home with you again in no time."

As much as Malcolm wanted to believe the cousin he'd known all his life, he couldn't stop picturing the way Giselle's face had gone slack when she'd passed out on him that second time. "You aren't just saying what I want to hear now, are you? Telling me whatever it takes to get me to continue willingly answering more questions for your investigation?"

Fletcher clasped his arm. "You're family first, Mal, not some stranger—or a suspect. I swear to you, I'd *never* do that. And especially not on this lake, of all places."

Pulling away, Malcolm starting walking, Scarlett trotting at his heels. Raking his hand through the disordered mess of his slightly longer hair, he strode to the railing and knotted his hands around the sun-warmed metal. When he heard

Fletcher walk up behind him, Malcolm screwed his eyes shut against the images resurfacing from the past.

Instead of pushing him again with more of his damned questions, Fletcher appeared content to bide his time and give Malcolm a chance to pull himself together. When Malcolm looked around again, he saw his detective cousin squatting down, sitting on the backs of a pair of well-shined shoes, to rub Scarlett's floppy red ears and play with her a little.

Noticing Malcolm's regard, Fletcher asked, "So who's this cutie? New little sister for Pacer, maybe? I can see she's definitely not one of Kiki's charges."

Malcolm shook his head, knowing that since Fletcher's partner, Kiki Shelton, was a puppy-raiser for Crosswinds, the couple had the inside track on many of the young dogs that Sebastian and Della took into training. "She came to Sebastian via an out-of-state puppy raiser for potential airport sniffer dogs. But she's a—"

"Ouch—watch it there, Miss Mouthy." Wincing, Fletcher gently pried a pair of determined jaws open to extricate his fingers from the sharp puppy teeth that had clamped down on them. Looking up at Malcolm, Fletcher said, "Sorry to interrupt."

"That's fine—and a perfect illustration of the problem. Scarlett's a little homework training project from Sebastian," Malcolm said. "She's been something of a wild child around the kennel—but she's taken a real shine to Giselle."

"From what I've observed, she's not the only one." Fletcher rubbed at his fingers. "You've been spending time with Giselle, I take it?"

When Malcolm gave him a hard look, Fletcher patted the pup once more before standing again to look his cousin in the eye. "Whatever your relationship, I promise you, I'll be the last person to pass any kind of judgment."

"I never intended to see her again, much less drag her

into this Markus nightmare. But running into her again—it's brought up so many…complicated feelings. Feelings I can't afford to let take hold." Malcolm grimaced, shaking his head at the impossibility of the attraction. "And right now, we have bigger worries. And not only Markus Acker."

Fletcher frowned and shook his head. "What are you trying to say?"

"We found out just this morning that the boat responsible for the accident three years ago—the boat that killed Kate—may have turned up. At least there's good reason to believe so."

"You're serious?"

Malcolm nodded before briefly explaining how the boat had been purchased out of storage and taken to a marine mechanic in Hadley, who claimed to have found information. "Detective Rodolfo from the sheriff's department's checking out the story he tried to sell me about someone possibly threatening him about it, but she didn't seem so sure this guy was on the up-and-up. Apparently, the mechanic has a sketchy record."

"What was *your* take on the guy?" Fletcher asked.

Malcolm shrugged. "I can't tell at this point whether he's in serious danger after finding evidence or he's really some kind of grifter with an agenda. But I'm afraid that after all the attempted scams and shakedowns, I wouldn't believe an honest person by this time."

Fletcher shook his head. "I tried to tell you years ago that putting up a big reward for information and trying to vet the calls yourself was a terrible idea."

"You and Max both did." Only now did Malcolm realize what an idiot he'd been to ignore the advice of both a seasoned detective and an ex-FBI special agent. "But at the time, I couldn't see any other way."

"For what it's worth, I probably would've done the same

in your shoes, in spite of knowing better from my professional experience."

Malcolm shrugged. "Apparently, when it comes down to love, all the reason in the world flies straight out the window, the way it did when Markus Acker, of all people, came charging at us out of nowhere, aiming his gun straight at us."

"On the *exact* day you heard that this boat had turned up..." Fletcher's forehead creased as he frowned.

"You sound skeptical about the timing," Malcolm said, "but that boat vanished more than three years ago."

"Yes...less than a year after Markus moved to Idaho and established the Ever After Church in Conners."

Malcolm felt a wave of nausea assail him. "You aren't implying, are you, that the former Reverend Acker—or whatever it was he was calling himself back when he was scamming people into signing over all their assets and their free will to him—could've had some possible connection to the accident?"

"I'm not necessarily suggesting—"

"You're thinking he might have been the person *driving* that red ski boat on that afternoon in August, aren't you?"

Raising his palms, Fletcher cautioned, "Let's hold up a minute there, Malcolm. That's *way* too big a leap to make at this point."

"But if Acker *was* responsible for Kate's death, in addition to injuring Giselle the way he did just now, don't you see, there's no way I can possibly stay out of this."

"Seriously, Malcolm. Do you hear yourself? You're letting your emotions regarding Acker overwhelm your judgment."

"We already know for certain that he was responsible for the deaths of your father and my mother, and he just shot Giselle right in front of me, so why the hell wouldn't I?"

"I see your point," Fletcher said, "but I wouldn't be allowed within ten miles of this task force if my professional detachment were ever called into question. And as I was saying, if you start off certain you already *know* your investigation's endpoint, you'll accept only evidence that backs up that hypothesis and ask only the kind of questions that could possibly take you there. That sort of tunnel vision results in a lot of terrible police work."

Malcolm forced himself to take a breath to consider what Fletcher was suggesting. "So you're saying we have to stay open to the possibility that the boat's turning up at this particular juncture has nothing to do with Markus?"

"It could certainly be coincidental. Or maybe Acker was nowhere near the scene of the accident itself but had some involvement with the cover-up of the boat's location later, or of its mysterious reappearance at this time. Or maybe he's somehow tied to this boat mechanic's possible attempt to scam you. We just don't have enough information to know at this point."

"I don't understand," Malcolm said. "If Acker *is* somehow tangled up with the call I received from the boat mechanic, what would be his point? And would that have any bearing on why he showed up pointing a gun at me today?"

"*Now* you're sounding like someone with real detective potential." Fletcher added a smile. "Or at least I'd say that if I didn't figure you'd pulverize Acker before you ever had the patience to pry the answers to any of those questions out of that slippery charlatan."

A darker-haired man in his mid-thirties jogged over, a slim six-footer with a trim beard wearing a navy polo beneath his Owl Creek PD jacket. "Sorry to interrupt," he said.

"You're fine," Fletcher told him before glancing toward his rancher cousin. "Malcolm, you remember Archer McKenzie? His Las Vegas PD experience and the fact that he's a real wiz, especially when it comes to evidence processing, has been incredibly helpful."

Malcolm and Archer shook hands, both men nodding.

"Sure. Hannah's introduced us," Malcolm answered, referring to Fletcher's widowed sister, who seemed happier than she'd been in ages since she'd gotten together with the Nevada transplant.

"Speaking of evidence," Archer said, looking at Fletcher, "I wanted to let you know the presumptive test on the dark stains you marked over here were positive."

Fletcher glanced back in the direction toward the parking lot. "So those are definitely bloodstains?"

Remembering the information he'd provided earlier, Malcolm felt his pulse accelerate. "Are you saying—you don't mean you've found blood over where I showed you Acker dropped and rolled after I shot at him? I could've sworn I missed him." He ran those chaotic few moments of the shootout back through his mind.

"Perhaps not," Fletcher allowed.

"I still have to run another test to confirm the blood is human," Archer qualified. "Then, if that one's positive, I'll cross-match it to a known sample from Ms. Dowling to eliminate her as the source."

Fletcher explained, "We don't want to take a chance of letting a defense attorney get him off on any procedural errors once we take him into custody. But I do think it's very possible you left Markus Acker something to remember you by—maybe even an injury serious enough to force him to seek help."

"If I did happen to hit him," Malcolm said, "I damned well hope he's finally getting a good taste of the pain he's cost so many others."

"I'll leave the worrying over retribution to a higher power," Fletcher said. "All I want right now is to get him off the streets before he can destroy any other lives."

"Of course, I understand that." Malcolm admired Fletcher's composure but doubted he would share it if he'd just seen Kiki hauled off in the back of an ambulance.

"I've already sent out alerts with Acker's photo and description to every hospital and clinic within a hundred miles."

Archer nodded his approval. "That warning could save some lives—but are you sure you don't want to expand the radius even farther?"

"I could, just out of an abundance of caution, but the task force is fairly certain that won't be necessary," Fletcher told them, "because *something's* clearly holding him in this area, whether there's something he desperately needs or worse yet, some revenge fantasy he's cooked up against members of our family."

"That's a chilling thought." Malcolm winced, thinking of his father and the aunt he thought of as a second mother, his siblings, half-siblings, and cousins, not to mention their partners and even the little ones who should never have to think about such evil.

"One I pray I'm wrong about," Fletcher said. "But with the possibility of his being injured, too—"

"You're saying that I might've made things even worse?" Malcolm asked.

"Worse, better—it's impossible to say what might set off a ticking time bomb." Fletcher gazed out over the lake's wind-troubled waters. "Or who exactly it could end up going off on in the end."

Chapter Thirteen

In the emergency department exam room where Giselle had been left to rest with a bag of intravenous fluids, she cracked open an eyelid and breathed a sigh of relief at the sight of Malcolm.

"Thank goodness it's you," she said, fumbling to raise the head of her bed. "I was scared half to death it would be a technician out for yet another blood sample. It's a wonder I have anything left for them to take by this time."

"No more needles here, I promise," he said, eyeing the fresh bandage now covering the graze wound on her upper arm. "Just a guy who's relieved as hell to see your color back and hear you sounding more like yourself."

When he bent to kiss her cheek, she couldn't resist the impulse to give him an awkward hug.

He returned it, his voice going rough when he said "Giselle," and squeezing her in return, hard enough that she understood how deeply she must have scared him at the park earlier.

Closing her eyes, she leaned her head against his shoulder, relief flowing through her to be in the strong arms of a man she knew she could always trust to look out for her interests—a man she knew she would always care about as well.

"I'm so glad you came," she said, telling herself that it

was perfectly appropriate to embrace a good friend—even a male friend she'd once kissed, in a moment of poor judgment that could never be repeated—as she pulled away. "When I asked the nurse to watch for you and let you back here if you showed up, I wasn't sure if—"

"I would've been here a heck of a lot sooner, but there were a lot of questions that needed answering to assist in the search."

"Of course," she said, immediately understanding that the manhunt had to be the number one priority, before anyone else could be hurt. "Any new updates yet on—"

"Before we get into any of that, I have to know how you are. What did they say about your wound? And are they going to admit you?"

"Admit me? Not for this," she said, shaking her head as she gestured toward her bandage. "All it needed was some cleaning and a little surgical adhesive. Shallow as it was, the doctor says it should be fully healed within a couple of weeks and not even leave much of a scar."

"That's wonderful. But you're sounding awfully nonchalant for someone who went lights-out on me more than once." He cast a worried look toward her IV bag. "I don't mean to pry, but you did mention something about your blood. And I was afraid that—I was just *afraid.* For you."

"I get that," she said, "and I'm really sorry. This bag's only hydration, just to perk me up a little."

"Graze wound or not, you don't need to apologize for being *shot,*" he said, sounding offended by the idea of it. "The shock alone, I'd imagine, would be enough to—"

"That wasn't what had me fainting," she said, frowning. "And I'm sure I had you imagining all sorts of terrible things with what I said about blood testing, but I promise you, it's nothing dire. Only my own negligence."

He shook his head. "I don't understand."

"Of course you wouldn't," she scoffed. "Not when I'm being cryptic. What I suspected—and turned out to be right about—was that I might be anemic again. It happens to some younger women, especially around their…their monthly cycles." She reminded herself that they were both grown adults and basic biological functions were nothing to be shy about discussing. "According to the doctor, my hemoglobin was low because I haven't been doing the greatest job getting enough iron in my diet."

"This has happened to you before, then? The passing out from not taking care of yourself properly? Because I'm totally prepared to reintroduce you to the joys of steaks and burgers. Or at least to chicken and fish, if the vegetarian lifestyle's not cutting it for you."

"Thanks, but no thanks," she said, having lost her taste for meat years before. "I've been given a supplement for the short-term to move the needle in the right direction. But in the long run, there are *plenty* of outstanding meat-free options that'll keep me in top form. I just need to remember that cooking for myself is no excuse not to pay attention to what's healthy."

"No, it definitely isn't," he said, "especially when I've tasted the evidence of what a fantastic cook you are when you put in the effort. But I think I understand. When you're alone the way you have been, it must be tough motivating yourself to do things that feel like they're solely for your own benefit. I know that during the past few years, there were a lot of days when, if I hadn't had family, Pacer, or ranch and SAR obligations to motivate me, I'm not sure I ever would've made it out of bed."

She avoided his gaze, not wanting him to get an inkling how often she had fought that very battle.

"Hey," he said, the tips of his fingers brushing her jaw,

"I hope you know that I would never judge you. I only want you to be healthy and happy."

"I *have* been taking steps toward the healthy part. Doing some weight work and trail running to build my muscle tone and stamina. Trying to get back into scratch meal prepping for myself the way I was when you came by the cabin," she said. "All I have to do is stay motivated to keep it up."

"That's an excellent start, and for the time being, I want you to consider me a partner in that effort."

"I don't need a babysitter, Malcolm," she said.

"That's great, because I'm in the middle of a full-blown crisis and don't have the bandwidth to babysit anybody while I'm working to keep my family safe from whatever Markus's next move might be. What I *can* be, though, is the kind of friend who'll have your back—especially if you'll help to keep an eye on mine."

"Sounds more than fair to me," she said. "Earlier, though, you put me off when I asked you about Markus. Please tell me there's been some good news about the search for him."

"It looks like I may have clipped him during the shoot-out," Malcolm told her. "There was enough blood found where he fell after I fired on him that an alert's been sent out to medical facilities. And while Fletcher was driving me over here, he got word about a possible sighting of my truck on the road to Owl Creek. Ajay's got everyone he has on it, even air support from the state."

Excitement zinged through her. "Do you think they might really have him this time?"

"For my family's sake—and the safety of the whole community—I hope they do. Especially after finding Claudette yesterday and watching you get hurt today."

"But I wasn't his real target, was I? It definitely looked to me like his attention was focused on you."

"Fletcher had the same thought when we talked about it."

"You don't think he was aware it was you before tracking him with Pacer, do you?" she asked. "Maybe he could've been watching you through a pair of binoculars on the mountain and seen the two of you and then decided you were a particular threat."

"That's not a half-bad theory," Malcolm said, "but I'm fairly sure Pacer and I didn't come nearly that close to him, especially with yesterday's poor visibility. And anyway, he would've been more focused on my K-9 as the threat instead of me personally."

"We passed him in the Crosstrek, as well," she said, "but it was awfully quick, and the visibility was awful."

"If we couldn't see him, I can't imagine he got a good look at either of us."

Shaking her head, Giselle asked, "What then?"

"Fletcher figured Acker might've spotted that Colton Ranch logo on the truck I was driving today and assumed I was one of the members of the same family that's been causing him so much grief lately."

"Oh, poor him," she said sarcastically. "Sounds like he only has himself to blame for whatever troubles he's run into, considering his scheme to kill your uncle and rob the Coltons blind."

"I don't imagine that the concept of fairness has ever figured into Markus Acker's thinking," Malcolm said.

"I suppose it comes with the territory when you're a homicidal narcissist with cult members willing to treat you like some sort of god on earth," she said.

"I need to tell you," Malcolm said. "Fletcher has a theory that Acker's crimes against our family may go back even farther than we ever imagined."

"What do you mean?" she asked.

He turned a somber look on her. "Before I tell you, you need to understand that this is only a very tentative working theory. The red boat's turning up right now could be exactly what it seems to be—a very lucky break after years of frustration in finding—"

"Wait. What are you—?" She shook her head, desperately trying to keep up with his change of subject. "You aren't saying that in some way, *Markus Acker* of all people could be—that he might have something to do with the—the *accident*?"

For the third time that day, black spots edged her vision. This time, however, Giselle fought them back, in spite of the nausea threatening to overwhelm her.

"I don't know *how* he might be involved," Malcolm said, "or if he has anything at all do with—"

"Murdering my sister," she said flatly.

His face blanching, he nodded. "Or helping somehow with the cover-up or even using the bait of the boat this morning, along with Kelsie's uncle Larry at the marina, to try to lure us—or probably just me—out where he could ambush me on my own. I'm only sorry you happened to be with me. If I'd had the faintest idea that I might've been being played—"

"Let's not either of us waste another second apologizing for things that weren't our fault. Now, I should try calling Detective Rodolfo," Giselle said. "We need to find out whatever happened to Larry Willets at Creekside Marine. We have to know whether he's tied up with Markus somehow or if instead he's one more of Acker's victims."

Nodding his agreement, Malcolm said, "Fletcher's out in the lobby trying to reach one of the sheriff's department detectives right now. Meanwhile, we should—"

He was interrupted as the emergency physician who had treated her earlier returned to talk about sending her home.

"I don't mind if my friend hears this," Giselle said, certain that whatever the doctor had to say would take only a few minutes.

"She'll be staying with me for at least the next few days,"

Malcolm said, darting a look her way that brooked no argument on the subject, "so the more I know about how to assist with her recovery, the better."

A leanly built, middle-aged man in navy scrubs and thick, dark hair streaked with silver, Dr. Avila glanced curiously at Malcolm's immobilized left hand and forearm but asked no questions before nodding. Returning his attention to Giselle, the doctor reviewed her wound care. After emphasizing the importance of her staying close to home for several days, he advised her to follow up with her family doctor for further care.

"I don't exactly have one in the area," she admitted. "It's been a few years since I've felt the need to go in for anything beyond some recent vaccinations at the mobile clinic."

"Well, then it sounds like high time that you found yourself someone. Do you need a list of possibilities?"

"I'll ask around," she said vaguely.

"I'll make sure she gets in to see Dr. Beecham," Malcolm put in.

"Cynthia Beecham?" Dr. Avila asked, brightening. "My wife swears by her. Good choice, but I hear it can be tough for a new patient to get appointments."

"I have an inside track there." Malcolm smiled. "My aunt's one of her nurses and works there a couple of days a week."

"That's perfect, then," the doctor said before going on to hand Giselle a thick sheaf of printed papers.

"I'm a vegetarian as well," he said, "so I've included some suggestions for plant-based iron sources, since a lot of people find food sources easier to tolerate than the supplements."

"Thank you." Giselle said as the nurse who'd come in while Dr. Avila was talking unhooked her IV. "But I'm actually feeling so much better now. And I'm already quite aware of what I should be doing. I only need to make a point to actually do it."

"The fluids, painkillers, and rest you've had here may have given you the false impression that you're completely back to normal, but you've still suffered a serious physical and emotional trauma," Dr. Avila countered.

"You said yourself that the graze wound on my arm was minor," she argued, feeling impatient to get this over with.

"While the injury shouldn't leave you with any long-term damage, your system was quite depleted. And it can be more upsetting than you might realize, once you've had the chance to process that someone's committed a potentially homicidal act of violence against you."

"I haven't—I haven't really thought about that," Giselle said.

"But you likely will, so I've included among your papers contact information for a victims' advocate who can connect you with resources such as counseling or—"

"As much as I appreciate all you've done, I don't need naps and I don't need to chat about my feelings," she insisted, ignoring the look that Malcolm gave her. "I just need out of here, so I can get myself prepared."

"Prepared in what way?" Dr. Avila asked her.

"Prepared to make certain that the next time I encounter Markus Acker, *I'm* not the one who ends up in your ER."

Chapter Fourteen

Malcolm wasn't certain which he found more disturbing, the thought that Giselle might be too passive to take measures to protect her own life or the idea that she might be actively looking forward to another violent confrontation with an unhinged killer. Between Claudette's murder and the shoot-out, she had reason enough to be upset, but he suspected the real trigger for her uncharacteristic outburst may have been his own suggestion that Acker could have been involved in Kate's death.

Noticing the alarmed look on the physician's face, Malcolm quickly explained, "The last couple of days have been an emotional roller coaster for both of us. But right now, the only things we're looking at doing are getting home where we can regroup, have a good meal, and meet up again with a certain puppy I know will be very happy to see you."

"Poor Scarlett. Is she all right?" Giselle asked, her expression turning anxious. "I'd forgotten all about her."

"She's fine. No need to worry. My brother Greg showed up with a change of clothes for me and then took her back to the ranch to hang out with his kids and Briony."

"Thank goodness."

Once Giselle had changed back into street clothes—with the exception of a scrub top one of the nurses had found for her to replace her own blood-soaked shirt—she and Malcolm were escorted back into the waiting area, where they were told Detective Fletcher Colton was waiting to see them.

"Do you see him anywhere?" Malcolm asked Giselle.

"I don't think so," she said, scanning the room, which was crowded with a variety of individuals, some holding ice packs to bandaged heads or towels to bleeding body parts. Another leaned over a trashcan, his greenish hue indicating the possibility that he might at any moment fill it, and a particularly alarming-sounding woman tried—and failed—to cover the sound of her deeply phlegmy coughs.

"Whoa," Malcolm said quietly, sticking out an arm to prevent Giselle from moving any farther into germ central.

"I'm with you on that," Giselle whispered.

"There's Fletcher outside," Malcolm said, gesturing toward a window, where his cousin stood near the edge of the parking lot, talking on his cell phone in the shade of a maple tree.

Spotting Malcolm inside, Fletcher waved, imploring the two of them to come outside to meet him. They quickly found an exit and left the emergency department.

"That was a good call, finding yourself a patch of green grass and fresh air," Malcolm told him. "Giselle, this is my cous—"

"I'm Detective Fletcher Colton." Fletcher offered her a hand after tucking his phone back inside his pocket. "We met briefly earlier right before you were loaded into the ambulance, but I don't expect you to—"

"It's a bit of a blur," she admitted, "but I do remember speaking to you."

"I hope you're feeling better now."

"Oh, definitely. Thanks for asking," she said. "But I was hoping we might be able to get some information from you."

"I know this isn't anything to do with the task force's investigation," Malcolm elaborated, "but we were both wondering if you'd heard anything from the sheriffs' department about whether they found Larry Willets safe at the marina?"

Fletcher nodded. "I was just giving an update on the two of you to Detective Rodolfo, since she reached out when she heard about what happened. She also asked me to let you know that Willets voluntarily came in to her office to answer some additional questions and turn in a piece of evidence that he claimed to have collected from the boat before it was taken in for further processing."

"So he wasn't harmed at all?"

"Didn't sound that way," Fletcher said. "But I got the impression from our conversation they're trying to figure out how he fits in with the other suspects they've identified."

"What do you mean, the *other* suspects?" Giselle blurted, beating Malcolm to the punch.

"I should probably let someone from the sheriff's department explain that to you."

"Don't do that to us." Malcolm looked his cousin directly in the eye, "especially since you and I both know there's no telling how long it might take for someone else to get back to us in person."

Clearly uncomfortable with the situation, Fletcher allowed his gaze to drift to Giselle.

"Please," she said. "After everything we've gone through, don't you believe we've at the very least earned the right not to be treated like small children? Or be bounced around from voicemail to voicemail for hours or days while we wait for answers?"

After a moment's hesitation, Fletcher sighed. "I guess you have at that, both of you. So, this morning, Deputy Rodolfo and her partner tracked down the couple who previously owned the facility where the boat was stored before it was sold to its present owners. The hope was that one or both of them might remember something more helpful than the phony name and address listed on the paperwork they filled out more than three years ago."

"And they hit pay dirt, I take it?" Malcolm asked.

"The husband seems to have been the one who helped them. He didn't recall anything helpful, but it turns out his wife remembered that one of the two *boys*, as she called them, was the red-haired son of someone she'd gone to school with. They dug out an old high school yearbook and came up with a woman's name, and from there they ended up setting up a—"

"So you're saying that they've *arrested* them?" Giselle all but shouted, her eyes wide.

"They've identified two men, both of them mid-twenties," Fletcher said. "Twenty and twenty-one that summer and only about a week out from heading back to the dorm at Boise State for the fall term."

"You mean they were—they were damned *kids*?" Malcolm burst out.

"Adults, in the law's eyes," Fletcher pointed out. "But we still don't—"

"Who the hell are they?" Malcolm demanded.

"Do they have them in jail yet?" Giselle asked at the same time.

"These suspects, at this point, have no idea the deputies are even aware of any such boat accident," Fletcher said. "For all they know, the sheriff's department may simply want to speak to them about their unpaid storage bill."

Malcolm frowned and shook his head. "They'd have to be pretty idiotic to voluntarily go in for a conversation about their 'missing boat' when they've been hiding it all this time following a fatality accident."

"You'd think so, wouldn't you?" said Fletcher. "But you'd be absolutely shocked at how many people will respond to exactly such an invitation—not so much because they aren't worried about what the authorities might know but because they've had a whole lot of time to sweat over what might happen to the lives they've been building since their original crime took place. The crime that they've long since begun to hope that people have forgotten about by this point since no one's caught onto it for this long."

"No one's forgotten a thing," Malcolm angrily insisted. "At least *we* never will."

"It's impossible," Giselle added, slipping her arm through his, "when the nightmares are always *right there*, just waiting for you to let your guard down."

Though the sadness of her statement hit hard, Malcolm felt something of a kinship in the way they stood together, lending each other strength in their shared trauma. Even if some part of him, a part that had stubbornly taken root and refused to be tamped down inside him, wished they might share more.

Fletcher nodded his agreement. "Of course, no one's forgotten Kate's death, for all their wishful thinking. But they'll be dying to find out what, if anything, the sheriff's department really knows and desperate for any chance to put their worried minds at ease."

"So what do *we* do now?" Giselle asked.

"Let me take you two back to the ranch," Fletcher said, "where both of you can get some much-needed rest and do some healing while we all wait to hear the outcome of these interviews and whether Acker's been arrested."

"You sound almost like you're expecting some news on that at any moment," Malcolm said hopefully. "I mean on Markus."

"Maybe it's because we got a credible tip on a sighting and location, still in your truck," Fletcher told them. "Or maybe I'm just thinking that no fugitive's luck can hold forever. But whether it takes minutes, hours, days, or weeks, they eventually always slip up, especially when they're under this much pressure—and if he's in pain, as the blood we found at the scene of the shoot-out seems to indicate, that only pushes the chances even higher that we'll soon be celebrating an arrest."

"As far as Acker's concerned, we've all had our hopes dashed more than once," Malcolm reminded him. "But exactly where is it that he was spotted?"

Looking him directly in the eye, Fletcher's voice turned firmly official. "In answer to that question, all I'm going to tell you is that I don't expect to hear another word about you going off on your own, doing anymore freelancing with Pacer. Or with anyone else, either, for that matter." He looked pointedly at Giselle. "Do we all understand each other?"

Recalling the hail of bullets that had not only grazed Giselle's arm but punctured the headrest so close to her neck and struck his own side of the pickup, Malcolm said, "I hear you, Fletcher, but I'll remind you, Acker was the one who came for *me* today and not vice versa. And if he comes again, I promise you, he's going to find me more than ready to protect myself and anyone who happens to be with me."

"Trust me," Fletcher said, "Acker's got enough to worry about avoiding the dragnet that's tightening around him right now to be trying to follow you two to a ranch where he's bound to run into one of any number of Coltons or hired hands who'll all be on the lookout for him."

"We've got everyone on high alert and putting the house's new deadbolts to good use."

"Good. So quit feeling like you need to do law enforcement's job for us and try to take it easy for a little while, both of you."

EXHAUSTED, HUNGRY, AND in pain, Markus Acker sat inside the idling pickup on a dusty back road two days later, knowing he was nearly out of options. After that freaking Colton cowboy had jumped out of his pickup and shot off a significant chunk of his damned upper *ear*, he'd wanted nothing more than to hunt down and kill the bastard for the insult— not only for the bloody injury he'd inflicted, but for permanently marring an appearance Acker had always taken so much pride in. Not only was the wound agonizing and disgusting, it would make him all too easily identifiable once it was discovered. Seeing his own reflection in the mirror now, gaunt and filthy, dressed in ragged clothes and with thick gauze peeping out from beneath the oversized stocking cap he wore in an attempt to conceal his clumsy efforts with the truck's first aid kit, he felt disgusted, diminished from the man he'd been before he'd been forced into hiding. The man whose followers had practically seen him as a god.

What he would do to have them all back, hanging on his every word as they competed for new ways to better please him. But by now, that had been ruined—most of his people likely turned against him as surely as Jessie the Betrayer. Yet he wondered if there might be one, at least, whom he might trust now, even at his lowest—one so blindly loyal that Markus, who had never had nor wanted his own children, had granted the younger man the extreme privilege of allowing him to call him Father. Just as he had, in private, when he'd needed something especially dubious, referred to his acolyte as Son.

He would do so again today, he decided, should his follower remain in the Wilderness Chapel of Contemplation, where he'd been sent only days before the meltdown that had led to the downfall of the Ever After Church. He could only hope that in the aftermath, no one had given a moment's thought to the nearly-silent acolyte who—it was just possible—remained there, completely isolated from all news from the outside world.

And completely open to performing one last, vital service to the man he considered the closest thing he still had to a father on this earth.

OVER THE COURSE of the three days following the shooting, Giselle struggled to heed both Fletcher's and the ER doctor's advice to focus on her recovery. Malcolm tried to keep things as low-key as possible, taking her for easy strolls, helping her fix healthy meals, and working to keep various family members from overwhelming them with visits to check to see how they were faring, since word of their ordeal had spread.

Soon the two of them fell into a routine of sorts, with Giselle's favorite part being Scarlett's training sessions, repeated in brief intervals three times daily to suit the pup's short attention span. Except for one morning, when a brief but heavy shower forced them to improvise indoors, she and Malcolm—and often Pacer, modeling his most dignified, grown-up-dog behavior—worked in a grassy outdoor paddock, with an expansive view of the mountains in the distance—more often used for training horses. With the excitable pup always on the lookout for opportunities to dart off snapping at some insect, bark her lungs out at any ranch hand who happened to ride past, or race over to roll in some smelly pile that would necessitate a struggle to get her in the bathtub later, Giselle couldn't afford to let her attention wander for so much as a split second.

Still, she found their efforts rewarding—even fun, since there was no way to spend any amount of time trying to outsmart the ornery Scarlett without laughing at her antics. The diversion served as welcome relief from the time she spent worrying over whether the Coltons would ever again be safe from worries over Markus Acker, who had somehow managed to disappear again.

Somehow, though, she was even more bothered by the sheriff's department's failure to make the swift arrest that she and Malcolm had both hoped for. Not long after the ranch truck was returned—its formerly flat tire changed—the prior day, Detective Rodolfo had come by the ranch for an in-person chat. She'd been quick to inform them that so far, they'd found no reason to believe that Larry Willets had been involved in any conspiracy involving the boat, its storage, or its reappearance at this time.

"Now that the threatening calls from that blocked number he claimed to have received have stopped, he actually appears interested in wanting to help solve the crime himself," she'd said, sounding equal parts amused and annoyed by this development. "That's just what we need around here, another wannabe true-crime podcaster."

Afterward, Rodolfo had spoken of the two suspects who'd rented the storage unit where the boat had been abandoned. The first had come into the sheriff's office with a story about how he and his friend were working at a lakeside marina one hot summer day when they were paid cash to trailer the red speedboat across county lines and store it under a name and address—both of which had turned out to be fictitious—scribbled on a scrap of paper. After he'd insisted that he'd had no knowledge of the boat's involvement in any accident, the detectives' questions had grown more pointed.

"At that point," Rodolfo told them, "he told us to direct all further inquiries to his lawyer and walked out on us."

"And you just let him?" Giselle blurted.

"We'd gotten what we were getting from him for the moment."

"What about the other one?" Malcolm had asked next.

Rodolfo shook her head. "I'm afraid the news is worse there. It turns out the other kid, the red-haired one the storage facility woman had recognized, was reported missing by his parents, just a few months after the boat accident, after leaving his dorm at Boise State and never showing up back home."

"Missing?" Malcolm blurted.

Rodolfo nodded. "Apparently, he'd had some significant issues during the early weeks of the semester. Disruptive outbursts in his classes—when he bothered showing up— tearing up his dorm room. But the last straw was when he jumped on the hood of a commuter's car in the parking lot and started shouting all kinds of nonsense at the driver."

"Had he always had these kinds of issues?" Malcolm asked. "Or was he using something that anybody knew of?"

"From what I've gathered, this was way out of character. This kid liked to party some, but he was on track to graduate with honors," Rodolfo told them. "He managed to disappear without a trace—but not before draining every penny from a family trust he'd gained access to after turning twenty- one. So we know he wasn't *completely* out of his mind..."

"You *have* to get that first guy talking," Giselle said. "I'll bet he knows what his friend was really running from."

"I'm sorry," Rodolfo told them. "We've tried everything we're able to. We've even been discussing an immunity deal with the DA, where we would agree to let Suspect One off for his role in hiding the boat if he'll only give up the real owner. But what if we sign off on something like that, and then it turns out that he's been lying about his true role in the accident? We certainly don't want to absolve him of the threat of prosecution if he's actually the one guilty of intoxi- cation manslaughter..."

As Giselle and Malcolm walked back toward the house now, with the dogs trotting beside them, Giselle shook her head. "Sorry. You were saying something? I'm afraid I was off chasing butterflies in Scarlett-land or something."

He smiled at her. "I was just saying you had that worried

look on your face again," he said. "I thought we'd agreed we were going to take the afternoon off from fretting over police business so we could go test-drive some possible new wheels for you."

"Can you honestly say you haven't been doing some worrying of your own?" she asked, unwilling to be sidetracked into another conversation about the pros and cons of various models. "I've caught you looking distracted more than a few times, especially since Rodolfo told us about those two guys."

Rather than denying it, Malcolm removed his cowboy hat to rake his fingers through his hair. "If only we could've talked her into giving us their names ... I'm sure I could've at least talked to that one who clammed up and personally persuaded him to come clean with what he knows."

She cast a sidelong glance in his direction. "I'm not so sure I'd trust you not to resort to methods that would end up getting you into serious trouble, if you ever got that close."

He snorted, smiling wryly. "So you think of me as the menacing sort?"

She stopped walking to face him, recalling all the times she'd seen him affectionately scratching Pacer behind the ears, scooping up Scarlett for a cuddle, or taking a couple of carrots or apples to the fence line to handfeed them to Sundance and his pinto pasture-mate, Ivy, while he stroked the horses' strong necks.

"Normally, I think that any kind of violence goes against your very nature," she said honestly. "But I know how painful it is to finally get this close yet still not have any concrete answers. I heard it in your voice the other day when you were on the phone with Willets threatening to, how was it you put it? Something about rearranging his bones?"

Turning toward her, Malcolm snorted. "I hope you don't

believe I'd have really done any serious damage. I'm not that kind of person."

"Says the man who whipped out a pistol and started blasting away at Acker before I could react to what was going on back at that park."

"Yes, and he *still* nearly managed to come close to killing you. I've been having nightmares ever since about turning my head to see you bleeding—and that bullet hole right by your neck."

Seeing him grimace, she laid a hand on his arm. "Hey, I understand. And I didn't mean to give you grief for saving both our lives. You did what you had to—and what *I* certainly would have been no help with—especially since we figured out that the gun in my bag wasn't even loaded."

"We can change that, if you'd like," he told her. "But I wouldn't feel comfortable arming you without giving you some serious training, both in safety and basic marksmanship."

She thought about it carefully, recalling how angrily she'd spoken at the hospital about never again wanting to be taken by surprise. But when her thoughts turned to guns, a deep-seated discomfort rose up in her, one that had her shaking her head. "I know how tough I talked before, and at the time I really meant it. But I'm not sure I could really pull a trigger. I mean—it seems so simple, the idea of him or one of us. But sometimes, the bullets don't go where they're intended, do they? So often I'll watch the news, and I'll see where one's ended up in a toddler sleeping in his crib across the street or an old man shaving at his bathroom mirror. And then, in the blink of an eye, not only the lives of the person struck, but every single person who loved them are changed forever, sometimes destroyed, and I can't help think about how our hearts were crushed, our souls stamped into splinters when Kate was taken from us…"

Seeing how intently he was staring at her, she shook her head. "You're probably thinking you'd expect no less than this kind of cosmic touchy-feely weirdness from someone who can't even eat anything that had a mama."

"Do you *really* want to know what I was thinking?"

"I'll probably regret saying so, but I've always been way too curious for my own good," she said, raising her brows expectantly.

"I was thinking, Giselle Dowling," he said, speaking with a quiet sincerity that made her lean in to listen to him more closely, "that your soul is as beautiful as the rest of you, and I hope you won't ever let the ugliness that exists in this world change you."

"It's not that I'm not flattered—sincerely—but you should know as well as anybody, this world dulls everybody's colors." She dropped her gaze, remembering the vibrant enthusiasm of the optimistic, often sassy younger woman she had once been. Perhaps, she realized, her gaze dropping to Scarlett as the pup jumped to the limits of her leash at Pacer, waving her paws and flashing white teeth in an attempt to lure him into playful combat, it was her nostalgia for the version of herself lost to the lake that had drawn her to the sweet and silly little beagle.

"I'm pretty sure there's an entire rainbow still inside you," Malcolm told her. "All you have to do is give yourself permission to let it shine again."

She looked up into the face of a man she'd grown to deeply care for, allowing a sigh to slip free as she did...

And wincing when Malcolm immediately reacted, asking, "What was that for? Am I embarrassing you, talking rainbows instead of barbed wire and billy goats like the simple rancher you've always had me pegged for?"

She shook her head, her shoulders shaking.

"What's so funny?" he asked.

"Only the idea that anyone who's ever had more than the briefest of encounters with you imagining you as a *simple* anything," she said. "What I was embarrassed about, honestly, was the thought of all the years I wasted hanging with a crowd who never saw anything in me beyond the long, blond hair, the trendy fashions, and whatever celebrity cache they imagined might've rubbed off on me from my work."

"I'm sure you had your share of fun running around town spending money and looking like a million bucks."

"What *passed* for fun, you mean." She shrugged, since even the memories of those days had lost their luster after her so-called friends had dropped her. "But the thing is, I doubt that any of those people, including the couple of men I was foolish enough to trust with my heart—ever *really* saw me. Not the way a rancher does who has not a single thing in common with me except the worst day of our lives."

"I'm pretty sure you're wrong on that count," he said. "We both loved the same woman, a woman who lived for both of us."

"I miss her *so* much." Giselle balled her fists, her heart breaking open with the memory of what it had been like to have someone in the world who had loved her so completely, someone who had been there for her from the moment of her birth. "I miss my family, Malcolm."

"I know you do," he told her, gathering her in his arms and letting her lay her head against his chest as the tears began to fall. "But I've got you right now. I've got you for as long as you need a pair of arms to hold you up."

As Malcolm stroked her back and supported her, he fervently wished that there was something—anything—more that he could do to ease her anguish. He thought about how effortlessly his dad—who always seemed to know the right things to say around his aunt and sister—had set Giselle at ease that first night he'd brought her to the ranch by assuring her that she was practically family. But he was smart enough to understand that being welcomed as an honorary Colton could in no way make up for her personal losses.

Stepping back from him, Giselle wiped her eyes with a tissue she pulled from the front pocket of her jeans. "Thanks for that, but I'm so sorry. I shouldn't be—"

"It's fine," he was quick to say as they both, by unspoken agreement, began walking back toward the house. "I'm sure this business with the boat turning up has brought things back for you, the same as it has for me."

She looked up to study him intently. "Are you—are you doing okay, Malcolm? This hasn't dredged up any of those feelings, like you had before…back when your father saw you…" Her glance strayed toward the working barn.

He shook his head. "I won't say it's been pleasant, but having my family, my work, even distractions like this little dynamo here help." He nodded his head toward Scarlett, who was entertaining herself flipping around a spindly stick she'd picked up somewhere while Pacer watched her with a look of mild interest. "They've given me a lot more to focus on. But I do appreciate your asking about that time. Even my dad mostly likes to pretend that nothing ever happened— because it didn't, really."

"But it might have."

He hesitated for a long time before admitting, "Yeah. I'll own that. Just like I'll own up to the fact that what I was dealing with for quite some time was clinical depression. Millions of people do."

Having given her that opening, he gave her the invitation of his silence to speak about her own lost years.

But after an awkward silence, she said only, "I'm really glad you talked to someone."

"Talking to the right person's good. And there're other

things as well, things that help a lot of people," he said. "If you're ever interested in—in discussing—"

"If you're trying to bring this around to me," she said, "I'd really rather not get into that now, Malcolm."

"Sure thing," he said, wondering why she couldn't draw a line between supporting him for getting the help he had needed and considering that such a thing might be a viable option for herself. But he'd heard that warning shading her tone, the one that told him that it was time to back off and give the seed he'd planted a chance to take root if it would.

They made it within about twenty feet of the house's back deck when Giselle lurched, saying, "Whoops, *Scarlett*!" as the pup—darting after a leaf blown by a puff of wind—tangled beneath her feet.

Malcolm grabbed at Giselle's arm but caught air as she plunged forward with a yelp before sprawling in an undignified-looking heap in a patch of grass.

"You all right down there?" he asked, amazed she'd been able to contort her body into such a position—with her shoulders down and her knees folded beneath her—to avoid squashing the beagle.

"Just *fabulous*," Giselle said, trying to push herself up to a kneeling position while at the same time fending off Scarlett's attempts to cover her face with kisses.

Malcolm knew he shouldn't have laughed, but Giselle's chagrin, combined with the small canine tornado's delirious joy at the chaos she had wrought, had him chuckling, even as he reached down to grab the pup and offered Giselle a hand up.

"Sorry I was too slow to catch you," he said, "but let me take this one off your hands for now. And maybe from now on."

"Wait—what do you mean?" she asked.

"I mean, you've been a really good sport these past few

days, but it's obvious that what this little hound needs is some one-on-one time with a real professional. So I wanted to let you know that last night I spoke to Della, and talked her into taking her over to her place for some one-to-one intensives in the evenings."

"No!" Giselle cried out before adding. "Sorry—I didn't mean to shout. It's just that I don't want Scarlett to feel like one more person's given up on her, especially not when…"

"Go on," he encouraged, Scarlett wriggling in his arms. Wriggling to get back to Giselle, just as he'd expected.

"Not when…" Giselle said, the plea in her tear-filled gaze as she held her arms out prompting him to hand over the beagle. "Not when I already love this little mess so much."

He reached out to touch her cheek. "I know you do. Just like I'm totally onto the fact that you've been letting her sleep with you at night instead of in the crate the way we discussed."

Giselle looked down into Scarlett's face. "Did you rat us out, girl?"

"She didn't have to. When that smoke alarm malfunctioned last night, and you came out to see what was up, I spotted all the dog hair on your pajamas while you were pulling on your robe."

"So you were checking out my oh-so-sexy pj's, were you?" she asked, her smile revealing a dimple he'd noticed the night before. A dimple he'd had trouble getting off his mind when he'd later returned to bed alone.

"Hey, how would I have figured out you liked baby pandas otherwise," he asked, "and that you'd been spoiling our houseguest?"

"I will *never* apologize for my baby pandas, but I *am* sorry if I broke some kind of serious Colton house rule by sleeping with the dog," she said. "You won't report me, will you?"

"To who, exactly—presuming that Mr. Pacer here's never

set a paw on any furnishing without an invitation?" He smiled at his own hairy sidekick, who'd been known to hog the sectional while he, his father, and a brother or two were all watching football. "For one thing, my dad's asked everyone to give us a break from any more visits for a little while."

"But I've enjoyed seeing Lizzy, Greg and Briony. And those veggie tartlets Hannah dropped off were delicious," Giselle said.

"It was great they came to check in on us," he allowed, "but even I'll admit my family can be a lot at times. And my dad could see it was getting a little overwhelming for you."

She blushed. "I hope I didn't hurt anyone's feelings."

"Don't worry. You were polite as could be to everybody. But you're also healing—and grieving your friend. So the only other family member we'll be seeing over the next few days will be Sarah, since she'll be briefly stopping by tomorrow to drop off something here at the house."

"Sarah's your mother and uncle Robert's daughter, right?" Giselle said, thinking back to what he'd told her about the two recently discovered Colton siblings.

He nodded. "You've got it. Anyway, back at the time her mother left my father, she took this old Victrola stand record player with her. I suppose it was to spite him since she always told Sarah and Nate it was some sort of valuable family heirloom. In truth, those things aren't actually worth that much, but this one has a lot of sentimental value to my dad since it belonged to his late mother. So Sarah's had it packed up and taken it to her place. She's just been waiting for a chance to bring it by here, to surprise my father."

"That's really thoughtful of her," Giselle said. "It's a shame your father isn't going to be here when she comes by."

"I know, but with Markus coming out of the woodwork

the way he did to attack us, he didn't feel right leaving Mama Jen alone at her home unprotected."

"He's so smitten with her." Giselle smiled. "And when she came by the other day, I could see she feels the same way about him."

Malcolm nodded. "I swear to you, it does my heart good, after watching everything they've both been through, to see them find so much happiness together. But I can see your friend there is getting restless." He nodded toward Scarlett, who was pulling at her lead. "So how about we head on back inside now?"

After opening the door and following Giselle and Pacer inside, Malcolm hung their jackets before they headed for the kitchen, where they always stopped to grab drinks following their training sessions.

Once Malcolm gave each of the dogs a chew and had them lie down on their mats in the great room, Giselle brought him a glass of water while holding another in her hand.

"Just look how well she's picked up on that after-training routine you've started with her," she said, clearly not finished advocating for the little beagle. "Look at her, enjoying her own treat so calmly instead of trying to jump on top of Pacer and grab his, too, the way she did at first."

Malcolm wandered toward the leather sectional. "I think we mostly have Pacer to thank for teaching her that bad canine manners aren't going to fly at all. There's nothing like a stable, mature dog for teaching a pup boundaries."

"And she's really picking up fast on going out when she should and releasing off-limits things she's grabbed and trading them for an approved toy," she continued, trailing after him, "so we've *definitely* made progress. And that's in just a few, short days."

Finishing a swallow of water, he lowered his glass but didn't sit. "I was thinking the same thing."

"What on earth?" She made a sound of pure exasperation. "Then *why* would you call Della and ask her to take Scarlett?"

Malcolm took a deep breath. "Actually, I *didn't* call her or have any such conversation."

Giselle scowled at him. "Are you serious?"

Immediately realizing his mistake, Malcolm said, "I'm sorry. I only meant to check the temperature on how close you two were really getting, but I can see now that I should've told you from the start it wasn't Della I really spoke with last night about you and Scarlett. It was Sebastian."

"Sebastian? I don't understand why you would—"

"Please, just hear me out," he said, holding up his uninjured hand. "It was because I saw something in the two of you. The spark of what could be an amazing bond, one of those perfect pairings you can't force and wouldn't trade for anything once you find it."

"Do those usually begin with the puppy leaving the human sprawled out in the grass?" she asked. "Because the way you put it sounds as if it ought to feel a little more like magic."

Malcolm chuckled. "Trust me, things didn't start out with Pacer the way you see them now. He was a cute pup, but a handful, and Kate loved to pamper him, so he started to look at me as the spoiler of all fun. But after the accident, once it was only him and me—"

When his throat clamped tight, Giselle went to him and put a hand on the small of his back. "I know," she said simply, in a voice as gentle and reassuring as her touch.

He slanted a look down into her gorgeous blue eyes. "I thought that maybe—maybe I could convince Sebastian that Scarlett could be for you...what Pacer once was to me, an anchor to help tether you to life."

Chapter Fifteen

As upset as Giselle was about Malcolm manipulating her emotions, the raw fear she saw in his gaze—so close to hers now that she saw his green eyes dilate as she studied them—short-circuited her anger. Not fear for himself, despite the risk he'd taken in exposing his greatest vulnerability in a way so few strong men would dare to, but a bone-deep terror of what he'd recognized in her—and refused to sit still and allow to go on. Because of an attraction so clearly written on his face and every action.

An attraction she felt burning in her own blood, as well, one she'd felt intensifying with every moment she spent in his presence these past few days, for all her efforts to picture Kate's face each time she found her gaze lingering on the solid masculinity of his movements or the working of his throat as he drank water. Moving her hand from his back, she dropped her gaze to avoid his, scrambling to summon a memory of her sister.

But Kate wasn't with them in this room. There was only Malcolm, the warmth of his presence and a lingering scent of sunshine and the outdoors still discernable, as close as they were standing.

Finally finding the courage to speak, she said, "I *am* getting attached to Scarlett—" *And* only *Scarlett…* "and of course, I've fantasized about having the kind of job and living situation where keeping her for myself would be the right and fair thing, if that were even remotely possible..." *Because* he *isn't possible...*

"I have to tell you," Malcolm said, "as sympathetic as Sebastian was to my argument, he did remind me that he has protocols for a reason. He didn't completely rule out the possibility, though, so I believe there's still a chance I might convince him, especially if he sees the two of you together."

She shook her head. "It's fine, really," she said, telling herself it would have to be. "I'll just love on her for the time I have her."

"But you *need*—"

"Stop it, please," she said firmly, prompting him to go still. "You're telling me what *you* needed, in those first truly horrible months after Kate's death. And I truly understand how deepening your bond with Pacer, in addition to your dad's making sure you got the other help you needed, was life-changing—maybe even lifesaving—for you."

He nodded. "Yes, and that's why I want to—"

"Malcolm, I *know* you're worried about me, and all right. I'll admit, I've allowed everything that happened—and how guilty I felt for living through that accident when it should've been Kate who made it—"

"Please, never say that again," he begged her, "because I'm *glad* you're here now, Giselle. Don't you understand that? I look at you and—I feel—I feel alive in a way I never imagined I ever could again."

She wanted to tell him that knowing how much he cared for her was opening the world to her, too, to explain how much it had meant to her, being invited into the warmth of his loving family's circle. But she didn't know how to say it—how to do anything except to reach up toward him and trust that he would meet her halfway between temptation and desire.

He pulled her into his arms, the kisses hungry, hot, and desperate to a degree Giselle could never remember feeling with any man before. For a split second, she told herself to slow down—to slow her questing hands and try to register the wrongness of what it was they were doing. But when Malcolm's mouth nipped her neck and he cupped her breasts, her body rebelled against the impulse, charging ahead in a desperate race to feel, to taste, to savor every bit of him before one or both of them came to their senses.

Yet only moments later, she was pulling him with her down onto the cushions of the sectional and pulling off her top.

MALCOLM HAD ALMOST forgotten what it was like to be overtaken by sensation—the demands of his body running miles ahead of anything that any lingering doubts might have to say about the subject. And his heart was more than willing to go along for the ride. It was pumping now, faster than ever as she reached behind her, clearly meaning to unhook that tantalizing rose-colored bra of hers, a lacy little number that held her breasts so temptingly just beyond reach.

"Hold up a second, will you?" he said.

"Why's that?" she asked, her blue eyes sparking with impatience.

"Just trying to imagine if you're this gorgeous now," he told her, "how much better the view's about to get."

Straddling his hips, she leaned in to kiss him nearly senseless, making him forget everything but the taste and heat and welcome pressure of her body bearing down against his pelvis, and his desire for far more.

When she came up for air and smiled down at him, he repeated, "Absolutely gorgeous…"

"I could say the same of you, but I'm not here for the compliments."

"You have something else in mind?"

She looked around the room, with its large, uncovered windows and the walkway just beyond it. "Something in my room I need to show you…"

Rolling off him, she hopped up and started walking toward the staircase. Before she reached it, he saw that she had the lacy, rose-colored bra trailing like a promise from her fingers.

He wasn't far behind.

Chapter Sixteen

Giselle snuggled deeply into Malcolm's arms, unable to recall the last time she'd awakened feeling so contented. But it wasn't only remembering how completely cherished he'd made her feel, with his unselfish attention to her pleasure, but the knowledge that she'd helped ease Malcolm's loneliness in the same way, that filled her with a happiness so intense and unfamiliar that she wasn't certain she could trust it.

"Hey there, you awake, sleepyhead?" Malcolm asked before gently kissing her temple.

"I am," she said, adjusting her position to lean back into the pillows.

As she pulled the sheet to cover her breasts, Malcolm grinned. "It's too late, you know. I've already committed them to memory for life."

"I'm glad at least one part of my anatomy made some sort of impression," she said.

Shaking his head, he told her, "I don't want you to have a single doubt about it, Giselle. I could rattle off a whole list of your body parts that I'm quite fond of, but it's *you* I've fallen for—no matter how hard I've tried to fight it."

"Malcolm, no. This has been wonderful—so much better than I ever could've imagined. But both of us have been alone for such a long time, so what you're feeling isn't really anything like what you had with—"

"Please, Giselle," he said, passion roughening his voice. "I'm not expecting you to feel the same way I do. That's all right with me. But don't try to tell me what's in my own heart."

"I'm sorry. It's just—this is all so new to me. My brain keeps wanting to default back to—to the way I've always known you." *As Kate's*, she thought. But she couldn't say that part aloud yet. Couldn't allow herself to name the chill that passed over her when she even thought about her sister, lying in another bed beside this man who'd loved her so deeply that he had vowed to make a life and family with her.

Malcolm nodded, his expression softening. "That's completely understandable. So let's talk about our plans for this afternoon, then, shall we? Did you still want to drive over to Conners to go car shopping the way we'd planned? Because there's still plenty of time for us to clean up and head that way."

She made a considering noise before saying. "I really *would* like to keep that test-drive appointment I made for that hybrid model I liked so much at four thirty. Those have been in such demand, it's been hard to even locate one anywhere to look at."

"Sure thing. And after we've finished up, how about if I take you out to Barbieri's? You still like Italian, don't you?"

On hearing the name of one of the area's finer restaurants, Giselle shook her head. "That's awfully nice of you to ask, Malcolm, but I don't have anything appropriate here to wear. And even if I did, I can't imagine being in the mood for anywhere so high-end while Markus is still out there somewhere—"

"You're right, of course. I'm sorry. I'm just—I feel like you deserve a nice distraction."

"You've done a pretty amazing job with that already," she reminded him, "but let's choose someplace a little more casual we can both agree on. And we'll celebrate at Barbieri's once Markus has been arrested, or over at The Tides if you like the food there better. Deal?"

"Sounds like a plan," he agreed. "Now what about a shower?"

"What? *Together*, you mean?" she asked, slightly taken aback despite the things they'd done already.

He shrugged. "Why not? I mean, it does stand to reason that someone as interested in animal welfare and the environment as you are would care, too, about water conservation."

She snorted at his reasoning. "You and I both know that if we tried it, the two of us would never make it past the lathering stage together without getting water *all* over that bathroom."

Grinning, he said, "That sounds like *such* an excellent idea—"

"But think of all the cleanup. *And* I'd definitely miss my appointment."

"I have some pretty good ideas about how I could make it all up to you," he said, leaning in to lay a blazing trail of kisses along her neck—before they were both distracted by the sound of both dogs barking from downstairs.

Sitting up on the bed's edge, he sighed. "As much as I hate having to give up my plans to sidetrack you, I'd better go check to make sure Scarlett isn't demolishing some major furnishing or disgracing herself on a rug."

"Oh, no! *Scarlett...*" Giselle felt her face heat. "I completely forgot she wasn't crated downstairs while we, uh—"

"Were otherwise occupied," Malcolm finished for her as he reached for his jeans. "Don't worry about it. I'll go down and deal with the situation and then take both dogs out to the outdoor covered run so they can enjoy this pretty spring afternoon for a little bit while each of us cleans ups in our own rooms."

Nodding, she said, "I'll meet you downstairs, then. Thanks."

When he bent to kiss her before leaving, though, something made her present him her cheek rather than her lips.

On her way to the shower a few minutes later, she happened to catch sight of Malcolm's phone peeking out from just beneath the edge of a blanket on the floor. Realizing it had probably fallen from the pocket of his jeans, she bent to retrieve it and saw a notification on the screen for a missed called from Ajay Wright.

Thinking that it might be something important, she stepped out into the hallway wearing only a T-shirt, meaning to call down to Malcolm. But at the same moment, she heard the back door close, and she soon realized that he must have gone ahead and taken both the dogs out to their enclosed run.

Remembering what he'd said about heading right back upstairs for a shower, she thought a moment before heading around the corner, where he'd previously invited her to knock anytime if there was anything she needed. Though she was wildly curious about what lay behind that door—and whether Malcolm was really as neat in his personal space as he appeared to be when working in the kitchen and picking up around the house's common areas—she couldn't bring herself to try the handle. So instead, after standing the cell up against the bottom of the door and telling herself he'd have to be blind to miss its safety-orange protective case leaning against the dark wood, she retreated to her own suite.

While she showered, she tried to tell herself the awkwardness she was feeling might be less a result of how very long it had been since she'd allowed any man to get so close than it was the fact that someone as caring, thoughtful, and attractive as Malcolm saw her as someone worthy of his attention. And not only his sexual attention—which, taken on its own, had made her realize how much pleasure she'd been missing out on with her choice of partners—but with his insistence that someone who'd lost everything that had once defined her as a person—her family, her career, and nearly all her friends—might still actually have value.

Of course he thinks that you have value, some small, mean-spirited voice inside her whispered. *You remind him just enough of the only woman he's really interested in having sex with.* But even as the thought occurred, she realized it was really just the self-loathing she had listened to for far too long talking. Or maybe it actually *was* some version of the same depression that Malcolm, too, had struggled with, like so many others.

But what if she'd had it wrong these past few years? If the so-called facts she'd been telling herself about her failures had been skewed so badly that they bore little resemblance to the objective truth of who she was: a woman with as many strengths as flaws. A woman who had made the best choices available to her during a time that she was weathering devastating losses. A woman worthy of the same grace that she herself had always been willing to give others she'd seen stumble.

By the time she left the shower, Giselle was determined to stop looking for reasons to doubt whatever happiness she felt and simply enjoy those moments that came to her. After choosing a pair of navy chinos and a pink top that helped to brighten her fair complexion, she fussed a little with her hair, something she hadn't done in some time, and found herself unexpectedly humming as she did so.

Pleased with the results, she dug out her purse, where she unearthed and actually made use of a few cosmetics she'd neglected to toss. Though she used a light touch, once she finished, she smiled, catching a glimpse of her old reflection, as if she'd just spotted an old friend for the first time after a long illness. Definitely changed, she thought, but surely on the mend.

As she returned her lip stain and mascara to her purse, the cell phone she'd had on the charger nearby dinged a notification for an e-mail. Hoping she wasn't about to find out the vehicle she was scheduled to test drive had been sold already, she picked up the phone, only to find a number of unread e-mails waiting.

Scrolling past the unsolicited automotive ads—which kept springing up like toadstools thanks to her online searches—she zeroed in on a message bearing the name *Colton* in the sender column before remembering how, just the evening before last, Malcolm's sister had pulled her aside during her visit to say, "I have some lovely photos of Kate I've been meaning to share with you—that is, if you'd like to have them."

"Absolutely, Lizzy. Thank you!" Giselle had immediately responded, giving her a hug. She'd meant it, too, since she treasured every opportunity to add to the trove that she'd compiled to preserve the memory of her sister.

But now, as her finger hovered over the message, with its paperclip-shaped icon indicating its attached files, Giselle hesitated, her usual excitement mixed up with dread and guilt. Because the Kate that Lizzy had known so well, the one she would undoubtedly be faced with, would be a woman brimming with love and hope, with trust and anticipation for a future with Malcolm that would never, ever happen.

Not for her, at any rate.

Delete them, all of them. Pretend you never got them, Giselle thought, memories cascading through her mind: Kate posing with her new fiancé, both impossibly photogenic as they flashed a pair of gorgeous smiles, or Kate alone showing off the beautiful diamond-flanked emerald engagement ring she had been so very proud of.

A click, and they go away. Giselle could then text a separate note to Lizzy: Thanks for the pix! Some nice ones in there!

Then, she could move on with her life. And a man who had been meant to be her sister's.

But Giselle didn't have the strength to make such a decision. Or maybe letting herself off the hook had been a right she'd ceded the day she had accepted a breath from Malcolm's lungs as the price of her survival.

So instead, she found herself sitting on the bed, looking through photo after photo, and smashing her own heart to pieces one image at a time.

WHEN MALCOLM HAD first headed downstairs to check on the dogs, he'd found no damage with the exception of a single crime in progress. He winced at the sight of one of the running shoes, which he recalled having kicked off somewhere near the sectional, being masticated beyond recognition by one very small but extremely contented-looking beagle.

Looking over at Pacer, who lay curled up on his bed pointedly ignoring the destruction, Malcolm said, "Man's best friend indeed. You could've at least *tried* to stop her."

Pacer chose to ignore him, too—probably sulking, Malcolm figured. His K-9 did perk up, however, watching Malcolm chase Scarlett around the room for several minutes before he was finally able to pry the slobbery remnants from the pup's jaws to assure himself that the little miscreant wouldn't end up choking.

"Glad to see you're entertained, at least," he told Pacer before looking down at the sharp-toothed beagle. "You'd better count yourself lucky that Giselle's so crazy about you. And that *I* adore Giselle. Let's go on outside for a bit, so both of you can enjoy a little playtime."

Once he headed back upstairs, he was surprised to find his cellphone lying propped up on the floor in front of his closed bedroom door. In the time it took him to wonder how it could've gotten there, the screen lit up, and he could see—although the sound was off—that it was Ajay calling.

Picking it up, Malcolm asked, "How's the search going?"

"You'd have a whole lot better idea, if you'd ever answer your phone," Ajay complained. "I've been trying to reach you for the past hour."

"Sorry about that. What's up?"

"What's up is I need you and that dog of yours to come over to the staging area as soon as you can get here," Ajay said.

"Meet you? But I thought—Aren't I suspended?"

"I promise you, I'll still be paying careful attention to how you handle yourself as a team member," Ajay assured him, "but right now, we have a critical public safety situation, and I can't afford to leave one of our top trailing teams sitting on the sidelines when we've got Markus Acker on the run on foot and headed straight for town—"

"What are you talking about?"

"We've found your stolen truck wrecked just off the road, in those tall timbers north of Owl Creek. After Archer collected a scent item from the cab, Pumpkin and I started trailing him down into that low creek bottom area—"

"The area where we found that Silver Alert woman last year?" Malcolm asked, speaking of an elderly person with memory issues who'd become disoriented while taking what had been meant to be a short walk.

"Right," said Ajay. "We lost the scent trail, but I'm almost positive he's headed back toward one of the residential neighborhoods near the river. Probably looking for someplace he can jack another vehicle—and we both know he won't leave behind a living witness if he can help it, either."

"You don't have to tell me. I've seen his handiwork in that department," Malcolm said, his thoughts turning toward the bloody handprint on the barn door. "So where exactly should I meet the team?"

"I've already texted the location of the city park where our team's staging. There'll be a law enforcement checkpoint at the entrance, but just tell them you're with the SAR team and they'll let you in."

"Pacer and I will be there as soon as possible," he promised, knowing Giselle would understand.

"Thanks. And, Malcolm?"

"Yes?"

"Before you head out on Acker's trail today, I want you to check in with Fletcher. He'll have a ballistic vest for you, and I want you wearing it."

Malcolm thought about it for a moment before asking, "Are you handing those out to our whole team—or only to the ones named Colton?"

"You're the *only* Colton on the SAR team, Malcolm—as well as the only member of the team Acker's already gone after. But you already know that, don't you? So quit worrying about whether I'm showing you some kind of favoritism or whatever strange idea you've got into your head and just trust that I'm looking out for a valuable asset, the same as I would any other."

"Got it," Malcolm told him, hopeful that he could live up to Ajay's expectations and still be a part of bringing down the man who'd cost his family so much grief.

Before he could start doing that, however, he would need to let Giselle know about the change in plans. When she didn't answer his knock, he decided she must be in the shower, so he headed to his own suite to quickly clean up and change into his SAR gear.

Afterward, another knock at Giselle's door went unanswered, even after he called out her name. Feeling the low hum of anxiety, he trotted downstairs, frowning with confusion when he didn't spot her in either the family room or kitchen. "Did you go check on the dogs?" he asked aloud, jogging over to the back door, his pulse picking up speed.

But he found the deadbolt locked, as were the other two doors—a safety measure his family members had all agreed to follow until Markus was finally behind bars, and he saw that both dogs were still outside lounging. Genuinely worried now, Malcolm headed back upstairs once more—this time at a run.

This time, he pounded on the door hard. "Giselle, can you hear me?" When no answer came, he pictured her lying on the bathroom floor, unconscious after falling after slipping on damp tile. "I'm coming in to check on you unless you tell me otherwise."

He barely waited another second before he was through the door, where, to his relief and bewilderment, he immediately spotted her. Though her back was to him, she was fully dressed and perched on the bed's edge as she stared down at her cell phone.

"Giselle?" he said, upset she would ignore him while surfing social media or something. "You scared me half to death. How did you not *hear* me?"

Her head snapped up, her red-rimmed eyes so miserable, he knew immediately that something was terribly wrong.

"What's happened?" he asked, his anger shifting to alarm. "Are you sick—or has someone sent you some sort of threat or—" He tried to imagine someone from her past, like the obnoxious Nico, attempting to make trouble for her at this juncture, but reasoned that the rock star had been distracted by any number of other, more outrageous scandals since the one in which Giselle had figured.

She shook her head. "I've just—I'm so sorry, Malcolm, but I've—I've made a terrible mistake."

"A *mistake*? I don't under—"

"With you, I mean. I just can't. I—I can't be Kate's sister and your—whatever you've convinced yourself this might be between us."

"What are you talking about?" he asked. Thinking of the phone in her hand, the way she'd seemed so fixated on it, he asked, "Did someone—did someone say or send something to you, something to change the woman I left here in this room such a short time ago into—"

She shook her head.

"Then just what was it you were staring at on your phone?" he demanded. "Seriously, Giselle. What is it? *Please.*"

"Only a reminder. Pictures of Kate that Lizzy asked me if I'd like to have."

"Oh, no. Not Lizzy and her pictures..." Malcolm ground the heel of his hand into his forehead. "I adore my little sister. Her heart's *definitely* in the right place, but I can remember a similar offering of hers sending me to a very dark place the Christmas before last."

Giselle sucked air between her teeth, looking sympathetic. "She sent you a bunch of photos of Kate at the *holidays*?"

"Right before them, yes," he said. "The thing is, as much as you and I both might want to remember, there are times it's dangerous, poking too much at the tender places underneath the scar tissue. Times when you risk undoing all the healing that's already underway."

"But maybe I'm not *ready* to heal yet, Malcolm. Not if that means betraying the love that I felt for my sister. And everything she felt for me."

After picking up her phone, she touched the screen and

showed him the photo she'd been looking at when he'd entered the room. Though he'd been steeling himself—and in some ways dreading—seeing an image of himself with Kate, it wasn't a photo of the two of them together. Instead, it was of Kate, taken on the day of their engagement cookout, reaching to pull in the visiting Giselle into a welcoming embrace. Both of them were so beautiful, so vibrant, and so filled with the joy of their reunion, it nearly took his breath away. The skirt of Giselle's summer dress was flared, captured mid-whirl with her movement, and her nearly waist-long blond locks were fanned out, glowing in the sunlight.

Visually stunning as the shot was, he had to look away, overcome by a gut-wrenching vision of that same long hair, floating detached in the waters of Blackbird Lake after he had cut it. Recoiling from the memory—and from the recollection of the loose strands left clinging to Kate's pale flesh as he'd pulled her from the water to give her mouth-to-mouth resuscitation—he realized, *Heaven help me, I can't do this either. Giselle's been right all along...*

Screwing shut his eyes, he struggled to re-center himself on the present. A present that required his strength, his courage, and all the determination he could muster not to let either Giselle or his SAR team down.

Focusing on those responsibilities, he forced himself to cover Giselle's hand with his. Ever so gently, he prompted her to turn the phone face down. When she looked up at him, a question in her eyes, he said, "I know we need to talk, and I'd like to be able to stay right here and have that discussion with you. But right now I really need to—"

"You're leaving, aren't you?" she asked, her expression changing as she shook her head. "I should've realized—I saw earlier, when I found your phone, that you'd missed a call from Ajay, and I see now that you're dressed for trailing. Is it—is it *him* again?"

Understanding that she meant Acker, Malcolm nodded before sharing the highlights of his phone conversation.

"Then you and Pacer had better get on the road right now," she said. "I'm only sorry I delayed you so long with my..." She gestured vaguely.

"You have absolutely nothing to be sorry for," he assured her. "I hate leaving you here on your own, though. What if I dropped you over to hang out with Greg and Briony at their place down the way on my way out? I'm sure they're home right now and—"

"They're really nice, and I'm sure those little ones of theirs are as adorable as the pictures they showed me the other day when they stopped by. But look at me—" She gestured toward her swollen eyes. "Do I look like I'm in the mood for happy-family company right now? Just let me lock the doors and veg out with some TV with Scarlett and try to forget that this day ever happened..."

He grimaced, hearing her say that. But there was no time to even sort through his own emotions, much less delay any longer, so he said only, "I'll pop Scarlett back inside her downstairs kennel before I leave, then, so you can get her once you're ready. But please, just promise me that you'll keep the doors locked and stay inside. And well away from those photos."

She nodded. "I will. But only if you'll promise me you'll be really careful out there, Malcolm."

"Don't worry. Ajay's insisting that I wear a vest like law enforcement, and all of us trailing will most likely be accompanied by an officer as well."

"That's good," she said, the sadness in her blue eyes holding him a moment longer, "because, no matter where I end up once all this is over, I'll always want to know you're back here, strong and safe and whole."

"We—we'll talk more later, all right?" he managed—

barely—now more upset than ever to hear the rejection of everything he'd tried to show her, everything he'd tried to tell her and meant to spend a lifetime proving, of everything they might have been together, that lay in ashes behind the goodbye he'd heard in her words.

It left him frustrated, too, not only with the circumstances forcing him to leave now, but with her, for allowing her own pain to blind her to her capacity to wound him.

So it was that when Giselle nodded and said, "Sure. Please, text me with updates when you're able," he didn't hug or kiss her, instead only answering, "Will do," as he headed out the door.

Chapter Seventeen

Giselle stared at the open doorway, a heaviness growing in the pit of her stomach as she heard his footsteps receding down the staircase. She thought of hurrying after him, throwing her arms around him, and taking back what she'd said. She'd seen it written on his face, how she was hurting him, yet she'd kept on digging the hole deeper. Telling herself he'd be better off set free of the encumbrance of someone who would only serve as an enduring reminder of the most traumatic moments and the greatest grief of his life.

Still, she felt a cold heaviness inside her, a growing doubt about the way they'd left things. Worried about him going off to face a killer who'd already come after him once with his mind on their issue, she finally rose from the bed and rushed for the stairs, intent on apologizing—or at least giving him the goodbye kiss he'd deserved.

But by the time she reached the landing, she could only sigh as she spotted his ranch pickup's lights receding down the long drive.

"That's what you get for dawdling," she scolded herself, wondering if she should call and try to speak with him while he was on the road.

But she had no idea what to say—how to make things right without giving him false hope for a future she couldn't honestly promise. And it wouldn't be right, or necessarily safe, to further distract him at a time when he needed to focus on both the road and his work with the SAR team. Better that she use this time planning her own next move—and think about what she wanted her future to look like after Markus Acker was captured.

One thing she knew for certain: returning to the isolated life she had been living before Malcolm showed up at her cabin was no longer an appealing option. She'd been floundering for too long—so mired in her grief, she'd been unable to even imagine that any of the skills she'd spent years honing would apply to any other career field, let alone exploring and acting on her options.

Maybe she could start by at least opening some of the unread messages she'd allowed to pile up in her email's inbox. Then she would thank those who'd taken the effort to check in with her and write a brief note asking if anyone had heard of any opportunities that might be a good fit for her, regardless of the location.

She decided the idea felt right, even if a new position required her to sell the family cabin to finally loosen the past's painful grip on her life. Daunted by the thought of leaving Owl Creek and everyone here that she'd come to care for, however, she instead headed downstairs to free Scarlett from her crate, deciding that for the moment, some puppy therapy sounded like her first order of business.

The two played and cuddled until the knot of anxiety inside her loosened. They then practiced Scarlett's commands—so successfully that Giselle wished she'd set up her phone to take a video to show off the pup's skills later.

Just as she realized she'd forgotten about canceling her test-drive appointment—now ten minutes past, she heard a low rumble. Looking toward the window, she noticed a couple of the hands headed toward the ranch gate in a pickup, towing a livestock trailer. Moments later, the phone inside her pocket started ringing.

Checking it, she saw that it was Detective Ariana Rodolfo from the sheriff's department. Eager to hear what more she might have learned about the two men who'd put the red boat into storage, Giselle was quick to answer.

"Please tell me this is good news," she blurted, the hope she'd worked so hard to manage bubbling up again in spite of years of disappointments.

"I'm doing quite well, thank you," Rodolfo said dryly. "I hope you're having a nice day, too."

"I'm sorry if I sometimes seem impatient with you," Giselle told her.

"Considering what you've been through, that's understandable," Rodolfo said. "And I hope you didn't feel I was making light of something that's so important to you."

"It's fine." Giselle hugged herself. "But please, have you learned any more about the suspects you and Detective Danvers ID'd?"

"I was hoping I might come by to speak to you and Mr. Colton—Malcolm—about that personally if you're available?"

Something important, then, Giselle realized, so anxious she could scarcely breathe. Shaking it off, she turned away from Scarlett's attempt to gain her attention by jumping up against her leg and headed into the kitchen. "I'm sorry, but he's just left to join his search and rescue team. They're assisting the task force right now, trying to keep Acker from reaching—"

"Our department's been updated, and we've sent every deputy we can spare to help cut off his access to the neighborhood where they believe Acker might be headed."

Giselle got herself a clean glass. "It sounds like they're pretty confident they know where he is, then,"

"There are never any guarantees, but it sounds as if this

time, Acker's boxed himself into a half-mile-wide, wooded wedge between a four-lane divided highway where he'll be immediately spotted either by helicopter or one of the drones they've sent up if he tries to cross the river."

"Couldn't he just make a swim for it?" Giselle asked.

"Not there he can't. Even if this past week's snow melt didn't have the river running so fast and cold that it would drown him, the opposite bank is so steep and rocky, you'd practically have to be a mountain goat to climb it."

"He has a gunshot wound as well." Giselle filled her glass using the fridge dispenser. "They're pretty sure that Malcolm at least nicked him in the parking-lot shoot-out."

"I hadn't heard that happy news," Rodolfo said brightly, over the sound of another phone ringing in the background and the muffled rumble of men's voices somewhere nearby. "But it certainly doesn't bode well for Acker's chances of pulling off another miraculous escape."

"I'm praying you're right," Giselle said, "and, selfishly, I'm hoping that someone in law enforcement slaps about six sets of cuffs on him before Malcolm gets within a mile of him." If anything happened to him, she'd never get over it, especially not knowing that she'd hurt him as she had.

"I'm with you on that," the detective told her. "Listen, I understand you're nervous right now, and you have every right to be, but I know Ajay Wright, who's not only working with the task force but the SAR team too, and I can't imagine him taking any chances when it comes to his people's safety."

"I know he cares," Giselle said.

"You'll see," Rodolfo told her. "Malcolm's going to come home safe and sound, and once the two of you have finished celebrating Acker's arrest, then you can call to let me know a convenient time to come out and see you about this other investigation—"

"Oh, no. Please, detective," Giselle said, nearly choking

on the water she'd swallowed before setting the glass back down on the counter. "Whatever you've found out, just tell me. Whether it's good news or bad, I can't deal with one more mystery hanging over my head."

"You—you're not alone now, are you?" Rodolfo asked, raising her voice a little to speak over what sounded like male conversation in the background.

Giselle glanced down at Scarlett, who was sitting politely at her feet, as she'd been taught, instead of jumping for attention. Her heart warming at the sight, Giselle squatted down to pet the pup. "I definitely have company," she said, though she realized she'd been played when the pup rolled over on the tiled floor and pawed at her hand, angling for one of the belly scratches that the beagle lived for.

"All right, then," Rodolfo said, "but let me step into this conference room so I won't have to out-shout my colleagues."

A door clicked closed, and she said, "That's *much* better. Now, I have what we believe to be some answers for you. Answers about what really happened regarding the red boat."

Giselle's stomach swooped. "You've tracked down the real owner?"

"Thanks to that faded receipt found by Larry Willets, we were able to determine that his name was Alan Broussard—"

"That's not the same Broussard who owns the big car dealership in Conners, is it?" Giselle asked, chills running down her spine at the realization that she was late for an appointment at the same spot at this very moment.

"It is, though I believe it's his brother who's running the family business these days—unless Broussard's widow's taken up the reins."

"His widow?" Giselle echoed, as Scarlett pawed a reminder at her to keep up with her scratching duties. "Then he's—"

"Money can fix a lot of things, but not the kind of cancer

that took him out last July. Although the way that his wife tells it, it was the disappearance of his only son that really did him in."

"Maybe his son wouldn't have gone anywhere if his father hadn't hired him and his friend to do his dirty work and hide that boat that killed my sister." Giselle gave the dog a final pat before once more rising.

"I'm afraid you have it wrong if you think it was the old man who hit you," the detective said. "Broussard's son, Zach, it turns out, was actually the one driving."

"That's the red-haired college kid who had the breakdown? How'd you figure that out?"

"The friend who lawyered up on us before came back. Only this time, Joss Ryan showed up looking like he hadn't slept in days, and he'd ditched his attorney. He took out some pictures of his fiancée holding their newborn baby daughter and told us that now that he's a dad, it's time for him to be a man, too. And a man would own up to the truth about what really happened on the lake that day."

"Wait a minute. So he's admitting he was *there* now? And that he was on board when the boat hit us?"

"Joss was there, all right, standing right next to his good friend Zach Broussard, who'd decided that instead of pulling the new speedboat his dad had just purchased out of the lake and trailering it back home the way he'd been asked to, it would be a lot more fun spending the day tearing around the lake and drinking with a couple of hot babes, as Joss put it, that the two of them had met at the marina."

"So you're telling me the accident—Kate's death—really was all about a couple of idiots joyriding and showing off for girls?"

"I'm sorry, yes. Apparently, the babes in question thought better of the whole thing and no-showed on them. According to Joss, Zach was furious about it, since he'd bought all this alcohol for the four of them to share. He started drinking pretty heavily, going off about 'entitled bitches,' and ripping around so close to water-skiers that Joss finally got scared enough to try to force him to take a break from driving."

"Or so he's claiming now, since Zach's nowhere around to contradict his story," Giselle said bitterly.

"I learned long ago in my line of work that you always have to assume that whoever's telling the story is going to try to make himself look better," Rodolfo told her.

"Same here," said Giselle, thinking about how the versions of the truth her celebrity clients gave her had so often failed to stack up to any fact-checking she might do with others who'd been present at the time of the events described.

"Joss may very well only be trying to get himself off the hook by claiming he tried to do the right thing, saying that Zach yelled how it was his father's boat and shoved him back right before they cleared that point and struck the towrope of the raft that you and Kate were riding."

Giselle felt the world tilt on its access as the truth she had waited so long to hear was finally laid bare. "And then they kept right on going, despite the screams and shouts for help."

"Joss says they both panicked. He was underage and had been drinking, and at the time, he claims Zach was terrified his dad would kill him for taking out his brand-new boat without permission."

Unable to hold her tears back any longer, Giselle asked, "Would *kill* him? But what about *us*? I was left trapped beneath the water. And when Malcolm had no one—no one to help him cut me free, my sister—she slipped out of her vest and drowned—because of the head injury from what they'd done!"

"I know, and I'm sorry," Rodolfo said. "Joss claimed he felt worse and worse, worrying about what might be happening. He tried to tell me he even attempted at one point to get his buddy to turn back."

"I'm sure..." Giselle scoffed.

"Whatever weak protest did or didn't come out of his mouth," Rodolfo said, "you and I both know that those boys pulled that boat out of the water that day. From there, they ended up hauling the thing back to Zach's parents' home."

Wiping her eyes, Giselle said, "I don't understand. I thought they immediately took it and hid it at that storage unit."

"Zach could be a bit of a hell-raiser, but he'd never cross his dad by simply making off with his new boat without explanation. Then the two boys heard about your sister's death, and they realized their troubles could be far more serious than they'd imagined. So they both went to Zach's father and basically threw themselves on the old man's mercy."

Detective Rodolfo then went silent, giving Giselle a few moments to process all she'd said.

Impatient as ever, Giselle couldn't help but focus on what remained unspoken. "So you're telling me it was the late Alan Broussard who put those two young men up to hiding the boat under a fictitious name?"

"So Joss Ryan is claiming. And after my conversation with Mrs. Broussard, I'm inclined to believe that her husband really was involved—and that he very much came to regret it, along with his insistence that neither of the pair even *think* of jeopardizing their futures by allowing their consciences to overwhelm their sense of self-preservation."

"So he blamed himself for Zach's breakdown later and his disappearance?"

"His wife claimed that he was acting out of love and fear for their son's future, but yes, he did blame himself. As she blamed him, when she found out about it later."

"Yet she didn't see fit to end my suffering and Malcolm's

by doing the right thing herself and reporting her husband's crimes or her son's to the authorities," Giselle said bitterly.

"If what she claims is true—and I happen to believe the woman—by the time she had all the facts, her son was missing and her husband was terminally ill," Rodolfo said. "I believe she was too caught up in her own pain and her family's to think beyond them."

"I hope she's not expecting sympathy from me, not after what her family's selfishness and silence cost me. And now—" Giselle shook her head as frustration washed over her. "I can't believe how much time I've wasted, imagining that getting these answers was going to somehow make things any better."

"I want you to know, we're not giving up on finding Zach Broussard and bringing him to justice, since he told his father as well that he was the boat's driver. If he's still alive, he can be held accountable. The DA will look at charging Joss, too, for his part, since they both bore a responsibility in the failure to render aid and in keeping the boat hidden for all these years."

"It's not that I don't appreciate all your hard work, you and everyone from your department, because I definitely do," Giselle said, "but how's any of this supposed to even feel like justice any longer?"

"I'm sorry, but the truth is, it probably never will, exactly. But that doesn't mean we should ever give up trying to come as close as we can get."

ALREADY SWEATING BENEATH a layered combination of T-shirt, ballistic vest, and SAR jacket, Malcolm was grateful when Pacer's nose quickly took the two of them into a deeply shaded patch of riverside wood. Though the visibility was poor—and would soon grow worse, as the sun was rapidly descending—he decided the relief of the cooler temperature was well worth the trade-off.

As Pacer pawed at a thick patch of ferns before pulling Malcolm deeper into the underbrush, he answered the question the young police officer who'd been paired with him for security had asked about how the SAR dogs worked.

"At this point, Pacer here's just seeking, filtering through an entire world of scents in the environment—the white noise of the scores of animals and humans who've recently hiked through here, along with all kinds of incidental odors, while trying to sniff out the proverbial needle in the haystack that matches the dirty sock collected from my wrecked pickup earlier this afternoon."

"Lucky thing the evidence team found a few of Acker's things abandoned in the wrecked truck today so we could track him, isn't it?"

"Very," Malcolm said. "It's a sign he's breaking down—whether it's from his injury, exhaustion, or the pressure of the three-week manhunt."

"In other words, he's making mistakes that'll make him easier for us to take down," Ramirez said eagerly.

"Easier could still prove lethal," Malcolm reminded him, somewhat concerned about how keyed up the younger man seemed. "Remember, you and I and the other SAR teams are here to narrow down Acker's position then send in the rapid response team for the take-down. They're the only ones properly trained and geared out to deal with the kind of threat he represents."

Ramirez nodded. "Yes, sir. I do understand that."

Dismissing his lingering suspicions about Ramirez's attitude toward being in a supporting role, Malcolm went on to tell him, "If one of the search teams working another area ends up picking up the scent first, we may hear the barking from here. Provided it's not drowned out by the noise from the river."

Ramirez shrugged. "Either way, they told us at the briefing the law enforcement member of the team will send out a GPS-tagged alert to everyone's cell. But that'll only summon the rapid response team and task force leaders—cutting out the working stiffs like us."

Malcolm reminded himself that he, too, had once been in his early twenties—although he didn't recall ever having been so irritating. "But if Pacer hits a scent, things here are going to start moving *very* quickly."

An eager grin erupted on the rookie's tanned and handsome face. "That sounds *just* like what I signed up for."

"I'll be doing my best to keep up with my K-9," said Malcolm, who cared more about getting the two of them and his dog through this safely than he did this rookie's hunger for excitement. "As soon as you've sent out the locater alert to the team, I'll be counting on you to try to catch up and keep up with me as best as you can. You'll definitely need to watch your footing, though. The last time I didn't pay close enough attention, I ended up with this brace as a souvenir."

Lifting his still-healing left hand as a warning, Malcolm surveyed the deeply shaded downslope to their right, which was thick with protruding stumps and understory vegetation.

"My legs might be a little shorter than yours, but I promise you, I'm plenty quick enough to keep up." Hand resting on the butt of his gun, Ramirez nodded toward the shadowed gloom, his dark eyes gleaming with excitement. "You just make sure to get down fast if Acker pops up, so you don't get hit in any crossfire."

"You don't have to tell me twice," Malcolm said. "But Pacer—he means a whole lot to me, too."

"I'll be looking out for your partner, too, I promise," Ramirez said.

You'd better. "And watch out for yourself, too."

As Pacer continued investigating on a loose lead, Malcolm kept an ear open for any signal from other teams. Soon, however, the background thrum of swiftly flowing water drowned out all other sounds as they moved steadily closer to the river, though it remained well hidden by the trees. Most of his attention, however, was centered on shifts in his dog's behavior as he began to pull, more and more insistently, along a rightward-leading track.

As they worked their way deeper into the woods, Ramirez's interest perked up. "Your dog seems to be moving faster. Is he on to something there?"

"Maybe just a skunk in heat," Malcolm said dryly, his standard line for when he wasn't certain. But before Ramirez could respond, the beautiful, rich sound of Pacer's booming howl startled some crows out of the nearby treetops.

Barking away, his dog pulled hard to the right, and for the moment, Malcolm forgot all need for conversation. Forgot everything except the pleasure of running with his best friend, joining Pacer in an activity that sent the pure animal joy of the chase thrumming through his veins as, even in the dark green shadows, he managed to jump logs and dodge saplings to keep up with his K-9 partner.

Remembering his instructions, however, Malcolm forced himself to pull up short, coming to a halt where the sloping depression began to run back uphill toward a ridge that he knew would lead them back toward the river.

"Hold up, Pacer, will you? Settle," Malcolm said, getting out some chicken treats to help distract him from his obsessive need to find his quarry.

"Giving him a rest?" The rookie panted as he caught up.

As Pacer ignored the treat and whined to go on, Malcolm shook his head. "Just waiting for you to catch up. But I think we'd better hold up here instead of heading over that ridge completely blind when we'll have help available in just a couple of more minutes."

Ramirez scowled at him. "But *we're* the ones who caught Acker's scent—and now you *really* want this rapid-response team to swoop in and hog the glory?"

"What I *really* want is my uncle's and my mother's killer apprehended without adding any more corpses to his body count. Including yours, you little—"

Before Malcolm could further escalate the situation, a breeze rippled through the woodland's understory. Pacer lifted his head and sniffed at the air before pulling in the direction of the ridge and barking wildly, his muzzle moving from left to right as if he were tracking—

Ramirez shouted, "I've got movement on the right! Gray jacket!"

Malcolm saw nothing at first. Then their target crossed a relatively open spot among the trees, sporting the same stained, hooded jacket Malcolm had last seen him wearing in the parking lot. Turning toward the river, Markus ran along the top of the ridge, sprinting faster than Malcolm would have imagined an injured, middle-aged man could possibly move. There was something else that seemed off as well, some troubling aspect that almost immediately evaporated as Malcolm tried to work out whether it was more dangerous losing sight of the man or trying to follow him.

Ramirez made the decision for him, racing toward the threat and bellowing, "Stop, police!"

Malcolm wasn't in the least surprised when Acker only accelerated, disappearing over the far side of the ridge.

"Hold, Ramirez! Don't go!" Malcolm shouted, his instincts—along with everything he'd learned about their adversary—screaming that the moment Ramirez crested that ridge, Acker would be waiting to deal him the swift death of a waiting bullet.

Instead of heeding Malcolm's warning, the rookie only tucked his head and continued charging forward, as if he were running for a winning touchdown. Clipping Pacer's lead to his belt, Malcolm drew his own gun for the first time and then raced after him with Pacer bounding at his side.

"If that fool rookie gets us killed, I swear I'm going to thrash him," he told his dog.

Though he'd been primed to fling himself to the ground at the first crack of gunfire, Malcolm was pleased to find himself still moving moments later. On the other side of the ridge, the ground was more level and the trees considerably thinner, allowing him space to run unimpeded and better lighting for safer footing. Led by Pacer, Malcolm soon caught up with Ramirez, who had stopped in a grassier area not far ahead.

Ramirez held up a hand before looking back over his shoulder and signaling Malcolm to come no closer. A moment later, the young officer pointed out Acker, about thirty yards ahead and slightly above the two of them, his back turned to them as he struggled to climb onto an overgrown embankment.

Just as Malcolm realized that Markus had decided to take his chances attempting to swim the dangerous river, the right sleeve of Acker's gray coat snagged in the thick brush.

Ramirez, who had his weapon trained on the fugitive, shouted over the sounds of Pacer's barking, "Hands up, now! Police!"

Ripping his sleeve free, Acker turned in their direction. As he raised a pistol of his own toward them, the hood he was wearing swung wide with his movement. Malcolm felt a superheated jolt go through him, causing him to hesitate at the deep-red hair he imagined he had spotted. But it was hidden again before he could be certain, and Ramirez got off a shot—followed by a second. Malcolm saw the man in the gray jacket twist around, spun to the left by the impact of a bullet ripping through his shoulder.

When the shooting ended, it took Malcolm a moment to register that neither he nor the suspect had gotten off a single shot. But both Ramirez and the man in the gray jacket had climbed up onto the weed-choked embankment.

"Colton! Hurry!" Ramirez called from somewhere among the weeds. "He's going to fall if you don't come help me hold him!"

After pausing to clip Pacer's lead to a thick tree branch to keep his dog out of harm's way, Malcolm climbed up and pushed through the tight space to join Ramirez where he was sprawled near the river side of the embankment, struggling mightily to hold on to the leg of the suspect, who was dangling above the torrent.

Tossing a desperate look back toward Malcolm, the rookie shouted to be heard over the thundering flow. "Get over here and help me! Grab him! Otherwise, he's going to fall for sure."

"Working on getting through these damned weeds," Malcolm said, briars snagging at his clothing as he maneuvered himself into position.

As the injured man's arms waved above the spray, the torrent crashed and tumbled its way among a gauntlet of boulders that Malcolm couldn't imagine anyone with at least one fresh bullet wound possibly surviving.

"Stop your thrashing, you damned fool, before you get yourself killed!" Ramirez shouted at him as Malcolm wormed his way closer.

Malcolm made a grab for the man's leg—only to get the side of his head kicked for his trouble, hard enough that his ears rang and the rushing water below seemed to be inside his head.

But something else filled his head as well—the certainty

that the young face and the red hair he'd glimpsed when the gray hood had swung sideways had not been Markus Acker's.

"Hurry, please!" Ramirez shouted. "His boot—he's coming out of it! He'll fall. And we can't let him—*Nooo*!"

With no time to weigh the odds of his own survival, Malcolm dove, both arms reaching desperately toward a risk he prayed would lead to answers.

Chapter Eighteen

Too nervous to do much more than pick at a few leftovers and try to delete some of the more obvious junk from among her backlogged emails, Giselle checked her messages for at least the tenth time to see if she might have missed a reply from Malcolm.

She'd known, of course, that he wouldn't see her text since he would have his phone zipped inside his pocket and his full attention on the dangerous mission he was part of. But she was hoping that at some point—whether because the search had veered in some other direction or, in the best of all scenarios, had come to a successful end, he would eventually pull it out and check it.

Mostly, though, she needed to know that he was safe, especially now that a look through the back door's window showed the rose-streaked twilit sky was fading into a soft violet.

When the phone did ring, however, the Caller ID showed the name of a Colton she had never met.

"Hi, this is Sarah Colton," a friendly-sounding voice said following Giselle's greeting. "I hope I'm not disturbing you, but Lizzy suggested I reach out when I couldn't reach Malcolm this evening. She did tell me he was likely occupied with the search for Markus."

"He is, but I'm happy to chat. Malcolm's told me a bit about you and Nate," Giselle told her. "Before anything else, though, I want you to know how sorry I was to hear about your mother's passing."

"Thanks," Sarah said. "It's been—our relationship could be…challenging. But in the end, she left me no doubt that in her way, she really cared about me."

"Hold on to that part, then. I understand you're dealing with her—with her things now—I'm so sorry. Please excuse me," Giselle added before covering the phone for a moment and shushing Scarlett, who'd begun barking furiously at something outside.

Picking up a toy, Giselle distracted her from a fat tabby-and-white barn cat out prowling in the grass outside. "Sorry for my puppy problem. Or maybe I should say my problem puppy—not that I'd trade her for the pick of any litter."

Sarah chuckled. "I'm sure you wouldn't. But the reason I'm calling is I was wondering, if it wouldn't be too inconvenient, would you mind if I dropped off that record player from my mother's house this evening? I know Malcolm and I talked about tomorrow, but it turns out, I need to cover a sick friend's shift at the library and then—"

"Of course you can stop by this evening. No one else is around at the moment, but I'll be happy to help with the unloading," Giselle said before, once more, Scarlett began barking at the window.

After returning to the phone, Giselle said, "Once more, sorry about the noise. I look forward to meeting you in person—and having what I hope will be our first uninterrupted conversation."

Laughing, Sarah said, "Can't wait to meet you and your puppy, too. Look for me in about an hour."

After ending the call, Giselle decided she'd better run upstairs and at least wash her face, which probably still bore evidence of smudged mascara. As she started through the kitchen, however, Scarlett yipped to get her attention and went running to the back door.

"I hope this isn't about that silly cat again," Giselle warned.

But when Scarlett sat and yapped again, Giselle realized that the pup was signaling her need to go out to relieve herself. Reassured by what Detective Rodolfo had said about Acker having trapped himself in an area Giselle knew to be some distance from the ranch, she hooked Scarlett to her leash before unlocking the deadbolt.

Outside, a smattering of stars had emerged, and a few automatic solar security lights had switched on to light her path. As she walked Scarlett out onto the grass, she spotted the front end of a truck parked around on the other side of the house. Deciding it must be the ranch pickup she'd seen leaving earlier, she wondered why the hands would have left it there this evening instead of at the working barn, as usual, upon returning from their earlier errand. Taking a few more steps to get a better angle on the silhouetted shape, she realized, *That's not the truck at all. It's an SUV.* At the same moment, Scarlett whirled around and started barking aggressively at something she heard moving behind them.

Instinct had Giselle scooping the dog up and bolting for the door, not knowing the how or why or how close the threat might be, only guessing *who* it must be. And knowing that her sole chance of survival lay in beating Markus Acker to the door.

Within seconds she heard the footsteps, hard on her heels and the panting sounds of his exertion—so close that she imagined she could feel the heat of his breath. As she imagined his fingers closing on her shirt, adrenaline gave her a burst of speed, and she surged ahead to reach the door ahead of him. A hot wave of relief cascaded through her as she fumbled with the knob to push it open.

As she was stepping through, he bulldozed her from behind, his bodyweight slamming her in a flying tackle. As she cried out, the last thing she was aware of was Scarlett spilling free from her arms. Then her head smacked down against the tile floor, and darkness overtook her.

SHOVING HIS DAMP hair from his eyes, Malcolm looked up from where he sat wrapped in a blanket after being checked out by EMTs and then encouraged to change into a pair of dry sweats supplied by one of his SAR teammates. Exhausted to his bones, he watched the Med-Evac helicopter disappear into the dark sky with both the suspect and Officer Ramirez, who had been sent along in the unlikely event the man came to in transit. As the sound of the chopper's receding rotors merged with the roar of the nearby river, Malcolm shifted his gaze—and spotted Ajay Wright and his Lab Pumpkin striding his way.

Ajay looked down and shook his head. "You know, just because you're the luckiest man in the state of Idaho doesn't mean you're not still out of your mind. When you dove in after your target, there's no way you could've possibly known that you and he would end up washed into the shallows where Fletcher and Officer Phillips would be able to haul you both out. You could've *died* in there—and then what would I have told your sister?"

"That I didn't actually *dive* in so much as I fell," Malcolm explained as he stroked Pacer, who had sidled up in front of him, offering both moral support and the warmth of his dry body. "I was making one last hail Mary of a grab for the suspect when I realized that he wasn't Markus, and his body weight ended up pulling me down after him."

Ajay's golden-brown gaze bored into his. "Because you took things one step too far, as always."

"That could very well be," Malcolm allowed as he climbed stiffly to his feet, his body aching in a dozen places. "But I knew that if he died here, we'd end up losing whatever information he might have on Acker and his plans forever."

As Malcolm was speaking, Fletcher, who'd been on a call nearby, rejoined them. "Sorry to tell you both, but it doesn't sound as if that gamble's going to pay off. That was Ramirez calling from the chopper. He tells me our suspect started crashing almost as soon as they were in the air. They're working hard to try to get his heart restarted, but things aren't looking very promising."

"Tough break," Ajay said.

"On several levels," said Fletcher. "I was pretty sure I recognized the suspect's face and that red hair when I saw him being loaded, so I took a quick pic and conferred with other detectives. They knew who he was right away."

"Let me guess—he's the red-haired college student reported missing three years back in Boise," Malcolm said.

"Zach Broussard, yes. How did you know?" Fletcher asked.

"I was never told the name, but this kid's disappearance from his college came up during the investigation of my fiancée's death at Blackbird Lake. Sheriff's Department Deputy Ariana Rodolfo can give you all the details. But from what I heard, this kid and one of his friends stashed the boat involved in the collision under a false name shortly before heading back to campus. A few months later, the red-haired guy vanished into thin air."

Ajay said, "Interesting how this kid goes missing and then turns up here, more than three years later, acting as some sort of stooge for Markus Acker."

Fletcher said, "I wasn't personally on his case back in

Boise, but I do remember hearing that he had some kind of a breakdown before disappearing. I know, too, that a pretty substantial inheritance he'd had access to went missing at the same time."

"Sounds a lot like Acker's M.O.—getting his hooks into a 'lost sheep' and draining them of all their assets," Ajay said. "In return, he would've given the kid a place to run to—"

"But run from what?" Malcolm asked. "Unless Broussard did a lot more than just participate in a cover-up for some rich boat owner to earn a little extra money—which, bad as it is, is hardly enough to trash your whole life over."

Fletcher's gaze connected with his. "I think you probably know, if you think about it, what the kid was *really* running from, Mal."

Malcolm nodded tightly. "So you're telling me I just nearly got myself killed trying to save the man who cost me— *Hell...*"

Ajay clapped him on the shoulder. "He might've taken the future you thought you had ahead of you, but you can at least be sure he didn't take your humanity as well."

"Even if it's kind of reckless at times?"

"I'm still grateful to have you as a friend—and a member of my team," Ajay assured him.

As glad as Malcolm was to hear it, before he could thank Ajay, the task force leader excused himself and stepped away to take a call.

Fletcher said to Malcolm, "I have to head off myself to check back in with Archer about how he's coming on getting that search warrant for the phone that was collected from your pickup—"

"Acker had a cell phone on him? I'm surprised you weren't able to use it to track him before now," Malcolm said.

"His personal cell was found smashed shortly after he went on the lam. This one's probably stolen—but the hope is, it'll yield enough data to give us information on his recent movements," Fletcher said, "or possibly lead us to other past associates he's recently reached out to for help."

"Or other victims—like maybe the owner of that cell phone and whatever vehicle he happens to be driving now," Malcolm added.

"Unfortunately, the thought's occurred," Fletcher said. "I'll check back in with you in a bit."

Instead of leaving, however, he stopped at the sight of Ajay heading back toward them, looking as if someone had slugged him in the stomach.

"What is it? What's happened?" Fletcher asked him.

"It's Acker, isn't it?" asked Malcolm, a chill that had nothing to do with the plunge into snow-melt-charged floodwaters he had just survived washing over him. "Please tell me this whole thing with the Broussard kid wasn't simply a diversion so he could go after another member of our family." He glanced at Fletcher, whose father's stroke a year before, had set off this entire nightmare.

"Just let Ajay speak," Fletcher ordered, his professional training overcoming the emotion Malcolm saw blazing in his green eyes.

"I'm sorry to have to be the one to tell you both this," Ajay said, his gaze moving from Fletcher to Malcolm, "but there's been a 9-1-1 call from the ranch. Your sister Sarah stopped by just a little while ago. She'd spoken with Giselle about three-quarters of an hour ago about a change of plans—an item she needs to drop off."

"Our late grandmother's record player," Malcolm said, his pulse pounding as his dread built.

"The thing is, though, when she arrived," Ajay continued, "Giselle didn't answer. But Sarah spotted a small, frightened-looking beagle running loose with its leash dragging."

"Giselle would *never* leave Scarlett unattended." Malcolm

tried to tell himself that, most likely, she'd accidentally lost the pup somehow and gone off looking for her. Maybe this was all some terrible misunderstanding and the same gentle Giselle who wouldn't put bullets in a gun or eat anything with a mother would show up at any minute laughing about how she had simply dropped the leash.

"Sarah thought the same thing," said Ajay, "which is why she went around back to see if she could spot Giselle out looking for her puppy. Instead, Sarah found the back door standing open. There were streaks of what looked like fresh blood, still wet, smeared across the tile inside. That's when Sarah locked herself inside a bathroom and called Greg from down the road, along with 9-1-1."

Malcolm had never been slammed by a tsunami, but for the second time in his life, he felt the earth ripped out from underneath him, replaced by a wave of fear and grief and regret so huge, it squeezed the breath from his lungs.

"I—I never should have let her stay alone," he said. "I should've known, after Markus came for me once, that he might—"

"We had every reason to believe Acker was right *here*, completely surrounded by dozens of law enforcement and search and rescue personnel," Ajay said. "And we had no reason at all to think the attack on you and Giselle earlier might be personal. But whatever mistakes any of us might've made, we can't afford to waste time on guilt or blame now. Do you hear me, Malcolm?"

Something in his tone cut through the ringing in Malcolm's ears, pulling him back from the spiral of guilt he'd been heading for. It was a damned indulgence, he warned himself, one he dared not give in to—not as long as hope remained.

Over the ringing in his ears, he heard Fletcher, somehow

functional enough to ask, "Have they searched the house and barn yet, do you know?"

Some detached fragment of Malcolm's shocked brain understood that those on the scene would be looking not simply for evidence but a body. *Giselle's* dead body, left behind like refuse, exactly as Claudette Hogan's had been following her murder. But he refused to allow himself to believe in the possibility that they would find it. He wouldn't, *couldn't* lose Giselle before he had the chance to make her understand that whatever pain their past held, in her, he saw a future worth staking his heart on a thousand times over. He felt only shame that he'd lost sight of that for even a moment before when he had seen her last.

"Greg and Sarah have done a preliminary search of the house's interior. Other than a single, round hole in one of the top kitchen cabinets, they found nothing—"

"A *bullet* hole?" Malcolm flashed on an image of Giselle's pale face, after she'd been grazed before.

"Unconfirmed at this point. First responders are still en route," Ajay said. "I'll be heading there with the rapid-response team to join them and take command of the scene."

"Pacer and I will be coming with you," Malcolm insisted. "Wherever that bastard's taken her, we're going to find her— and I swear to you, I'm going to bring her home alive."

Chapter Nineteen

Thirty-five minutes earlier...

"Wake up, damn you. Look alive." Markus booted the side of the unconscious woman's thigh, angry with her for running from him and forcing him to tackle her so hard that he was now left with this mess. Not only that, but he'd smacked down painfully against his wounded ear when he had jumped her—a pulsing, overheated pain that had been growing more miserable by the day instead of better, and now he felt something hot and thick and putrid-smelling dripping from his bandage.

"And, *you*, shut up." He kicked at the barking beagle, which deftly dodged his mud-caked shoe to race from the room with its tail tucked tightly between its legs.

Glad he wouldn't need to waste a bullet on it, he knelt down and rolled the limp blonde onto her back, eager to see which of the younger female Coltons he had gotten.

Whoever she was, he saw that she was definitely a looker, despite the large bump already going purple, high on the right side of her forehead. Definitely not Sarah—the troublemaking daughter that Jessie Colton had taken a bullet for rather than allowing him to shoot dead the way he wished he had—and definitely would if he ever saw her treacherous face again.

Whether this was Jessie's other daughter or some cousin didn't much matter, he supposed. Since the lot of them were all so pathetically attached to one another, he was certain she would serve as the hostage that he needed to finally reclaim the life that he deserved...

But if she were too badly damaged to speak into a phone—to cry and plead for her life before sharing his demands with her distraught family members—it was time to cut his losses and find himself a sturdier hostage. Eager to find out, he bent to scoop up the cell phone he saw she had dropped. After tucking it into his own shirt pocket, he reached over and roughly shook her shoulder.

"If you're only playing possum on me," he told the helpless woman, "I'm going to give you this one warning. An unconscious victim's as much use to me as a dead one right now, which is exactly what you're going to be if you don't open your eyes and start cooperating, right—*awfgh*!"

His shout transformed into an expletive as two sharp jaws—the small piranha of a dog's—clamped down painfully onto his bare ankle.

Kicking the beast free, he drew his gun and took aim at the barking, snapping menace.

"Don't you *dare* hurt her!" the woman cried out, shoving his legs out from under him so unexpectedly that he crashed down onto one knee, sending a wild shot into an upper kitchen cabinet.

With a shout of rage, he spun around to point the muzzle only inches from her pale face, a wave of dizziness making him realize the infection working on him must be worse than he'd imagined. "You ever lay another hand on me, and I swear to you, I'll leave what's left of you strewn across this kitchen for your precious family to find! Now get that barking stopped, or I swear to you that I will."

"Scarlett, hush, girl. It's all right," the woman pleaded, her voice reed-thin.

When the animal went quiet, he noticed the red smears on its muzzle. Realizing it was *his* blood on the dog's fur, he gave it a glare that sent it darting behind the kitchen island, at least for the time being.

As he returned his attention to the woman, Markus wiped away the sweat dripping down into his face. "Have you—have you seen an antique record player lately, from Jessie's home? Do you know what's happened to it?"

"An old record player? Why would…" She sounded so bewildered that he wondered for a moment if either shock or the blow to her head had rendered her incapable of comprehension.

Then she shook her head. "I'm sorry, but I've never been inside her place. But if there's something you were particularly attached to that was accidentally packed up, I'm sure I can help you get it back, if you'll only tell me where to have it sent—"

"Are you joking?" His laughter sounded like a dry wheeze. "And I don't give a damn about your stupid Colton family heirlooms, only the—"

"*My* heirlooms?" she echoed.

He eyed her with suspicion. "You *are* a Colton, aren't you?"

She seemed to weigh her answer momentarily before her blue eyes turned disdainful as she looked him over, from the hat that partly obscured his dripping ear to the clothes that he suspected were by now only being held together by the layers of grime and sweat embedded in their fabric. "Oh, I'm Colton enough," she said, "to know *exactly* how big of a mistake you're making in daring to come here, Acker. And if you imagine that one little dog and I are trouble, just you *wait* until you see what's coming for you next."

Furious to be treated with such contempt by a woman whose life he could snuff out in an instant, he rounded on her once more, pressing the gun's muzzle to her temple as he hauled her up off the floor. "You're damned lucky I need you for a hostage for the moment, to trade you for what I'm really after, do you know that?"

"A hostage?" she echoed weakly.

"But you're right about one thing, though," he said. "It's time that you and I get moving. First, though, I'm going to bind these hands of yours and cover your eyes. If you fight me, I may need to tape your mouth, too—"

"Please, no…" she said, her eyes gone huge and glassy.

Empowered by her helplessness, he felt a hot surge of satisfaction. "Only, the thing is, I can't guarantee you I won't get sloppy with it. Sloppy enough that I won't accidentally cover up your nose, too, with that tape and leave you to smother underneath the blanket in the back of the SUV where you'll be riding. Then maybe I'll dump your body in the lake before I turn around to find myself a more compliant Colton. Or will you save me the trouble?"

She only stared in answer, completely unresisting as he bound her, her lips slightly parted and her face as pale as death.

I'LL DUMP YOUR body in the lake…the lake…thelakethelakethelake…

The words looped endlessly, the soundtrack of Giselle's dread and horror as she lay curled on her side beneath a musty-smelling—and profoundly itchy—blanket in the SUV's cargo area with her arms bound tightly behind her. The rough ride of the speeding vehicle—an older model whose engine was a throaty rumble—was brutal, battering her head, already throbbing from its impact with the kitchen floor, against what felt like bare metal as they jolted over every bump.

Willing away her nausea, she told herself that whatever happened to her now, she could at least take some comfort in knowing that Acker had taken her away before Sarah had shown up with the very record player he seemed so eager to get his hands on. Guessing that there had to be something critically important to him hidden inside—and that the moment that he had it, he would have no more incentive to keep her and Sarah breathing—she'd told whatever lies she'd thought might buy her a little more time. Time to come up with some hope for extricating herself from this nightmare.

She held out hope that Sarah would quickly raise an alarm over her failure to be at the house as they'd arranged this evening. But Giselle had no idea whether there were any cameras around the ranch property that might have shown the vehicle that she'd been loaded into. She thought about her cell phone, with its GPS, but she couldn't feel it pressing into her body when she rolled from side to side, so she supposed that Acker must have taken it from her pocket while she was unconscious and tossed it somewhere to make it impossible to track them.

Desperately, she fought against whatever he'd used to tie her up. Her bonds barely gave at all. He'd tied her wrists so tightly, the rope or cord felt as if it was cutting into her flesh, and her hands ached with the restricted circulation. Frustrated by her inability to loosen the binding, she instead wriggled around and used her shoulders until the blanket finally slipped off her. Pushing her face against it even harder, she gradually forced the torn tea towel he'd used to blindfold her down from her eyes until the still-tied cloth dropped down around her neck.

Blinking in the darkness, she peered all around her but

saw little, other than a few hazed reflections through the SUV's filmed rear windows. Her exertions must have stirred the dust, however, for she sneezed reflexively. Afterward, she froze, terrified that he might have heard and that he'd pull over and beat her bloody for making a sound, the way he'd threatened when he had dumped her back here. Fortunately, however, he'd turned on the radio—she'd caught the muted tones of some advertising jingle and now, a couple of male voices chatting about the forecast for the upcoming weekend.

Would she be alive to see if they were right about their prediction of "great weather for tennis, hiking, or boating," she wondered, or would that only matter to the searchers out looking for her remains?

A wave of grief washed over her as she pictured Malcolm out with Pacer, knowing he'd insist on being part of the operation, even though she was certain he would be beside himself with worry. And knowing that, if he did find whatever Acker left of her, it would certainly destroy the man she'd come to love.

Her heart breaking at the thought, she told herself, *No. I'm not doing this to him—and Markus isn't destroying our chance to make things right between us. Whatever I have to do, I can't let this happen...*

She wasn't certain whether minutes or hours passed her by in the rear of that SUV, only that time seemed glacially slow as she came up with and discarded dozens of plans— each one wilder than the last—to plead, bargain, or fight for even the slightest chance of saving her life. Eventually, however, they turned, and the jouncing battered her sore head worse than ever as the ride grew rougher and the truck took a tight corner.

This is it, she sensed, a moment before she heard the loud squeak of the brakes, and she heard as well as felt the SUV's shift into park. Her every nerve ending standing on alert, she strained her ears, listening as he shut off the engine and opened his door.

As an eddy of fresh air reached her from the front, Giselle dragged in a deep breath, desperate for any clue of what might be coming. But all she smelled was the acrid scent of her own terror mingled with the damp breath of a lake that chilled her to the bone.

Chapter Twenty

Markus had driven around and around the back roads, the plan that had seemed so clear in his mind a few hours earlier fraying at the edges as waves of heat and chills vied with the pain for his attention. If it were only the discomfort, he told himself, he would fight straight through it to head to the Wilderness Chapel, where he knew that a secure supply of clean and edible, if not gourmet, food and a medical kit he'd personally ordered kept well-stocked to protect his church from lawsuits lest some member of his sect perish while left to contemplate the error of his or her ways on the isolated island.

But Markus hadn't beaten the odds his whole life—and outmaneuvered the authorities for most of the last few decades—by being stupid, and he was smart enough to know that, with pain, fever and fatigue nipping at his heels, he wasn't thinking straight now. That he was forgetting something. That this plan for exchanging the sealed pack containing his passport and a million-dollar ransom for the location of the Colton woman, which he would offer to provide via text message once he was safely beyond the country's borders, was as full of holes as a wasp's nest with an even greater potential to end up with him getting fatally stung.

So he continued driving, mentally running through each

step, trying to come up with where he'd gone wrong. Soon, however, he became sidetracked, imagining the Coltons opening the photos he meant to send the worried family from the phone of their loved one. Bruised, bound, and terrified, the young woman would make quite the horrifying picture. Or better yet, he thought, he could tear her clothes off before he started—add that layer of humiliation to punish her for the way she'd dared to shove and threaten him back at the ranch house instead of simply cowering and complying the way a woman ought to from the start.

On some level, he knew there was something dangerous about using her cell phone to send such messages. But now that he'd come up with the idea of playing god once more, shocking and hurting the Colton family with the kind of photos they could never erase from their minds, the less he could focus on the risk and the more excited he became about the idea of getting started with his plan.

By the time he finally parked the old Suburban beneath the low-hanging limbs of the huge black walnut tree near the dock where the Ever After Church kept several rowboats tied, a fresh wave of anticipation had him floating high above the pain. Hurrying around to the vehicle's rear hatch, he popped it open and gestured with his gun at the still-bound woman—who was staring at him with the blindfold dangling down around her neck—and sitting propped up on one elbow.

Ripping the blindfold off her, he slapped her hard enough to knock her over—less because he was angry than because he imagined that another mark on her face would look good for his explicit photos.

"Did I *tell* you you could take that off?" he demanded. "Did I?"

"I—I'm sorry," she said quickly. "I swear I didn't mean to. It just—it fell off. From all the bumping around these roads."

Another lie, he knew, but at least he'd shocked her enough that she gave him no trouble when he pulled her from the rear of the vehicle. Grabbing one of her bound arms, he began forcing her quickly downhill, frog-marching her ahead of him through the overgrown grass.

As they approached the lakeshore, she dug in her heels and shook her head, staring at the half moon's reflection off the inlet's shimmering waters. "If you're—if you're planning to drown me, j-just go ahead and shoot me here. Because I'm not going one step closer."

"You think I've driven you around for hours just to toss you in the damned lake? If that was all I wanted, I would've killed you back at the house," he said. "Now get moving. Boat's right over here to take us where we're going—then you and I have some proof-of-life pictures that need taking."

"Proof-of—for your ransom?" she asked.

He sent a cruel smile her way, warming even more to the thought of repaying a fraction of the suffering this family had forced him to endure. "For the ransom, a few porn sites—there's honestly no telling where the sort of shots I have in mind might end up...not that you'll be alive to worry about your precious reputation."

Predictably, she tried to bolt then, but he slapped her again before dragging her down onto the pier. When he tried to fling her in the boat, though, he fumbled the gun he had been holding on her.

In an instant, everything sped up: Markus ducking and reaching for the dropped gun—the woman kicking it out of reach and into the dark water before diving after it to avoid his fist arcing through the air above her. And then there was the sound of shouting from the shoreline—deep-voiced men barking out harsh orders.

But Markus Acker wasn't about to end his life withering

away in some prison, so with a roar of pure rage, he made one more wild leap in the direction the woman had taken…

Only to have a hail of bullets catch him before his body hit the water.

"I'VE GOT HER!" Malcolm shouted to the others, his heart pounding like a piston as Pacer bounded into the shallow water just ahead of him. The K-9 grabbed Giselle by the shirt where she struggled, facedown, a moment before Malcolm lifted her, coughing, choking, and sputtering in his arms.

"You're all right now. You're safe. You're safe," he kept telling her as Fletcher came to help him carry her to the grassy bank, now illuminated by the headlights of several emergency vehicles.

At the edge of his awareness, he caught sight of Ajay on the dock, directing two of the strike force team members, who were hauling an inert form from the wine-red water. But Malcolm returned his attention to lowering Giselle—who continued coughing—gently before noticing, with a flare of fresh rage, the way her arms were bound behind her.

"Her wrists," he said, his voice rough with emotion and the understanding that she would have certainly drowned had it taken them even a few minutes longer to track down her location after requesting an emergency ping from her cell phone provider. "You have a knife to cut her loose?" And for just an instant, he was back again on that deadly August day, sawing through her hair.

"You keep her supported so I can reach her hands. I'll get this," Fletcher said, pulling a blade from his pocket.

Nodding, Malcolm let him free her, instead focusing his energy on reassuring Giselle as he held her. "Fletcher, Ajay, and I are all here with you. You're safe now, safe forever. I promise you, he can't hurt you or any of us any longer."

Glancing back over at the dock, he saw no activity to indicate that Ajay had ordered any resuscitative efforts, and realized with a start that Markus Acker would never again threaten any of his loved ones. Still, when Malcolm got his first look at the bruising on Giselle's face, he felt a surge of such overwhelming rage that it still took all his restraint not to rush straight over and beat the living hell out of the lifeless corpse.

He shook off the foolish impulse, reminding himself that right now, the living woman in his arms deserved every scrap of his attention. She gave a moan of relief as her wrists were finally freed.

"There you go," Fletcher told her gently. "I see a pretty good-sized knot on your forehead. Any other injuries we need to know about right now?"

"Don't think—so—no—" Her words splintered into another round of coughing.

Patting her shoulder, Fletcher said, "Let me go check on the ETA for the ambulance and see if I can round up a blanket for you. Anything else you need or want, just name it, and I'll do whatever I can to make it happen."

"Th-thank you," she choked out.

Concerned about how much lake water she may have inhaled, Malcolm gently gave her back a few thumps. Pacer chose that moment to move in and sneak a couple of face licks before Malcolm was able to push him back.

"All right, you. Give her some space," he complained, pulling the dog back from her cheek. "I haven't even scored my own kiss."

"So now..." Giselle wheezed out a laugh as she reached to pet the shepherd. "So now you two are in some kind of competition?"

"I've already accepted that I'll always be runner-up behind that handsome mug of his," Malcolm said. "You know, he led me straight to you—even after—after Acker threw you in the water."

"He—he didn't throw me in. I—I dove in myself. Because he was going to kill me. I saw it in his eyes when I—when I punted the gun he'd dropped off the dock."

Pulling her into his arms, he let her cry, gently stroking her hair and telling her, "I'm so sorry that he hurt you, that he ever laid a finger on you."

"It was—it was all my fault. I thought it would be safe to take out Scarlett. Oh, no—Scarlett! I know the door was left wide open, and she—" Giselle coughed briefly before quickly regaining control. "She was so frightened when he tried to shoot her. I think—I think she might've bitten him—when he was hurting me."

He drew back to look into her face, still so beautiful to him despite the marks of violence. "First of all, Scarlett's safe—Sarah and Greg found her. And if she *did* bite Markus, she deserves a big, fat T-bone."

Giselle's face contorted. "She might need an extra rabies shot, though. He was *so* horrible! I never should've let him take me—"

"Please don't say that. No part of this is in any way your fault. Why would you imagine for a moment that—?"

"Scarlett was crying to go out, and I thought, since Detective Rodolfo had told me on the phone that Malcolm appeared to be surrounded at the search location miles away, it would be more than safe to take her for a quick walk."

Malcolm grimaced, shaking his head. "Believe me, we were *all* fooled. But it turned out we were chasing an impostor. Acker had sent the missing red-haired guy Rodolfo was looking for, Zach Broussard—who's apparently been in hiding all this time as one of his cult members—to lead us on a wild goose chase in my truck."

"Broussard's a member of the Ever After cult?"

"He *was*," Malcolm said. "He ended up shot by an officer himself. Our last update was a text on the way here saying that he'd just been pronounced dead at the trauma center."

"Detective Rodolfo said—she told me that Broussard—that he was the one who was piloting the—"

"I've already put together that he had to have been out joy-riding with his buddy in the red boat that day," Malcolm said, drawing her in closer once more as he felt her shiver. "But now that we know the truth about the past, the real question is, are we going to keep allowing it to keep us from claiming the kind of future we deserve? Because we *do* deserve to know real happiness, Giselle. I think we both know that Kate would want that for us."

"Of course she would, because she loved us." Giselle sighed. "So maybe what's been getting in the way is that we haven't been willing to show ourselves a measure of that same love…"

"I think so, yes," Malcolm said just as Fletcher returned, tearing open one of the emergency space blankets that so many first responders carried in their vehicles.

He passed it to Giselle. "About five minutes on that ambulance."

She thanked him before he excused himself when Ajay called him over.

Returning her attention to Malcolm, she said, "When I was tied up in the back of that SUV, all I could really do—other than dream up a lot of really unworkable ideas for how I might overpower and escape an armed psychopath—was regret how afraid I've been of my own feelings for you—"

"Afraid?" he echoed.

She nodded. "Afraid of trusting in the positive things you saw in me, since I couldn't even see them in myself. And believing that after years of settling for immature, self-centered men when I was younger, I might really deserve to love someone so driven, so focused, and so absolutely loyal to the bone—because I *do* love you, Malcolm. I can't help but love who you are. I even love seeing my mess of a self through your eyes."

In the distance, he spotted flashing emergency lights approaching. But his attention remained riveted on Giselle.

"You're absolutely perfect as you are to me," he told her, "but if there are some issues for both of us to work through, what do you say the two of us throw in our stakes and tackle them together?"

"Together?" she asked.

"Absolutely," he said, as someone directed the ambulance to pull up nearby, "because whatever challenges life hands out, it seems to me, they'll be a whole lot easier to face, knowing I have someone as brave and bright and beautiful as you are standing by my side."

She stared at him a moment before gesturing toward her face and muddy clothing. "You *really* need to have that ambulance crew give you an eye examination if you imagine I look beautiful covered in lake muck, bumps, and bruises—"

"And one more thing," he said, reaching over, as if to pull something off her shoulder.

"What's that?" she asked, looking down to see what he'd found.

"Just this, my love," he said, lifting her chin to claim a kiss that began sweetly, only to tip quickly toward a heat that he took as a promise of far better days—to say nothing of the nights—to come.

Chapter Twenty-One

Two Weeks Later...

A satisfied grin stretching across his freshly shaven face, Malcolm looked down from the window of the bedroom suite he and Giselle were now sharing and pointed out the long line of vehicles coming up the ranch's drive and heading for the house. "Judging from the response to his Saturday-afternoon summons, the old man's definitely still got it. Looks like every single member of the family's arriving for the Buck Colton Show right on time."

Giselle finished affixing an earring and smiled back at him, her healing bruises now scarcely distinguishable beneath the light dusting of powder she'd applied—mostly, he knew, because she was more than ready to move on from discussing her abduction with anyone besides him and the counselor she'd begun seeing last week, a woman who specialized in the processing of trauma.

"You sound almost surprised to see them," she said as she straightened the lower hem of the pretty spring top she was wearing with a pair of ankle jeans. "Was there ever really any doubt this family would be ready to celebrate, after nearly a year of the kind of stress you've all been put through?"

Malcolm patted Pacer, who had walked over to check on

the action outside the window as well. "Oh, I'm sure everyone's more than ready to let their hair down for once. It's just the *on-time* part that's left me so impressed. Let's just say we have a few chronic stragglers among our ranks—and between those juggling little ones and my cousin Frannie being so close to her due date, I'm sure that's added an extra layer to the challenge of keeping to a schedule."

"Speaking of Frannie, I ran into her at the bookstore a few days back. She looks amazing."

"I'm surprised she was even there. Dante's told me that she's been a bit uncomfortable on her feet just lately, and the doctor's advised her to take it easy for the duration."

"Dante has nothing to worry over. She was sitting in a comfy chair, enjoying her time visiting with everyone and looking positively radiant while the staff and the store manager handled all the real work. I kept trying to ask her about the baby, but everyone there was too excited about that big Cami Carlson TV interview to talk about anything but my 'big moment.'"

Malcolm couldn't help but smile at the way Giselle rolled her eyes. "I don't know why you find it so embarrassing. People are proud of you. *I'm* proud of you—and have been, since long before 'My Lioness' became such a megahit."

"It's a wonderful tribute to her mother, who's devoted her life to teaching her daughter how to become her own independent woman, and Cami really deserves the success she's found with the song becoming such a huge crossover hit. But it was *totally* unnecessary for her to publicly name me as 'the other lioness' in her life, especially in front of one of the biggest interviewers out there. I became a ghostwriter for a reason. I've never personally wanted this kind of attention. It's been crazy."

"I'll admit, it's not at all what I expected either," Malcolm said, thinking of the avalanche of requests for interviews from other media outlets. In addition, so many cards, bouquets, and gifts had been sent by Cami's grateful fans that Giselle had been having a ranch hand check her cabin for them daily and donate everything that was appropriate to a local nursing home.

He said, "Once the media sees you're not willing to trade in juicy stories to get your face and name splashed worldwide—"

"Heaven forbid." She made a face.

"They'll move on to their next target."

"Now that it's been announced that a certain previously unnamed 'wolf' is facing multiple charges related to his history of 'mentoring' other musically gifted girls, they can focus on the whole sordid history of his scandals instead. Then I'll be able to quietly get on with working on Cami's book helping other young people figure out how to become the lions and lionesses in their own lives—and to recognize and avoid those looking to exploit them."

"So you've decided to go ahead and ghostwrite for Cami?" he said, not at all surprised by her choice, though he knew that Giselle's new agent had received at least two other celebrity tell-all offers, either of which would have paid more up front.

Giselle smiled. "How could I say no to something with the potential to make a real difference in so many young lives?"

"I think it's the perfect choice—especially since you'll be able to do most of your work from here," he said. "Speaking of which, we'd better hurry up and get downstairs before everyone else beats us inside and we end up getting counted as the late ones."

"Or worse yet, missing whatever this huge announcement is your dad keeps teasing everyone about."

"I've been wondering exactly what he has up his sleeve myself," Malcolm said.

Giselle squatted to give Scarlett a final pat before opening her crate door. "In you go, my sweet girl. I'll be back to check on you soon."

When the pup trotted in obediently, Giselle gave her a fresh chew and sighed happily. "I still can't believe she's really mine. That was so nice of Sebastian, bending the rules to let me keep her."

"He couldn't technically allow anyone else to adopt her, since she'd bitten Markus," Malcolm told her. "But I think we would've come up with some way to make sure you got her regardless, considering the ordeal you'd been through together."

"This is why I adore you both," she said, giving him a quick kiss before they hurried downstairs to join the joyful chaos of Malcolm's siblings and his cousins, their loved ones and their littles. For the next half hour or more, there were numerous hugs and greetings, reunions and introductions, laughter and the rising din of happy chatter as drinks were passed around and the pre-meal snacks set out.

Malcolm couldn't believe how much he'd missed the wonderful normalcy of it all, after all these months of stress and danger. Or maybe it just seemed better, having Giselle at his side.

Then his father, looking more at ease and—somehow—younger than he had in ages, in a new pearl-button denim shirt, and a pair of neatly creased jeans went to the antique brass dinner bell that hung on the wall. When the crowd failed to quiet in response to his throat-clearing, he rang the bell so loudly that all those nearest him clapped their hands over their ears and Pacer gave a single hound-like howl of protest.

As everyone fell silent, Buck put his arm around Mama Jen, who was all smiles in an embroidered turquoise dress that complemented her silver-streaked dark-blond hair.

"All right, everybody," Malcolm's father said. "Simmer down, or *next* time, I'll make a bad noise even worse by singing along with it."

There were answering calls of "Please, have mercy!" and "We'd rather hear more howling!" followed by laughter as Buck pretended to peer around angrily in an attempt to find the culprits.

Malcolm—who'd been one of them—bit down on the inside of his cheek as Giselle elbowed him in the ribs and then returned a wink sent to him by his cousin, Ruby, from across the room, next to Sebastian, who held their infant son.

"All kidding aside," his father said, "Jenny and I wanted to thank all of you for taking time from your busy lives to be here today. We thought it was important to mark the memory of the struggles we've shared and observe a moment of silence for those we've said goodbye to this year."

They did so, a solemn stillness descending until, a short time later, baby Sawyer cooed and babbled, prompting an outbreak of smiles and then giggles from Greg and Briony's children and Hannah and Archer's daughter, Lucy, as the contagion spread.

Always a pushover with the youngest Coltons, Buck Colton didn't scold, but instead asked in a teasing voice, "What's all this, during our serious moment?"

Answering for him, Mama Jen said to everyone, "It's a wonderful reminder that along with its challenges and sorrows, this past year has also brought us so many blessings. Some fine new grandchildren to love with all our hearts; delightful new daughters-and sons-in-law or in-love, and I can't tell you how very happy and proud we both are of every single one of your amazing choices." Her gaze and Malcolm's father's traveled from one couple to the next, brimming with a full measure of love, pride, and approval that excluded no one.

"And now it's time to tell them, my love," Buck said, "that we've made some choices of our own. This coming June, Jenny and I would like to invite you all right back here for…" He drew out a long silence, milking every moment of the building anticipation before booming out the very words that everyone present had most hoped to hear: "our wedding!"

Wild cheers, whistles, and shouts of congratulations erupted, with so many rushing toward them that Malcolm found himself protectively pulling back Giselle, explaining at her protest, "Sorry, but I was afraid I'd lose you in the crush!"

Squeezing his hand, she smiled and assured him, "In case you haven't figured it out yet, Malcolm Colton, you couldn't lose me if you tried."

He was kissing her when the dinner bell rang out once more and his father shouted, "Everybody, back off for a minute, please. Because we aren't quite done with the announcements."

From near the back of the scrum, Malcolm's brother Max called, "Let the luckiest man in Owl Creek speak!"

As the room once more fell silent, Buck beamed, saying, "I really *am* the luckiest man, aren't I?" and locked lips with his bride-to-be, provoking another round of applause.

Coming up for air, he said, "While I still have your attention, I wanted to let you know, too, that Jenny will be moving out here to the ranch with me—just a hop, skip, and a jump from the new place that Malcolm and Giselle will soon be breaking ground on. And as much as I know it means to everyone, I'm afraid that for practical reasons we've decided to put Jenny's home on the market—unless any one of you here would like to buy it for your own family."

A hush fell, and when people began whispering, Malcolm told Giselle, "I have so many fond memories of all us cousins running around that place as kids together. It's going to be really tough to see it leave the family, but it's awfully big for most—"

"We want it!" came a familiar voice. Malcolm turned his head just in time to see that it belonged to his *very* pregnant cousin, Frannie, who was being helped from her seat by her husband Dante, whose dark beard bore the slightest trace of silver.

At the moment, however, they both looked excited and perhaps a little nervous as his blond cousin went on to explain, "We could definitely use the space, you see," she said, "because we've been holding back some big news of our own. News we had to—shall we say—*process* for ourselves for a little while before we were ready to finally share it with everybody."

When she inhaled deeply, as if for courage, the whole packed room seemed to hold its breath in anticipation.

Dante grinned and blurted, "Send diapers, everybody, lots and lots of diapers!"

Frannie cut in, finding her voice to add, "Because…we're having triplets!"

Once more, the household erupted into a riot of cheers, hugs, laughter, and congratulations. Only this time, no one even tried to shut down the ensuing celebration, which kept right on rolling through the afternoon and well into the happiest of nights.

* * * * *

COMING SOON!

We really hope you enjoyed reading this book.
If you're looking for more romance
be sure to head to the shops when
new books are available on

Thursday 16th January

To see which titles are coming soon, please visit
millsandboon.co.uk/nextmonth

MILLS & BOON

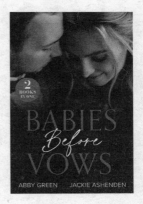
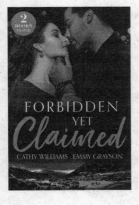
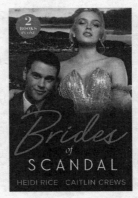

LET'S TALK
Romance

For exclusive extracts, competitions and special offers, find us online:

[f] MillsandBoon

[X] @MillsandBoon

[◎] @MillsandBoonUK

[♪] @MillsandBoonUK

Get in touch on 01413 063 232